I0664649

The Knights of Langerwitz: The New King

Patrick Kennedy

Copyright © 2016 Patrick Kennedy

All rights reserved.

ISBN: 0692821902
ISBN-13: 978-0692821909

DEDICATION

This one is for my students who keep me
telling stories every school year. They are the reason
I love my job.

CONTENTS

ACKNOWLEDGMENTS

Thanks to my parents, family, and friends who read the early edition of this book. Thanks also to everyone who read my first book and any of my other works. Finally, to everyone from my old writing troupe who pushed me forward.

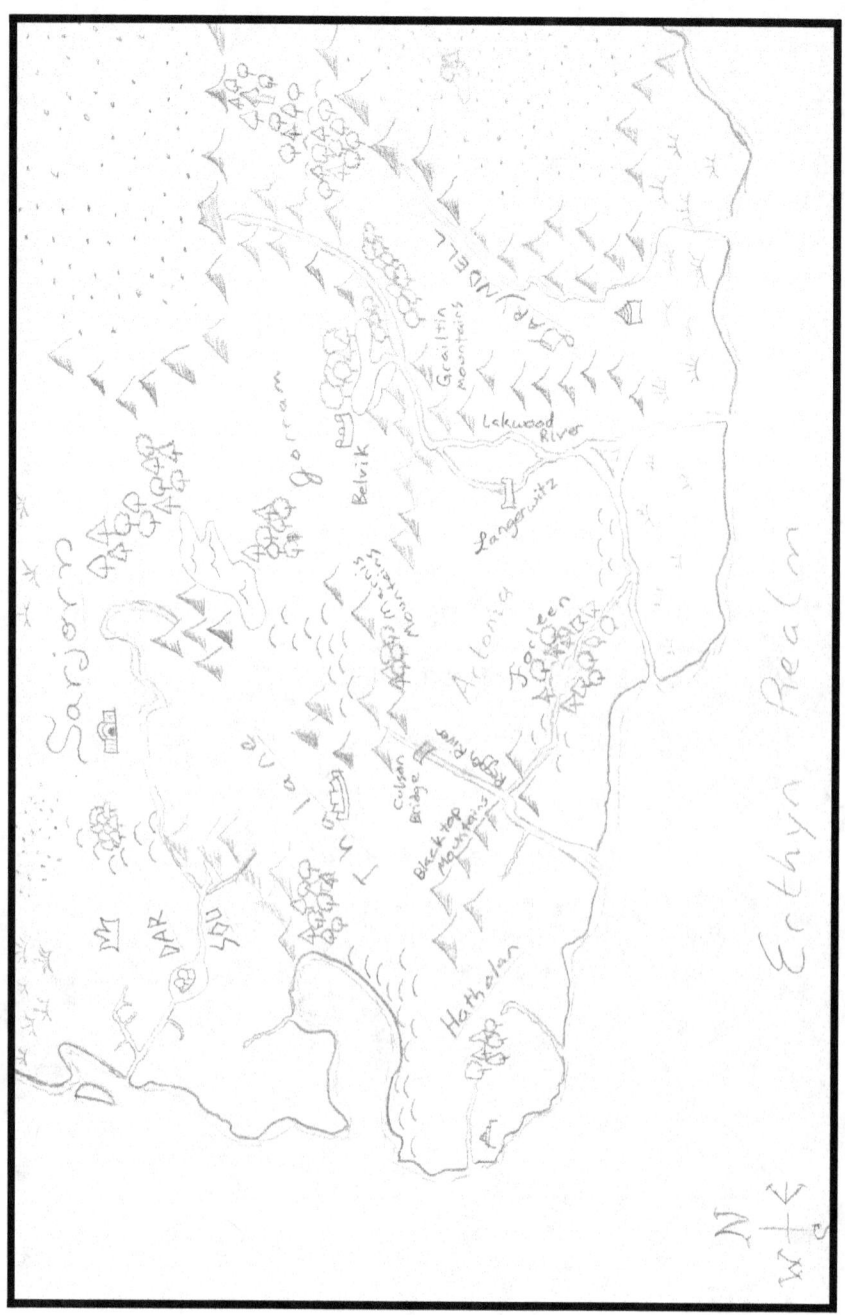

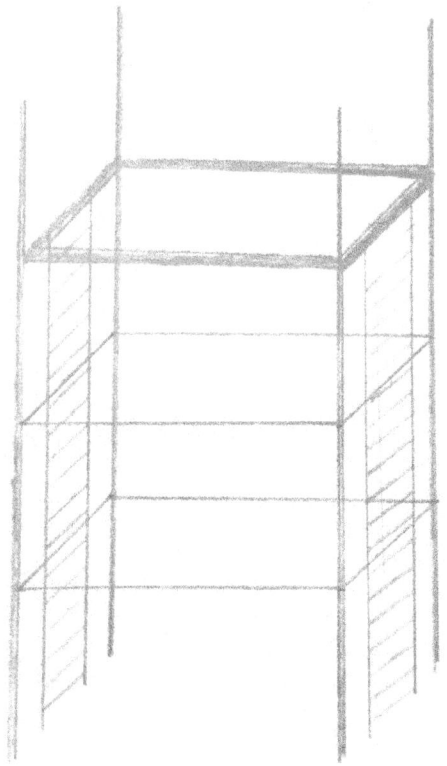

Verti-Dueling Structure

PREFACE

Just within the castle wall
    Where autumn leaves do fall
There sits alone,
    A single, white stone
To mark the grave
    Of one so brave.

And all who know his tale
    Believe without fail
His deeds would be unmatched
    If death had not snatched
From this good earth
    A boy of such high worth.

For glory, he sought none,
    Greatness he did shun
Rather than the royal art
    He stayed loyal to his heart,
Let love lead the way
    Rather than pride's sway.

Thus, his life he gave
    When an'ther he could save
A light that shone so bright
    He embodied more than a knight.
Forever he will be renown
    As the best never to wear the crown.

INTRODUCTION

The histories of the world do not record when the family of Wuhlfies first came to Artonia. Nor does it record why Cerk, the first king of Artonia, broke from the rest of the Erthyn Realm and established his own kingdom. From what is known of him, it would be easy to understand why so many would follow him as a leader. He was charismatic and selfless. Though not the most powerful in the world, he could delve into the magical arts. He was a skilled speaker whose power of articulation could turn the masses to his views. Fortunately, the man in power showed kindness and acted benevolently. He did not use his gifts to enslave those who followed him to his will; he bettered the world around him to the advantage of all. No, history does not show why Cerk chose to create his own kingdom, but it does show that Artonia became a most prosperous land and benefited greatly from its place in the world.

With cities along the southern border to establish harbors next to the Great Sea, the fishing trade blossomed. Sandwiched between the Reggen and Lakwood Rivers, the peoples of the south could send their product further north and set up shops all through the land. For the Lakwood River is the great river of the land – stretching beyond the lands of Artonia, into the neighboring kingdom of Jorram, and beyond. All along the river sit townships and villages set up to send supplies and food into the heartland of Artonia where farms and manufacturing cities reside. East of Lakwood, the land extends to the Mountains of Grailtin, mountains which separate Artonia from the mystical kingdom of Daryndell. Daryndell has had little contact with its neighbors over the last thousand years. Few venture beyond the peaks of the mountains, and those who do rarely return. The mountains follow the Lakwood River except for a small range which runs away from the river to create a border between Artonia and Jorram. A great valley between the Grailtin and Marnis Mountains provides the only roads to pass from Artonia to Jorram. But for the last several centuries the roads have been largely abandoned. Jorram and Artonia stand at odds with one another. An ancient feud which stemmed from the origins of Artonia. For while Cerk Wuhlfies wished to build a better world for his people, he did not count Yunul Grepportorn among them.

Grepportorn sought to better only himself and increase the wealth of his own family. He did not view the world in the same way Cerk did, but he did have many things in common with the first King of Artonia. He could command the masses as well, and those not enthralled with Cerk Wuhlfies stayed with Grepportorn in his kingdom. For many years, the kingdoms would have nothing to do with one another. An uneasy peace lingered between them. Then, Jorram fell on hard times. Their crops did not produce. The kingdom lost much of its wealth. In a desperate hour, Jorram turned to Artonia. While many Artonians would rather scorn their neighbors to the north, the descendants of Cerk Wuhlfies remembered the generosity of their original monarch and opened a treaty with the land of Jorram. For years, the kingdoms worked together until Jorram could once again support itself. It would take fifty years for Jorram to reach a place where it could stand on its own. Once prosperity returned to Jorram, the amount of trade between them lessened. In time, hardship would come to Artonia. Only, when they turned to Jorram to help, Jorram would close their borders and the ill-will returned as many people in Artonia suffered and died of starvation and disease.

Luckily, Artonia could look to other lands. On the western front, where the Reggen River ran as a border and in coordination with the kingdom of Thalane, the largest kingdom in terms of land, Artonia built the Culson Bridge as a last effort to save its people. The Bridge would facilitate trade between not only Thalane and Artonia but the kingdom to the south, Hatholan, and the two kingdoms to the north, Dar Sou and Sarjorn. These four kingdoms would work to continue the prosperity of each land over the centuries. While from time to time, the other kingdoms would try to broker some peace with Jorram, Artonia remained apart.

As each kingdom maintained its stability, the alliances between them dissipated. Not because they wished for a neighboring kingdom to fall, but because they wished to secure their own people and deal with their own struggles. The kingdoms were self-sufficient and able to run on their own, so they did. The kings who followed in the line of Wuhlfies continued to reign and lead Artonia over the years. The only thing that changed was the kings' reliance on magic.

King Cerk was well-versed in magic and used his powers to benefit his people. He taught his sons, and the magic passed on through the ages. Yet the great famine and disease which so crippled their lands caused the kings to doubt the true power magic held. When the construction of the Culson Bridge and trade with other kingdoms restored Artonia to its place in the world, they relied more and more on the reality they could see rather than the magic they were once told of. Eventually, the use of magic stopped in the royal family though some in the kingdom still held to their long-held beliefs.

Though King Cerk's belief in magic would not hold, the city he built as the capital of Artonia would. As the Lakwood River comes down from the mountains in Jorram, it splits in two. Along the western stream Cerk built the city of Langerwitz. Atop the one hill in the area, which would come to be called King's Hill, he constructed his castle. The easy access to the river allowed the people to travel downstream where the river would reconnect and continue running. Thus, Langerwitz could get supplies from all over the kingdom. Being on the western side of the river allowed them access to the farms. As the Lakwood traveled south, it would split again, but this time, one section of the river would continue straight south while the other cut across the land in a more westerly direction. Because of this western stream, the merchants and tradesmen of Langerwitz could reach the harbors along the Great Sea as well as the marshes in the southern and eastern most parts of the kingdom. Not many people lived there, but they served a valuable purpose. Where the Lakwood River cuts across the land, the northern bank is slightly more treacherous to travel than the south. There are hills, the Forleen Forest, and the southern tip of the Blacktop Mountains where the Reggen River splits and begins its journey towards the Lakwood.

In the city of Langerwitz, King's Hill sits in the middle of city. It stretches more East-West than it does North-South. There is a high wall around the whole city. It is a vast city which holds markets, homes, farms, and even a small forest in the eastern part of the city. Most who live there serve the castle. The royal guard have their homes in the areas closest to the castle. The farmers in the western part of the city keep a close working relationship with the rest of the farmers in the land. Those in the southern part of the city deal more with the merchants and harbors along the Great Sea. Most of the families who live in the city have been there for centuries as knighthoods for the royal guard are normally passed down from generation to generation. However, during the hard times, King Cecil Wuhlfies opened his doors to other knights from other towns and cities in the kingdom. When Artonia recovered fully, the tradition continued.

Within the last fifty years, Artonia has seen its prosperity diminish slightly. For most, it was unnoticeable. At the worst, people had to tighten their belts a little more. Very few starved, and very few went without. Things became more difficult however, when King Colten Wuhlfies and his queen, Penelope, both died from an illness contracted on a journey to the southern harbors. They left behind an heir to the throne in their son, Cyrus, and a daughter, Crystalynn. Though he was young and needed the whole of the council to guide him, the kingdom seemed to be in good hands. It became even more tragic when the doctors of the capital discovered Cyrus had an illness which would shorten his life greatly and make it unlikely for him to produce an heir. At best, he would live to his twenty-seventh year. By then, Crystalynn would be twenty. She would be ready to rule, but the decision of who would be her king was unknown. It would signal the end of the Wuhlfies' line of kings. Which family should take the crown will be under debate until the day Cyrus passes. There is one family which seems to be in a prime position to ascend to the throne. They are a noble family who have served the crown well. Even now, the head of the family serves in the highest position a knight of the land can serve. As if the fates smiled upon them, the knight and his wife have a son the same age as the princess. However, there is another boy of the land who wishes to win the princess's heart.

At the northern base of King's Hill sits a small cottage erected by order of King Colten. There live Elle and her three sons. Elle was born in the village of Vilrill, north of Langerwitz, and lived there for the first sixteen years of her life. During her fifteenth year, she met a young man training to become a knight named Armous. He was instantly taken with the young maiden though she showed little interest in him. Refusing to be deterred, Armous courted the young girl whenever he came to town. Eventually, she came to find the man charming and sweet, so she gave in to his requests. Within the year, they were promised to one another, and Elle's parents agreed to let her move to Langerwitz so she could live closer to her love.

For more than a decade, the two lived in happiness and began a family while Armous worked his way into the king's royal guard. All seemed to be well for the happy couple and the children they raised together. Then, tragedy struck when Armous surrendered his life in service to the king in a battle with the forces of Jorram.

In honor of his sacrifice, Colten decreed the knight's family be forever taken care of by the king and his court. For seven years, Elle and her family have wanted for nothing. Though they have struggled with the loss of their father, the boys have grown up well and proven themselves to be of the most honorable in the city. The youngest, Calvin, now aged ten, holds little memory of his father but is well taken care by his older brothers. The middle brother, Steel, three years older, has recently begun his training towards knighthood. It is Elle's oldest child, however, who finds himself at the turning point of his life. A handsome but shy young man, Lyosan is an athletic-looking youth. With blue eyes and straight, blonde hair, he doesn't quite look the part of a knight, but there is something truly admirable and honorable in him. Now seventeen, Lyosan is but a year from earning his knighthood and possibly becoming part of the king's royal guard like his father before him. He is not the most skilled trainee of his age group nor does he possess the sharpest mind. His effort and his heart cannot be questioned, but many of the other youths have a better skill set. At times, this makes Lyosan feel inferior. This is furthered by the fact that, outside of his father's courageous sacrifice, his family name does not have much panache. Part of him even fears he'll make a subpar knight and be given a token position rather than earning his place among his peers.

The other cause for turmoil in Lyosan's life stems from his friendship with Crystalynn Wuhlfies. Perhaps, if not for the unusual circumstances of needing to find a new king, the situation would not be as distressing as it is for Lyosan. Growing up, he probably wouldn't have spent any time around the princess. However, as they are of the same age and Cyrus must make the final decision of who will succeed him, they have spent a great deal of time together. Many of the youths in the capital who are of the same age have been accelerated through their training and have received extra training in kinglier affairs. The effect of all this attention has shown in the princess's demeanor. While she understood she would have to be ready to rule, she was not eager to consider so constantly the impending death of her beloved brother and king. Thus, she would often need an escape from the castle. Since Lyosan lives so close to the castle, she would turn up at his front door more often than others. The proximity to the castle always put the guards at ease, and Lyosan had an easy way about him which appealed to Crystalynn. Over the years, the two would run into each other often. Quickly, their friendship blossomed. As he grew, Lyosan's love blossomed for her as well. Though he knew little of love at this stage in his life, he came to believe early on that his heart belonged to her.

During the course of his comings and goings at the castle, Lyosan made many friends among the other youths. There were two, Shaylynn Storm and Fallon Welms, who stood out among the others. Though it would be improper to place wagers on which youth would be selected to be king, many would place a substantial sum on Shaylynn Storm, for it is his family which holds such a high place in the minds of so many. He is bright, athletic, and a handsome young man. With brown hair and brown eyes, his chiseled features draw the eyes of many a young maiden in the land. He keeps his face clean shaven but is ever the outdoorsman. Beyond his impressive stature, he possesses skills far beyond the normal youth. His father, Feylynn, is the High Knight of the Royal Court. To the pleasure of many, Feylynn also has a deep respect for the magical arts which he passed down to his boys. As some suggested the line of Wuhlfies is ending because they had forsaken magic, it looked promising to have magic back on the throne. Also benefiting his cause, Shaylynn has an older brother, Beylynn, whom many thought would rise to the position of High Knight when their father steps down. This would give Shaylynn a loyal captain of the army. Lyosan knew however, that the princess would often grow weary of Shaylynn. Though he was very accepting and open, his skills made him arrogant and over-confident. It was very easy for him to come across as condescending and patronizing though he would eventually see his error and work to make amends.

The one person who would always help Shaylynn see his errors was Fallon Welms. Fallon and his family lived next to Shaylynn in Langerwitz, and his father, Degon, served alongside Feylynn. Shaylynn and Fallon grew up together, played together, and trained together. With wavy, raven hair and brown eyes, Fallon grew up to be a handsome young man himself. His family heritage and bearing made him destined for a great life in service to the crowd. He was also bright and skilled – though not as skilled as Shaylynn. That fact never stopped him from facing Shaylynn in duels during training. There were not many willing to square off against Shaylynn, but Fallon would never back down. Many believe Fallon would make a good king if he was chosen, but all who knew him well knew it would be a difficult transition to the throne. Fallon would serve in any capacity, but he would rather prefer to be out of the spotlight or, at the least, have a friend to share the spotlight with. Shaylynn was always willing to do that. But Fallon was the more socially aware of the two. He knew when Shaylynn was getting too big of a head, and Fallon knew how to bring Shaylynn down as well. Unlike Shaylynn and Lyosan, Fallon had no siblings. Fortunately, Shaylynn and Lyosan were willing to be like brothers to him.

Once Lyosan became their friend, it was very much like they were brothers. The only time they were apart was when they were performing chores at their respective homes. When they were training, they were together. When invited to the castle for lessons, they went together. At times, Lyosan would break off to spend more time with the princess, but he would quickly be back with his friends afterwards. Given all the time they spent together and the fame within each family's name, the trio became well-known throughout the city. At times, it was for more nefarious reasons, for they were still young after all. They remained well-liked by adults and peers alike, save one – Pythyn Ornol. From an early age, he wanted to be the one everyone looked up to, but Shaylynn had that spot secured. When it became clear Shaylynn greatly preferred Fallon's company to Pythyn, Pythyn took great offense. It became the last straw when the two of them befriended Lyosan. Pythyn looked down upon Lyosan and saw him as living off his father's act. From what Lyosan showed in training, Pythyn saw nothing to put Lyosan in the same class as the rest of them. Shaylynn and Fallon, however, knew Pythyn had no idea what he was talking about and saw something truly special about the young man who lives at the foot of King's Hill.

CHAPTER I

As the sun rises one morning, Lyosan feels the first rays of light on his eyelids. As he has always done since his father's passing, Lyosan rises at the crack of dawn to perform his morning chores. Steel and Calvin have their chores as well, but they do not need to rise quite as early to complete theirs. Furthermore, their schedules for the rest of the day are far less hectic. Lyosan must complete a good portion of his chores before going to training at the castle.

The chores are nothing too strenuous for a boy Lyosan's age. He checks on the animals Elle keeps at the house. He makes sure they have food and water. He takes eggs from the chickens and gets milk from the cow. He also does some light cleaning around the outside of the house. By the time he gets in, Elle is up and has the kitchen ready to cook. While Lyosan changes for training and wakes his brothers, she prepares breakfast. Lyosan has just enough time to clean his plate when he hears a knock at the door.

"Did you save us any?" Shaylynn asks when Lyosan opens the door.

"Very funny," Lyosan replies.

"I've plenty if you need it," Elle calls from the table.

Fallon smiles. "Thank you, ma'am, but we haven't the time. Besides, Shaylynn has eaten already this morning."

Shaylynn rolls his eyes and waves at Elle. The younger boys and she wave back as well. Lyosan puts a few things away, then joins his friends outside. They turn down the road and begin the slight climb to the castle on King's Hill. At first, none of them have much to say, but a matter does weigh on Shaylynn's mind.

"Did you happen by the castle yesterday?" Shaylynn asks Lyosan.

Lyosan shakes his head. "They kept the doors closed all day. The princess never came out."

Fallon chuckles, toying with the idea that Lyosan only cares about the castle when the princess shows herself. Shaylynn and Fallon have teased Lyosan about the matter in the past. Years ago, it would've riled him up, but now it only bothers him slightly. He gives Fallon a little shove to show him.

"I should not have mentioned her," Lyosan admits.

"She's always on your mind," Shaylynn teases. "I'm sure it's difficult to keep her name off your lips at all. You should be commended for not mentioning her more."

Lyosan rolls his eyes and moves ahead of them briefly.

"Now, don't pout," Fallon chides. "It's not very becoming – in a royal sense."

Lyosan stops and glares at them. "Why I ever befriended the two of you is beyond me."

"Yes," Shaylynn says mockingly, "the decision was entirely yours." He shakes his head a few times before getting back to the point on his mind. "I only ask because my father was late returning home."

"You think the king grows ill?" Fallon asks.

Shaylynn shrugs his shoulders. "It is possible. I also know my father has been concerned as little has been heard from Jorram."

Fallon grunts. "An enemy remains silent and that gives him cause for concern?"

"They know the transition of power could take place any time," Shaylynn explains. "Artonia will be vulnerable while we argue over which family should succeed the Wuhlfies. The only question is when they will make a move."

Shaylynn worries about these affairs more than he lets the world know. Around other company, he would never broach such matters. Conversely, when alone with Lyosan and Fallon, he will discuss politics as if he already serves on the King's Council. Fallon cannot take these talks seriously. In some ways, Fallon still thinks with the mind of a child. He knows it will change in time, but for the time being, he would rather fill his mind with more innocent concerns. Lyosan, always eager to follow Shaylynn's lead, tries to stretch his mind and widen his horizons.

"Surely, it is too early for that," Lyosan suggests. "It would do no good to attack when the king's health remains strong."

"If it is so strong," Shaylynn replies. "What's more, they could attack as a means to further the argument. Try to make us focus so much on the problem we become blind to all else."

"Well," Fallon says, "if we focus so much on that problem, we will be blind to what Jonas attempts to train us."

Jonas Barr is the man in charge of training the youths; a charge he has performed for well-over twenty years. When Cyrus was young, Jonas even trained him. For his years of service, Jonas keeps a chair on the council though his duties require him to miss most of their meetings. In cases of emergency, Jonas must heed the king's call. In those cases, Shaylynn's brother Beylynn fills in as the trainer. Today, however, Beylynn will merely assist as he normally does.

As the boys approach the door to the training area, they see Jonas awaiting them. An older man, with some wrinkles around his eyes, Jonas's face rarely holds anything but a scowl. Despite his age, he is as daunting a figure as he always was. He is a man of average height, but he is a stone wall. Having fought in past wars, Jonas is a hard and demanding man. Praise does not come often, and he has little room in his heart for pity. Standing in the frame of the door with his arms crossed, he does not move as the trio approaches.

"Glad you could grace us with your presence," Jonas says.

Lyosan fears they've arrived late. "Are we tardy?"

"We cannot be," Shaylynn replies. "Stefen and Darrow were still in their homes when we left."

"A leader should show initiative," Jonas says turning his attention to Shaylynn. "A leader should always be first when he knows he will one day command the lives of his company. He will ask for their loyalty; surely, he can give them his time. Especially one whose brother arrives hours in advance."

Shaylynn nods in understanding. He does not appreciate being chastised like this, but he knows it comes with the territory. Fallon must hide a smile. It always pleases him to see Shaylynn grounded in such ways. But were he to show it, Jonas would happily give Fallon a lecture as well. Lyosan doesn't have such concerns. He doesn't take pleasure in this. He'd rather slide on by.

As Shaylynn apologizes to Jonas and moves on, Beylynn approaches with a smile on his face. It only deepens the scowl on Shaylynn's face and brightens the smile on Fallon's. With Jonas now behind them, Lyosan even lets himself revel in the moment. Beylynn may be ten years older than Shaylynn, but he does not stand but a couple inches taller than Shaylynn. He possesses more size than Shaylynn, a sign of his years and training.

"I tried to make you come with me this morning," Beylynn reminds his brother.

"Why should this morning be so different?" Shaylynn asks.

Beylynn looks around him and sees a small crowd. They are not eavesdropping, but Beylynn does not want to give them the opportunity to. He motions the three boys to the side. In truth, he'd rather speak with Shaylynn alone, but he has learned over time the difficulty in splitting the three of them apart. Furthermore, Shaylynn will tell them later regardless of the restrictions Beylynn gives him. Once the four of them are safely away, Beylynn gives his explanation.

"The king has opened discussion over which family should marry into the throne," Beylynn admits.

"Why the change?" Shaylynn asks.

"His disease progresses," Beylynn replies, "not to the point where his life is in danger, but enough to hasten him towards action."

"Discussion counts as action?" Fallon asks.

"When it comes to handing over the throne, yes." Beylynn explains. "For years, he'd kept the conversation to a select few. Now, he invites leaders from all over the kingdom."

"He needs to bring in leaders of the land to tell them he'll select someone from within the capital?" Shaylynn questions.

Beylynn smirks. "Already measuring the throne, brother?"

Shaylynn rolls his eyes. "I doubt I'm the man for the throne. But with all the training we've received and lessons we've been given, it is clear the king wishes for someone close to the princess to take the throne."

Beylynn nods. "I concur. But the transition will be smoother if he at least hears the others out. They are leaders in their own right after all. Loyal to the throne, yes, but worthy of the respect an audience with the king grants."

As more of the youths enter the room, Beylynn returns to his duties and leaves the boys to ponder these new developments. They do not have much time to think them over though, because as their friends arrive, new topics of conversation arise. Very soon, they put aside the whole matter regarding the king and lose themselves in the topics of their peers. They joke and jest for nearly thirty minutes before the last of the trainees arrive. Not one for wasting time, Jonas rushes the last ones in to begin the session.

"Stand at attention!" Beylynn yells.

The youths quickly form ranks. Shaylynn, Fallon, Pythyn, and three others stand in the first line. Lyosan takes a spot directly behind his friends but several rows back. The order in the ranks was never specifically set, but it had remained the same for several years. Shaylynn and Fallon tried to move Lyosan up in the ranks, but he always refused. So long as he had a place behind them, he was perfectly content. As soon as Jonas feels every eye in the room focused on him, he begins.

"I feel a certain lacking in your dedication lately. No better example of this can be seen than in the tardiness many of you showed this morning. It used to be I'd have you waiting at the door in the morning. Sometimes, many of you were here before the crack of dawn. You were beating down the door to have a go at whatever I put in front of you. And when you were put in front of a challenge, you attacked fiercely with the passion of a Knight of Langerwitz.

"As time has gone, your passion has waned." He pauses for a minute to let the idea sink into the minds of the youths. As each reflects on this truth, many refuse to meet his eye. "Complacency, gentlemen, is a dangerous thing!" He booms the statement in a manner which causes many to jump a bit. Then he brings his voice back down and continues. "Wars do not begin when you decide you're ready. Tragedy does not announce itself before it strikes. You must remain ever vigilant, especially when the world around you tries to lull you into a sleep.

"Those of you who have the good fortune to become knights of the castle will be given a title and a duty and for years, your life will be the same. You will think monotony will be your whole life. And if you let that thought become your reality, you will fail in your duty, and it will cost you your life or the life of someone you love."

Though Jonas is a hard man who takes the training seriously, he rarely lectures so severely. Only when the youths have failed to meet his expectations in an important manner does he resort to these tactics. In the past, when the lecture ends, the punishment begins. Usually, it's a hard day of training with many cuts and bruises to be had. So not only have the harsh words from Jonas struck them at their hearts, but the possibility of a long day awaits them.

But Jonas is a smart man and remembers they are still but children. At times, when children need to be reprimanded, it requires a strong word and some action. Other times however, it requires a strong word and an opportunity to change. The youths seem to be at the perfect age for such an opportunity to be given. For this opportunity has not been selected at random, nor has Jonas thought it up recently. It is one which stands as a tradition for the youths in training. Those who take advantage of the opportunity begin to climb up the ladder of success. Many end up on the King's Council, and several end up serving as the High Knight of the Royal Court. This group, however, may have one youth who will serve a much higher purpose. One who will ascend to the throne of Artonia. And while Jonas may have his opinion on which youths are better for the throne, he will need more than his thoughts to support a decision should the king ask him.

"Fortunately, for you, you are not knights, yet," Jonas says. "You are boys learning to be men. You still need to figure out how to fight off monotony and maintain vigilance. You need to further your journey towards manhood. Another step in that process will take place tomorrow. In preparation for this step, we will end today's session before lunch, and you shall have the afternoon off."

A sigh of relief echoes through the room. Beylynn chuckles.

"But we will still have a tough morning," he informs them. "Your training has covered a lot of ground. You've learned to handle a sword, shield, bow and arrow, spear, crossbow, and dagger. You've fought hand to hand, on the ground, on a horse, and even in water. You've been placed in scenarios when the odds were with you and against you. Starting today you learn to tackle a new challenge."

With a wave of his hand, Beylynn commands the doors on the side of the room be opened. Two guards open the doors and Jonas calls for the youths to follow. In their eagerness to see what lies ahead and the excitement of a free afternoon awaiting them, they break ranks and crowd through the door. As they enter the adjacent room, Jonas commands them to stand along the wall. The room is large enough for the youths to stand shoulder to shoulder and make one ring around the room from door to door. Jonas and Beylynn move towards the center of the room and give the youths a moment to take in the room.

The room has an abnormally high ceiling compared to most rooms in the castle. There are no decorations or banners on the walls though there are plenty of windows in the higher parts of the wall. Weapon stands encircle the room along with shields. Mostly there are swords, but there are a few spears as well. Past the stands is the most fascinating element of the room. Four posts, each rising at least forty feet into the air, stand as the four corners of a square. The square's sides are twenty feet. On two sides of the square are a ladder which goes to the top. Crossbeams create a square around the posts at ten, twenty, and thirty feet respectfully. The first two squares do nothing more than provide support and decoration. The third is quite different. Though the vertical posts rise above the square by about ten feet, the rest of the borders of the square are solid wood. The beams are thicker and slightly wider than the rest. They are maybe two feet wide. On the ground surrounding the structure are piles and piles of hay. Beneath the hay are cushions and matting. Upon seeing the structure in the room, every one of the youths knows what it is for.

Verti-dueling is the favorite sport of the capital. Two participants ascend the ladders and take their place on the highest square. Each takes a sword and a shield. Once the match begins, it only ends when one of the two yields or falls from the top square to the ground. Because it can be a dangerous sport with the participants falling from a high perch, tournaments are not held often. Instead, only a select few participate in challenges and exhibitions of the sport. Aside from the great level of skill it takes to fight, verti-dueling requires the highest level of balance and awareness. Each challenger must be in total control of his faculties. He must use his weapon to defend, attack, and maintain position on the square. And just because one of the duelists loses his weapon does not mean the other has won. If an unarmed participant can use the vertical posts and the square to his advantage, a weapon in the hands of a lesser opponent becomes meaningless.

This is a big step in the training, indeed. While dueling with weapons always possesses a level of danger, it is nothing compared to what will happen when the verti-dueling begins. If all of them, the entire group of trainees, will attempt to master this skill, many of them will fall multiple times. Some could be seriously injured. It is a thought already crossing Lyosan's mind because he thinks he could become one of those injured souls. His mastery of dueling isn't the highest, but worse than that, he is not very comfortable with heights. Being consistently suspended thirty feet above the ground while trying to fend off an opponent does not sound like something he will excel at.

As he scans the room, Lyosan sees many faces with the same show of concern. He is not alone in his fears in terms of the whole, but when it comes to those he tries to keep up with, he is alone. Shaylynn's face beams with confidence as though he was waiting for this day to finally arrive. Fallon, though not as confident as his friend, does not seem overly perturbed by this revelation.

"Gentlemen, welcome to the sport of verti-dueling," Jonas announces. "It is the king's sport – the maker of champions and legends. The man who can master the square can tackle the greatest challenges life can throw at him.

"It is a sport which challenges every facet of your training and requires the highest level of creativity. We can show you the basics and suggest ways to better yourself, but the truth remains that success comes from places beyond the training room."

Jonas begins walking around the posts as he speaks. Beylynn steps away, smiling knowingly, as though he remembers every word of Jonas's speech and loves hearing it. Jonas looks at every boy standing around the edge of the room. Each boy seems to feel as though he is being measured by Jonas. As though Jonas holds the truth of their ability in his gaze and is telling them here and now whether they have the ability to make it or not.

He is an excellent judge of character, Jonas. It was the reason Colten named him to train the youths of the capital. In many ways, he could see the measure of a man with but a look at him. He could spot weakness in a person, sometimes even before that person had a chance to discover it for him/herself.

"If you fear it, you may succeed, but only if you don't let that fear control you. Even though the kingdom loves the sport, it is a very dangerous sport – only for the best and the most determined. It will test you in ways we cannot. And if you conquer it, you will discover the best you could possibly be."

Taking a shield and a sword from the stands, Jonas tosses Shaylynn the equipment and motions for him to ascend the ladder. With a nod Shaylynn walks towards the dueling stand and starts up the ladder. On the other side, Beylynn has procured a sword and shield as well. Shortly after Shaylynn reaches the third tier of the structure, Beylynn climbs and joins him at the top square.

"Take a moment, Shaylynn," Jonas instructs. "Get your bearings with the weight of the shield and sword. Take a few steps around the square."

Shaylynn does as instructed. His first steps are slightly uncomfortable. Though he teeters a bit, he never looks as though he'll fall. He walks to the corner of the square, then steps to the next beam. Stepping quicker now and taking a few practice swings, he moves down the next beam and leaps to the next – the same beam Beylynn continues to stand on. Unfortunately, Shaylynn's enthusiasm betrays him somewhat. His jump is too wild and uncalculated. He lands on the beam, but the combination of the weight of his equipment and his error in judgment shifts his momentum to a point wherein he is about to fall. As the crowd below gasps, Shaylynn struggles to regain his balance. Beylynn watches, ready to react, but he doesn't advance on his brother's error.

After a few tense moments, Shaylynn regains his balance and steadies himself on the beam. A few deep breaths show his concern in the matter. Once he regains his composure, he faces Beylynn. Beylynn smiles coyly as he swings his sword circularly from side to side. Shaylynn just shakes his head.

"No concern for your younger brother?" Shaylynn asks.

"If you'd have fallen and landed on your head, it might have done you some good," Beylynn remarks.

Shaylynn smiles. "Is that what happened to you?"

"I wasn't foolish enough to try a jump my first time up."

"Or you were frightened."

Before they can further their brotherly banter, Jonas interrupts them. Having watched these two grow up, he knows their arguments and bickering can go on for hours on end. "You can settle your argument later. Get on with the exercise."

Shaylynn turns to Beylynn who holds his sword out ready for the duel. A smirk still sits upon his face. Normally, Shaylynn would return the look, but given his new predicament, he will wait to show his confidence.

"How is this to go, then?" Shaylynn asks.

Beylynn chuckles. "Just a simple lesson. Show the others how it works. Test your abilities in a new arena."

"Doesn't really seem fair to test someone before he's had a chance to prepare."

"It may not be fair, but it is the most telling."

With no other words, Beylynn advances on Shaylynn with a quick strike. Shaylynn goes on the defensive and blocks the strike. As he backs up, he quickly finds himself against the corner post. Beylynn continues the attack, knocking away Shaylynn's shield. Staying on the attack, he relieves himself of his own shield to focus on the attack, which becomes harder and harder for Shaylynn to fight off. To give himself some breathing room, Shaylynn lashes out with a strike. Beylynn blocks it easily enough, but Shaylynn gets the time he needs to step to the adjacent beam and get away. Beylynn runs around the other side of the square to get a better attack point.

However, Shaylynn has enough time to meet Beylynn at the corner, and the two continue to exchange strikes. Neither hits their mark and both maintain their balance upon the beam. After a few exchanges, Beylynn wraps around the outer edge of the beam and attempts a strike. Shaylynn counters and swings his sword to retaliate. He has not realized that Beylynn has set a small trap, and by swinging, Shaylynn has sprung it. Retreating to the inner side of the beam, Beylynn allows Shaylynn's blade to strike the post. Shaylynn has swung hard enough to embed the blade in the wood slightly. As Shaylynn struggles to get it out, Beylynn jumps behind him and attacks. Shaylynn must duck to avoid the first blow. But in doing so, he puts himself in a submissive position below Beylynn's blade.

From the ground, the exhibition has been quite the sight. Every youth who watches Shaylynn fight his brother is greatly relieved to be on the ground, rather than on the dueling square. Each has had to bear the brunt of Beylynn's blade before. He is an excellent fighter, who has such command of his skills that he can be trusted to test yet never seriously wound a trainee. Never has he had to hold back in order to protect. He can be as ruthless and calculating in training as he would be in battle. As such, he becomes the perfect challenge for the youths – a wonderful way for them to hone and perfect their own skills. For the best of the youths anyway. Lyosan, who watches with wide eyes, feels he'd never be able to last two minutes up there with someone as skilled as Beylynn, let alone win a duel. For all Jonas claims this sport can do, Lyosan can't help but consider it will only show him more clearly how he doesn't belong.

Beylynn holds the tip of his blade a few inches from Shaylynn's neck. The smirk he's held since the start of the duel seems larger than before. Shaylynn, a bead of sweat dripping down his face, begins to slow his breathing to get a handle on the situation again.

"You can yield," Beylynn suggests.

Jonas watches with bated breath. It is moments like these where Shaylynn tends to impress most. And if he can do something more, anything more here, he will do so. For just a brief moment, he scans the room. The youths who watch have a look of anticipation in their eyes. They suspect Shaylynn will be able to succeed still. Fallon even has a smile on his face. He knows his friend will not yield. Such faith and belief in a leader. It is everything one would look for in a captain and a king.

The plan has been forming in Shaylynn's mind. The plan Fallon suspects has been brewing though he can't fathom what it would be. While Beylynn has been basking in the glory of his advantage, Shaylynn has worked to take it away.

"Why spoil the fun?" Shaylynn replies.

Rolling off the square, Shaylynn leans back and grabs the adjacent beam with his hands. Allowing his momentum to do the rest, he swings around the beam and comes up on the other side. Beylynn lunges to attack, but Shaylynn sidesteps the attack and goes for his blade. Ripping it free, he swings down and knocks Beylynn's sword away from him. As Beylynn's sword drops to the ground, the youths gasp and cheer Shaylynn on. Beylynn has to recoil and keep his footing. The smirk which had been on his face moves over to Shaylynn's. Suddenly, the sport which seemed so daunting moments ago has turned into another exercise to be conquered. With his blade a few inches from his brother's chest, Shaylynn moves to end the duel, his confidence rising every second.

"You can yield," he suggests.

And this is the second trap Beylynn has set. Knowing how quickly Shaylynn's arrogance can betray him, Beylynn allows this scenario to play out to teach Shaylynn a valuable lesson if needed. And after his 'suggestion,' it is clear to Beylynn that it is needed.

"The duel does not end when one is without a weapon," Beylynn says, and the smirk returns to his face.

Beylynn turns and runs. Annoyed by what Shaylynn perceives as Beylynn's arrogance, Shaylynn runs after him. Beylynn leaps into the air and grabs the corner post with both hands. Using it a slingshot, he swings around the post, feet together and ready to strike. Before Shaylynn can even think to react, he realizes he's come too close. He catches Beylynn's feet square in the chest and goes toppling off the beam. Moments later, he crashes into the hay.

As soon as Fallon sees Shaylynn fly off the beam, he starts moving towards him. Lyosan follows shortly after with a couple of the other youths. Just because there is a mound of soft hay does not mean the landing is soft. Moving quickly to Shaylynn's aide, the youths surround him but do not move him.

"Are you okay?" Fallon asks.

Shaylynn grunts in reply. "Would you be?"

"Could've been worse."

"How?"

"Your father could've been watching."

With a chuckle, Shaylynn starts to get up. Fallon and Lyosan give him a hand and pull him to his feet. Almost as soon as Shaylynn is on his feet, Beylynn is leaping down next to him.

"Nothing wounded but his pride," Beylynn jokes. "Fortunately, he's got plenty to spare."

Once the youths get Shaylynn out of the hay, Jonas addresses the group again.

"Notice how quickly the tables can turn in this sport," he says. "The most skilled fighter with the greatest advantage can be outdone by an unarmed opponent who understands the value of his surroundings."

Jonas stares at Shaylynn as he speaks, so as to direct his comments directly at him. Shaylynn shies away from Jonas's gaze and tends to a bruised back. Once Jonas is certain the lesson has set in, he continues.

"But mastery is for another day. Before you can learn to run, you must be able to stand. In groups, you will ascend the dueling square and perform simple balance practices. Those not on the dueling square will practice dueling techniques on the ground using the squares marked out with chalk."

The morning flies by for the youths. Shaylynn and Fallon remain together, but Lyosan keeps to a group he feels more reflects his skill level. When Lyosan is on the ground in the practice squares, he feels comfortable enough. He struggles to stay within the confines of the square, but so do many of the people he is with. When he gets on the actual square, however, things are much worse.

Beylynn trains them on the square. He works as patiently as he can, but when Lyosan hesitates and constantly has to regain his footing, Beylynn's patience wears thin. Fortunately, the training only lasts through the morning.

Though every youth loves a short day of training, they also recognize that a short day usually means a significant challenge tomorrow. For that reason, Lyosan wishes to get home immediately so he can take care of chores quickly and assure himself a good night's sleep. He knows; however, his friends will have drastically different plans. Most likely, Fallon would be okay with simply returning home, but Shaylynn would never allow such an easy day.

After putting his things away, Lyosan sees Shaylynn and Fallon approaching. The smile on Shaylynn's face confirms he has something in mind. Lyosan looks away to suggest he has not seen his friends yet. They know better.

Taking a seat on either side of him, Fallon and Shaylynn warmly smack Lyosan on the back. He jolts a bit as this greeting has never been one he prefers. Nevertheless, they continue to use it.

"You did well today, Lyosan," Fallon says.

Lyosan does not agree, but he would also rather not argue the point. "As did you my friend," he says and then turns to Shaylynn. "I doubt I need say anything about your performance, Shaylynn."

"Indeed, you do not," Shaylynn says, "but it is always nice to hear."

Lyosan rolls his eyes, but Fallon merely smiles and speaks for Lyosan. "You did very well today, Shaylynn."

Shaylynn shakes his head as though the adulation is unwarranted. "Oh come now. We needn't dwell on the past...no matter how spectacular it was. Indeed, gentlemen, we should only concern ourselves with the here and now. We've a long afternoon ahead of us as we've been granted a small reprieve from training."

Lyosan quickly says his piece. "And I shall use the time to end my chores and get some needed rest. You two may do as you wish, but I have no intention for mischief."

Shaylynn and Fallon lean back so they can see each other. Fallon holds a smile as he sees the feigned insult on Shaylynn's face. "Mischief?" Shaylynn says a bit dramatically. "Dare he accuse us of getting into mischief?"

"He did indeed," Fallon says. "I heard as much."

Lyosan sighs as he realizes the error in his thoughts. It is not a matter of being honest – indeed his words are true as true can be. His error is in giving Shaylynn an opportunity to use Lyosan's own words against him. Had he merely said he wished to be left alone, he'd have stood a better chance than maligning their endeavors.

As Lyosan moves to leave, Shaylynn clasps his shoulders and forces him back to his seat. Lyosan rolls his eyes and looks at Fallon hoping for some manner of escape. Fallon merely shrugs to suggest this problem is Lyosan's entirely. When Lyosan turns to see Shaylynn looking at him, Shaylynn holds a serious, though comically so, expression on his face.

"You accuse me, your oldest and dearest friend, of mischief?"

"Does that surprise you?" Lyosan asks.

"Surprise me?" Shaylynn repeats. Then he places a hand over his heart. "It hurts me, Lyosan. It hurts me deeply that you would suggest I, in my diligent efforts to better our quality of life, would reduce my efforts and sincerest workings to mere mischief."

"Then, please," Lyosan says, hoping this will be the end of it, but knowing far better, "allow me to apologize for my rash comment."

Shaylynn gets up off the bench and steps away. "I do not know if a mere apology can mend the wound to my heart."

Lyosan sighs, not really wanting to ask this question. "And what would?"

Shaylynn turns back to the pair of them with a smile on his face. Fallon pats Lyosan's shoulder in sympathy. "I'm so glad you asked," Shaylynn replies. "I was thinking of considering a small incursion into the castle tonight."

"Into the castle?" Lyosan repeats.

"We've done it before," Shaylynn replies.

"Once," Fallon corrects him, "when we were but children. And I believe your father had you performing three times your normal chores for a month after our little prank."

"Chores," Shaylynn shrugs, "I didn't really mind them, anyway. I needed something to do since I couldn't sit for that month."

Lyosan chuckles.

"See," Shaylynn says, "you are in high spirits for this challenge."

As Shaylynn continues to attempt to goad his friends in mischief, Beylynn approaches from behind. Loudly dropping some training materials to attract their attention, Beylynn clasps his brother on the shoulder.

"Perhaps, you should reserve your spirits for the challenge tomorrow," Beylynn suggests. "You will not want to approach it on a few hours' sleep – especially after the fall you suffered."

Shaylynn shakes his head. "You merely wish to stifle my enjoyment."

"Dear brother," Beylynn replies, "if I wished to do that, I would merely alert father of your plans."

True as it was, it still grinds at Shaylynn that Beylynn injects himself in Shaylynn's affairs. Fortunately, Beylynn will be let off the hook by Shaylynn's cohorts.

"All the same," Fallon says, "I would rather attend to some chores as well. Harvest will be coming in soon. I must ready the barns."

Finding none willing to join him in is endeavor, Shaylynn concedes the idea.

"Another time perhaps."

"As crazy as it seems, Shaylynn," Beylynn says. "I would not object to your breaking in to the castle."

"And why is that, brother?"

"As a future guardian of the throne, it behooves me to know its weaknesses."

"Then, someday, I shall perform for you a great favor."

"I look forward to it."

The boys retire for the afternoon and complete their chores. With Beylynn's warning in their minds, they are early to bed. While they cannot imagine the task that awaits them nor anticipate the need for an early night, they soon receive a small indication of what awaits.

CHAPTER II

Early in the morning, before the sun rises, Beylynn stirs Shaylynn from his slumber. Saying nothing more than rouse the troops, Beylynn sends Shaylynn out the door and tells him to be at the castle in ten minutes. Three other youths have received the same instructions. It is a common tactic for the knights to use – spreading the word from one to another to gather together and prepare for battle. Only here, there clearly is no battle. There is only the challenge.

Shaylynn goes on his usual route, leaving Fallon and Lyosan for the end. Of the two, he awakens Fallon first. Having taken the word of Beylynn to heart, Fallon needs little time to prepare for the morning task. Within minutes, they leave and race to Lyosan's house. Running up the walkway, they come to the door and bang hard. Minutes later, Elle comes to the door.

"Boys!" she cries, "why the ruckus?"

"Our apologies, ma'am," Shaylynn offers. "But we have been summoned to the castle. Lyosan must come at once."

"Very well, then," Elle replies. "Wait here! I don't want his brothers disturbed."

Elle goes to Lyosan and rouses him. Saying little, she instructs him to dress for training. She also informs him Fallon and Shaylynn are outside waiting for him. Lyosan scrambles out of bed as quietly as possible. He also wishes for his brothers to remain asleep. Less than a minute later, he steps out of the door to join Shaylynn and Fallon.

"What is this about?" Lyosan asks.

"I don't know," Shaylynn admits. "Beylynn woke me up and told me to get everyone to the castle."

"This does not bode well for the rest of the day," Fallon comments.

"Take comfort in the fact that we received warning." Shaylynn reminds him.

"Not much of one," Lyosan says.

"Far more than the others received," Shaylynn says.

Wasting no more time, they race for the castle encountering more and more youths along the way. Knowing time is of the essence, they say nothing. As the castle comes into view, they see Jonas standing at the doorway with a torch in hand. Already many have come, but more will arrive. Beylynn also stands with a torch in hand.

"Prepare yourselves," Beylynn instructs. "We have a small breakfast for you. Eat light, for you will not want to be weighed down."

"What is this about?" Shaylynn asks his brother.

"Patience, Shaylynn," Beylynn replies. "The answer will come in due time."

"Our good friend has arrived," Fallon says sardonically.

Shaylynn turns to see Pythyn passing through the door. Shaylynn and Pythyn have known each other all their lives and hated each other most of them. While this may seem a tragedy, it is worth noting few can stand to be around Pythyn. He does not garner much in the way of friends – nor does he wish to. Ever the loner, Pythyn looks for any advantage he can gain. Though he is a handsome youth with abilities which place him towards the top of the class, he cannot stand to be considered less than the best.

Unfortunately, for Pythyn, the best remains Shaylynn. All the youths and knights of the land know it. Even Pythyn knows it. Hence, when the opportunity arises, he cuts corners, takes cheap shots, and fights dirty whenever he can get away with it. Many fall victim to his tricks, but Shaylynn never has. And whenever Pythyn attempts to pull one over on him, Shaylynn always manages to overcome him and settle the score. Often, that means getting violent.

Beylynn watches for a moment as Shaylynn stares at Pythyn. Though Beylynn must remain impartial in the matter, he also thinks little of Pythyn. Always the studious one, Beylynn cannot stand it when Shaylynn allows Pythyn to become a distraction.

"Keep your focus, Shaylynn," Beylynn tells him. "You needn't worry about him. The more you concern yourself with him; the greater the likelihood of your sinking to his level."

"I know," Shaylynn responds.

Beylynn then turns to Fallon and Lyosan, who often receives the brunt of Pythyn's taunts.

"That goes for the two of you as well," he says. "Focus, it is what will save you in a desperate hour."

"Yes, Beylynn," they reply.

The boys take a seat inside the hall. They eat together while discussing with the other youths what this could be. A full half hour passes before Jonas addresses them all.

"Young knights, I thank you for your diligence. Though we must better our efforts in the future. When the Knights of Langerwitz receive the same summoning, they arrive at the castle in less than ten minutes. I have an hour glass set for ten minutes which I had to turn before you all arrived. Nonetheless, I come before you this morning with another challenge..."

The term does not elicit a warm welcoming from the youths apart from Shaylynn. While he holds no joy for a challenge, he does always welcome a chance to upstage the works of his elder brother. Not since the days of their father has there been a knight with the qualities of Beylynn. Growing up, Shaylynn heard all about the deeds and performances his brother perpetrated. For the longest time, it only bred resentment, but after a while, Shaylynn used the ill-feelings as motivation to drive himself. Thus, when a challenge comes forward, Shaylynn always prepares himself for a chance to outdo Beylynn.

"...This is a test of your endurance and character. The Bridge of Anwar rests some ten miles outside the walls of Langerwitz. Though it can be reached by many roads, the easiest path to the bridge is by following the river. This, naturally, takes you through many challenges including: trees, rocks, hills, and deep sand. The youth who can navigate the terrain, reach the bridge, and return to the castle doors first will be declared the winner and receive a special token from the princess..."

At the mention of the princess, many of the youths perk up. Chief among them is Lyosan. Though he does not find comfort in such a race, he will risk nearly anything to win an audience with Crystalynn for his prowess as a knight. Pythyn also finds this opportunity intriguing. He can defeat Shaylynn, taunt Lyosan, and curry favor with the princess, all in one act.

"…The test of endurance obviously comes from the race to the bridge," Jonas continues. "The test of character comes from this: no one from the city will be able to know whether you actually reached the bridge or not." This comes as a shock to the youth. They look from one to the other uncertain of what this could mean.

Finally, Stefen raises a hand in the air. Jonas nods in his direction, to which Stefen replies. "Sir, do you mean you're not going to be watching us?"

Jonas scans the room for a moment to give them time to consider the reasoning behind this. When enough time has passed, he turns back to Stefen.

"That is correct, Stefen," he finally says.

The crowd immediately begins murmuring to each other. Many question whether it could be true or not. Several suggest this is merely a test and they will be monitored as they race. Others consider the possibility of being able to shirk this challenge and merely take the afternoon off. Pythyn stands alone with a smirk on his face. Shaylynn, Fallon, and Lyosan agree he is up to something.

Unsure whether or not he believes in this tactic, Shaylynn turns to Beylynn with a questioning look. Beylynn looks back at his brother with a diffident smile. Try as he might, Shaylynn cannot gauge any measure of truth from his brother. Beylynn knows. He undoubtedly went through the same process when he was in training. Now, it becomes all the more pleasing to get to inflict this enigma on a new group of students.

"Now," Jonas continues, "we still start the race when the hour comes up. It will be seven in the morning. If you run steady, pace yourselves, and use your breaks intelligently, you should be back in plenty of time for lunch. For those of you looking to make a name for yourselves…" Suddenly, the attention turns to Shaylynn. "…let it be known that the record for this challenge stands at four hours and forty-two minutes, set by none other than Beylynn himself."

Jonas raises an arm over Beylynn's head to put him on center stage. The youths applaud Beylynn's efforts while a pit of competition festers in Shaylynn's gut. Having the time in his head, Shaylynn already begins strategizing his movements through the race. As the look of determination grows more concrete, Lyosan's spirits sink. If Shaylynn goes after the record, as he clearly intends to, Lyosan has little hope of being able to claim the prize. Fortunately, he has Fallon to defend him.

"I recognize that look, my friend," Fallon says to Shaylynn.

"I suppose it has become a rather common one by now," Shaylynn replies.

"Perhaps your thoughts should lie with something more important than a chance to upstage your brother."

Shaylynn ponders the words while the instruction from Jonas goes on.

"And while it would be magnificent to see that record fall this day," Jonas says, "there are far more important victories to take from this day. For indeed, I have stated that no one in the city will be aware of your doings once you leave the walls. Thus, you could run out of the northern gate, turn to where you are out of sight, and stop for the day. Then, to avoid detection, you could hide in the trees until the group who does run to the bridge returns. Once they pass, you can follow them on in, and we will be none the wiser. Who knows, maybe you'll set the record without ever even setting your eyes on the bridge. It could happen, but the victory you achieve will be hollow. If that's all your looking for, then so be it. If you wish to be nothing more than a name on a page, then you will fulfill your dream today.

"However, if you truly wish to become something better. If you wish to earn a place among the finest knights in the land, nay, the world, you will complete this task in full. Only if you earn the privilege will you become the name the other youths aspire to. Furthermore, you will gain the confidence to achieve where so many others have been unwilling to try. For I can say, and Beylynn can say, that many of you will cut corners today. Many will give up on the task and merely decide to call it a day. I have seen it; Beylynn has seen it. You will see it. What matters is, will it be you?"

Saying nothing more, Jonas leads the youths out of the chamber and to the starting line. Most of the youths let Shaylynn, Fallon, and Lyosan come to the front of the pack. They understand Shaylynn will attempt to break his brother's record. They have no doubt Fallon will be close behind him, and they know, at least for the opening burst, Lyosan will be with them as well.

Pythyn also works his way to the front of the pack. The other youths are less willing to let Pythyn by, but none wish to cause distress before the race begins. As they exit the castle and step out into the light, they see the princess standing at the starting line. Jonas stops the group, and they bow respectfully. Lyosan's heart begins to beat faster the moment he sees her.

She is a regal sight. The princess does not stand taller than most of the youths before her, but she does have a much more commanding presence. She is small, though not fragile in the slightest sense. Her dark hair flows from her jeweled tiara and cascades behind her to the mid of her back. In her green eyes, there hides the beauty and enormity of nature's wealth. Her porcelain skin and smooth features capture the eye, and her smile softens even the hardest heart.

"Rise, young knights," the princess commands.

With smiles on their faces, they raise their heads. As the princess scans the group, she smiles at Lyosan, Shaylynn, and Fallon. Lyosan cannot help but look away for a moment to catch his breath.

"It is an admirable feat you attempt today," Crystalynn says. "I would hope my presence at such an early hour would support that claim. And I wish you good luck. No doubt Jonas has already informed you about the token the winner shall receive from me." Though none have noticed it yet, the princess holds a precious stone in her hand. It is round, translucent, and as blue as the cleanest ocean waters. Holding it up now for them all to see, she explains its importance. "This stone, which we call an Allolyst, comes to us from the farthest parts of the known world. When our tradesmen ventured out into a more peaceful world, they discovered these stones in the caverns of the Eastern Expanse. Though they are simple to look at, they are believed to bring luck and happiness to those who possess them. We give them to youths as a symbol of their promise and eventual place in the kingdom."

Though the stone possesses no owner, it still seems that the princess speaks directly to Shaylynn as she goes on.

"For it takes a special kind of person to achieve the task in front of you. Someone with speed, endurance, and will. But also, someone with the strength of character to do what is asked of him even though no one will work to ensure it happens. It is only for the best, and, I believe, the best shall receive it today."

With a nudge to Lyosan's arm, Artimous jests. "That counts you out, Lyosan."

Lyosan turns away, having no retort. Shaylynn, having heard the remark, begins to understand Fallon's comment. Winning this race would clearly mean far more to Lyosan than it would to Shaylynn.

"Can you beat the rest?" Shaylynn asks Lyosan.

"What do you mean?" he asks.

"If we run this race together," Shaylynn explains, "do you think you'll be able to beat the rest of the youths?"

"I'm not sure," Lyosan replies. "Why does it matter?"

Fallon overhears the entire conversation as well. As Lyosan seems unable to see the gift at his feet, Fallon decides to explain it to him.

"If you can keep up with us," Fallon says, "you'll win the race at the end."

Lyosan does not believe this logic. "It would take a small miracle to outrun the others. It would take the hand of God to see me beat Shaylynn."

"If you can keep pace with us," Shaylynn says, "I will let you win the day."

"You mean that?" Lyosan asks.

"Will you follow?" Shaylynn asks, almost as though he hates the idea.

"I will try," Lyosan admits.

"Then let us fly my friends."

"I can barely see the road," Fallon admits.

"Just stay behind me," Shaylynn says.

"That'll be helpful; I can barely see you!"

As the hour comes, Jonas raises his arms in expectation. Keeping a close eye on the clock, he drops his arms as the hour arrives. Immediately, the flood of youths takes off towards the northern gate. Though many attempt to take the lead, Shaylynn holds on to it easily. Fallon follows with Lyosan in step. At times Fallon struggles to keep an eye on Shaylynn. It doesn't help when a shadowy figure cuts in his way.

"Don't tire yourself out, Shaylynn," Pythyn, the shadowy figure, says.

"Three times a week I run to the river and back to my home within the hour," Shaylynn replies. "I do not think this is beyond my scope. Unlike some."

"I can accomplish anything you can and better!" Pythyn snaps.

"I look forward to seeing that," Shaylynn admits. "As it is, I need to start racing now." Shaylynn calls over his shoulder. "Let's get going!"

Shaylynn darts forward with Fallon and Lyosan close behind. Pythyn considers following at their pace but quickly realizes it would be folly.

"If you get lost," Fallon cries, "just follow our footsteps! By the time you reach the gate, the sun will be shining anyway!"

Within the first few minutes, the trio separates themselves from the pack. They rip down the road past the still sleeping houses. Through the first stretch of the race, they have a remarkable pace going and are well ahead of the pack. Better yet, the first rays of light are seeping over the horizon.

"Finally, some light!" Fallon cries.

"We'll be out of the city before the sun rises," Shaylynn projects.

"You sound certain," Fallon replies.

"I am."

Lyosan begins to calculate the time required to run at this pace. Though he feels fine for the moment, he doubts his ability to maintain once they reach the city limits.

"Do we really mean to keep this up?" Lyosan asks.

"Why do you ask?" Shaylynn asks.

Lyosan shrugs. "I fear the tempo will claim me."

"We shall rest halfway to the bridge," Shaylynn explains. "We can take another rest once we reach the bridge and another on the way back."

"Three respites seem risky," Fallon says. "Especially if you mean to capture your brother's record."

"I must admit I yearn to make it my own," Shaylynn says. "But I feel our friend could benefit more from this win."

Lyosan smiles at the thought. Even Fallon cracks a smile.

"Such a turn for you, my friend," Fallon says to Shaylynn. "Putting aside petty records for a friend in love!"

"Someday, I shall collect on this favor!" Shaylynn says.

As the gate comes into view, the boys notice the gate remains closed. The men guarding the gate did not expect any of the youths to arrive so quickly. When they see the three coming at them, they scramble to action. It will take a few minutes to unlatch the gate and swing the doors open far enough for them to pass. At their current rate, the boys will arrive just in time. But Shaylynn realizes that would work too well. Why not have a little fun with it?

"Shall we test fate?" Shaylynn asks over his shoulder.

"What does that mean?" Lyosan asks.

"You shall soon see," Fallon replies.

With a smile, Shaylynn quickens his pace. Fallon immediately follows suit, but Lyosan takes a moment to piece it together. As they race towards the door, the guards lift the beam off the braces. Shaylynn speeds towards the gate as the two guards attempt to move the beam off to the side. Looking over their shoulders, the guards see Shaylynn coming at them. They try to ward him off by waving their hands to slow him. Instead, Shaylynn leaps in the air, lands momentarily on the beam, and springs off the board. Doing a quick flip in the air, Shaylynn lands on the ground and keeps running on the far side.

Fallon turns to Lyosan and gives him a wink. Lyosan shakes his head, not wanting to upset the guards and uncertain he can make the jump without hurting himself. But Fallon ignores him and sprints on. Lyosan reluctantly joins in.

The guards are teetering on their feet from Shaylynn's antics. When Fallon and Lyosan approach, they yell for them to desist. Fallon ignores them, and Lyosan goes along, and the two leap, landing on the ends of the beam, and spring off as well. Fallon makes the jump with ease and bounces off a moment later. Lyosan stumbles a bit and almost falls off. With the slightest of corrections, he restores his balance and leaps from the beam. The guards tumble to the ground under the weight of the beam. The others around them curse the youths for their recklessness, but none chase after them.

Fallon and Lyosan soon catch up to Shaylynn. He and Fallon revel in their antics, but Lyosan does not find their games so amusing.

"Can we not do that again?" he begs.

"Depends on the opportunity," Shaylynn replies.

"Besides, we only react to the guards' lack of preparedness," Fallon informs. "We have performed a service in ensuring they are no longer lax in their responsibilities."

"They do not see it that way," Lyosan says looking back over his shoulder.

Shaylynn and Fallon burst out in laughter. For the next hour or so, they race along the river towards the bridge. Though they stumble from time to time over the rocky terrain, they do not lose their pace. By Shaylynn's calculations, they still have an opportunity to break the record. While he believes he can maintain his pace, Fallon finds it hard to believe he can continue. Lyosan knows for a fact he cannot. If it were someone other than Shaylynn, he would have already voiced his disdain for their speed. However, he knows Shaylynn wishes to keep the rest of the youths at bay, especially Pythyn.

Perhaps sensing the tiring of his comrades, Shaylynn decides to take the first break a little sooner than anticipated. They stop on a small bank by the river. Shaylynn grabs a few handfuls of water. Lyosan dunks his head into the current and comes up refreshed. Fallon watches behind them to ensure they keep their lead.

"What's the outlook?" Shaylynn asks.

"I see no one," Fallon replies.

"Good," Shaylynn says, "take some water, Fallon. We shall leave shortly."

Lyosan hears the plan but does not share in Shaylynn's desire to get back on the path. By his estimation, Lyosan will need a good rest if he is to continue at his current pace.

"If no one is coming, we needn't be so hasty," Lyosan says. "Surely, they will need a rest at this point as well."

"Perhaps," Shaylynn concurs, "but the sooner we complete our task, the sooner we can take a full rest."

"You forget, my friend, not all have your fire to drive them," Fallon reminds him.

"Too torrid a pace, I take it?" Shaylynn guesses.

"For all except you," Fallon says with a wink to Lyosan. "Do not forget you have already promised the victory to another…"

"If he can up with me," Shaylynn corrects.

"A promise made when it is known it can't be kept is hardly a promise at all," Fallon says.

Shaylynn sighs deeply, having been caught in a deception. Perhaps he did not mean for it to happen, but now faced with it, he cannot deny it. If he is to let Lyosan win, he cannot run to win himself. In the back of his mind, Shaylynn has been trying to win the race and break his brother's record. None of his party share this ambition. At the same time, he must push Lyosan past his normal limits. Even Fallon would agree that Lyosan cannot win at his preferred speed, but as Shaylynn pushes him to extremes, he cannot push him over the edge.

"Very well," Shaylynn concedes, "we will slow our pace to meet our collective needs." Lyosan smiles at the news. Fallon nods in agreement. However, Shaylynn will not come completely to Lyosan's side. As Lyosan rises, Shaylynn puts a finger in his face as warning. "Do let it be known we will not slow to a snail's pace. It will still be rigorous, and I will not let another man pass me. If you cannot win, I shall!"

"I understand," Lyosan says, "and I swear to you if I cannot keep with you, I will let you pass me by."

"Does no one think I have a chance?" Fallon asks. Shaylynn and Lyosan turn with a smile. "I only mean to say I am keeping up with you now, Shaylynn. What's to say I'm not saving up for a late push?"

"Because you were the one who asked for a slower pace," Shaylynn replies. "Though you asked for it for Lyosan's sake, you need it yourself."

"So you say," Fallon says.

After a minute or so, they ready themselves for the next stage of their journey. Each knows they will run until they reach the bridge. Until that time comes, they shall find themselves overcoming a great many obstacles. The rocks loom larger and the hills rise higher. With the sun climbing higher into the sky, the heat only adds to their troubles.

In good time, they reach the bridge and take another rest. With the sun high in the sky, the boys get a good look at the lands around them. Displaying the promising crop the year will bring, the rolling plains of Artonia stretch out in front of them. Though their lungs ache and bodies yearn for inactivity, Shaylynn and Fallon find energy in the beauty around them. Lyosan takes a seat on the bridge and attempts to catch his breath. While it would make sense for Shaylynn and Fallon to join him, they climb atop the bridge wall to get a few feet higher in the air.

"I rarely journey here," Fallon admits. "I must wonder why."

"We've our own matters to attend to," Shaylynn explains.

"But the world gives us this beauty, and we do not even lift our eyes to it."

"Then we must give it its due now. Don't you agree, Lyosan?"

Lyosan turns from his seated position to see his friends on the wall. Though he's been working to calm himself, he still has not entirely accomplished his goal. Instead, he takes a few more heavy breaths before answering. Fallon cannot help but chuckle at his friend's struggle.

"I cannot imagine taking in beauty that was not the princess at this moment."

Shaylynn is surprised at his candor. "He grows honest as he grows tired." Shaylynn hops down from the wall. Fallon follows. "Perhaps it is unwise to let him finish the race first. When he goes to collect his prize, he may profess his love for the princess. One can only imagine how the king will react."

Fallon looks Lyosan over and sees the heavy panting still being perpetrated by Lyosan. Despite wanting to see his friend succeed, he cannot, at this moment, see success in his future. Perhaps, Lyosan still requires a bit of a push to carry on in his pursuit.

"I doubt it will matter, Shaylynn," Fallon ribs. "Based on his current condition, I daresay Lyosan will not be able to keep up with you."

Lyosan stirs at the words, but he cannot bring his words out to retort. He does shake his head and force a bit of resolve into his veins. He cannot tell if it will be enough, but he will at least try to prove Fallon wrong. After a few more breaths, he musters a reply.

"I expect doubt from Shaylynn but not from you, Fallon. Did you not champion my cause a few minutes ago?"

"If you mean when we first paused, that was well over an hour ago."

"And what has changed your heart so?"

"Nothing has changed in my heart. It is only in my mind things have crystalized."

"And what does your mind tell you?"

"Only that you grow tired in the shadow of a better man."

Fallon points to Shaylynn, which only irritates Lyosan further. He would show them both the error of their ways. Only, in his heart, he knows in a true display of ability, he would not measure up to Shaylynn.

"When last I checked, we stood in this cause together," Lyosan says. "It matters not how much greater he is than I. All that matters is the promise he has made to me."

Though he usually revels in hearing of his own prowess, Shaylynn furls his brow when Lyosan responds. Something Lyosan has said strikes hard at a nerve in Shaylynn's mind. And now is as good a time as any to voice his grievance.

"You speak of greatness within me," Shaylynn begins, "as though it is some foregone conclusion I have any..."

Fallon snorts. "You, who claim to be better than any his age, show doubt in your greatness?"

"I believe in my abilities," Shaylynn corrects, "perhaps with more zeal than deserved. I am not foolish enough, however, to claim any of it to be greatness. What have I done? Won races? Outdueled my peers? What of it?

"Many who win early fail to succeed later as they become eclipsed by those who lost and yearned to win." Then, he turns to Lyosan. "Tell me, my friend, what greatness lies in me that is so far beyond your reach?"

Lyosan chuckles to himself. If he could, he'd thunder at Shaylynn for this madness. Not a youth in the kingdom would deny the greatness Shaylynn remains destined for. None would measure themselves against him and honestly say they were on the level. Shaylynn knows this…he must. Yet, he attempts to humble himself, quite poorly at that, by suggesting what he can do is nothing great. What Lyosan would give to have one day to bask in the limelight in the manner Shaylynn does every day. Instead, he must bite his tongue and focus on the task at hand. This is his friend after all. He still means to see Lyosan win this race.

"You could have left me in the dust an hour ago," Lyosan replies. "Undoubtedly, you could set a record none of us could dare reach. It is only because of our friendship you even give me a chance to run with you."

Shaylynn turns aside and shakes his head. Fallon, like Lyosan, does not understand the look upon Shaylynn's face. Everything Lyosan has said, Fallon agrees with. Yet, Shaylynn seems to be thinking an entirely different way than them.

"You do not run with me because I allow it," Shaylynn explains. "You run with me because you seek the prize this race affords. You forgo any concerns about greatness or showing yourself better than the others. All you think of is proving yourself to the princess. And through that love does your greatness show.

"You blush and hide from your emotions. Yet, they make you strong."

"They are the impossible dreams of a peasant," Lyosan responds. "They do not better me in any way."

"Do you think I have slowed my pace?" Shaylynn demands.

Lyosan shrugs. "Clearly, you have. You promised at our first break you would meet my ability rather than display your own. How else could I maintain my position?"

"Look around you," Shaylynn commands. "See the place of the sun in the sky. Think of how quickly we've arrived at this spot. I have not slowed since we first stopped. You have not noticed because your mind remains focused on the endgame."

Lyosan and Fallon study the sky and focus momentarily on the sun. Indeed, its placement stands early for as much as they believe they've accomplished. They doubt truly the day stands so young when so much has transpired.

"This is merely a bit of your magic," Lyosan guesses. "You fool our eyes with this view of the sky."

Shaylynn chuckles. "Again, you place too much faith in my abilities. You think I could keep the pace I keep while maintaining magic upon you."

"If you could, I'd rather you use the magic to revive us," Fallon says, "give us strength to finish at the torrid pace you've set us on."

Shaylynn jests. "I cannot do that either."

Lyosan continues looking towards the sky, attempting to clarify the situation in his head. Shaylynn speaks the truth; they do stand at the bridge at a remarkable time from when they left. If they can continue this pace on the way back, they will all set a record for the time taken to complete the race.

But, as he stands at the bridge, Lyosan feels his legs turning to stone. Even now he can barely lift them to walk. The idea of being home in his bed before the day ends seems a lost dream. Shaylynn and Fallon will soon depart on their return journey to the castle while he attempts to gather himself for a less than stellar attempt to get home. The others will catch him soon. He'll sink to the back of the pack – perhaps to where he belongs.

They continue to rest for a few minutes. Shaylynn does so hoping Lyosan will be ready to move sooner rather than later. Fallon stands pretty much ready to go. He'd wish for more time to rest, but he would rather follow Shaylynn's lead.

Though Shaylynn has not used his magic to this point, he begins to use a bit to sense the progress of the others. Extending his vision down the road they followed, he sees a band of eight youths roughly ten minutes from the bridge. Other groups are a little way behind, but the one he really searches for is Pythyn. Surprisingly, Pythyn lags behind the other groups a good way from the bridge. From what Shaylynn can tell, he does not strain himself greatly in this endeavor. Something seems amiss in Shaylynn's mind.

Aside from that, the pace Shaylynn wishes to maintain stands about to fall. They must be on their way soon if they will reach the castle in his time. Granted, he does not need the pace to win at this point, but Shaylynn did not make the promise to Lyosan for his own reasons. In his heart, Shaylynn wishes to show Lyosan that Lyosan is capable of succeeding in ways he does not believe.

"Come then, let us be off," Shaylynn says slapping Lyosan on the back. "The day is wasting."

"Surely, we have some time still," Fallon replies, thinking more of Lyosan than himself. Though, the difference is small.

"I measure ten minutes before the next group arrives," Shaylynn informs them.

"Then give us ten minutes," Lyosan pleads. "Even if we leave when they arrive, we shall win by ten minutes."

"I'd rather win by twenty," Shaylynn replies. "Besides, that mark of yours only works if none turn back before they reach the bridge."

Fallon scoffs. "Surely none will attempt something so foolish. Even though Jonas says they have no way of knowing, the trainers will know somehow."

"I can think of one who will turn back."

Shaylynn turns to begin back towards Langerwitz. Fallon stands ready to follow, but Lyosan hesitates.

"Give us a moment more, please."

"You said you would keep my pace," Shaylynn reminds him. "You promised as much."

"Very well then," Lyosan concedes, "begin without me, and I shall catch up."

Fallon and Shaylynn both know the dangers in giving in to this request. The first being the unlikelihood that Lyosan would be able to catch up. If he is tired now, he will surely find it difficult to make up the difference in their pacing. Also, there's no telling when Lyosan would actually get back on the road. If he cannot recover by the time the next group of youths arrive, he will lose his nerve and fall behind.

"You've held your own with us so far," Fallon says, "don't lose it now."

"You've held faith in me so far," Lyosan retorts, "don't lose it now."

When it does little to calm Fallon's concerns, Lyosan adds. "A mere moment more is all I require. You shall see. The sight of you going shall will me forward."

As Shaylynn looks to the trail, he sees the distant dots of other youths coming. Believing Lyosan will either hold to his word or lose the race, Shaylynn sees no need to tarry any longer.

"Very well, then," Shaylynn says. "Let's be off, Fallon."

"We cannot leave him!" Fallon cries.

"Leave him or carry him," Shaylynn replies. "I've done enough of the latter. It's up to him now."

Shaylynn says no more and leaves the bridge. Fallon holds for but a moment to try to give Lyosan one last opportunity to go with them. He only shakes his head and waves Fallon on.

"See you at the finish," Fallon says.

"I'll be waiting for you," Lyosan jests.

Fallon smiles, though halfheartedly. He cannot continue to believe Lyosan will keep his word. Holding back the words he wishes to say, Fallon turns his head and runs after Shaylynn. Lyosan watches as his companions tear down the trail and eventually disappear into the shrubs. Try as he might, he cannot get himself rested to his satisfaction. Every time he believes himself ready to rise, a hard cough rips through his chest and causes him to rethink leaving. He realizes, however, that he must be on his way soon. His legs grow weaker by the second. He can feel a slight shake in his hands. Attempting to ready himself, he rises to his feet and takes a couple deep breaths. His steps are shaky; his gait hectic.

There is nothing really at stake here, he tells himself. *Merely a race amongst my friends. Who cares if I don't finish first? I will still finish before many of the others. Considering how little they believe in my ability, it will be a good first step towards gaining some respect.*

The more he lets the thoughts enter his mind, the more he resolves to rest until he is truly rested. All the while, the distance from Shaylynn and Fallon grows.

CHAPTER III

With Lyosan out of the pack, Shaylynn carries on at a torrid pace. Fallon, who knew this would occur, manages to keep up with Shaylynn though with greater difficulty than on the way to the bridge. He fears he will be unable to keep the pace for long. He shall have to attempt to slow Shaylynn in some manner. As always, the best way to distract Shaylynn is to get him talking.

"Do you think he has left the bridge?" Fallon asks.

Shaylynn glances over his shoulder but does not break stride. "I doubt it severely."

"You are too hard on him," Fallon says. "He kept pace with you for hours."

"And if he would've believed in himself, he could've done it for hours more."

"Why do you demand so much of him?"

The question catches Shaylynn off guard. Truly, there is little reason as to why he should expect great things from Lyosan. They have lived very different lives. Lyosan has toiled his whole life to keep his family going. Shaylynn, while working hard in his own right, has been able to explore aspects of life Lyosan would not understand. Shaylynn has been trained for these kinds of exercises. He has been bred to be a knight and a champion. Lyosan has not. He merely wishes to attain such an honor. Many in his place would never reach such a position. One could assume that without the benefit of Lyosan's father's place in the kingdom and his close association with Shaylynn and Fallon, Lyosan would not be considered for knighthood. And yet, something still emanates from him which causes Shaylynn to hope.

"He is my friend," Shaylynn finally replies, "dear to me as my own brothers. I only wish for him to succeed."

"Humph," Fallon grunts. "You never show such concern for me!"

Shaylynn smiles and turns to face Fallon. "As if I've ever needed to!" he says. "I daresay I'd be more likely to be jealous of your skill before I feared your shortcomings."

"Sounds like you fear the competition," Fallon jests.

"I never said you were at my level," Shaylynn retorts. "I only said it was the more likely of the two occurrences. The litany of likelihoods to come before both of them runs longer than the Lakwood."

As they continue down the path, they begin to encounter the other youths. Leading the pack are Stefen and Shawl. When they see Shaylynn and Fallon, they almost lose their footing they are so surprised.

"You've already reached the bridge?" Stefen shouts as they come near.

"And are on your way back?" Shawl adds.

"We'd tell you all about it," Fallon says, "but we've still a stretch to go."

"Don't be too long yourselves," Shaylynn says as they pass, "wouldn't want to waste an entire day on such a simple task!"

The youths race on in disbelief. One, Mitan, cannot help but notice Shaylynn and Fallon have lost a member.

"What of Lyosan?" Mitan asks. "Does he still draw breath?"

"He did when we last saw him," Fallon replies.

"If he's still at the bridge when you reach him, "Shaylynn says. "Remind him we do have to get back to Langerwitz for the challenge to end!"

"Do not remind us," Brynnal pleads. "We've still the first leg to finish."

With no more time together, the two groups go off in their different directions. Indeed, Lyosan has not yet left the bridge. Though he continues to stand and walk a bit, he cannot force himself to start back to the castle. He realizes he should have left with Shaylynn and Fallon. Having them in front of him would've given him something tangible to chase after. Now that he stands alone, it all seems so trivial. Another group will be approaching soon. He will simply run with them. If he can be one of the second wave to arrive at the castle, it will be a great feat.

A few minutes later, the wave arrives. Stefen and Shawl still lead the pack. They wave to Lyosan when they see him. He reciprocates as he jogs in place for a moment. He quickly stops as his legs ache.

"Not injured, are we?" Stefen asks.

"No," Lyosan replies with a chuckle, "just readying myself for the return journey."

As the youths come to a rest at the bridge, Nycolas turns to look down the path. He remembers seeing Shaylynn and Fallon not that long ago, but long enough to suspect Lyosan has had plenty of time to recover.

"It was some minutes ago we encountered Shaylynn and Fallon, "he informs Lyosan. "They, no doubt, are well on their way back."

Lyosan nods. "They did seem anxious to commence their race. Shaylynn would not say why, but I suspect he believes something foul is afoot."

"No doubt you mean Pythyn," Mitan says.

"You know something of him?" Lyosan asks.

Mitan shrugs. "Only that he does not strain himself like the rest of us. Perhaps he has no intention of making it to the bridge."

"Well, I suppose I'll have that over him, then," Lyosan says with a smile. "I completed the task better than he."

"Until you reach the finish, I do not think you can boast about completing anything," Refgen comments.

Lyosan lowers his gaze before he replies. "I suppose you are right."

A twinge of failure begins to strike Lyosan's heart. Indeed, he cannot talk as though he has completed the race. As it stands, all he has done is lose pace with his friends. And as honesty begins to settle in, he also begins to think he will not be ready to leave the bridge any time soon.

Sensing the distress in Lyosan, Stefen attempts to right the ship and get Lyosan back on task.

"Come, enough of this," he says. "We will be off in a few moments, Lyosan. Run with us."

Lyosan appreciates the offer but does not think it will happen. He still thinks back to Shaylynn's claim regarding the pace they ran to reach the bridge. It cannot be true that Shaylynn continued at his typical speed. There is no way Lyosan could keep up or Fallon either. Though Fallon remains a better runner than Lyosan, he cannot hold a candle to Shaylynn. No,

Shaylynn lied when he said Lyosan truly kept up with him. It was a ploy to keep Lyosan with them – only that and nothing more.

"I will try," Lyosan finally says.

"Good," Darrow replies offering Lyosan a hand. "After running with Shaylynn you will know the best path to run. We've tried keeping in his footsteps, but that is no easy task."

A sentiment Lyosan knows all too well.

Though he leaves with the second wave, Lyosan quickly finds himself falling behind them on the return trip. And they are not willing to slow to allow others to keep up with them. They know they cannot catch Shaylynn, but they also will not allow a mediocre time for the task.

Still, the race continues. As Shaylynn and Fallon burn the trail back to Langerwitz, they pass the youths still making their way to the bridge. Most are clustered together, running in waves much like Lyosan does now. Every now and then, they come across a single youth running on his own. Usually these are greatly out of breath and struggling with each step. They spot a few stopped and at the river. All look greatly tired and weary from the race. Some have broken down in tears over the exercise.

Though Shaylynn makes note of every face he encounters, he searches more definitively for Pythyn. He sensed him at about the halfway point when they left the bridge, but he has not encountered him yet.

"Where is he?" Shaylynn says more to himself than to Fallon.

"Does it really matter?" Fallon asks. "You'll beat him in any event."

"He's planning something," Shaylynn replies. "I'm sure of it."

"So it comes down to your skills and intelligence against his?" Fallon asks assessing the situation. Then, he sarcastically adds. "Yes, you are clearly at a disadvantage."

"Even the best laid plan can outwit the best opponent," Shaylynn retorts.

"I wait on pins and needles to see it happen."

In truth, Pythyn has not made it to the halfway mark. He took a short repose to let others pass him by, then hid in the bushes to ensure none would see him. Though Shaylynn could not read the full of Pythyn's scheme, he could see something devious in his mind. If he had the time or the discipline, he would attempt to locate Pythyn and delve deeper into his thoughts, but he cannot spare his focus.

Instead they sprint on. His mind back on point, Shaylynn picks up the pace, which Fallon reluctantly adopts. With a new rigor running through him, Shaylynn loses sight of everything else around him. Indeed, Pythyn has been lying in wait for Shaylynn to happen by, but his plan will not come full circle yet. He knows if he overtakes Shaylynn too soon, it will look suspicious. Shaylynn will need to be close behind him if his victory is to look legitimate.

So rather than jump out and attempt to surprise Shaylynn or Fallon, Pythyn gives them a good lead, then follows. Since he is well rested and his two victims have been going all morning, he will be able to keep up with them until the time comes.

Sadly, Lyosan loses sight of the troop he set out with. He also finds himself stopping often to catch his breath. Were Shaylynn and Fallon with him, they'd never be so tolerant of so many stops. He sees many others pass him on the road. Though each offers encouragement, their progress provides greater hindrance. Confidence flees like rabbits before a wolf. It may be nightfall before he reaches the castle.

As Shaylynn and Fallon approach the city wall, Shaylynn begins to distance himself from Fallon. Fallon knew it was coming. He only hopes the distance doesn't grow too great.

As Shaylynn pulls away, Fallon begins to hear footsteps from behind. At first, he thinks it to be children running along with them. He can remember doing the same when he was a child. However, as the steps coming closer and closer, he begins to realize it couldn't be a child. Rounding the road into the city wall, he catches Pythyn out of the corner of his eye.

"Shaylynn!" he yells.

No avail. Shaylynn either cannot hear him or is too focused. In any event, Fallon attempts to run faster to keep Pythyn at bay and reach Shaylynn in time. As he races through the streets of Langerwitz, he believes he may stand a chance. Though Pythyn is closing in on him, it is not by leaps and bounds. Shaylynn remains a decent distance ahead.

As the castle comes into view, Fallon turns to see Pythyn only a few feet away. Fallon turns to give one last attempt to warn Shaylynn, but Pythyn catches him and knocks him to the side. Fallon falls to the ground as Pythyn turns his full effort towards catching Shaylynn.

With the castle a mere three hundred yards away, Shaylynn feels a record coming his way. He remains oblivious to Pythyn and Fallon's 'mishap' along the way. Only when a foot collides with his and he begins toppling to the ground does Shaylynn realize what is happening.

While falling forward, he sees Pythyn overtaking him with a wicked smile on his face. Not to be outdone, Shaylynn wraps his body into a ball and rolls with the fall. As his feet touch the ground, he springboards back to his feet and continues the run. From behind, Fallon sees the event go down and stops in amazement.

Shaylynn, however, must continue his torrid pace. With Pythyn a few steps ahead and running his ease, Shaylynn must ignore his fatigue and the pain from his tumble. Knowing Shaylynn still runs, Pythyn works hard to stay ahead, but Shaylynn cannot be stopped and pulls ahead of him in the homestretch.

When he comes racing into the castle, the princess awaits the arrival of the youths.

"Congratulations," she says to Shaylynn offering him a drink. "I daresay you broke your brother's record of time."

Shaylynn bows to the princess and accepts the drink, though he says nothing as first Pythyn and then Fallon soon join him in the castle. Pythyn wears a sharp scowl on his face. Shaylynn matches his look as Fallon smiles. The discourse between them is always heated, but whenever Shaylynn foils one of Pythyn's unseemly attempts, it brings a smile to Fallon's face. The princess, however, remains oblivious to the tension and concerns herself with another matter.

"Is Lyosan not among you?" she asks. "He did leave with you."

Shaylynn is glad for the opportunity to turn away from Pythyn without reprisal. Though he is not glad for the news he will deliver.

"He did indeed," Shaylynn replies. "However, he needed to take a rest."

The princess, guessing the amount of rest Lyosan would take, frowns at the news. Pythyn chuckles.

"The run too much for him?" Pythyn chides.

"It is amazing what happens to those who run the full race," Shaylynn replies.

Pythyn frowns. "Are you accusing me of something?"

"If he doesn't, I will." Fallon adds.

Before the matter can truly be settled, Jonas enters with Beylynn in tow. Shaylynn knows better than to accuse Pythyn of anything now. He has no proof in any event. Should he voice his grievance, Beylynn would see it as little more than the petty battle forever being fought by the two. Whether he likes it or not, Shaylynn must remain silent. Fallon too for that matter.

"Do nothing of the sort," Shaylynn says to Fallon.

"He cheated," Fallon replies.

"A fact we cannot prove."

"How much more obvious can it be?"

"It matters not."

Beylynn walks over to Shaylynn with a playful smirk on his face. Though he rose early with his brother, he has been able to rest while the youths ran. With a rested mind, he wishes to jab his brother for the early rise Shaylynn had.

"I was beginning to worry," Beylynn says.

"I'm sure," Shaylynn replies already bored of the game.

"Well, so little sleep, I wasn't sure you'd have the energy to complete the race – let alone challenge my record. If only I had known, I would have warned you, so you could prepare."

Knowing he has bested his brother's time, Shaylynn smiles at the comment. Now it only becomes a matter of how to break the news to him. Even Fallon lets go the incident with Pythyn to listen to the brothers converse. They remain more competitive than ever. Each would brave the fires of hell to show the other up. How Daylynn has managed to avoid their rivalry is a mystery to Fallon.

"Slow me?" Shaylynn finally repeats. "I daresay not. It did not stop me from beating your old time."

Beylynn steps back, somewhat impressed. At the same time, he cannot tell if Shaylynn speaks the truth or merely eggs him on. He cannot make a scene for something so frivolous. Yet, at the same time, he does not want to see his record fall.

"You've confirmed this, of course?" Beylynn asks.

Shaylynn chuckles. "I do not need confirmation for something I know."

"We shall see if your knowledge is so absolute."

Beylynn walks away as a cluster of youths come racing towards the finish line. Stefen is the first of the pack. Athen and Shawl are not far behind. All who cross immediately double over from the exhaustion they feel. Jonas and Beylynn are quick to scold them for this. The instructors remind them they only impede their recovery by collapsing their lungs. With groans and complaints, they quickly stand tall and place their hands over their heads. Shaylynn and Fallon take comfort Beylynn and Jonas were not yet present when they crossed the line and did the same as the others.

They also keep their eyes focused on each boy who crosses the line. They look for Lyosan, silently pleading for him to be among this grouping, but he is not. Instead, Lyosan finds himself just outside the city walls. He still must make the run to the gate and through the town, but he feels as though the hardest part of the race is over. Despite weary legs and a pained chest, he feels instinct has taken over and will not let him fall. He barely thinks about running as he moves down the path. Instead, his thoughts move ahead to when he crosses the finish line and must face Shaylynn and Fallon.

It will not be easy to see the disappointment on their faces. They will try to hide it, but it will be there. After staying with them for so long, Lyosan will come crawling in with the last of the troop. After promising a short respite, he will be exposed for having taken a short holiday in getting back on track. Most likely, they will comfort him. That will almost make it worse. A harsh word is never appreciated, but it would at least show how much they want to believe in him.

As the gate approaches, Lyosan begins to make his final turn. He feels his legs give a bit, and he stumbles. Suddenly, the confidence he felt in finishing diminishes. He manages to keep his footing, but now he must wonder how much longer he can continue to do so. His pace is far from impressive, and he feels as though he's pulling his legs from mud with each step.

While his struggles grow, he sees more youths pass him by. In his mind, he knows he should use this as motivation to keep moving, but the drive to do so evades him. Instead, he reverts to a snail's pace as the castle incrementally moves closer. There cannot be many more behind him. Even with the enormous advantage he held, he's witnessed most come back from it.

After a few desperate minutes, he passes his home – the last marker before the castle. He looks up the hill to the gate which he must reach. He can see so many of the youths waiting for the rest to get there. As he scans the faces, he catches Shaylynn and Fallon among them. They would raise their voices to him, but such favoritism is forbidden among them. They cannot value one youth, one brother of Langerwitz, over the other. In their eyes, they must see each other as equal. None of them can truly profess this idea as a truth in his heart, but each can pretend while being watched.

As Lyosan begins his ascent, he spots someone he had not counted on seeing – Crystalynn. She has watched the entirety of the troop come in. From the moment Shaylynn returned first to this moment, she has watched. On some level, she has waited for him. When he did not return with Shaylynn and Fallon, she feared he might not return at all. Now that she sees him, a look of relief washes over her. At the same time, a small amount of pity shows. It is this element Lyosan cannot help but notice. The look on her face crushes what little spirit he had left. Had he been able to hold his own with Shaylynn or Fallon or even find himself slightly behind their pace, he would have been able to impress her and the others. Instead, he displays his foolishness. Having taken up their cause and failed to keep it so miserably, he stands where he should – a great deal behind them. He still manages to finish. Shaylynn and Fallon are still first to greet him when he does. They get him a drink and a place to sit. His legs have finally given out.

During his recovery, a few other youths make their way to the finish. Yet, Lyosan can take no comfort in defeating them. Thankfully, Shaylynn and Fallon do not try to boost his spirits by telling him he didn't lose to everyone. Perhaps they do so in anger of his fall, but in any event, he appreciates the silence. They stay with him while Jonas and Beylynn check to see who remains on the path. A great number have returned, but they still seem to be missing a few. This roll call gives Lyosan a needed chance to regain some strength. While he rests, the princess approaches. He is greatly pleased, yet discomforted by her presence. She will undoubtedly ask about falling off from Shaylynn's pace, and he will not be happy to give his answer.

"Quite a journey, it seems," Crystalynn says.

Lyosan nods with a smile.

"Do you need anything else?" she asks.

"No," Lyosan manages. "I'll be just fine after a few minutes."

"I may be wrong," she says, "but I recall you initially running with Shaylynn and Fallon. Could you not keep up?"

The question is a painful one. It is a reminder of all the ways in which Lyosan has failed. "Yes," he says, "I did fall off their pace. It was quite grueling."

Crystalynn concurs, "So grueling it set a new mark in time."

The news does not surprise Lyosan in the slightest, yet he still feels a slight twinge of anger when he hears it. Of course Shaylynn would go on and set the record once Lyosan broke their arrangement. When Lyosan fails to impress, Shaylynn adds to the disgrace by impressing even more than usual.

Yet, he is not the last to finish the race. Over the next hour, the last of the youths arrive. Many are on the brink of exhaustion. Still, Jonas calls for the youths to gather around him. He allows them to take a seat on the ground to help recover from their ordeal which everyone takes advantage of. Encircling their trainer, Beylynn, and the princess, the youths gather and await the awarding of the prize from the princess. Before the princess speaks, Jonas addresses the youths.

"Congratulations young knights," he says. "You have passed an important test this day." Shaylynn almost grunts when he hears the remark. Not because he means to diminish the accomplishment he and many of his brethren have completed, but because he knows at least one of them did not truly meet the qualifications of the task. Pythyn will be congratulated for almost winning the race when he barely ran half of it. And Pythyn will use his hollow victory to demean Lyosan. "When you reached that bridge today, you followed the same path of every great knight who came before you. You took a task which many of you would've thought impossible and did your best to complete it anyway. The time may come when you are faced with such a situation in your duty. When you face that day, remember well the sights of today."

Jonas steps away and bows to the princess. She nods to him and steps forward. In her palm, the stone she promised to the winner of the race rests. She shows it to everyone seated before her. Then, she beckons Shaylynn to rise and join her. Fighting his frustration towards Pythyn, Shaylynn stands and walks to the princess's side. She smiles at him, which he respectfully returns. In the crowd, many gaze on with great envy – chief among them are Pythyn and Lyosan.

Pythyn needed this victory to show his equivalence to Shaylynn. In the past, Pythyn has always fallen when it came to him and Shaylynn. In every aspect, Shaylynn would show how he was better than Pythyn. Even when Pythyn managed to squeak out the smallest of victories, it would eventually be stolen away from Shaylynn in a later exercise. In his own mind, Pythyn believes he can earn the crown one day. But before he can do that, he must displace Shaylynn as the best of the youths. For years, he has been waiting for a chance, but he has yet to capitalize on his opportunities.

While Pythyn's envy directs itself at the prize, Lyosan's goes to the girl. He cannot blame Shaylynn for what he did because Lyosan agreed he would keep up, but he could not. Still, he cannot help but feel a tinge of jealousy seeing Shaylynn standing beside Crystalynn. The smile on her face is a smile Lyosan never receives. There is admiration and reverence. Even though she is a princess and he is merely a knight in training, she looks at him like he is so much more. Though she has never outwardly said it, Lyosan believes there is also a certain amount of attraction for Shaylynn coming from Crystalynn. He may be arrogant and an annoyance. He may clash with the princess at times. Still, she cannot overlook the positives he possesses. For his part, Shaylynn has never shown an interest in the princess, but he could not deny her beauty.

"As promised this morning," the princess begins, "a token for the winner. And in this very special circumstance, not only do we have a winner, we have a record setter. Only a handful of times has this record been broken over the years. I feel extremely special as this is the second time I've seen it broken in my lifetime, and both times it has been broken by a member of the same family. It seems like just the other day Beylynn Storm broke this record and received a stone like this from my brother. Now, I am proud to give it to, not only a worthy champion, but a young man whose future seems brighter than any other's."

Crystalynn turns to Shaylynn, and he to her. Respectfully, he lowers his head and goes down to a knee. She takes his hand in hers and places the Allolyst in his palm.

"Shaylynn Storm, son of Feylynn, accept this token with my highest esteem," Crystalynn says. "May it be the first mark of a great legacy to our country."

Shaylynn takes the stone and rises to the applause of the other youths and the instructors. In a spontaneous moment, the princess steps forward and kisses Shaylynn on the cheek. The response from the rest of the boys picks up into chorus of cheers and roars of approval. Jonas steps forward and yells for them to cease, but the princess does not seem to mind. Instead, she says goodbye to the crowd and promptly exits.

Jonas gets the rest of the group back under control and continues with the day's lesson. While the race was the biggest aspect of the day, there is more to come.

"Hopefully, your zest will not ebb when you see what else is in store. Come with me."

Jonas leads the crowd back outside to the courtyard. A dueling square has already been set up. Four dueling swords sit at the center of the square. Beylynn pulls Shaylynn, Fallon, Pythyn, and Stefen aside while the others encircle the square.

"Just because you are tired does not mean you will get to take things easy," Jonas explains. "When you are at your weakest, your enemies will seek to take advantage of your fatigue. It is in these moments you must use your cunning and intelligence to ensure you can still complete your task.

"Shaylynn and Fallon will face off against Pythyn and Stefen. No doubt each of them is quite tired from the race. Still, we are going to see which pair can coordinate and work together to gain a victory. So, boys, grab a blade, take a minute to plan with your partner, and then come out fighting."

Shaylynn and Fallon grab their weapons and come to a side of the dueling square. In Fallon's mind, the strategy for this duel is easy. The fact they are facing two opponents will actually make it easier. Basic strategy would suggest they either separate their opponents and stand back-to-back or try to corner them both to remain on the offensive. However, with Pythyn involved, the method becomes much simpler.

"He's gonna come after you," Fallon notes.

Shaylynn agrees. "That he will."

"So, how do we use that to our advantage?"

"I'm thinking I'll square up against Pythyn to begin. You stand across from Stefen. I'll advance towards Pythyn, and he'll no doubt follow. When he gets close, I'll shift my focus to Stefen. He'll be unprepared, and I'll disarm him easily. Meanwhile, Pythyn will come after me, so you can come from behind and disarm him."

The simplicity of the plan belies its assured success. Fallon smiles already thinking of the look on Pythyn's face when Shaylynn shirks him. If he could, Fallon would merely sit back and watch the events unfold. But he knows he has a key role to play.

Jonas calls for the duelists to take their marks. Shaylynn takes his position and looks to Pythyn across from him. A satisfied grin sits on

Pythyn's face. Next to Shaylynn, Fallon stands looking over at Stefen. Stefen looks back with just the slightest bit of relief in his eyes. Facing Shaylynn right now is certainly not on Stefen's list. Especially after Pythyn merely said he would handle Shaylynn while Stefen was to do what he could with Fallon. Stefen's hope is for Fallon to disarm him quickly or manage to disarm Fallon quickly. Either way, if the duel goes long, he will not fare well.

Moments later, Jonas calls for the duel to begin. Shaylynn twirls the blade in his hand and charges towards Pythyn. Pythyn returns the move. Fallon takes a couple steps towards Stefen who retreats. As Shaylynn comes closer to Pythyn he swings his blade. Pythyn goes to block, and in his mind, he plans his counter. However, the time for his counter never comes. Instead, Shaylynn spins away from Pythyn and goes for Stefen. Stefen barely has time to register before Shaylynn swings at him. Weakly, Stefen puts his sword up, but the force of Shaylynn's blow knocks his sword away. To finish him off, Shaylynn places the point of his blade at Stefen's chest and forces him out of the square.

Meanwhile, Pythyn's curt grin has changed into a raging frown. By the time Stefen has bowed out of the duel, Pythyn has begun a charge at Shaylynn. As Shaylynn predicted, Pythyn ignores Fallon and focuses completely on Shaylynn. Sword raised, he charges at Shaylynn. As he swings forward, Fallon comes in, blocks the blow, and delivers a swift kick to Pythyn's gut. Pythyn falls to the ground as Shaylynn whips around, and both he and Fallon point their blades at Pythyn's face. With the rage still burning on his face, Pythyn yields and the duel comes to a quick end.

Jonas steps forward and raises the arms of the victors. The other youths cheer, and even Stefen applauds their efforts. Only Pythyn remains silent as with a huff, he stands up. In his rage, he turns to Stefen, suddenly blaming him for the loss. After a hard shove, which knocks Stefen to the ground, Pythyn stands over him menacingly.

"You would cheer for them who bested you so easily?" he asks. "Perhaps if you had the courage of a maggot, we could've stood a chance!"

Always willing to stand up for his comrades, Shaylynn quickly comes to Stefen's defense. Giving Pythyn a shove, Shaylynn steps between them. The rage Shaylynn felt from before now gets the better of him.

"And perhaps if you had the slightest amount of integrity, you'd admit you don't even deserve to be in this duel!"

Pythyn knows exactly what he means. He was only chosen to be in this duel because of his second-place finish in the race. He could walk away from the argument, but he sees an opportunity to chip at Shaylynn. Jonas has said neither he nor any of the other trainers will accuse the youths of not completing the full course. As long as Pythyn's denies cheating, Shaylynn's anger will grow and grow. Soon, Shaylynn will lose his composure and look the fool in front of Jonas, Beylynn, and the others.

"What are you accusing me of?" Pythyn asks.

Shaylynn's anger blinds him to the trap, but Fallon sees it clearly. Had Pythyn not attacked Stefen, perhaps Shaylynn would be more level-headed, but once Pythyn goes after someone else, Shaylynn loses sight of what's important. Wanting to stop this before Jonas and Beylynn have to step in, Fallon grabs Shaylynn's arm.

"Don't let him get to you," Fallon pleads.

Shaylynn ignores his friend and rips his arm free. He now stands eye-to-eye with Pythyn, ready to do whatever he needs to get the truth from his enemy. Even Stefen has risen from the ground and tries to stop the madness, but Shaylynn will not be deterred.

"You cheated in the race!" Shaylynn yells.

Pythyn pretends to be insulted. "How dare you!"

"How dare I?" Shaylynn repeats. "You made it perhaps half way to the bridge before turning around and waiting for Fallon and me to return. Then, you coasted in behind us and tried to overtake me at the end – even going as far as to trip me before making it to the castle!"

"This is absurd!" Pythyn yells. He then turns to Jonas. "Surely, you will not believe this. I did just as much as every boy here."

Finally, at the end of his line, Shaylynn lunges at Pythyn and tackles him to the ground. The two grapple with one another for a few moments. The other youths quickly jump in trying to separate them, but the two combatants are too incensed. Finally, Jonas and Beylynn step in. Jonas grabs Pythyn and throws him back into a group of youths who grab him by his arms and legs. Beylynn does the same with Shaylynn who ends up held back by Lyosan, Fallon, and others. Fallon talks quickly to calm Shaylynn.

"Enough!" Jonas screams.

The wrestling stops and all action ceases. Jonas, trying to calm himself before speaking again, goes back and forth between the two. Glaring and with arms folded, Beylynn stands in front of Shaylynn. Shaylynn refuses to look his brother in the eyes. After a few tense minutes pass, Jonas finally speaks again, directing himself to Shaylynn.

"You take umbrage with your fellow trainee," Jonas says, and as he speaks, his voice rises, "but do you have the slightest bit of proof beyond what your eyes have seen?"

Shaylynn knows he cannot win this portion of the argument. His emotions have bettered him and left him embarrassed. But after all that has happened, he knows he will not be able to avoid admitting his wrong. All things considered, he would rather let his silence be proof of his error, but Jonas will not have it.

"Have you?" Jonas demands.

"No, sir," Shaylynn replies. "Not in regards to the cheating."

"And the tripping?"

"I've other witnesses," Shaylynn says meekly. "Other youths and no doubt someone in town saw it."

"And what good does all that do you, Shaylynn, son of Feylynn?" Jonas asks rather calmly. "You won the race, received the reward from the princess, and you take this victory and turn it into defeat!" By this time, Jonas is yelling again. "You besmirch your name and your father's name by tussling with your peer over a petty grievance!"

Shaylynn would bring up Pythyn's assault on Stefen, but the look on Beylynn's face tells him to hold his tongue. Besides, Jonas is about to turn to Pythyn, and Shaylynn need not bear Jonas's wrath any further.

"And you!" Jonas bellows. "You attack your partner because of your shortcoming! Perhaps if you had listened to my instruction rather than be so focused on facing Shaylynn, you would've made a better plan and been prepared."

Pythyn can muster nothing in his defense.

"And what of his accusation that you tripped him in the last leg of the race?"

Pythyn looks at Fallon who makes it clear he will speak up if Pythyn denies it. Reluctantly, Pythyn tells the truth – at least his version of it.

"It is true our feet became tangled, and he fell," Pythyn claims.

"Did you stop to see if he was okay?" Jonas asks.

Pythyn opens his mouth to speak but realizes he will only further his peril if he is not careful. After a moment, he admits, "I did not."

"So, you attack one of your own and leave another to fend for himself."

"In my defense, he did recover with ease."

It is in these moments that being on his own greatly hinders Pythyn. Had he a brother or a close friend as Shaylynn does, he would have someone to tell him when to quit. Unfortunately, he has neither and continues to bring himself nothing but trouble and distain.

"And so the ends justify the means, do they?" Jonas asks. "Because no real harm came to him, your misdeed can be forgiven. Had you won the race, you would've repented and suggested Shaylynn receive the honor. Is that what you mean to say?"

After years of working with young men, Jonas's talent for twisting their words has refined itself to a deadly asset. Allowing them to work themselves into trouble serves a valuable tool to remind them they have much to learn. When they can no longer say anything to defend themselves, they remember why they need the work this training provides.

Shaylynn remains silent because he knows his words will only greaten his punishment. Pythyn remains silent because he has used every possible angle he had. Nothing has really come of it. His plan to shame Shaylynn has succeeded with the unintended consequence of shaming himself as well.

"Both of you strive for leadership," Jonas says. "One these men would easily follow; the other still needs to gain their trust. One would serve as a fine leader if he did not abuse the privileges afforded him. If the other would accept his place and not strive for things currently beyond his reach, the entire class would be better off. Instead, we find ourselves here."

After the fight between Shaylynn and Pythyn, Jonas takes the boys to the armory and gives a stern lecture over the proper use of equipment and the need for calm and honor while in battle. Beylynn stays near Shaylynn with his arms folded, undoubtedly attempting to show the disdain their father will have for Shaylynn's actions when he comes home. Shaylynn does his best to ignore his brother's presence by folding his arms as well and begrudgingly paying attention to Jonas's lecture.

Of course, many of his words are directed at Pythyn and Shaylynn. Knowing this will not affect him any more than it already has, Pythyn ignores the talk. He will go home, tell his uncle of the encounter, and that will be the end of it. It almost makes the whole ordeal worthwhile knowing how much Shaylynn will suffer from their conflict. If it would not incur the wrath of Jonas, Pythyn would smile at the sight of Beylynn standing over

Shaylynn's shoulder. Surely, Beylynn will make Shaylynn explain the entire incident to their father. Feylynn will not be happy and will punish Shaylynn severely. Pythyn can only imagine what will be in store for Shaylynn's punishment. The chores he will have to do. The training he will have to go through. The time he will have to spend away from his friends. Perhaps Shaylynn got the better of the fight, but he will also get the better of the punishment. He will pay for their scuffle for weeks beyond this day. Pythyn knows it from the look on Shaylynn's face. Every now and then Jonas says something everyone knows is specifically for Shaylynn. When that happens, Shaylynn turns away slightly. He will not completely look away because then he would see Beylynn and the stern look he has for him. Even Fallon and Lyosan look uncomfortable from time to time. They stay right by Shaylynn to show their support for him, but they know he feels embarrassed at this point.

After an hour or so, Jonas finally relents and sends the knights home for the afternoon. Beylynn walks out of the room with Shaylynn not far behind. Shaylynn says goodbye to his friends, and they part ways. Fallon and Lyosan walk out together, but they say little about what occurred. Eventually, Fallon heads for home as he has work to do.

Waiting to see if Crystalynn is around, Lyosan lingers around the castle for a few minutes. Aside from their short talk after the race, he has not seen her for a few days, and he wonders if things are picking up within the castle. When it becomes apparent she is not coming, he returns home as well. He does have a few chores he needs to get done before the day ends. Plus, it is doubtful Steel and Calvin will be home, so he will be able to work without any distractions. The most difficult task he has to do is mend the fence to the chicken coop.

CHAPTER IV

As Lyosan works, the sun begins to set. He sees many of the knights of the royal guard returning to their homes. Though he sees Fallon's father, he does not see Shaylynn's father walk by. In his mind, Lyosan begins to think of the scene at Shaylynn's home when Feylynn returns.

What breaks him from these thoughts is the arrival of Crystalynn. At first, he does not see her approach. His eyes are on the road to the eastern wall. No real thoughts run through his mind. He merely loses himself in the scenery.

"You look conflicted," Crystalynn says.

Lyosan recognizes her voice immediately and turns surprised to see her. He smiles at her though he is taken aback. She smiles as well, happy to have surprised him so.

"Not really," Lyosan finally replies.

"I hear there were some interesting happenings at your training today," Crystalynn says.

"To say the least," Lyosan confirms.

"What happened?"

Lyosan tells the story from what he saw. Of course, Lyosan could not see the finish of the race, but he did see the argument which took place afterwards. He tells of how Pythyn and Shaylynn eventually squared off after Shaylynn could not get Jonas or Beylynn to believe Pythyn did not complete the race.

As he tells the story, Crystalynn starts looking past him for brief moments. At first, he ignores it, but after she does it a few times, he begins to wonder. He turns and sees a figure running towards them. It doesn't take him but a minute to realize its Shaylynn. Perhaps, this is part of the punishment already happening.

Shaylynn comes to a stop when he comes upon Lyosan and Crystalynn. He is already out of breath and sweating profusely. He quickly catches his breath before nodding to the princess.

"Nice to see you out and about, my lady," he says.

"I would say the same to you if it were under better circumstances," she replies.

Shaylynn chuckles and turns to Lyosan.

"You told her, I take it," Shaylynn says.

Lyosan shrugs. "She already knew to some extent."

"Yes, I suppose it would warrant some attention," Shaylynn replies. "Apparently, my father already knew before Beylynn had the chance to tell him."

"Is that why you are out running now?" Lyosan asks.

"Indeed it is," Shaylynn replies. "In fact, I must keep moving. I must make it to the eastern wall before sunset. Then be back home before father goes to bed."

"How will he know if you've reached the wall?" Crystalynn asks.

"He has his ways," Shaylynn replies.

Without a word more, Shaylynn takes off down the road against the setting sun. As he disappears into the distance, Crystalynn lowers her head and looks at the ground. She takes a deep breath and sighs. Lyosan sets his tools aside and steps towards her.

"Is something the matter?" he asks.

Crystalynn looks down the road again where Shaylynn now seems but a dot in the distance. She shakes her head slowly.

"I worry for him," Crystalynn finally admits.

Lyosan scoffs at the notion. "Worried?" he repeats. "About Shaylynn? What on earth would you be worried about him for?" Were it anyone but Shaylynn, Lyosan would probably not react so strongly. However, having to consider Crystalynn feeling sympathy for Shaylynn puts Lyosan on the defensive and his normal sense of decorum out the window.

This change in tone does not come without consequences. Crystalynn does not appreciate the manner in which Lyosan treats her concern. Perhaps she fears where none is warranted. Perhaps she knows little about a subject and, as a result, jumps to a hasty conclusion. Nonetheless, it is unkind to treat her concern as folly. Especially when it is such a close friend who does it.

For that reason, when she answers Lyosan's question, her voice comes out more stern than usual. However, the harsh tone goes unnoticed by Lyosan, who still finds great humor in this concept. He knows if there were one youth in the city who did not need a single ounce of concern, it is Shaylynn.

"His father mistreats him so," Crystalynn says to explain herself. "Puts pressures many would not put on themselves on a child. It is one thing to punish a boy for insolence, but to make him run himself into the ground goes beyond the common decency of parentage."

"Shaylynn can handle what his father demands of him," Lyosan says in Feylynn's defense.

"That does not matter," Crystalynn snaps. Only now does Lyosan begin to realize how offended she is by his reaction. And yet, this does not register as something he should cease doing. Instead, he finds himself angered by her concern for Shaylynn. "All that matters," Crystalynn continues, "is that he is a child – not a knight."

Lyosan rolls his eyes. "You make it seem as though the father does not love the son."

Fed up with his demeanor, Crystalynn turns away from him and begins to leave. "I am entitled to my own opinion," she says. "Whether you agree with it or not."

Before Lyosan can say anything more, she leaves him to his work and returns to the castle. Lyosan watches with frustration for a moment as she makes for the castle doors. He is angry with her for feeling so much sympathy for a boy who needs none. He is angry at Shaylynn for garnering such sympathy when he truly stands in the wrong. Picking a fight with a fellow trainee under the watchful eye of Jonas and Shaylynn's own brother. It is preposterous he could come out better in the eyes of others for making such a spectacle of himself. What of the times Lyosan endured the wrath of his mother for spending time with the princess? What of the times he lessened himself in the eyes of the king and the knights because he allowed himself to be roped in with the princess in some reckless childhood-tomfoolery? Was there no sympathy for him?

Despite his anger, Lyosan finishes the fence. It is not his best work and, sooner rather than later, he will probably be forced to mend another break. Another thing Shaylynn has cost him this day. Calvin and Steel return home shortly before nightfall. They seem to be in merry moods, which picks up Lyosan's spirits a bit. They ask about the day. Lyosan tells them the tale though now his compassion for Shaylynn's lot vanishes in the telling. Instead, he paints Shaylynn as quick to throw the first punch, hot-headed, and emotionally compromised in the battle. Steel is not one to be tricked by the telling. He does not believe Shaylynn would act so rashly nor so foolishly. Calvin too finds it hard to believe Shaylynn would act so. Still, Lyosan does not waver from his opinion in the matter.

Feeling something more is at play, the two brothers leave Lyosan to his tasks and go into the house. As they do, Calvin adds one more comment to the story which hits Lyosan hard. "I bet he only did what he thought was right," he says. After hearing it, the truth comes back to Lyosan. He remembers more clearly the events which took place. Thus, he becomes angry at himself for ignoring his friends and letting jealously cloud his own judgment. Whatever he wishes to be between himself and the princess, he cannot wish for it at the expense of his friends – especially not one as valuable as Shaylynn.

He says nothing more on the matter though it preys on his mind. His relationship with the princess will be strained for some time after his treatment of her. In time, surely, it will all come to pass. In the meantime, however, he must be mindful of his remarks and the manner in which he phrases them. It is one thing for Lyosan to know the way Shaylynn lives as he has seen it ever since they were children. It is quite another for someone on the outside to understand the complexities of a relationship between father and son. Indeed, it becomes more difficult with a family as unique as Shaylynn's. They play by their own rules while still dedicating themselves to the needs of the crown. Lyosan understands it, as does Fallon and others who are in such good standing with them. Those on the outside, however, cannot even begin to comprehend it.

The next day, Lyosan finds himself concerned with the concept of mending fences with the princess. In his heart, he knows the opportunity will not come immediately, but when it does come, he will want to be ready to make the most of it. If he is being honest with himself, that will mean discussing the matter with Shaylynn and Fallon. However, he still bears some ill-will towards Shaylynn for being part of the rift between him and the princess. He accepts responsibility for his own part in the matter but also knows that, if not for Shaylynn, he would not have dug himself such a hole.

Shaylynn and Fallon find Lyosan early in the morning. In fact, they linger outside his front door waiting for him to journey to class. Fallon sits on the front step while Shaylynn lies on a bench with a hat over his eyes. Lyosan jumps a bit when he sees Fallon sitting on the step. For a moment, Shaylynn goes unnoticed. Sad as it is, this pleases Lyosan a bit. Perhaps he can discuss the matter with Fallon alone and there will be no need to bring Shaylynn in on the matter.

"I'm surprised to see you," Lyosan admits.

"I can't imagine why," Fallon replies. "We always attend training together."

"Never just the two of us," Lyosan says.

"Who says it's only the two of you?" Shaylynn asks from the bench.

Lyosan jumps again and turns to see Shaylynn. Shaylynn smiles a bit without lifting his hat off his eyes. Already, he knows he's caused a shock, and it pleases him to know he can go so unnoticed. Fallon finds it amusing as well.

"Tired from your evening?" Lyosan asks when he recovers himself.

Shaylynn groans as he rises from the bench. "I daresay not," he replies. "I've not yet seen the worst of it."

Lyosan rolls his eyes and heads for the castle. His reaction does not go unnoticed by Fallon and Shaylynn who exchange curious glances between themselves. Then they quickly catch up to Lyosan.

"Something wrong, Lyosan?" Fallon asks.

"I don't know what you mean," Lyosan replies none too convincingly.

"Shall I read your mind and find out?" Shaylynn asks.

Lyosan stops in his tracks and drops his arms in dismay. Fallon and Shaylynn step in front of him, both smiling with mischief on their minds. Lyosan, however, does not wish to play this game and hopes they will understand this soon. From the look on their faces, Lyosan does not feel too lucky.

"You wouldn't," Lyosan says.

"Wouldn't I?" Shaylynn replies. "I do find it pleasing you believe my claim with the simplest of ease. That you do not question whether or not I could actually read your mind, but you accept it as inevitability."

"Can I take comfort in the fact you can't read minds then?"

"Why spoil the fun?" Fallon asks. "How about you think of something – perhaps not the thing that bothers you so – and Shaylynn will attempt to guess it?"

"I love it!" Shaylynn exclaims. "How about it, Lyosan?"

Lyosan thinks of protesting for a moment, but then gives up the charade and simply walks away. Only then do Shaylynn and Fallon realize the severity of his melancholy. For his sake, they give up the game and take on an air of sincerity.

"Our apologies old friend," Fallon says. "We merely wish you wouldn't take matters so seriously."

"Even when it is a serious matter?" Lyosan asks.

"Oh, especially those," Shaylynn replies. "For in the end they hardly end up being so serious at all. Tell us and together we can all deal with this matter to rob it of its severity."

Lyosan looks to Fallon for a moment. Fallon nods that Lyosan should indeed divulge the matter to them. If it were only Fallon, Lyosan would not hesitate, but when he glances at Shaylynn and sees the carefree look in his eyes, he hesitates again. He trusts his friend to treat the matter delicately, but he does not want Shaylynn to know of the princess's concern for him. For one, Shaylynn will not look upon the concern as endearing but foolish. For another, he will tease Lyosan about this. Perhaps not this day, but some day in the future.

"Before I explain everything," Lyosan reluctantly begins, "I want to make it clear I know I am at fault in this, though I blame you as well." Lyosan points to Shaylynn as he says this. Shaylynn is taken aback by the accusation as he cannot fathom what he might have done to offend Lyosan so. Fortunately, Lyosan jumps into the story before Shaylynn can inquire more. "Last night, when you passed by my house, you stopped to talk to the princess and me before continuing on your run. While your conversation was short, it was enough to make the princess admit she worries about you..." Lyosan hesitates knowing his friends will be distracted by this revelation. Indeed, they look to each other with smiles on their faces. Truly, they find the idea more amusing than anything else. A reaction Lyosan knows all too well. "I know," he says. "I reacted much the same. Apparently, that was my undoing. She took exception to my reaction, and we argued on the matter. She left very displeased with me."

"And this is somehow my fault?" Shaylynn asks.

"If not for you, we would not have quarreled," Lyosan replies.

"Speak plainly," Fallon interjects. "What exactly did you say to upset her so?"

Lyosan sighs. "After Shaylynn went on his way, she looked after him with great worry in her eyes. I asked what was wrong, and she said she was worried for you."

"I am touched," Shaylynn admits.

Fallon smirks, but Lyosan rolls his eyes in frustration. Shaylynn playfully shoves him to indicate he is merely joking. Lyosan is still not in the mood.

"What exactly concerned her?" Fallon asks.

"She felt his father was too hard on him," Lyosan explains.

"Well," Shaylynn says jokingly, "maybe we have a common bond there."

Lyosan continues with his story. "I told her there was no need to be worried and may have suggested it was unnecessary to worry about you."

"Unnecessary in what regard?" Shaylynn asks.

Lyosan hesitates to answer this question. This is the point where he must incriminate himself in the matter. It was easy before when everything fell on Shaylynn. As Lyosan knows, not everything falls on Shaylynn.

"I laughed at her," Lyosan admits.

Both Fallon and Shaylynn sigh and drop their heads in shame. Of all the mistakes Lyosan could make, this stands close to the top of the list. He has disregarded her emotions and made her feel stupid for her beliefs. More importantly, he cannot hope to make up for this mistake easily. He will have to put in quite a bit of time to atone.

"Why would you make such a degrading error?" Fallon asks.

Another tough admission. The main reason behind Lyosan's reaction stems from his jealousy towards Shaylynn. If Crystalynn were concerned about Fallon, Lyosan would not have reacted as he did. Perhaps he still would have felt the concern was unwarranted, but he would not have scoffed at the notion as he did with Shaylynn. Rather than open that door, Lyosan skims over the truth.

"It just didn't make sense to me," Lyosan says.

"Perhaps it doesn't," Shaylynn explains, "but it makes less sense to react as you did. You are friends, yes, but she is still royalty. You've rules you must follow – considerations you must consider. What's more, do you believe she came to her conclusion lightly?"

"No," Lyosan replies.

"And yet you would treat it as if she had…"

Lyosan, appreciative of their concern, is not confused about the mess he stepped in; instead, he wants to know how to fix it. "I understand my folly," Lyosan interjects. "Let's concern ourselves with how I can fix it."

"There is little you can do," Fallon replies.

"You will have to apologize of course," Shaylynn says.

Lyosan nods in agreement.

"And in the future," Fallon suggests, "when she offers her honest opinion on something, even if you disagree with it, you should at least be open-minded towards those opinions. Don't forget, she is a princess. She isn't used to being insulted for her opinions – especially by a close friend."

Lyosan nods again. When he looks up, he sighs aloud and comes to a stop. Shaylynn and Fallon furl their brows, uncertain for his reaction, then look forward as well. Standing in the middle of the road, with a devious smirk on his face, is Pythyn. Clearly, he wishes to continue what was started the day before.

"How was your evening, Shaylynn?" he asks.

"Better than yours I'm sure," Shaylynn replies.

"Doubtful," Pythyn retorts with a snort, "I didn't have to run to the eastern wall before bedtime."

"You have a bedtime?" Fallon says with a chuckle.

Pythyn frowns and clinches a fist but will not be deterred. After a quick glance at Fallon, he turns his focus back to Shaylynn.

"Must make you awfully tired this morning," Pythyn says.

"Slept like a baby," Shaylynn explains. "Which is a lot better than acting like one."

"I did not throw the first punch!" Pythyn exclaims.

"No, but you did trip someone who was about to beat you," Fallon adds.

"If I wanted to talk to you, I'd address you," Pythyn replies. "As it is, I need none of your considerations."

"So what do you need, Pythyn?" Shaylynn asks. "Surely, you've not merely come here to chat."

Pythyn shrugs and begins pacing casually. Believing some plot is afoot,

Lyosan takes a small step back. Fallon looks to Shaylynn to see how he reacts. He is somewhat disappointed to see Shaylynn standing normally with no intention of preparing himself for what Pythyn has planned.

"I believe I've made my move," Pythyn says. "I engaged you in a fight and made you look bad in front of your family."

"Bad?" Shaylynn repeats. "You think a little skirmish will diminish me in their eyes? Though my actions may have been out of order, they were for a larger purpose. While my father would not acknowledge the validity of my course, he does respect my ability to choose for myself. He was also glad to hear I won."

At this, Pythyn stops pacing. "I don't believe we finished our bout."

Shaylynn smiles coyly, "Indeed, you are correct."

A sense of dread coming over him, Pythyn starts to back away. He means only to humiliate Shaylynn; he does not wish to engage him further.

"Well, for another day perhaps," Pythyn says. "We wouldn't want to upset our superiors further."

"There's only one problem with that," Shaylynn says.

"What's that?"

"Our superiors aren't around."

In a flash, Shaylynn bolts forward and knocks Pythyn to the ground. Pythyn puts up his hands to surrender, but Shaylynn is not finished. Taking the sword from Pythyn's sheath, Shaylynn raises it high and pins the blade into Pythyn's tunic. He buries the sword as far as he can into the ground and walks away.

"Shaylynn," Pythyn calls. "Shaylynn, don't leave me here!"

Lyosan hurries along to catch up with Shaylynn. Fallon strolls by with a smile.

"Shall I tell Jonas you'll be tardy?" he asks.

Pythyn swings at Fallon but cannot get close to him. Fallon then trots away laughing while Pythyn tries to reach the handle of his sword.

Shaylynn, Fallon, and Lyosan join the others at the castle. They begin the day's lesson, which is more to do with verti-dueling. About an hour into the training, Pythyn finally arrives. Jonas scolds him greatly for being late. Pythyn glares at Shaylynn, Fallon, and Lyosan the entire time, but he never mentions their names. Shaylynn keeps focused on his task, but Fallon and Lyosan can't help but revel in the sight for a few minutes. Their amusement comes to an end rather quickly when Beylynn, wondering why they aren't training, barks at them.

Clearly, the embarrassment of the day before has taken its toll on Shaylynn. He never takes a moment to bask in the glory of his victory over Pythyn. At one point, when the two square off for a demonstration, Shaylynn even shows respect to Pythyn. While on a practice beam, which stands a little over a yard off the ground, Pythyn loses his balance and falls. While the other youths laugh, Shaylynn jumps down and offers his hand to Pythyn. Knowing he is being watched, Pythyn takes the help and gets back to his feet. Otherwise, he'd have swatted the hand away.

In the end, the reason for Shaylynn's change of heart becomes apparent. Every youth present knows that before they close the day, Jonas will put them through a grueling physical activity as punishment for the actions of Shaylynn and Pythyn the day before. Sure enough, in the afternoon, Jonas takes them to a room full of heavy bags of grain and wheat and barrels of ale.

"The King will be entertaining a group of Counts from the Northern Province." Jonas announces. "The supplies you see before you need to be taken to the cooks, so they may prepare the feast. Normally, the serfs would perform this labor, but since some of you seem so willing to take on roles beyond your age, you will perform the task. And you will not have the benefit of their tools."

The youths all turn to Pythyn and glare. True, Shaylynn played a role in this as well, but the youths know Shaylynn would not have acted unless Pythyn had first. However, before any can take a step to the items, Shaylynn steps forward.

"Respectfully, I ask to undertake the task for everyone here," he says.

Beylynn smiles with pride, but Jonas remains unimpressed.

"An empty offer?" Jonas asks. "A hope I will remove the task because of your supposed selfless act?"

"No, sir," Shaylynn replies. "Regardless of what you do, I will perform this task with all of my peers or none of them."

Jonas stays his response for a moment to gauge the sincerity of this offer. It is expected in many ways. No doubt, Feylynn would have coached Shaylynn to offer this atonement. Perhaps not directly, but after all Shaylynn has seen, he would have this move firmly planted in his pocket. At the same time, Shaylynn does possess many of the natural talents a leader would possess. This move, while in some ways a show, is also sincere.

"Very well," Jonas says. Then he turns to the other youths. "What say the rest of you?"

Fallon is the first to step up.

"I'll not let him perform this feat alone," he says.

"I am not at all surprised," Jonas replied.

Before he can go any further, Lyosan also steps up. "Nor will I," Lyosan adds.

Others step up as well until all but a handful of the youths stand with Shaylynn. Pythyn is among those who do not step forward at first, but after a while, he concludes staying behind will make him look even worse in the eyes of those he needs to impress. If Shaylynn makes the selfless play and Pythyn lets him, he'll never be held in the same esteem.

By the end of it, all the youths stand with Shaylynn. The pride still beams on Beylynn's face. On some level, Jonas remains suspicious of the motives behind this, but he will give the benefit of the doubt.

"So be it," Jonas says. "Begin your work, and I'll have some carts sent to make it go quicker."

The youths immediately get to work. They spend the next hour or so moving the supplies to the kitchens. Jonas and Beylynn leave them to their business and attend a meeting in the King's Court. As they get close to the end, some of the youths begin to exit. With the last load to be taken by Shaylynn, Fallon, and Lyosan, most take their leave and go home.

Once all the supplies are delivered, Shaylynn returns the carts to their place and then the three start off for home. As they leave, they find Pythyn still lingering about the castle. However, instead of waiting to engage in further squabbles, Pythyn has found something else to capture his attention – or rather, someone else.

The true reason Shaylynn has never looked at the princess with any romantic intension is Sarin Athimere. She is of the same age as Shaylynn, Fallon, and Lyosan, and her beauty rivals any girl in the land. She has dark hair, blue eyes, pale skin, and red lips. Her slender frame hides her strength and intelligence. And her beauty is matched only by her wits which can top Shaylynn any day of the week.

Sarin is the only child of a knight on the King's Council, and she will become a Lady of the High Court in time. Her mother works as an ambassador and is often away from the city. Because of her father's closeness to the crown, he spends a fair amount of time with Feylynn. As their fathers have become close, the children have spent a good deal of time around one another. Since they were children, Sarin and Shaylynn have tormented each other mercilessly. And yet, they cannot help but find each other. No matter how much anger Shaylynn feels towards her at a given time, he'd not spend a minute with any other girl not in his family. To further their connection, Sarin befriended Shaylynn's cousin Faith years ago, and the two girls became inseparable.

Faith, who is a couple years younger than the others, is a beauty in her own right. It is her mother who shares blood with Shaylynn's father, but her looks come from her father's side. Being a part of Shaylynn's family, she is tougher than most girls – more of a tomboy. Yet, her place in the social order requires she maintain the qualities of a lady. She has caught the eye of Fallon. Shaylynn knows of this and mixes his reaction to Fallon's interest. At times, he seems pleased with it. Other times, he scorns the idea. Perhaps it is coincidence, but Shaylynn seems to despise the pairing when things between him and Sarin are at their worst.

At the moment, Shaylynn is the least of Sarin's concerns. Knowing how Shaylynn feels about Sarin, Pythyn always attempts to inject himself between them. Even now, he flirts with Sarin though he does not know Shaylynn is around. And Sarin is not at all impressed with him. But rather than rescue her from Pythyn's advances, Shaylynn is content to sit back and watch their interaction.

"I'm just letting you know," Pythyn explains, "Shaylynn won't be around. He's a little busy working off a punishment for attacking me yesterday. So, if you need anything, I'll be glad to help you."

Sarin rolls her eyes and gives Faith a look to suggest she can't believe Pythyn is even trying. "There are many flaws with your comments, Pythyn. First off, I've already been told what happened yesterday by several youths. You provoked the attack – I've no doubt. Secondly, my presence here today does not insinuate I am seeking Shaylynn. But perhaps of most importance, even if I were here to see Shaylynn and he could not provide assistance, having you stand in his place would be the least likely of outcomes…"

Seeing Pythyn shot down and having his own ego inflated sparks Shaylynn into action. "You flatter me so," Shaylynn says.

Faith and Pythyn jump at the remark. Sarin, hiding a smile, turns to see Shaylynn standing triumphantly. Faith beams at her cousin's arrival. Any time Shaylynn could help bring Pythyn down a peg and scare him away from her and Sarin, Faith would welcome the effort. The usual look of anger floods Pythyn's face. There are a million crass remarks Pythyn would like to make, but before he can say a word, Shaylynn jumps in.

"I must say, Pythyn," Shaylynn says, "I couldn't understand why you were so anxious to leave the rest of us to finish our task, but now that I see you here, I understand you wanted to give us something to laugh at when we finished."

"Perhaps I left because someone decided to make me late to the lessons today," Pythyn explains.

"Now, who would do such a thing?" Shaylynn asks facetiously.

"Shall I venture a guess?" Sarin asks.

Pythyn knows Sarin isn't standing up for him by asking this question. Rather, she's impressed with Shaylynn's actions and wants to see him bask in them. Mostly so she can cut him down and see him lose his cool. But after so many years, Shaylynn has learned to avoid the obvious bait. The game between them has evolved quite a bit, and in truth, Sarin is still better at it.

"I'd rather you didn't," Shaylynn replies. "You were saying such nice things about me."

"Perhaps if you acted better, I'd be able to say more," Sarin comments.

"Perhaps if you said more, I'd have a reason to act better," Shaylynn retorts.

"Since when have my words had such an effect on you?"

Rather than let the two continue, Pythyn decides to interject. The events of this morning cannot go unrectified. This is two days in a row Shaylynn has bested Pythyn in a physical bout. Even though this second one wasn't around a lot of people and it only made him late, it still has left Pythyn embarrassed. For Shaylynn to show up now and embarrass him again, around Sarin this time, he has pushed his luck.

"Perhaps you should concern yourself with your actions rather than her words," Pythyn says.

"Are we back to this?" Shaylynn whines.

"Am I bothering you?" Pythyn asks.

"Does that really need to be answered?"

"We've business to deal with!"

Shaylynn motions to Sarin.

"And so do we," Shaylynn says indicating him and Sarin.

"I've no business with you," Sarin remarks.

Shaylynn has fallen in the trap. He had avoided slipping when he was talking to Sarin directly, but the distraction of Pythyn left him vulnerable. Now, Sarin uses the opportunity to send him off the edge.

"You were looking for me, no?" Shaylynn asks.

"No," Sarin replies, "if you were listening to my words that weren't about you, maybe you'd have heard I had no intention of finding you."

"And yet you did."

"Yes, you served a nice distraction and managed to get Pythyn to leave us alone, but now that you've served your purpose, I'm content to go."

Sarin turns to Faith and nods to move on. Faith agrees for the moment, but she suspects they won't actually leave. Faith doesn't like it when Sarin toys with Shaylynn this much. She'd rather the two stop playing around and be true about their feelings for each other. In part because it would give Faith a chance to be true to Fallon about her feelings for him, but more because she loves Shaylynn so dearly. She has no brothers, but Shaylynn has always been one.

"What if I'm not content with you leaving?" Shaylynn asks.

It's a moment of honesty which Shaylynn doesn't normally show. They are one of the few actions Shaylynn can take which stop Sarin in her tracks. If Shaylynn will show some emotion, then she will as well. It hasn't always been this way. She used to show her emotions to him quite frequently, but he would always shoot her down. Ever since then, she has made him earn her emotions. At times, he won't give in, but in this moment, he has.

"What are you saying?" Sarin asks.

Pythyn still doesn't want to go ignored.

"Do not ignore me!"

Pythyn steps up, but Shaylynn quickly jabs and hits Pythyn in the nose. Pythyn falls back and grabs his nose in pain. Fallon and Faith laugh while Lyosan prepares for the battle to escalate. Pythyn charges at Shaylynn, but Sarin steps between them. Pythyn won't make a move with her standing in his way. Without a word, he backs up and runs away.

"That was unnecessary," Sarin says.

"But effective," Shaylynn adds.

"Get to your point," Sarin demands.

"What point?"

"I will leave."

If he had his way, Shaylynn would only speak these words when Sarin and he are alone. Fallon would use the words to heckle him, and Faith would use them to shame him. Only Lyosan could hear the words and not let them affect the way Shaylynn looked. But now that he's broached the subject, Shaylynn has to say something to impress Sarin.

"I was just saying I wouldn't like it if you left," Shaylynn says.

Sarin smiles. "You'll have to do better than that."

Shaylynn basically growls as he looks away for a moment. When he looks back, Sarin's smile has grown, and Shaylynn can hear Faith giggling behind her.

"I've not seen you much recently," Shaylynn admits. "And after the past couple of days, I could use a welcomed sight."

Since he's already down, Sarin feels it appropriate to keep kicking.

"I saw you running yesterday evening," Sarin says. "You must've been in quite a bit of trouble."

Shaylynn rolls his eyes. She would show herself simply to taunt him after his father punished him. Sure enough, she has prepared for quite a showing.

"The best and brightest of the youths reduced to a mere boy throwing a fit," Sarin continues. "And all because one of the other boys cheated and didn't play fair."

"If this is how you treat me, I may have been incorrect in my assertion," Shaylynn replies.

Sarin teases and taunts Shaylynn even further.

"Well, if you'd dare risk your father's wrath, perhaps you could join us this evening. Faith and I were planning on a stroll through the trees within the eastern wall. With mother away and father tending to business in the castle, I should be able to sneak away."

Before Shaylynn can answer, Crystalynn approaches.

"Is the invitation open to anyone?" she asks.

Surprised by her appearance, Sarin and Faith both curtsey. With a smug smile on his face, Shaylynn bows as Fallon and Lyosan follow his lead. Their formality immediately creates discomfort for Crystalynn.

"Please, we have no need to stand on occasion here," she insists. "Besides, Sarin, Faith, you will be ladies of the high court no doubt." She then turns her attention to Shaylynn, Fallon. "You two will serve in a high place in the council." Finally, she turns to Lyosan. "And you are one of my dearest friends."

"Who does not always act as one," Lyosan admits. "I am sorry for the last time we talked."

Crystalynn smiles. "We needn't speak of it," she says. "We cannot see eye to eye on all things." Crystalynn then turns back to everyone else. "But I would hope you all see me as a friend. I hope to remain close to each of you in your servitude to the crown."

"If one of you is not wearing it that is," Faith interjects.

Shaylynn, more for Sarin and Lyosan's sake than the princess's, chides Faith for her brash comment. "Cousin," he remarks, "know your place."

Faith lowers her eyes as she begins to blush. Fallon, believing Shaylynn too strict, scowls at his friend. Sarin remains quiet though she cared little for the insinuation made by her friend. Like most in the kingdom, Sarin has entertained the possibility Shaylynn will indeed marry the princess and become the king of the land. It is not the future she hopes to see come to pass, but it may very well be unavoidable. Crystalynn, hoping to return the conversation to a more genial tone, touches Faith's arm.

"Do not concern yourself," she says. "The statement is quite accurate as you all are aware. My brother has given the matter much thought, and turning the crown over to a citizen of our country has crossed his mind. If I were to take a husband from our land, I would be honored to have any of you."

Shaylynn and Fallon hesitate, hoping Lyosan will take the opportunity to dote upon the princess. However, words elude him, and the moment almost passes when Shaylynn finally speaks out of courtesy.

"The honor would be ours," he says with a bow.

Sarin sighs at his words.

"You are too kind, Shaylynn," Crystalynn replies.

Knowing full well his words may have upset Sarin, Shaylynn turns the attention back to her.

"A rendezvous after night fall then?" he asks.

Sarin, quickly masking her emotions, smiles brightly. "Only if you can manage it," she says. "Wouldn't want to put you out or anything."

"Not at all," Shaylynn replies. "Father leads the watch tonight. He'll not even know of my absence."

Sarin rolls her eyes. "So willing to chance it when there's nothing to chance."

"If you'd like, we could sneak through the castle on our adventure."

"An adventure now, is it?" Sarin asks.

"Would there be any point in it if it wasn't?" Fallon asks.

"I know I wouldn't bother otherwise," Faith adds.

"Surely, you wouldn't risk being discovered in the castle for such a simple outing," Crystalynn says.

"We've done it for less before," Lyosan admits.

As the plan solidifies, the six cohorts look at each other, brimming with delight at the mischief they might find themselves in. When night falls, Fallon and Lyosan sneak out of their houses to meet outside Shaylynn's window. A minute or so after their arrival, Shaylynn crawls out the window and joins them.

"You're late," Fallon informs him.

"Sorry, big brother had to tell a bed-time story," Shaylynn admits. "Apparently, one wasn't enough."

"Well, let's get going," Lyosan insists. "We agreed to meet by the butcher's just after sunset."

"So, let them wait," Shaylynn replies. "I think we're worth it."

With a wink at Fallon, Shaylynn takes off down the road with the other two in tow. They sneak around the darkness to the butcher's where they discover they have arrived early. After a few minutes of conversing, Sarin and Faith arrive out of breath.

"We've been waiting," Shaylynn says with arms folded across his chest.

"And I'm not worth the wait?" Sarin asks.

"Time will tell," Shaylynn says with a smile.

Shaylynn turns away as Sarin follows him. Fallon stays near Faith.

"Did you get away easily enough?" Fallon asks.

"Oh yes," Faith responds. "It's very easy when I have the room nearest the road."

"Fortunate indeed," Fallon agrees.

"Yes," Faith reiterates, "I'm basically free to come and go as I please. Or others could come and go as they pleased."

Fallon quickly glances to see if Shaylynn is paying attention to their conversation. Shaylynn has not made it clear in the past if he cares if Fallon courts his cousin, so her forwardness is more than Fallon expects.

Fortunately, Shaylynn and Sarin are focused squarely on each other.

"Besides, it's not like we're the only ones holding us up," Sarin says. "It doesn't look like the princess has arrived yet."

"No, but it may be difficult to escape the castle as easily as our homes," Lyosan offers in her defense.

"You'd be surprised," a voice says from the darkness. They all jump as Crystalynn steps forward into the light of their lanterns. "As long as I say I wish to be left undisturbed, my guards will not enter my chamber. It makes it pretty easy to go unnoticed."

As the princess says hello to Sarin and Faith, Lyosan pulls Shaylynn and Fallon aside.

"How long do you think she was there?" Lyosan asks.

"Difficult to say," Fallon replies.

"We didn't say anything embarrassing, did we?" Lyosan asks.

"Have I ever?" Shaylynn replies.

The ladies interrupt the conversation before it can carry on, and the six of them make their way through the rest of town and into the trees. They gallivant about until they come to the river. With many torches already lit, they extinguish their own lights and sit at the bank.

Together, they form a small circle. Shaylynn sits with his back to the river. Sarin sits a few feet away with Faith next to her. Fallon, resting against a rock, has taken a seat next to Faith. Lyosan sits next to him, and Crystalynn sits next to him on the other side of Shaylynn.

"I've not been out here at night in many years," Sarin says. "I'd forgotten how beautiful it is."

"It's the torches that really add to the atmosphere," Crystalynn says. "It's been a tradition in the land for many generations."

"If you don't mind my asking, how did it start?" Faith asks.

"You needn't ever worry about asking me a question," Crystalynn says. "Although, Shaylynn may know the answer better than myself. According to legend, it was actually started by the mages of the land when they held places in the court."

Shaylynn nods to confirm her explanation.

"Well, don't keep us in suspense," Sarin says. "Please, tell us the tale."

Shaylynn glances at Sarin with a soft smile which she reciprocates. For a moment, they tenderly gaze at each other and forgo their usual conveyances. Rather than quips and witty remarks, they allow a moment of civility and caring. It is in these moments they say more than they dare speak aloud.

It goes unnoticed by the others. They view the silence as Shaylynn's normal manner of grasping the attention of those around him. Patiently, they wait for the moment to pass and hear the story they know is forthcoming. For her part, Crystalynn wonders if she's done the right thing in handing the tale over to Shaylynn.

As she prepares to tell the story herself, Shaylynn draws a deep breath and ends the silence among them.

"The way my father tells it," he begins, "it was one of my own ancestors who started the tradition. I've found nothing to confirm his allegation, but I doubt he would fabricate a story for mere adulation…"

"Perhaps he wouldn't, but you would," Sarin interrupts, proof that the moment has passed.

The others smirk and chuckle. Even Shaylynn allows a smile to cross his lips. She endears herself to him with the remark. So simple, so honest, and so trusting. He knows she means nothing by it, and yet, she'd stand by it steadfastly.

"…In any event," Shaylynn continues. "According to my father, before the town walls were built, there was some concern amongst the townsfolk that the trees could provide haven to thieves and criminals of the like. Or that, in times of war, they would aid intruders by sheltering them from view until it was too late to enable defenses.

"To that point, the townsfolk came to the king, King Arlan IV, I believe…"

Shaylynn furls his brow at the name and glances at Crystalynn. He does not want to speak out of place. The smile on Crystalynn's face shows he is correct.

"You are correct," she says to alleviate him of his concerns. Though it does not show, she finds his knowledge base rather impressive. He has shown himself a man of detail and in turn, a man with caring in his heart.

"…And the king could provide no reasonable retort for keeping the trees, but he wished to hold on to them nonetheless. It is a principle of the order to keep nature, in turn for it keeping you.

"Finally, my ancestor, Veylynn, spoke to the crowds and courts asking they not rob the land of the trees. When the people spoke of their fears and doubts, Veylynn made a promise that those who kept the order would never allow our fortunes to become our undoing. He vowed from that day forward any who called him friend or family would keep the river safe and protect those who considered it home.

"To show the earnest of his word, he purchased the torches from a vendor and raised them into the trees. With a spell, he lit them and kept them from setting the branches aflame. Once the town saw his sincerity and the magic of the torches, they abandoned their cause and indebted themselves to Veylynn. For his part, he journeyed to these trees every night for the rest of his life, lighting them and keeping them. When the night came and the sun set for rest, he patrolled the river for hours into the night.

"When the task became too great for him, others took up the cause. Among them, his family, but mostly, the knights of the court. His majesty Arlan decreed the torches would burn brightly for generations to come. He ordered they be kept and allowed to burn every night as a reminder there were those resolved to keep peace in the land."

When Shaylynn finishes the tale, everyone there turns to the flames dancing in the night air. As they gaze into the bright beacons, a warmth enters them as though the measure of the vows made years ago still reach to them today. Through those simple torches, they feel the security and protection of a thousand men who came before them, who patrolled this riverbank, and who kept these borders. For all the words which bring war and destruction and incite fear, these words bring calm and serenity.

For some, serenity is fine when it is time for sleep, but this is not what has brought them out this night. They were promised adventure, so adventure there must be.

CHAPTER V

Taking the lead, Sarin rises from the ground and steps towards the nearest tree. After gazing at the torch upon a high branch, she turns to Shaylynn with mischief on her mind and playfulness in her heart. As if anticipating her intent, Shaylynn drops his eye line as well. The others soon follow, feeling the tide of this evening is about to turn.

"And so, Shaylynn, son of Feylynn, descendant of Veylynn, do you keep the word of your more noble ancestor?" she asks.

Fallon smiles as he turns to see Shaylynn's response. Faith chuckles under her breath. Lyosan smiles as well but is more concerned with the princess's response. She is not around them that often and is unfamiliar with Sarin and Shaylynn's typical interactions. The surprise on Crystalynn's face, a look not of displeasure but simply alarm, confirms Lyosan's suspicions.

"I merely said my father claims him as an ancestor," Shaylynn replies, the playful spirit finding his heart as well. "I never said I claim him as one."

"And well you shouldn't," Sarin retorts, "for he proves himself your better from beyond the grave."

Alarm grips Crystalynn stronger, as though she expects Shaylynn to respond in a fiery defense. With what she knows of Shaylynn's father and family, she cannot imagine he will let them be tarnished by such words. The others, though, know better than to believe Sarin would brandish Shaylynn so severely with any measure of sincerity. She simply means to antagonize him into playing her game. However, after so many years, he's become quite adept at the rules, which only means she has to change them more often.

"You strike so hard," Shaylynn says. "Why this concern for my name?"

"It is not concern," Sarin assures him, "merely a commentary on your place in your family's legacy."

"I believe I have time to find my place."

"I would not look in too high a place."

"As though height places some bearing in significance?"

"Only in that those among the clouds are looked up to, while those in the dirt are looked upon."

Fallon chuckles. "She speaks so soundly I feel I must give her my approval."

Shaylynn jokingly scowls at his friend while Sarin keeps in step with one of the tree's branches. It is a long, arching branch that leads out to the river. On appearance, it seems to be reaching out for a caress from the running waters, but it dares not touch them. For the river is angry tonight, running fast and without thought. Storms from beyond the city walls have agitated the river sending a torrent of fallen rain down the mountain through the plains searching for the great seas.

It is an anger juxtaposed with the anger in Shaylynn. He always grows weary of Fallon taking sides against him for mere amusement. Mostly because Shaylynn knows Faith will not come to his aid, and Lyosan strives to be forever impartial. Even more so tonight as Lyosan's attention holds on the princess.

For her part, Crystalynn is slowly acclimating herself to the brand of conversation had by her friends. Though it is quite unusual and forward, she does rather enjoy it. Especially since, in some way, Shaylynn seems to have met his match. There are few things, physically or mentally, in which Shaylynn can be bested. While it speaks greatly for his place among the future knights, it can be rather unpleasant in the moment to have one so highly situated among the rest. Whenever he comes back down to earth, everyone wants to see such an occurrence.

Perhaps, that is why Fallon, Faith, Lyosan, and Crystalynn align themselves with Sarin in her torment of him. They look to Shaylynn and bait him into offering his reply knowing full well Sarin has already planned what she will say next and how she will continue to ruffle his feathers.

"I say let her have it then, Fallon," Shaylynn replies. "Surely, I know I do not need it at all."

A chorus of guffaws ring out into the night from all but Sarin. She remains true to her course. She means to rattle the champion – a feat which cannot be done halfheartedly. True, she found the remark amusing and quite poignant, but she would not allow herself to show it. Not now. Now, she must use his lashing against Fallon to further her cause.

"So sad you speak so ill of a friend," she says. "I dare say you prove my point before I even try to."

"You still think less of me?" Shaylynn asks.

"I know I do," Faith interjects.

Shaylynn points a long finger in his cousin's direction. "Remember, love, that you are family, and family should not be parted so simply."

"Even if I love thee less, 'tis more than I love any I would call friend," Faith responds.

Shaylynn, smiling, turns to Sarin. "I've one to stand by my side."

"All the good that'll do her," Sarin says.

Quietly, Crystalynn leans over to Lyosan. He is so engrossed in the argument he does not notice her movements. To gain his attention, she touches his arm so that no one else will see. Lyosan reacts to her touch immediately but draws no attention. Her touch is so soft, so warm he forgets himself. He forgets where he is at the moment and dreams the dreams he sees when asleep.

An instant later, he reminds himself of his station in life. He assumes too much he tells himself. Indeed, for the time being, he does. For her thoughts, as his just were, are on the exchange between Sarin and Shaylynn.

"Are they always this lively?" Crystalynn whispers.

Lyosan smirks. "Actually, they're more civil than usual tonight. Perhaps they are bettered by your presence."

Crystalynn lightly slaps his arm. "You speak too kindly," she says.

"Yet truthfully," Lyosan adds.

She smiles again, this one entirely for him. Then, she leans back to her place and takes in the rest of the festivities. Lyosan, still lost in the moment of her touch, tries to calm his racing heart.

He has missed the new development. Sarin has ascended the tree and stands further out upon the branch that leads out to the river. For the moment, she still holds at the trunk, but no one believes she will be there long.

"You mean to prove yourself then, Shaylynn?" Sarin asks.

"You mean to test me then, Sarin?" he asks in reply.

"On some level," she answers, "if you feel up to the task."

Shaylynn extends his arms to give her the floor. "By your lead," he says.

Sarin steps away from the trunk along the branch. She still stands above ground for the moment, but she nears the bank with every step. The others, somewhat concerned by her intentions, lean forward from their places in the grass. Only Shaylynn remains constant.

"Do you mean to protect these lands?" Sarin asks.

"By my life," Shaylynn responds.

Sarin takes another step along the branch. She stands at the precipice of the river's edge. Again, the others harken to her movements. Shaylynn smiles as she weaves her magic. Truly, this is a power he shall never possess.

"And those who call it home?" Sarin adds.

"By my death," Shaylynn replies.

Again, Sarin steps out on the branch now clearly standing over the river's current. With her step, unheard by most, the branch begins to crack. Shaylynn hears the cry of the tree and doubt enters his mind for the first time tonight. Yet, he knows if he voices his concern, it will only provoke Sarin further.

Fortunately, the others do not need the warning of the tree to provoke their objection to this course of action. Faith, meaning to be kind and pleasant, rises to her feet and stands beside her cousin. Fallon, Lyosan, and Crystalynn rise as well.

"Sarin," Faith pleads, "end this now, I beg you."

"Indeed, I do not believe this to be a safe course of action," Crystalynn adds. "The river runs wild this night."

Sarin is having none of their concerns. She still believes this to be a game, and she thinks herself winning. Their concerns, though heartfelt, stand as merely an obstacle to overcome. Although her actions may seem reckless to all but her, she has chosen them with great care. They are the gambit to bring the endgame.

"Calm yourselves," she says, "we stand in the presence of one whose family keeps the light of these torches burning. Surely, he will not allow harm to come to me."

"I cannot stop that which is so strongly invited," Shaylynn says.

Sarin smiles, still feeling herself the victor. "You yield then, sir?" she asks.

"Not at all," Shaylynn replies.

Sarin steps further upon the branch. She is mere feet from its leaves now. A slightly louder creek echoes in the air. Only one hears it, and he cannot convince her that it is true.

"He's as good a man as any before him," Fallon says meaning to end the debate. "We all know this. We know those of our age would follow him into battle and worse. His measure needs not to be tested."

"Is that so, Fallon?" Sarin asks. "You, who gave me your approval mere minutes ago, say this."

Never missing the opportunity to bask in other's misfortunes, Shaylynn turns to his friend. "Your actions do not seem so wise now, do they?"

"Shut up," Fallon replies.

Though he realizes the severity of the moment, Shaylynn cannot break character without alerting Sarin. She expects him to battle to the end. He will do so. While he does, he shall keep a sharp eye and ear on her. At less than a moment's notice, he must ready himself to take action.

"Sarin," Lyosan says, "please, let us find another way to test his valor. A venture into the castle perhaps? He shall pass right by his father…"

Shaylynn interrupts, "I'll do no such thing."

"You will stop this!" Faith cries.

The others cannot understand why Shaylynn does not forgo the charade and work more diligently to bring Sarin back to safety. Though he has never outwardly said it, he cares for her a great deal, does he not? How can this be the manner in which he chooses to show it?

"As if I perpetrate it?" Shaylynn asks.

"He speaks correctly, Faith," Sarin calls out from the branch. "This is my doing, so I am the one to be stopped."

"So you yield then?" Fallon asks.

The answer cannot come fast enough. At the bend in the branch, the arm of the mighty oak cracks. Though not a clean break, its fingers dip into the waters so suddenly that Sarin cannot brace herself. The violence and suddenness of the action drops her from her perch and casts her into the river.

Immediately, the current captures her and drags her along. Though she struggles, she cannot overcome it. Instead, she hopelessly grabs the air above her, hoping some rescue will find her. For she only has moments before tragedy will befall her. Ahead lie sharp, unforgiving rocks which have anchored themselves into the middle of the river. Given the speed of the current tonight, a collision with them will be fatal without question. If she is to live, she must avoid them.

From the bank, Fallon, Faith, Lyosan, and Crystalynn stand in horror of the events unfolding. Faith clings to Fallon, burying her face into the hidden shelter in his arms. She will not watch her friend come to her end – not one as grizzly as this. Lyosan stands with them wishing he knew of a course of action to take. For the first time this night, his thoughts do not dwell upon the princess. In truth, he would sacrifice whatever graces he'd been bestowed this night to save Sarin from this fate. Crystalynn watches, hands over her mouth, begging for some reprieve from this moment. When the moment strikes her, she turns to Shaylynn in hopes he will know what to do. But when she looks for him, she cannot find him. He has gone – vanished! As she turns in a desperate search to locate him, she hears a splash in the river some yards ahead.

For the instant the crack occurred, Shaylynn had darted ahead of the scene knowing he had but one chance to save Sarin. Without thought or hesitation, he dashed along the bank of the river to keep pace with the damsel in the current. When he was slightly ahead of her, he took one deep breath before leaping into the waiting arms of the river.

The others now become aware of his actions and watch in shock. With swift speed, he forces himself to the center of the stream where Sarin waits for him. Within moments, he has her in his arms and is helping her stay above the waves, but he cannot stop the current from taking them. At the bank, the others begin to fear the worst.

"Shaylynn will die with her!" Crystalynn cries.

Faith unveils herself from her hiding spot at the sound of her cousin's name. Searching the river for him, she watches in horror as he speeds towards the rocks. The harsh thoughts she bore him only moments ago are still fresh in her mind. What she would give to take them back. She could not bear to watch her friend die; she cannot believe her kinsmen will die here.

"Cousin!" Faith yells.

She steps to the bank and waves strike at her feet. Fallon steps forward and braces her, unwilling to risk another venturing into the waters. She immediately tears away from him and runs up the bank towards the rocks. The others quickly follow.

In the currents, Shaylynn keeps Sarin above the water while he struggles to fight the current. For flashes and instances, he can see the rocks coming upon him. Desperation fills him as he attempts to formulate their escape. Time is short and options continue to shorten. He cannot escape the current with her, and he will not abandon her to this fate. Forgo any damage to his name, his heart could not stand the separation. He knows he must save her, but as time trickles away, he knows not how he will do it.

Clinging to Shaylynn as though he were life itself, Sarin cannot force herself to look about. She knows the danger which lies ahead and fears her reaction to seeing it with her own eyes. She curses herself for dooming them to this fate, but she finds solace in the fact he will be with her when they go. Yet, for all they've done and meant to each other, she has never plainly told him the workings of her heart. She will not allow her life to pass without making it plain and true.

Against the crash of the water, she turns her head and forces her eyes open. She sees him valiantly attempting to thwart the river's current around him. As he gives his last breaths to protect her, she falls deeper in love with him.

"Can you hear me?" she asks.

"Always," he somehow replies.

And his words are clear to her as though they stood on land together with nothing between them but air. Somehow, he manages to find her amongst this chaos and doom.

"I love you," she says.

For a moment, his fight ceases. Through the torrent of the water pouring over him, she sees him look into her eyes. With a push from unknown forces, she lunges forward and thrusts her lips into his. The warmth of his kiss fills her with a hope she clings to in what she believes will be her last moments. As his arms tighten around her, she feels a place more special than anywhere she'd ever called home. In this moment, in this embrace, she finds everything she'd ever wanted and ever could. She feels a feeling that overwhelms her emotions and defies all which could be considered logical.

Shaylynn feels it as well, and suddenly, he demands for this to be only the beginning and not the end. They've defied logic with their love; he will do it again to keep it alive.

In an instant, Shaylynn spins in the river. Sarin pulls away from his lips and tucks herself onto his chest. Bringing his legs up into him, Shaylynn summons a power to him greater than any magic he'd brought forth in his life. Conjuring the power and majesty of the river into one blow, he kicks forward and brings his feet into the rocks a moment before they'd have claimed the pair.

As soon as he makes contact, the rocks explode with the violence of a thousand blows. Shattering into countless bits, the rocks scatter from their place and fall into the river, a mere shell of their former selves. Shaylynn and Sarin pass through the debris unscathed and the danger dwindles away. Shaylynn draws them to the river bank as the current yields to his prowess.

Those along the bank can only watch in amazed stupor as the shower of pebbles rises in front of them and harmlessly drops away. The measure of the moment cannot even reach them until they see their friends wash upon the shore.

Sarin, still resting on top of Shaylynn, coughs violently to expel some water as she drops off him. Shaylynn merely comes to a stop at the bank and refuses to move further. He has drained himself completely and looks as if death may take him. Sarin sees it in his eyes. After all she has suffered, she will not suffer this.

"Help me!" she demands of her friends.

Snapping into action, they race to her side and pull Shaylynn to safety. When he drops to the ground, he snaps awake and begins coughing violently. At his first movement, Sarin cups his face in her hands and attempts to steady him.

"Quit your thrashing," she commands. Then her tone turns much softer and loving, "you're safe, now."

Though he would normally jest and remark at the absurdity of her comfort, Shaylynn now welcomes it dearly. After all he has endured in a short time, he will not scorn emotion. She admitted her love of him while he found no opportunity to reciprocate – in words anyway. With the others around, he will not do so now. Still, he must acknowledge her admission somehow.

"Are you?" he asks weakly.

"Of course I am, you fool," she responds warmly.

Immediately, he ceases his convulsions and breathes deep to calm himself. Sarin kisses him again and buries her head into his chest. As soon as she moves away, Faith jumps upon her cousin and throws her arms around him.

"Don't do that again!" she demands.

"Tell your friend not to give me reason," Shaylynn replies.

Shaylynn remains on the ground for many minutes. Lyosan stands to the side with Fallon. Both speak silently to each other about the fear they felt at Sarin and Shaylynn's possible loss, the relief of their safety, and the awe of his actions. All they had seen prior to this night suddenly turned to nothing at the sight of his act.

Only one stays away from the scene. She cannot believe her eyes and cannot accept what has come to pass. Stories. That's what it has all been until now. Tales that fathers tell their sons and daughters to inspire hope and pride. Surely, they cannot be true. Those matters of magic they spoke of were imagined or exaggerated. Or so she has thought. For this is not imagined or exaggerated. Shaylynn had cast himself into the river, rescued another, and destroyed the rocks which got into his way. Everything that was fiction suddenly fit into her reality.

Lyosan eventually senses her trepidation and turns to her. Her eyes, wide and alarmed, focus on the man resting on the shore. Fear fills her. Uncertainty claims every thought which comes from her. All this is plain on her face.

"Princess," Lyosan says stepping towards her.

She does not react to his call at first. When he calls her again, she cannot stop her thoughts from spilling out.

"He obliterated stone," she says. "With nothing but his feet, he turned solid rock into dust and sand. Before that, he ran like lightning, swam like a creature of the sea. Yet, he sits there, breathing as if having completed a race or hard day's work."

"So he does," Lyosan says.

"That cannot be."

"There are many things about that man which cannot be," Fallon says. "But with each task, he proves they can."

Slowly, Shaylynn rises to a seated position and braces his arms behind him to hold him up. Faith kneels behind him and supports him as well.

Fallon and Lyosan come over and offer a hand, but Shaylynn asks to rest a bit longer. The mood lightens for most, but Crystalynn cannot manage to rationalize what she had seen. With great hesitation, she approaches Shaylynn where he lays. She looks upon him as though he is an apparition. There is a slight level of horror in her gaze. She attempts to mask it but in vain. Fortunately, none present hold her reaction against her.

As Shaylynn continues to breathe deeply in an attempt to collect himself, he senses the distress around him and looks at the princess. A faint smile crosses his lips when he sees the look in her eyes. He knows it well. He has seen it from every one of his friends before.

With a look to Sarin, he takes one more deep breath and finally recovers from his ordeal. She smiles at him and takes his hand in hers. The gentle squeeze she gives represents the only thanks he will receive. He would have it no other way. To show his contentment, he pulls her hand to his mouth and kisses her hand. She blushes at his brazenness, which only causes him to smile more. Then, he turns his attention to the princess again.

"You seem concerned, my lady," he says.

As the attention shifts away from the spectacle, Crystalynn's discomfort increases. Being new to these happenings, she does not want to cast aspersions or seem judgmental. At the same time, she does not want to appear an outsider who doesn't belong. She thoroughly enjoys her time with her friends and hopes to continue her association with them.

"Not at all," she utters none too reassuringly.

Shaylynn chuckles. Having not fully healed from his ordeal, he coughs and winces in pain shortly thereafter. Sarin gently touches his face.

"Not exactly convincing, your highness," Shaylynn replies.

"Perhaps not," Crystalynn concurs, "but it's the best I can do considering the circumstances."

"I suppose they are quite shocking," Sarin says.

"From your perspective perhaps," Shaylynn jests.

Sarin rolls her eyes and drops Shaylynn's hand. She stands, and Shaylynn starts to stand as well. His movements are slow and rigid. Fallon grabs one of Shaylynn's hands and helps him to his feet. Once upright, Shaylynn stumbles a bit. Before he can fall, he grabs Fallon who braces him and holds him up.

"Worth it?" Fallon asks.

Shaylynn glances at Sarin, who smiles at him in spite of herself.

Shaylynn smiles as well. "I'd say so."

Fallon shakes his head and helps his friend along. Lyosan comes forward as well and supports Shaylynn from the other side. Together, they slowly make their way back to town. They still hope to go unnoticed in their endeavors.

"This was quite the eventful evening," Lyosan comments.

"Good to hear you say it," Shaylynn replies. "I was beginning to feel the night was going stale."

"I hope the princess did not regret her decision to join us," Fallon says to change the subject.

"I doubt she did," Lyosan says. "To be witness to such an event outweighs any discomfort the night brought."

"There, Fallon," Shaylynn says, "I've proven the worth of my actions even further."

"Just what you needed," Fallon replies, "more assurances in your actions."

Silence pervades the night until they reach the town limits. The more they walk, the more Shaylynn regains his strength. Eventually, he unburdens himself from Fallon and Lyosan. Sarin stays at his side for precautionary measures.

"I'll be fine," Shaylynn assures her.

"I don't recall inquiring," Sarin replies.

Fallon, sensing their relationship returning to its customary pleasantness, steps away and stands next to Faith. Considering all that has taken place, she has remained remarkably calm through this whole ordeal. Fallon has no doubt she has been witness to events like this before. Still, being that close to death cannot be pleasant.

"He mends quickly," Fallon says referring to Shaylynn.

"It's good he does," Faith replies. "For all he puts himself through, he should probably be dead a hundred times over."

"You don't seem worried."

Faith hesitates before answering. Fallon feels as though he's touched a sensitive area, but he was attempting to. Faith takes a deep breath before giving her answer.

"I've learned to mask my worry from him," she replies. "If he knew how much his actions upset me, he'd leave me at home."

"Is it worth the anxiety just to spend time with your family?" Fallon asks.

Faith takes Fallon's hand. "It's not the time with him I value."

The need for discretion closes all conversations. Now at the first stretch of houses in the city's limits, the group goes silent as they move through the streets of Langerwitz. With every movement, they seek to hide in the shadows. At times, they hold their position for minutes before making their next move. They exaggerate the need for their secrecy, yet it amplifies their enjoyment of it all – none more than Crystalynn.

With the uneasiness of the events in the river behind them, she finds herself again entranced by the jubilant air of her company. Now that she can view everything in hindsight, she cannot remember a time when she had such fun. Furthermore, all the romance pervading the air captures everyone's heart. In total honesty, she cannot bask in the glow of it, knowing the love between Shaylynn and Sarin has cemented itself this night. Though she has never explored her feelings for Shaylynn, she always found him to be quite handsome and believes he would be a good choice to take the throne.

She can bask, however, in the glow of the feelings between Fallon and Faith. Lyosan has spoken often of the love Fallon feels for her. Sarin, speaking out of turn as she often does, has made clear the feelings Faith has for Fallon. Now, watching them walk hand in hand, she sees the love she hopes someday to acquire. While she knows she may have to sacrifice her love for the sake of the kingdom, she also knows she may be lucky enough to wed a man who loves her and whom she could come to love. Though she cannot give the thought its due right now, Lyosan could be such a man.

Lyosan shields her and protects her with every move. He knows more than anyone the reaction her escape from the castle walls will garner. Many are the times he found himself receiving a harsh word from the king for housing the princess while on leave of her security. Though his actions and willingness to take the king's scorn endeared him to the princess, he attempts to avoid such moments whenever possible.

After several near misses and close calls, the troop comes to the moment to go their separate ways. Faith agrees to take Shaylynn home the rest of the way and ensure he makes it there safely. Shaylynn objects at first, but his cousin quickly shows she will not be dissuaded from her course of action. Fallon agrees to see Sarin home even though she'd clearly rather go with Shaylynn. But, as they must view this situation with some strategy, she eventually agrees to this design.

As Lyosan lives closest to the castle, he stands the likely candidate to see the princess back to her chambers. Shaylynn and Fallon choose him for other reasons than that, but they need not be mentioned. Faith and Sarin silently understand and consent to this as well.

"You're sure you'll be okay, Shaylynn?" Crystalynn asks.

Shaylynn nods and politely bows. "Right as rain by morning I assure you," he says. "If not by my own means, then by my family's."

Shaylynn nods to Faith, who smiles and nods in agreement. Shaylynn then turns to Sarin to say goodnight.

"I'm not sure I want you as you were," she muses. "That might suggest things would be as they were."

"After this night," Shaylynn replies, "nothing will ever be the same."

"I would concur with that statement," Faith adds with a glance at Fallon.

Fallon smiles and kisses Faith on the cheek. "I rejoice at the notion."

Faith starts down the road, but Shaylynn lingers and gives a stern look at his friend. There is no sincerity to his reaction, but he plays his part flawlessly.

"I'm not sure that was called for," Shaylynn says.

Before Fallon can respond, Faith comes back and grabs her cousin by the arm. "Come along you fool."

Pulling him down the street, Faith bows courteously to the princess and calls quietly to her. "A good night to you, my lady."

"And you as well," Crystalynn replies.

A moment later, Fallon and Sarin go on their way as well. Lyosan lingers a while in the street to ensure they still have safe passage. Soon after Faith and Shaylynn and Fallon and Sarin disappear into the darkness, Lyosan turns his attention to the castle. In his abruptness, he turns and collides with the princess. He quickly steadies himself and catches her as well.

"I am sorry," Lyosan says.

"Not at all," Crystalynn replies, "it was my fault. I stood too close to you."

"I have no objection to that," Lyosan assures her.

The innocence of his comment quickly turns in his mind. He understands that perhaps he has spoken to brazenly. The likelihood of his possibility increases when the princess gives no reply and her eyes widen. Quickly, Lyosan attempts to correct the misunderstanding.

"That is to say…" Lyosan stammers, "I didn't mean…I…"

Crystalynn, having found no offense to his comment but understanding his caution, smiles and gently touches his arm.

"Think nothing of it," she says. Then, she turns to the castle as well. "But you do flatter me too much."

"I only mean to be honest," Lyosan explains.

"Then perhaps you exaggerate the truth from time to time," Crystalynn says.

"Not when it concerns you," Lyosan says.

She smiles again though his stubbornness remains somewhat annoying. Yet the nuisance of his steadfastness is overwhelmed by the sincerity of his words and dedication to his perceived cause. His is not the fighter Shaylynn is nor does he possess the innate abilities of his friend, but surely Lyosan's heart holds just as strong as Shaylynn's if not proving itself the better of the two.

Once the time shows itself, Lyosan and Crystalynn start towards the castle. With guards along the walls, it will be difficult to go unnoticed. Luckily, they have the advantage of knowing the patterns of the guards' surveillance. Each has mastered the guards' path over time. A time and place will present itself, but they must hit the window the first chance they get.

"You do not have to accompany me," the princess says as they breach the outer wall. "I can assume the risk from here."

"I am too far in my training to allow such a thing," Lyosan jests. "Besides, two sets of eyes eliminate the risk."

"So what about when you make your exit?"

"As you have proven time and time again, it is far easier to get out than it is to get in."

"As you will have it then," Crystalynn concedes.

With the princess in the lead, the two slip along the wall avoiding the guise of the watchmen above them. Within minutes, they find themselves across from her window. Unfortunately, their journey has been too slow. Two knights patrol the wall directly above them. She could not go unnoticed up the wall and into her chamber. It may be as much as an hour before she has her opportunity.

Staying within the safety of the shadows, Lyosan and Crystalynn settle in for a short wait. They position themselves directly underneath the knights knowing detection will be all but impossible. Only they can surrender their position at this point. Having made that mistake before, they know what precautions will protect them now. As Lyosan recalls similar instances from their past, his heart lightens from the memories. Since they need to pass the time, he turns to Crystalynn and whispers quietly.

"Do you remember the night we snuck out in the rain?" Lyosan asks.

A smile crosses Crystalynn's face. "How could I forget?"

"You told me the day before you never ventured out into the rain," Lyosan recalls. "Your father never allowed you to venture out when the weather was anything but dry…"

Crystalynn picks up the story from there. "So when it rained the next day, you came to my window and asked me to join you. I asked what we would do, and you gave no true explanation to your intentions. You merely assured me I would enjoy myself…"

"And as I recall, for a while anyway, you rather did…"

Crystalynn chuckles lightly as the memories come back to her. "I truly did. I'd never felt the rain on my face before, and it was quite wonderful. It is just unfortunate we lingered too long, and the temperature became our enemy…"

"I don't think the wind was on our side either," Lyosan adds. "It turned horribly cold in a matter of minutes. When it finally became too much, we raced back to the castle. The patrols were lessened due to weather, so it was easier to sneak by…"

"But we found ourselves in the same position as tonight. The guards above us preventing me from scaling the wall undetected…"

"And the cold continued to worsen…."

"So you held me in your arms to try to keep me warm…"

"I didn't fare so well in that…"

"Perhaps not, but your efforts were not unappreciated."

Suddenly, she remembers how fiercely he tried to keep her safe that night. The strong grasp of his arms around her as the rain fell upon them. Even though he shivered as much as her, he refused to look to himself. Not until she made her move to the wall did he let her go. The same holds true today. He stays at her side until the time he can be assured of her safety.

She does love him. The extent of that love is yet unknown. He could be a brother, a dear friend, something more? Perhaps she does not wish to explore it because of the strong possibility that another will be crowned king. Should that day come to pass, these moments will be no more. She will not be able to sneak out with him. She could not risk being seen with him in what might be considered a compromising position. The attacks on her would be fierce; on Lyosan, they would be devastating. Yet, as she sits with him this night, she knows he would risk such attacks to be with her.

The moment begins to build on her. She wishes to avoid the unpleasant feelings rising within her. So, she turns back to Lyosan and continues the recanting of their adventure.

"We were so certain we'd gone undetected," she says. "Then I suddenly came down with the chills. My maid found the drenched clothes, and father raised hell finding the truth behind my illness…"

"He came to my house two days later, asking if I had anything to do with it," Lyosan adds. "I had him convinced I was innocent in the matter, but then a sneeze proved otherwise. We were not to see each other for a fortnight as punishment…"

"But you were at my window two nights later."

Before they can go further, they hit a stretch of luck. A commotion from within the castle brings the guards from their posts. The path to her chamber clears, and Crystalynn readies herself. Moments later, she sprints across the courtyard to the base of the wall beneath her window.

"I suppose our night is at an end," Crystalynn says as she finds her footing in the wall.

"Be safe princess," Lyosan says.

"And you as well, Lyosan," she replies.

He watches as she ascends the wall. Upon entering her chamber, she looks out one last time and waves to him. His concerns alleviated, Lyosan makes his way through the castle and back to his house.

As Lyosan heads for home, Shaylynn finally arrives at his. Having recovered from the ordeals of the evening, he sends Faith on her way and takes to sneaking into the house on his own.

Silently and quietly, he goes to his window and slides it open. At every creak, he stops and waits to see if he has alerted anyone. After a couple, careful minutes, he slips through the open window and into the room. In the blackness, he feels a small amount of apprehension as he cannot recall what lies on the ground. Closing his eyes, he opens up his other senses and allows for a different level of sight to guide him. Moving quickly but stealthily, he removes his boots and shirt before making it to his bed and laying down on the mattress. As he rests his head on the pillow, he hears the snap of fingers. Opening his eyes, he looks across the room to see a lit candle resting on his dresser. In the chair next to the dresser sits his father, Feylynn Storm.

Feylynn looks every part the knight. Though he does not wear his armor, he has his courtly cloak on. He is not an overpowering figure in stature, but he is an intimidating presence. A thin, brown beard covers the chiseled features of his face. Given the time of day and demands of his position, his face looks worn and tired. Still, he carries a cheery disposition as he stares at his surprised son.

"I must admit, you are better than I was at your age," Feylynn says.

Shaylynn sighs, "I can't be that impressive if you caught me."

Feylynn chuckles. "Don't be so disappointed in your skills. It was not your attempt to sneak in which alerted me to your...venture."

This statement leaves Shaylynn concerned. How much did his father know of his exploits tonight? How much worse would this punishment get considering his behaviors the last few days? Before he can inquire further, Feylynn steps in.

"The entirety of your agenda this evening does not concern me. But you did something, and it nearly killed you."

"How do you know that?" Shaylynn asks.

"I felt it. The power you exerted. The drain on your life." Feylynn pauses for a moment before he continues. "I even felt your life flicker for the briefest of moments."

When the matter was contained between only Shaylynn and his cohorts, he had given no thought to the danger on his own life. His only concern lay with saving Sarin. He cared nothing for his own life. Now that knowledge of the event clearly extends beyond those there, he feels the pain his actions might have caused.

"Have you told mother?" Shaylynn asks.

"No," Feylynn replies, "but I feel it will not be long before she realizes something is bothering me. I don't know if I can hold it from her forever."

A tear forms in Shaylynn's eyes. "I am sorry."

Feylynn rises from the chair and sits on the edge of Shaylynn's bed.

"I do not think you would use your magic foolishly. I have no doubt you acted from a place of need and a desire to do good. But you must understand where you are at in your training. Your powers are growing in ways I did not expect."

"What do you mean?"

"The power you showed. The concentration of magic goes beyond what I have seen for a boy of your age."

"And that is a bad thing?"

In truth, it is. At the same time, Feylynn does not want to frighten his son with what he has to say. It has been a desire for him and Kandessa to shield their sons from the truth of the world. They may be at the end of the line with Shaylynn.

"It very well could be," Feylynn finally admits. "When you exert the kind of power you did, it can be felt from very far away. Anyone tapped into the magical powers, as we are, can feel what you've done."

"Isn't Daryndell the only country who holds closely to the magic? They wouldn't care if…"

"They are the greatest power we know of," Feylynn interrupts. "They are not the only power. There are some, a small contingent, within our borders who hold to the magical traditions. While they are not a threat, they do not necessarily hold our beliefs. And then there is Jorram…"

Now Shaylynn interrupts. "Jorram has not been a threat in magic for centuries."

"Because their king has been strong enough to keep the magic at bay. Those who want to bring it back to power have no sway. However, should a threat arise in another country, like ours, it may be all they need to bring magic back into prominence."

"And I could be that threat?"

"In reality, maybe. But as long as they can perceive you as a threat and use that perception to further their cause, therein lies the danger."

Shaylynn feels the overwhelming possibilities flooding over him and can think of nothing to say. It wasn't anything he planned to have happen. A situation arose, he reacted, and now all of this is happening.

Feylynn sees the look of concern of his son's face. And while he does not mean to overwhelm Shaylynn, he does need to make clear the severity of the situation. Feylynn's powers are known to the world at large, and the manner in which he uses his powers are well-known. He has no desire to extend the rule of Artonia to other lands and kingdoms. He is not seeking a dynasty of his own, nor is he looking to delve into the true depths of magic. He merely seeks to defend his home and protect his family.

Shaylynn, however, could very easily end up on the throne of Artonia. A king with such innate magical prowess could very easily see his priorities shift once he gained his power. In his heart, Feylynn would like to believe wholeheartedly in Shaylynn's good nature, but he cannot be so naïve to ignore possibility. For those who cannot entertain possibility invite ignorance into their minds. And ignorance leads to the destruction of all.

"I didn't want to show myself," Shaylynn finally explains. "I only wanted to save Sarin."

It's a piece to the puzzle which Feylynn did not know. To this point, the reason behind the show of magic was immaterial. As Feylynn said, he believed Shaylynn would only act out of necessity. While he hadn't imagined what that necessity would be, hearing Shaylynn's admission changes everything.

"Tell me what happened, son."

Shaylynn sits up in bed. "There were six of us. We were in the woods by the river. Sarin fell in, and the current was strong. I went in after her, but I could not get her out of the way of the rocks in the river.

"For a moment, I assumed I would die there. Then, suddenly, I felt a … almost like a burning in my chest. Time seemed to slow, and a thought formed in my mind. I … knew … that if I focused everything I had and timed it just right, I might be able to break through the stone and save her."

The story makes sense. Feylynn has experienced the same kind of phenomenon when using his own magic. However, it appears Shaylynn is holding something back. Perhaps it is just the age of a young man which causes the hesitation in total revelation, or maybe Feylynn is only imagining it. But it is worth prying to find if it is the truth or not.

"Son, I do not wish to embarrass you in any way, but did something else happen to perhaps instigate this feeling?"

Shaylynn hesitates for a minute and then nods.

"Sarin…admitted she loves me."

Shaylynn looks away at the revelation, and Feylynn smiles knowing the difficulty a child can have in discussing such a matter with a parent. Were there a better way to broach the subject, Feylynn would definitely use it, but as it is, it will serve them both well this night.

"Son, do not be afraid or embarrassed by the love you share with another." Feylynn says putting a hand on Shaylynn's shoulder. Shaylynn turns back to his father – still somewhat uncomfortable with the conversation. "I am happy you have found such a beautiful thing with such a wonderful girl. You and Sarin have been close since you were children. I cannot imagine a day when you do not remain close."

Suddenly, the thought Shaylynn normally refuses to entertain jumps to the forefront of his mind. And before he can stop it from escaping his lips, he says the words.

"What if I am made king?"

The question stops even Feylynn. It is a thought he has spent a great deal of time discussing and considering. The knights of the high courts, dignitaries from around Artonia, other friends, and family have all posed the idea, but Feylynn never thought he'd have to have the conversation with his son so soon. And yet, it is not the conversation he assumed he'd have. It is not about what Shaylynn might gain should he be named king, but rather, it is about what he might lose.

"The greatest honor bestowed upon any citizen would be to be granted the throne. It is a duty which we all must be willing to accept with the highest levels of dedication and humility. To have an entire kingdom of people look upon you and decide they would follow your lead would be a true gift, my son.

"And you know the princess, well. You would surely make each other very happy.

"But, at the same time, I believe we all have a role to play in our destiny. We affect the outcomes of our actions. If, in the future, you are faced with the decision of serving as king or knight, I've no doubt you'll make the best choice."

"And if it's not my choice to make?"

"I pray you'll not have to face such a terrible day."

Feylynn says nothing more as he rises from his son's bed and gives him one more smile. He quietly leaves the room, and Shaylynn lies back down and drifts off to sleep. He has a great deal to consider, though, in reality, little will be resolved in the near future. The throne may very well await him, but it will not be his tomorrow.

CHAPTER VI

Indeed, the next day greets him as any other day. He rises early when Daylynn comes bounding into his room and jumps on Shaylynn's bed. Given his activities from the previous night, Shaylynn isn't exactly eager to rise as early as he usually does. Daylynn, however, will not be deterred.

"Get up, Shay!" Daylynn demands.

In all the world, there is only one person who gets to refer to Shaylynn as Shay. No one else has tried more than once. Not even Sarin, who can rarely resist the opportunity to jab at Shaylynn, dares jest about the nickname. It is a privilege reserved for Daylynn and Daylynn alone.

"Leave me alone, Daylynn," Shaylynn says, not really as a warning, more of a plea.

"But it's time to get up!" Daylynn informs him. "Mother is already making breakfast, and you're gonna be late if you don't get up now!"

"So I'll be late," Shaylynn concedes, "what's the worst that can happen?"

"Beylynn says he'll eat your portion!"

"Beylynn needs to get his own life already," Shaylynn mutters.

Unbeknownst to Shaylynn, Beylynn is standing at the door, listening to the entire interaction. As is normally the case, it was Beylynn who sent Daylynn into the room to wake Shaylynn. In his earlier years, Shaylynn would get up when Beylynn came for him, but now that he is older, Beylynn has to rely on other techniques. But now that Shaylynn has so eagerly changed the subject, Beylynn can use other methods to his advantage.

"If you look down on my presence, I will have to make it more known," Beylynn says.

"I would never," Shaylynn says drowsily, "look down on the presence of family. I just wonder if my oldest and dearest brother will ever look to find a family of his own. Surely, it would not be a hard task for one of the finest and bravest knights to find a suitable wife?"

"Now you mean to flatter me?"

"I only speak the truth."

"In truth, we do not all have suitable partners thrust upon us in the days of our youth. Ones who love us immediately without cause and without reservation."

Daylynn begins to giggle. It is well-known amongst the brothers that Shaylynn's soft spot is Sarin. In the past, Beylynn has been merciless in his teasing of Shaylynn's feelings for her. Thank goodness he was not around to hear her declarations of love for him. Still, there is enough without that knowledge to get under Shaylynn's skin.

"Shaylynn loves Sarin!" Beylynn calls, which causes Daylynn to laugh more.

"Stop it!" Shaylynn demands.

Daylynn stops laughing for a moment to repeat, "Shaylynn loves Sarin!" and then continues laughing.

Shaylynn pops up from the bed and tackles Daylynn playfully with one arm. Beylynn joins in the fray and leaps onto Shaylynn. Pinning him down, Beylynn frees Daylynn, who immediately jumps on top of both his brothers. Their laughter and cheerfulness permeates the air, but Kandessa cannot have their rough housing getting too far out of hand.

"Enough!" she calls from the kitchen. "Get to the table already. Father will need to leave shortly, and all three of you are going with him!"

At this news, Daylynn, always excited for a trip to the castle, jumps off the bed and runs for the kitchen. Beylynn finally relents and lets Shaylynn up. The two linger for a moment. Beylynn rubs his brother's head and leaves him. Shaylynn changes clothes for the day and then joins the family for breakfast.

Feylynn sits at the head of the table with Beylynn on his right. Shaylynn sits to his father's immediate left, and Daylynn sit next to Shaylynn. At the other end of the table sits Kandessa. Or at least her plate sits there because she often is up and about while the family eats.

"We've business in the castle?" Beylynn asks.

"Indeed," Feylynn replies, "dignitaries from the southern realm will be arriving. Sir Victer Erurt, mayor of O'Lyn, will arrive with his sons and main council. The king will meet with them most of the day. I will be directly involved in the meeting. Daylynn will stay with me as a page. Beylynn, you will serve as ambassador for the children. And Shaylynn will keep an eye on the horses in the stables."

Shaylynn sighs a bit.

"A problem with that duty, son?" Feylynn asks.

The concerns of the previous night cannot linger. Feylynn must carry on as usual if the two are to maintain their secrets. And so must Shaylynn. In truth, the duty is one Shaylynn has undertaken before, and he appalls it every time. But he cannot expect his father to deviate from their normal responsibilities just because Feylynn is aware of the strain Shaylynn has endured.

"No, father, of course not." Shaylynn replies.

"I know you hate to be pulled from your training, but this is an important responsibility." Feylynn replies. "To be placed in a dignitary's position, regardless of how meaningless the position seems, is to be awarded a certain level of importance and standing among the rest. You, perhaps the only in your age, will be known to the mayor of the largest city in the south. I know Sir Victer. He will remember you, and to be remembered is a great honor."

The family finishes their meal and prepares for their day. The boys leave first, with their father in tow. Before he leaves the house, he stands in the doorway with his arm around his wife.

"Can you believe it?" he asks. "Three healthy, wonderful sons."

"We are blessed," Kandessa replies.

"I only wish you had a daughter to care for," Feylynn admits.

"And give up one of them? Never! Besides, they will bring others into the family in their time."

"It seems one is already set."

Kandessa smiles and looks at Shaylynn. A mother knows when her child finds love. And while she does not happily give Shaylynn away, she is happy to see him find love.

"She is a wonderful child," Kandessa says. "I believed this day was coming from the moment they met."

"So wise you have always been," Feylynn says, kissing his wife's forehead. "I eagerly await the day they become one."

The remark strikes hard at Kandessa. She holds a secret of her own – one which has reared its ugly head only recently. Unlike her husband and son, she cannot so easily withhold the emotions it brings. After a hard breath, a tear drops from her eyes. Feylynn notices immediately.

"What brings this sadness?" Feylynn inquires.

"Just a feeling," Kandessa replies, "a fear."

Feylynn takes his wife's face in his hands. "Tell it to me now," he says, "that I may dispel it immediately."

"I see these moments we have – together – as a family. Something in my heart tells me there will not be many more of them. I feel something is coming which will tear us apart."

"Hear this now," Feylynn commands. "There is no power – in this world or the next – which can tear me from you. I am now, and forever shall be, with you. And you with me."

The two kiss, and Kandessa's fear lessens a bit. If he could, Feylynn would stay and comfort her even more, but he must see to his duties.

When the four arrive at the castle, Shaylynn breaks off to go to the stables while Feylynn takes the other two inside. Within two hours, the troop arrives, and Shaylynn begins his watch. His introduction with Sir Victer is brief but positive. Victer has nothing but glowing things to say about Shaylynn, even though in truth he means to set one of his own sons into a position with the princess. Nonetheless, Shaylynn feels he makes a good impression with the mayor.

As the morning drifts away, Shaylynn keeps to his tasks. With his father's permission, he keeps a training sword on his person so the day away from training won't be a total loss. In between feedings and waterings, Shaylynn hones his craft. Still not fully recovered from the previous night, he tires himself out rather quickly and rests against a post. His one saving grace is in knowing his mother will be bringing him lunch at some point. At least then, he will have someone with whom he can converse.

When lunch arrives however, it is not the company he anticipated. After hearing the rustling of feet approaching, he opens his eyes to see Sarin standing in front of him with a basket of food. She smiles at him – not in her usual manner but rather with a look of great relief.

"I did not expect to see you," Shaylynn says standing to greet her.

At first, she says nothing.

"Is something the matter?" Shaylynn asks.

"No," Sarin says as a tear drops from her eye. Shaylynn steps forward with concern, but she stops him. "No, honestly, it's nothing. I was at the castle today since the dignitaries were here, so I peeked in on the training. You obviously were not there, and Fallon did not know where you were. I feared you maybe hadn't recovered from last night, so I went looking for you."

The amount of concern is quite flattering to Shaylynn, but rather than tease her about it, he merely takes the compliment.

"I felt so silly, I ran all the way to your house, and your mother explained what you were doing. I should have known, of course. You always aid in these matters. Anyway, she insisted I bring you your lunch, so I could see for myself you were alright. She couldn't understand why I thought anything might be wrong with you."

"I was able to avoid telling her what happened," Shaylynn explains. "Father knows, but he would rather not worry mother considering what almost happened."

"Yes, what *almost* happened."

The fear and shock of the previous night comes back to Sarin and grips her once again. When Shaylynn sees the look in her eyes, he takes her hand.

"Are you alright?"

"To be honest, I don't know," Sarin replies. She looks down at his hand holding hers and smiles. "At times, I feel as though it was all a dream, and I am still sleeping. It's not just the magnitude of what took place – the feat you performed. But that I told you I loved you, and you showed me you loved me." She looks into Shaylynn's eyes. "I've wanted it for so long but am not sure it was real."

"It was," Shaylynn assures her. "And if you are uncertain, I'll do whatever it takes to remedy your fears."

Sarin laughs for only a moment. "If this is real, then why are you not teasing me? Where is the wit that cuts me to the bone and leaves me furious at you?"

"It is there," Shaylynn says with a smirk, "but with only you here, I do not wish to hide behind the teasing and the wit."

Sarin smirks now. "Does this mean you'll only profess your love in private? When we're in public, you'll hide your emotions?"

Shaylynn tries to jest a bit if it will make Sarin feel normal. "I must admit I am not perfect."

"Then why do I not see your imperfections?" Sarin asks. "Why, even when they are there in front of me, do they pass over me like the flow of wind? Why, even when I feel it, does it vanish and leave me wondering if it was ever really there?"

"I do not know," Shaylynn says. "I cannot speak of imperfections in you because for all my efforts, I have not found one."

More tears come from Sarin's eyes, but they are tears of joy now. The moment from last night did not pass on into oblivion. It remains with them here and now.

"You flatter me now?" Sarin asks.

Shaylynn leans towards Sarin. "Yes," he replies.

Just before Shaylynn can kiss her, Sarin backs away slightly. "You're a better tease than flatterer," she says.

Shaylynn smiles. "I'll work on it."

The two kiss again, and Sarin drops the basket to the ground. Now removed from the danger of the night before, they can merely revel in the revelation of their love for one another. For just one more moment, nothing else matters.

Then, as it so often does, reality steps in. A clamoring of feet comes rushing towards the stables. Shaylynn recognizes most of them as the troop which accompanied Victer Erurt. There are panicked looks on their faces and a flurry of comments flying back and forth between them. Shaylynn and Sarin move to the side to let them attend to their needs. At first, Shaylynn fears the talks between the king and Sir Erurt have ended badly. Yet, the concern on their faces makes it seem like it's something else entirely.

"My lords," Shaylynn says, "are you leaving?"

One of them, a Sir Gankin Torr, who was very pleasant with Shaylynn when they arrived, stops to address Shaylynn. "I'm afraid we must," Gankin explains. "Word has come down from the north. Jorram attacks."

The news hits hard. An attack on the north puts everything in jeopardy. Cyrus will have to send aid to the north. No doubt Feylynn will be part of the cavalry. Still, Shaylynn must attend to the visitors and ensure they can make a quick exit. Even though the south will not be under attack, they may be able to send fighters to help along the northern border.

Once Shaylynn finishes his tasks, he turns back to Sarin. While he would like to run to his father's side and see what is happening, he's not sure it is his place to leave his post and enter the castle. While Sarin, whose father will not be leaving the city because of his business within the walls, does not truly understand the feeling and concern Shaylynn has, she understands Shaylynn needs to find his father and know what is happening.

"Go," she says.

Without a word, Shaylynn turns and runs out of the stables. At first, Sarin lingers behind, for even she feels the effects of this news. The turmoil this throws the country into will be felt for months to come. And though it feels a little selfish, and she wishes her mind did not go there first, Sarin fears this will only escalate the movement to make Shaylynn king.

But those concerns must be relegated to the background because she needs to be there for Shaylynn at this moment. Leaving the stables, she heads for the castle to catch up with Shaylynn.

He has already made it to the castle and is heading for the knights' hall. With all the commotion and need to make quick efforts, none stop Shaylynn from making his way through them. In all the clamoring and the commotion, Shaylynn finds it difficult to find his father, but he will not give up. As he wanders to and fro, he hears a voice calling from somewhere around him.

"Shaylynn!" the voice calls.

Shaylynn turns around, hoping his father will be there to talk to him, but he cannot see him. Again, the voice calls out to him, and Shaylynn turns again. Finally, Fallon appears from the crowd and stands in front of his friend.

"Where have you been?" Fallon demands.

"Serving as stable boy for the visiting dignitaries," Shaylynn replies.

"A page from the north arrived not half an hour ago. He spoke of villages on fire and pillagers from Jorram running wild. The king means to send the entire royal guard to investigate."

"Investigate?" Shaylynn repeats. "What is there to investigate?"

"These actions are rash, Shaylynn," Fallon replies. "If we are lucky, it is not an act of war from Jorram."

"If we cannot see this as war, we will be beaten and in submission before we realize the battle has begun," Shaylynn replies.

He continues to scour the room with Fallon not far behind. After several minutes of searching, he finds his father conversing with Fallon's father and many other knights. Feylynn looks pleased to see Shaylynn.

"It's about time you found us," he says. "I was worried I wouldn't have anyone to leave Daylynn with."

Feylynn begins to walk away, and Shaylynn follows. Fallon stops to converse with his own father.

"You know I ride with the others," Degon explains.

"Of course, father," Fallon replies.

"You'll tend to your mother. The duties of the house will fall to you. Your uncle will be around, but he must see to his own family."

"I can handle it," Fallon says. "Besides, you won't be gone long."

With a smile, Degon reaches for his son and draws Fallon to him. Fallon grasps his father and holds him tightly.

"Indeed, my son," Degon finally says. "I love you, my boy."

"And I, you, father."

Feylynn leads Shaylynn out of the hall and into the chamber reserved for the High Knight of the Royal Court. Daylynn sits in the chamber with tears running down his face. Now that they are alone, Shaylynn can ask the question he feared to ask when they were in the main hall.

"Why would I need to be placed in charge of Daylynn?"

Feylynn ignores the question and continues with his instructions for Shaylynn. "In our absence, the king will bring in troops for the wall. It will be on you and your peers to aid in the general safety of the city. It is nothing too daunting for you, of course, but you may have to inspire your friends to do better than their normal duty."

"Why am I in charge of Daylynn?" Shaylynn asks again.

"You know the answer," Feylynn replies as he readies himself.

A minute later, Beylynn enters the chamber, fully dressed in armor and ready to ride out. Shaylynn cannot stand the sight. Beylynn sees the look of concern and terror on his brother's face, but he cannot do anything to steady him.

"The guard is ready," Beylynn tells their father. "We await your orders."

"Excellent," Feylynn replies. "If we leave before the hour ends, we shall arrive within two days. Ready yourself. Say goodbye to your kin."

A harsh command from a father. But a harsh world awaits them.

Beylynn rides on his first mission as a Knight of Langerwitz. The time for childish things has truly passed. So cruel it is that only hours ago, he played with his brothers in their home with their mother calling for them to come to breakfast. Now, he faces the trials of a man.

"Well, dear brother," Beylynn begins, "you wanted me out of the house."

Shaylynn grunts. "I wanted you married, acting as a husband and father – not fighting in a war!"

"Do not be so quick to assume," Beylynn chides. "And do not frighten Daylynn. He will need you to be his comfort."

Shaylynn turns to see his younger brother sitting on the edge of a chair, hands shaking and eyes panicking. It is all the things Shaylynn wishes he could do at the moment, but he knows he cannot. With the two eldest men of the house leaving, Shaylynn will assume some of their responsibilities. Still, when he turns back to Beylynn, a tear is in his eye.

"Do not fear, brother," Beylynn says placing a hand on Shaylynn's shoulder. "This will prove the actions of a few – not of a country. We will deal swift and righteous justice to the guilty and return within a fortnight."

"I've never wanted you to be right more in my life," Shaylynn replies.

Beylynn laughs and brings his brother to him. Daylynn leaps off the chair and joins his brothers in the embrace. After a moment, Beylynn breaks the hold and kneels down to face Daylynn.

"Do not make things easy for Shaylynn now that you must listen to him," Beylynn commands.

Daylynn smiles a bit. "I won't."

"Good," Beylynn replies. "I expect a full report on how terrible you were while father and I were away."

Daylynn nods but can say no more.

"I love you both," Beylynn says as he leaves.

Shaylynn walks Daylynn out of the chamber and sees Feylynn waiting for them. Daylynn leaps into his father's arms, and Feylynn lifts him happily off the ground.

"Goodness!" Feylynn cries. "You are getting so big! I imagine I won't be able to hold you when I return!"

"You will win," Daylynn replies. "You can do anything!"

"I certainly hope you are right," Feylynn replies. Then, he kisses Daylynn on the cheek. "My beautiful boy, be good for your mother and your brother, yes?"

"Beylynn made me promise to be bad for Shaylynn," Daylynn admits.

Feylynn roars with laughter. "Well, I suppose that'll be acceptable, but be good for your mother, eh?"

Daylynn nods and hugs his father tightly.

"My beautiful boy," Feylynn repeats. Then he kisses Daylynn again and sets him down. "Say, Fallon is just around the corner. Why don't you go wait with him while I talk with Shaylynn, okay?"

Daylynn nods and disappears around the corner. Once he is out of the way, Feylynn takes Shaylynn by the shoulders.

"I know you are scared, my son," Feylynn begins. "But you must be strong. The king trusts our family, and you are the highest ranking of us to stay behind."

"I am just a child," Shaylynn replies.

"No," Feylynn remarks. "No, you are not. All the talks we have had, the wisdom you have shared. These are not the qualities of a boy. They are makings of someone great … a … a …"

Feylynn does not want to the say the word because he knows it injures his son so. Yet, at the same time, it is the truth. Shaylynn possesses many of the qualities necessary for a king. It is merely a matter of whether he would accept the crown or follow his heart.

"A king," Shaylynn finally finishes.

"Perhaps," Feylynn admits. "Or perhaps just a great man. Either way, you will be needed for this kingdom to survive."

"Why would you tell me this now?" Shaylynn asks.

"A fear grows in my mind," Feylynn explains. "One your mother shares, though I'd not admit as much to her. I do not know what this journey holds for us, Shaylynn, but I fear it is something we are not ready to face."

More tears form in Shaylynn's eyes. "Then do not go."

"I must," Feylynn replies.

Shaylynn throws himself into his father.

"Be brave, my son," Feylynn says. "I've been wrong many times in my life. I'll happily admit I was again when we return."

Taking his father's words as a promise, Shaylynn pulls away and lets his father join the others. When Shaylynn comes around the corner, he sees Fallon sitting with Daylynn close by. Lyosan has joined them as well.

Shaylynn continues to follow his father out of the hall and into the courtyard. There, the rest of the knights wait on their horses for their captain to arrive. Feylynn mounts his steed and prepares to lead the group. Before he does, he turns back to Shaylynn one last time.

"Give my love to your mother, will you?" he asks.

Shaylynn nods.

Then Feylynn smiles. "And don't forget my love for you."

"Never," Shaylynn replies.

Then, Shaylynn watches as his father turns away and commands the others to ride out. Beylynn holds Shaylynn's gaze for but a moment and then joins his comrades. As they ride away, Shaylynn begins to chase after them. He runs out of the castle and stands atop the hill, watching the riders head for the northern gate. There he stands and watches as they fade to the point where he can no longer see them.

As he watches, a hand slips into his. Without looking, he knows Sarin has found him and stands with him now. He gives a little squeeze as a sign of appreciation. For a few minutes, the two stand in silence. When it becomes too much for her to bear, Sarin breaks the quiet.

"You must know they will return," she says.

"After all that has happened in the last day," he says, "I feel I know precious little. But I have your love, so I won't ask for anything more at the moment."

"That is good. I fear I've little else to give."

Shaylynn finally turns to look at her. "It is far more than I deserve."

Sarin smiles. "I agree."

Shaylynn laughs for the first time since the news broke. With Sarin at his side, he finds Daylynn and takes him home. Training is canceled for the rest of the week, though Jonas encourages the youths to practice in their own ways.

Lyosan lingers at the castle for a bit. He doubts he will see the princess given all that has happened, but if she should need his ear to bend, he will have it ready. After waiting for an hour or so, he assumes she will not be leaving the castle. What's more, Lyosan surely has some chores to attend to at home. Somewhat disappointed, he leaves the castle and walks down the hill.

As he approaches the house, he sees the princess walking towards the castle. His heart jumps at her sight, and she seems greatly relieved when she sees him. He races to her side.

"Is something the matter, my lady?" Lyosan asks.

"Please, Lyosan, your formality usually gives me discomfort, but today, it drives me up a wall."

"I am sorry," Lyosan replies, "but I must act as a man in my station."

"I know," Crystalynn replies. "Perhaps I hate it so because I envy your knowledge of your station. You always know what to do and how to act. You never seem lost and out of place."

"I assure you, I often am. Perhaps I hide the truth well, but I often find myself at a loss when I'm with you."

Crystalynn smiles as his attempt to empathize. But in truth, he cannot hope to understand the difficulty she faces. Her only family is the king, who is too busy to help her with her concerns. She has no mother or sister to show her the way to respond to such a difficult situation. And the attendants who attempt to assist cannot offer more than suggestions or recall a memory of something the queen once did. Crystalynn knows she is not her mother, and when she tries to be, she feels a failing all too real.

"My brother does not know what to make of this attack," she tells Lyosan.

"He is not the only one," Lyosan informs her. "In the midst of all the commotion, I did not hear a single knight speak with any confidence in the matter. They all hoped it was not a sign of war, but each understood the likelihood was greater than they wished to admit. Even Shaylynn seemed distraught with his father and brother riding off to fight."

Crystalynn did not know who all was riding to the aid of the north. She assumed Feylynn would ride, but she did not think Beylynn would go as well. Given Lyosan's desire to keep matters regarding Shaylynn to a minimum, he will not be pleased when her reaction surfaces.

"They both ride!" Crystalynn cries.

Lyosan sighs.

"Why would Beylynn ride with them?" Crystalynn questions, more to herself than to Lyosan.

Regardless, Lyosan seeks to answer her concerns. "Beylynn was knighted more than a year ago. He is a member of the Royal Court. What's more, he probably asked to go if he knew his father was riding."

Crystalynn continues to think silently. It is possible she didn't even hear Lyosan's response. When she speaks again, it seems very likely.

"I hope Feylynn left on good terms with Shaylynn. After Shaylynn's actions days ago, I fear there may have been lingering tension between them."

"You are kind to worry for him," Lyosan says, "but I feel it will be moot when the knights return."

"I sincerely hope it will be," Crystalynn replies.

After a few silent moments, Crystalynn turns to Lyosan.

"This must be odd for you," she says. "You see the torment on your friends' faces in losing their fathers, yet you lost your own not so long ago."

Lyosan nods. "It is difficult. I never wish to garner their sympathy, but I find it difficult to feel any for them. They've had so much time with their fathers, and I have a small collection of memories of mine. Still, I would never wish them pain."

"You are a good man, Lyosan. You must promise me you will stay that."

Lyosan smiles. "You have my word."

Crystalynn smiles back. "And I shall hold you to it."

The princess does not stay much longer. With so much going on, she will have duties to attend to at the castle. Cyrus will have to bring in a different patrol, as Feylynn alluded to, and the duties of those coming in will have to be reallocated as well. For the next few weeks, everything will run quite differently. They can only hope the matter will resolve itself quickly, and normalcy shall return.

CHAPTER VII

Unfortunately, a great number of days pass without any news from the north. Everyone knew immediate response was impossible. It would take days for the riders to reach the north, let alone assess the situation and send word back to the capital. So, for the first few days, everyone acclimates to the new order and says little about the absence of their loved ones. In short time, however, the subject becomes too difficult to avoid. The youths can no longer train with the same vigor and focus. What's more, their new duties leave many of them fatigued and depleted. Yet, Jonas cannot excuse them – especially while their contribution to the city holds such value. Rather, he must be ever vigilant – as a hawk on its prey. He must continue to push and strive to keep them in line. Fortunately, he has Shaylynn to assist. Ever the leader, Shaylynn keeps spirits as high as he can while the training continues. Many are quick to follow his lead – Fallon, Lyosan, Stefen, and Darrow. Others take more prodding. And, of course, Pythyn is ever the thorn in Shaylynn's side. But life carries on, nevertheless. Not the same life of course, but a life all the same.

The days begin to pass more slowly as people await news of the knights. So many days have passed without word from the north. Cyrus sends a rider once every five days, but they return without word or not at all. The training of the youths has stalled since many are now needed at home to keep their houses running. Nothing has changed for Lyosan of course. Having gone without a father for so many years, his family and he are well accustomed to being on their own. Others are not so prepared. Fallon manages with his mother, mostly because he has no other siblings to care for. He only looks after his mother, and she looks after him. As long as one has the other, they need nothing else. Yet, they yearn strongly for Degon to return to them.

Shaylynn, on the other hand, has seen his responsibilities grow twofold. He tends to the work of his father and his brother. At times, his duties grow even further because of the strain placed on his mother. She misses Feylynn greatly and worries so much for Beylynn she cannot compose herself at times. What's worse, she devotes herself to Daylynn who has never been so long without his father and brother. For all the effort she puts forth, it does not alleviate his concerns.

And so, one morning, when Kandessa wakes later than usual, she scrambles in search of her youngest boy. Shaylynn, who rose some hours ago, toils outside with the chores normally slated for his brother. Kandessa searches the house and areas behind the house, but she cannot locate him. In her frenzied state, she begins to worry greatly as to what may have become of him. She fears the worst though her fears are unwarranted. Still, with all that is happening, she cannot think or react rationally to anything that happens now.

"Shaylynn!" she calls as loud as she can.

From his place, he cannot hear her cries. When she goes unanswered, she fears more evil has befallen her. She runs frantically to the door and throws it open violently.

"Shaylynn!" she calls again.

This time, he hears her and immediately drops his things. Hearing the fear in her voice, he turns his full attention to her.

"Mother!" he replies.

Now that she sees him, her fear turns to anger.

"Why did you not wake me earlier?" she demands.

"You need the rest, mother," he replies.

"Do not assume for me!" she scorns. "You are but a boy. There are things you cannot understand!"

Shaylynn knows his mother speaks from a place of frustration towards the disappearance of the knights. She is not really angry with him, nor is she upset about the lateness in which she awoke. So, he says nothing in reply, and takes the brunt of his mother's frustrations.

"And where is your brother?" Kandessa asks.

"He tends to the chicks as he's supposed to," Shaylynn replies.

"So certain you are," Kandessa mocks. "When last did you check on him?"

Shaylynn begins to understand the problem. In truth, he's been focused on his own work for the better part of an hour. Daylynn may easily have escaped his sight and gone where he could not know.

Shaylynn now fears his answer, not for the recourse upon him, but for the effect his words will have on his mother. She is already in a place of great unrest. This will only worsen her cause.

"It has been too long," Shaylynn replies.

"Then you know not where he is?" Kandessa asks.

"I do not," Shaylynn says with a lowered head.

Kandessa steps into the yard and slaps Shaylynn across the face. He does nothing in response though some part of him wishes to speak up. Too much has been placed on him. She calls him a child but expects him to be two men on top of it. Surely, she cannot hold him responsible for all the world's grief.

"Your brother is just a child," she lectures. "He misses his father and his brother. He looks to me to protect him and assure him all will be well. And I cannot know these things! I cannot make the world better for him!"

She begins to cry as she speaks. Any ill will Shaylynn momentarily felt now vanishes without a trace. He embraces his mother, and she embraces him as well.

"Oh, my boy," she cries, "I am sorry. I was wrong to strike you."

"These times bring many ills greater than a reddened cheek, mother," he replies.

"I cannot lose him, too, Shaylynn," she pleads.

"He will come back soon, mother. I know he will. He's merely gotten into a small bit of mischief he'll tell us all about at lunch. He tries to put father out of his mind for a few hours. He's fortunate to be able to."

In truth, Shaylynn is mistaken. Daylynn has not gone out on some childish adventure lost in his own happiness and imaginative delights. Instead, he crouches on a tree branch a few hundred yards away from the northern gate of the city. Hoping to see some sign of his father, he had left home when he found the first opportunity. For two hours this morning, he has sat in that tree waiting for the slightest sign his father will come back this day. When it becomes clear it will not happen, he leaves the tree and runs for home. Along the way, he begins to cry as the despair he feels overwhelms him.

Despite the distance, he runs all the way home. He is so distraught he doesn't even stop when his mother begins to scorn him for being away from home. Instead, he runs straight into the house and into his room. Shaylynn and Kandessa hear his door slam shut from outside. They have no way of knowing what has upset him so greatly, but they both have a good idea. Unfortunately, Kandessa has exhausted her bag of tricks. She feels she cannot reach him.

"Go to him, will you Shaylynn?" Kandessa asks.

"And say what?" Shaylynn asks.

"If I knew, I'd say it myself," Kandessa replies.

With great hesitation, Shaylynn walks into the house and steps up to his brother's door. He pauses there for a minute trying to think of something to say to Daylynn. To be honest, the pain in his heart is blinding as well. He's tried with every ounce of himself to keep it locked away so he can help his mother and Daylynn. But this may be one thing he cannot help with.

Finally, he knocks on the door. "Daylynn."

"Go away!"

"You cannot tell me what to do," Shaylynn replies. "I am older and stronger than you."

"I don't wanna talk."

"Very good, then you can listen."

Shaylynn tries to open the door, but something blocks the door from the inside. When he feels the obstruction, he sighs and steps back.

"Mother was worried about you," Shaylynn says.

"I was fine."

"I'm sure you were. But, she would feel better if I could just see you and know for certain."

"No!"

Shaylynn hits his head on the door. He can get in the room if he must, but he'd rather not break into his own brother's room – not for this.

"You know I can get in if I want to," Shaylynn warns.

"Don't!"

"Then let me in."

Shaylynn stands at the door for a few moments and listens carefully. A few seconds later, he hears something being drug away from the door.

Then, the door opens slightly. Daylynn stands in view. His eyes are red from crying.

"May I enter?" Shaylynn asks.

Daylynn nods and steps away from the door. Shaylynn pushes the door open and slowly walks in. By the time Shaylynn closes the door, Daylynn has thrown himself on his bed. Shaylynn takes a seat on the edge of the bed.

"Where were you?" Shaylynn asks.

"At the castle gate…looking for father," Daylynn replies.

"You shouldn't have done that."

"Why?"

"Because, you're needed here."

"No, I'm not. I just watch the chickens so I'm not in the way."

"That's not true."

Daylynn lifts himself off the bed and faces Shaylynn. He still has tears in his eyes, but his face frowns deeply at Shaylynn.

"Then why do I need to be here?" he demands to know.

Shaylynn sighs. "Because mother needs to know you're safe. Father and Beylynn are off protecting the kingdom. You and I are all mother has of her family. She needs us close, so she knows the rest are okay."

"What if they're not?"

"They are," Shaylynn replies. "They are fine, and they will come back to us very soon. But, until they do, we need to carry on as though everything were normal. That way, when they come home, everything will be as it was for them."

Daylynn nods as if he understands, but it is more likely that he doesn't. Still, Shaylynn has helped in some small way. As proof, Daylynn throws his arms around his brother and buries his face in his side. Shaylynn embraces his brother and kisses the top of his head.

A few moments later, Kandessa comes into the room. The look on her face tells Shaylynn something important is afoot. Slowly, he starts to stand up from the bed. Daylynn looks up and sees his mother standing in the door. She immediately comes to her son's side and puts her arms around him.

"I'm sorry I ran away," Daylynn says.

"We needn't talk of it," Kandessa replies. "So long as you don't do it again."

"I won't."

With that, the matter resolves itself. It will never be talked about again. This is good because, as Shaylynn suspected, there is more going on than just his family. As Kandessa comforts Daylynn, she turns her attention to Shaylynn.

"There is a royal sentry at the door," she informs him. "He says your presence is required at the castle."

"What could this be?" Shaylynn asks.

"I do not know," Kandessa replies. "However, with the knights out, the king's court is greatly lessened. He often called for your father when he was in need of council."

"Surely, he would not need my council," Shaylynn retorts.

"You are wise beyond your years," Kandessa says. "Your father has told as much. Besides, if you can calm a crying child, a king should be a simple task."

She smiles to calm his nerves. He smiles as well and then leaves. While preparing his horse, Fallon arrives on horseback.

"I see I am not the only one called upon," he says. "And here I hoped I had something to lord over you."

"Better luck next time, I suppose," Shaylynn replies.

Before they set out with the sentry, Lyosan approaches on foot. He is greatly concerned when he sees the sentry with them. As soon as the sight enters his eyes, he races to Shaylynn's side.

"What has happened?" he asks.

"We do not know," Fallon replies, "we've been called to the castle."

"Just the two of you?" Lyosan asks.

"We do not know that either," Shaylynn replies.

Lyosan begins to fear what this might mean. He also feels somewhat slighted that he has not been called as well. Usually, whenever the youths in training are summoned, he is part of the gathering as well. In this instance, where he has been left out, he cannot help but wonder if this is some commentary on his abilities. And yet, he cannot ask to come along, nor can he attempt to ascertain more information about this meeting they have been called to. Fortunately, his friends are willing to do that work for him.

"What do you know, sentry?" Fallon asks.

"Only what I've been commanded to do," the sentry replies. "I was bid find Shaylynn, son of Feylynn, and Fallon, son of Degon, and bring them to the castle posthaste."

"Were you told to exclude those in our company?" Shaylynn asks.

"Not specifically," the sentry replies after some thought.

"Then it is possible the king wants others to come as well?" Fallon asks.

The sentry thinks it over some more. He follows what Shaylynn and Fallon are trying to do. The sentry cares not who accompanies them to the castle unless the sentry would be punished for allowing it. Fortunately, he can rely on the reputation of these two to avoid any brandishing from the king.

"Possible," the sentry replies, "though unlikely."

"Well," Shaylynn replies, "I prefer to err on the side of caution. I think Lyosan must come with us. If the king decides he should not be there, then the king can send him away."

"I agree," Fallon concurs.

"There you have it," Shaylynn concludes. "Lyosan, ride with the sentry. We'll enter the castle together. If your services are not required, the sentry shall return you home."

Lyosan smiles and shakes his head as he climbs aboard. They ride through town to the castle. An official stands – waiting for them as they arrive. Though he seems surprised by Lyosan's appearance, he gives no comment on the matter. Instead, he hurries them along to the royal conference chamber. When they enter, they see ten other youths awaiting their arrival. The king seems most pleased when he sees them.

"Very good that you have arrived," Cyrus says to greet them.

He approaches Shaylynn and Fallon and lets them kiss his ring. Then, he escorts them to the table where the other youths are seated. Darrow, Stefen, Artimous, Brynnal, Mitan, Athen, Shawl, Dragoon, Nycolas, and Pythyn have been called as well. Lyosan, having been looked over by the king, remains at the door. While the others acknowledge him, they will not speak to him. Only Pythyn means to bring attention to his presence but not for honorable reasons.

"I was to understand only the best were summoned," Pythyn scorns.

"You should have known better when you were approached," Fallon retorts.

The king, unsure where this outburst has come from, scans the room and spies Lyosan standing off to the side.

"Indeed, I do not recall asking for your services, Lyosan," Cyrus explains.

Lyosan says nothing and looks to his friends to calm the situation. They are happy to come to his aid again.

"An honest mistake sire," Shaylynn explains. "We were together this morning when the sentry came for us. Understanding there was some urgency to the matter, we set off before he could provide us with all the details. However, in knowing how you value Lyosan among the youths, we were certain his presence would not be frowned upon by you."

Cyrus considers Shaylynn's explanation while staring hard at Lyosan. He did not wish for the matter to extend beyond those present. He called such a small number because he wishes to control the information he is about to release.

"Sire," Pythyn says, "if he is not needed, the journey home will not be too much for him."

"Indeed it would not be, but since he is here, his council will be given," Cyrus decides. "Come Lyosan, join us."

The king extends his hand to Lyosan who exhales for the first time since entering the room and joins his fellow knights-in-training. They welcome him with handshakes and kind words. Except of course for Pythyn, who broods from his chair.

"They say a thirteenth guest will invite the evil serpent," Pythyn comments.

"No bother," Shaylynn replies, "we've already a snake among us."

Pythyn opens his mouth to retort, but the king commands silence. His matter cannot be delayed by such tomfoolery. They cannot know this now, but the news he has could change the course of the kingdom. If they are to provide any use to him, they must view the situation as dire.

"I have called you here in great urgency, as you have suggested Shaylynn," Cyrus begins. "There is an opportunity at my door – a chance I cannot look upon lightly. Yet, at the same time, I cannot bring myself to accept the conditions brought to me." Cyrus pauses for a moment to prepare himself. This news shall not be easy for any to hear. "Word has reached me from Athorn of Jorram. He would have me believe his forces stand ready to begin a war with our lands. As a show of his strength, he claims to have captured the royal guard. What exactly is their fate, we cannot be certain. Whether Athorn speaks the truth, we cannot know.

"What we do know is he offers a means to bring about peace." None of the youths are eager to hear the terms. Each begins to understand the price is too high for the king to accept. Yet, he would not have called them here if he did not consider taking this deal. "He means to unite the kingdoms through the union of Crystalynn, princess of Artonia, and Dreilon, prince of Jorram."

Upon hearing the news, the youths immediately murmur amongst themselves. Only Shaylynn, Fallon, and Darrow speak directly to the king.

"You cannot accept this!" Shaylynn barks.

"Surely, you mean to deny this request?" Fallon inquires.

"No peace is worth this price!" Darrow cries.

The only one who remains silent is Lyosan. Inside, his heart breaks at the very possibility of Crystalynn being taken from this land. True, she would retain her dominion of Artonia, but as the Queen of Jorram, she would live at the castle in Belvik. More importantly, she would marry another and be with him for all her life. He cannot deal with this notion. While he hopes to dispel this idea from Cyrus, he cannot speak the words to make it happen.

"I know this seems more than our land can spare," Cyrus admits after calming the youths. "But if this union came to pass, then the hostilities between us would come to an end."

Most of the youths are too timid to speak against the king's words. They silently pass looks between each other unwilling to accept the king's logic. Of those who would speak against the king's words, Shaylynn steps forward.

"I cannot agree with this, my liege," he begins.

"Oh, you would speak against my word?" Cyrus asks.

"Only with great care, my lord," Shaylynn replies.

"Then speak your peace, son of Feylynn."

Cyrus takes his chair at the head of the table and offers the floor to Shaylynn. After a moment of preparation, Shaylynn rises from his seat and turns to address the king. Upon seeing Cyrus's stern gaze fixed on him, Shaylynn pauses again and collects himself. Pythyn quietly smirks to himself. Shaylynn takes a breath to refresh his courage, then speaks his mind.

"The peace which Athorn speaks of would extend to his kingdom alone. They would not attack us because they would have no need. All the resources of our land, all the efforts of our toil would become the rightful property of Jorram. While the princess could fight for our rights, she would eventually have to buckle under the pressures of her would-be-king.

"What's more, the land of Jorram would use our soldiers as a shield against any who would oppose our union. Whether from Thalane, Hatholan, or Dar Sou, Jorram would put our troops on the front lines. We would no longer prosper in the ways we do now. There would be great unrest amongst your people, and eventually, they would revolt against the tyranny of Jorram."

"You speak quite ill of Jorram, Shaylynn," Cyrus replies.

"As well he should," Pythyn says. All in attendance gasp at the fact that Pythyn stands with Shaylynn on this matter. True, he does agree with Shaylynn but not for the same reasons. He simply does not want to see the crown go to another. He means to have it for himself one way or another. "Jorram has ever been the enemy of this land. They bring death and destruction to its people. There is no reason to believe they would not bring the same even if they claim lordship with your sister. They merely look to grow their own strength through our own."

Cyrus takes what he has heard into consideration. "Do you all feel this way?" he asks of the others.

Slowly, they all concur with Shaylynn's logic. Though they see the possible benefit to this situation, they see the larger problems which would ensue. One by one, they nod in agreement.

Once Cyrus sees they all mean to follow Shaylynn's cause, he nods in agreement with them as well.

"I thank you all," he says. "You are making fine progress in your studies. Indeed, the union with Jorram would be a hollow promise. The princess will remain here and prepare to rule this kingdom."

The youths rejoice at the proclamation. Lyosan leaps up and shakes Shaylynn's hand. Shaylynn smiles at Lyosan's reaction, and Lyosan quickly tempers his enthusiasm. With the meeting adjourned, most take their leave with the king's permission. Only Shaylynn is asked to stay behind.

"I fear for our kingdom," Cyrus says once the room is cleared.

"We are ever strong behind you, sire," Shaylynn replies.

Cyrus laughs. "And yet, I am not strong, Shaylynn. Who's to say that without your council I would've made the same decision? If not for your level-head and sound logic, maybe my sister would be on her way to

Jorram?"

"An unpleasant thought indeed," Shaylynn admits. "But a foolish notion given your unflinching character."

"Flattering a king," Cyrus remarks. "I never tire of it, but I cannot abide it at the moment. I grow weak, Shaylynn. Something must happen and soon to ensure the future of this kingdom. A successor must be named."

The conversation Shaylynn would mean to avoid at all costs stands on his doorstep. With the king having it, he cannot turn away. His life with Sarin – the true love of his life – stands on the edge of a cliff, ready to be pushed.

And yet, the rule of the kingdom – the lure of power – stands before him as well. To marry the princess and take over the rule of Artonia sounds more pleasant than he would've imagined it would. With the possibility directly in front of him and the decision out of his hands, he feels a certain freedom. If the king names him successor without giving him a choice, he cannot be blamed by Sarin or Lyosan. Crystalynn may not be happy with the arrangement at first, but she will accept her brother's ruling – especially if it is his dying decree.

On the throne, Shaylynn could be a more decisive ruler. He could put to rest the danger Jorram shows by prepping an army. Not that he wants a war, but he will not be weak and walked over. Nor will his people. They will rise beside him as a power in the world once again. A testament to the way Artonia was in days of old.

All this passes through Shaylynn's head in but a few moments. And before it can sink in, he tosses the thoughts aside. The lure of the throne is indeed powerful and dangerous. The more he feels it, the more he detests it. The more too, he realizes it pales in comparison to the love of Sarin.

So, after the briefest of moments in which he aspired to the throne, Shaylynn now stands hoping the king will make some other request of him. Rather than being a candidate for the throne, Shaylynn could be an advisor. He could keep the promise he made to Lyosan about assisting him in gaining favor with the princess.

"I did not realize your illness was this bad, my lord," Shaylynn says.

Cyrus shrugs. "It is difficult to assess. Some days I feel as though I am myself. Others, I feel but a shell of what I was. Today, when I first heard of the offer from Athorn, I must admit it felt tempting."

"All offers do from time to time," Shaylynn replies. "Especially when they are merely theory. But when examined, we see the flaws in the theory and better understand why the offer should not stand."

Cyrus smiles and chuckles a bit to himself. Shaylynn is not certain how to take this reaction, so he remains silent.

"Shaylynn, you speak with the wisdom of a king," Cyrus admits. "Sometimes, I feel as though I'm hearing my father through you. Tell me, if I offered you the throne, would you take it?"

The lure of power asserts itself again. The possibility of ruling a kingdom just there at his fingertips. From somewhere deep inside him, a voice cries out to accept the throne, but a larger voice, a sounder voice, says just the opposite.

"I do not know," Shaylynn replies.

Cyrus smiles again. "The wisdom of a good king. On the one hand, he desires the power a throne could bring. He knows the good he wishes to do and believes he could accomplish all ends. On the other hand, he fears what he may become when placed on the throne. With no one to check him, what would happen?"

Shaylynn can say nothing at this moment. Cyrus seems to understand Shaylynn's hesitation, even if he does not know all the reasons why.

"And then," Cyrus continues, "there is always the riddle of your heart." Here, Shaylynn feels his chest tighten up a bit. Does the king know of Shaylynn's love for Sarin? "For in becoming king, it means losing the choice of marriage. It is thrust upon you. You marry my sister whether your heart desires her or not. And a good king knows he would have to abandon any notion of true love he came across. Loyalty – he asks it of his subjects. But if he cannot give it to his own wife, then why does he deserve it from an entire kingdom?"

Again, Shaylynn can offer no reply.

"The truth is, he does not, Shaylynn," Cyrus finishes. "Not that you would have to worry of such things. After all your father has taught you, I am certain you would be an honorable king if the duty befell you."

"Sire, your words are too much." Shaylynn finally says.

Cyrus turns to Shaylynn and smiles. "And yet, they may only scratch the surface."

Cyrus dismisses Shaylynn, who returns home. Shaylynn tells no one of his discussion with the king. He carries on as though all is normal despite the fear in his heart that all is about to come crashing down around him. When he is with Sarin, he holds her a little closer. When he trains with Lyosan, Shaylynn pushes him a little harder. But he finds the princess around him more as the days go on. He hopes it is because of Lyosan, but he finds it far more likely Cyrus is ensuring their proximity for a much different reason.

CHAPTER VIII

The absence of the knights brings further despair to the city. Each day without word from the north creates more unrest within the city walls. Some fear the lack of communication foreshadows a grim fate for those still in the city. They fear the knights have been defeated, and the force which defeated them will soon lay siege to the city. Most, however, fear for the safety of their loved ones. They care not for the political ramifications of this occurrence; they wish only for their loved ones to be returned to them.

The king, sensing the unrest among his subjects, sends forth a decree he hopes will bring some joyous feeling to the air. He calls for a great feast to be held in the great courtyard of the castle. All of the city, save a small number to patrol the city walls, are invited to the soiree. The king promises a night of revelry and merriment. No expense will be spared to ensure a great time for all. Along with the celebration, so the decree continues, the king will make an announcement which will alter the course of the kingdom forevermore.

As soon as the decree is posted, the city buzzes with anticipation for the feast and the announcement. Many believe the king will finally make clear the manner in which the next king will be chosen. Others say he will name a successor as is his given right. To that end, the rumors begin to circulate about who will be named next in line for the throne. The name that jumps to the forefront of most minds is Shaylynn. In the days before the feast, he finds himself under siege from well-wishers and gossips who wish to know his reaction to becoming king someday. At first, he laughs off the notion, saying the honor is too great to imagine. That he would, of course, accept the throne if the king deemed him worthy of possessing it. He makes no mention of the consequent marriage to Crystalynn should he come to the throne. Most now know of the love Shaylynn bears for Sarin. They know he wishes to marry her and live his days with her. But the call of the throne and the duty of every man of the kingdom surely must come first. As he hears the question asked over and over, he soon tires of the attention suddenly thrust upon him. He seeks seclusion from those who would torment him and only welcomes his closest and dearest of friends. Yet, even in their company, he cannot find peace. He can sense with ease the displeasure Lyosan feels from the rumors as well. Lyosan, who wishes not for the throne but for the heart of the princess, now finds himself dealing with the possibility that his closest friend will have the hand of the only woman Lyosan has ever loved. The tension of it all causes more trepidation than the concern for the knights who have not returned.

Fortunately, the night soon arrives where the feast takes center stage. The preparation lasts all day, but by nightfall, the festivities begin. There is dancing and feasting for hours. The tension amongst the youths dissipates, and their hearts bask in the wonder and majesty of the night. Shaylynn takes Sarin in arm and dances the night away. Fallon and Faith dance as well. Lyosan passes the time, dancing with a different partner here and there. From time to time, he approaches the royal table and converses with the princess as she desires. He cannot linger too long however, as the princess has her own affairs to look to.

As the night carries on, Jonas makes his way amongst the crowd and finds many of the knights in training. He informs them their presence will be required at the third chime of the bell. He offers no reason for his instruction but promises all will be made clear soon.

Until such time, the feast carries on. Shaylynn delights his friends with tales of his magical encounters and his skills with the dance. Always he keeps Sarin on his arm as a subtle tell of where his heart lies. All who watch them make note of the closeness between them. As they watch, they come to the thought that their love should be allowed to flourish in a perfect world. Though Shaylynn may be the best candidate for the throne, he should not have to sacrifice his love for Sarin. Nor should she have to bear witness to a lifetime of torment in watching her love be at the side of another.

At the same time, they cannot remedy their love with the sacrifice that would be asked for. A true king Shaylynn could be. They see the royalty in his blood. Such honor, such wisdom, such strength. He could restore the glory of the land and ensure a bright future for it as well. The line that followed him would be strong for generations to come. None would stand against their kingdom so long as one of his progeny sat upon the throne. Who else could bring such prowess to the throne? Who among the youths of the land could stand as tall as he?

There are some who deem themselves worthy. First among them, Pythyn. Though he makes no scene this night, he has made his intentions known in the past. The bitter rivalry he has created with Shaylynn still shows itself at every moment. His ill words for Fallon and Lyosan, a mere extension of his hatred for the middle son of Feylynn, highest of knights in King Cyrus's court. Now, he watches his nemesis with bitter eyes. Every other eye holds admiration for the boy. Every other mind holds him in such high esteem. None do the same for Pythyn, however. He proves himself at every turn, but none choose to see it. He tries to raise his position among the land, but he is turned away at every chance. Soon, he believes, soon he will have the chance to prove himself, once and for all.

Three chimes pervade the air. The king calls for the youths to join him. Some three score and four youths gather at the head table of the feast. King Cyrus asks all subjects to return to their seats for the announcement to be made. The rumors stir again as the possibilities fill the minds of those there. They whisper to each other trying to keep some secrecy among them, but the king has heard word of the rumors which made their way through the city. He knows what has been said of Shaylynn and his sister. He must put some of these rumors to rest and let the others become the truth they were meant to be.

Rising from his seat, the king raises his arms high and calls to the crowd. "My loyal subjects!" he begins.

His voice is strong and clear as a king's should be. It carries from his place at the royal table to the entirety of the crowd. The clamor among the crowd dissipates and soon settles into a respectful silence. Though he is a boy himself in comparison to others who have sat on the throne, Cyrus seems well beyond his years.

The king smiles and lowers his arms folding his hands in front of him. "It does my heart good to see the merriment in your eyes," he continues. "Watching the youths of our city restore the innocence and splendor of our kingdom through their dancing and singing reminds me of much simpler times…" The king pauses as the memories swarm through his mind and the minds of all those in attendance. They long for those days now. As wonderful as the night has been, their hearts begin to ache with the wantings of their souls. To keep their spirits high, the king presses on before the ache becomes too great. "…And we will have those simpler times again, my people. I swear, before my reign should end, we will have those times again…" A small row of cheers rises from the crowd. In a few moments, the cheers peter out and the king continues, "…But, some time, my reign shall end. When it does, my sister shall need a husband to aid her in the ruling of this kingdom…"

As the announcement begins to unfold, the anticipation of the crowd reaches a fever pitch. The rumors quickly return; whispers echo through the crowds about who shall be named king. Shaylynn's name can clearly be heard by many. As he hears the crowd discuss him, Shaylynn becomes uneasy – not for himself but for Sarin. He knows the rumors have caused her great distress. She has always imagined this possibility and given it more credence than he has. Shaylynn also fears for Lyosan's reaction to this turn of events. If Shaylynn is named next in line for the throne, their relationship will be greatly strained.

To silence the chattering, the king raises his arms again to calm his subjects. Within moments, the commotion ends, and the announcement continues.

"While rumors have run wild that I would go beyond our borders to find the new leader of our kingdom, I have decided such an action would be unwise."

The citizens seem pleased with the decision, but the news only increases Shaylynn's concerns. With panic in his eyes, he searches the crowd for Sarin. When he sees her, her head is down, and he believes he sees a tear running down her cheek. He wants to leave his place and console her, but he could not dare to do so with the spotlight on him so clearly. He lowers his head as well. Fallon, standing next to him, pats his friend on the back to comfort him.

"Furthermore," the king continues, "as I have studied the youth of our kingdom, it has become clear to me their quality surpasses that of any common man…" The king turns to the youth behind him and motions to them with a wave of his hand. "…Before you stand the finest of our future.

Sixty-four young men, expertly trained in the arts of valor and bravery, each honorable enough to hold the throne.

"But, as only one can be king, one must show his place above the rest. To that end, we shall hold a tournament in the favored sport of our kingdom, Verti-dueling. Each man before you shall have equal opportunity to claim the crown for his own..." The gathered youths quickly perk their ears at this announcement. None more than Pythyn. "With the help and efforts of Jonas, each has been given a seeding based on his skills and abilities. They shall be pitted against one another in a contest until only one remains unbeaten. One defeat shall remove a man from contention. While we shall not unveil all the rankings this night, we shall make the first position known..."

Without looking, Shaylynn feels a thousand sets of eyes fall upon him. He uselessly attempts to hide himself, but it does no good. Then, from the crowd, one voice, unknown to Shaylynn whom it belongs to, calls out.

"Good king! We know Shaylynn Storm is the best of any who stand with him. Name him king!"

A chorus of cheers resounds to agree with the idea. Shaylynn sternly glares towards the source of the original cry. Many others do too, among them: Lyosan, Pythyn, Sarin, and Faith. Fallon looks to Shaylynn to calm him from doing anything too rash.

Jonas steps up from his spot and bangs on the table to silence the crowd. He will not have the king upstaged in such a manner. Cyrus calms Jonas first and then the crowd.

"Your notion is well-taken good sir," the king says in reply, "for indeed Shaylynn is a fine young man – perhaps better than any who has come before him..." Cyrus extends a hand in Shaylynn's direction to beckon him forward. Reluctantly, Shaylynn steps to the king's side. The king clasps Shaylynn's shoulder. "...Indeed, under different circumstances I would have no hesitation in naming this boy king. After all, my parents named my sister as an homage to the great deeds of the Storm family. It would then seem fitting for Shaylynn and Crystalynn to join in marriage," he says. Shaylynn shies away from the notion but quickly smiles so as to not insult the king. Cyrus then extends his other hand to Crystalynn and beckons her to him. She steps forward, unsure exactly what her brother has planned. She's quite certain Sarin is already upset by the king's announcement. She doubts anything said now will help her trepidations.

Upon taking his sister's hand, the king continues. "My sister speaks often of Shaylynn and the great quality he displays." Suddenly, both are embarrassed for themselves and their friends. Shaylynn is unaware of the words Crystalynn has spoken to the king about him, but so long as they are positive, they shall create uneasy feelings. Crystalynn, on the other hand, knows full well how her words could exacerbate the situation. "Though she is too young to know for certain and their relationship is so early in its development, I believe, based on her talks with me, he could make her happy in life."

Shaylynn worriedly scans again for Sarin. She hides her face from all around her. She will not even look at him, so he may assure her of his love for her. Instead, the king carries on.

"However, for something as vital as the throne, mere notion cannot be the sole criteria. The man who is to be king must prove himself worthy." There is little comfort in those words. Shaylynn takes his first breath in several minutes and turns to Fallon. The relief on his face is great as well. Lyosan, on the other hand, shows no relief on his face. Instead, his disdain for Shaylynn at this moment displays itself clear for any to see. Shaylynn would assure Lyosan of his feelings at this moment, but his reasoning would fall on deaf ears. Lyosan's anger needs to work itself out.

"Still," Cyrus says, "Jonas and I agree Shaylynn has the qualities and skills needed to emerge as the champion of this tournament. He is, indeed, the top seed in our tournament."

Cyrus raises Shaylynn's hand victoriously. The crowd cries out in cheers of jubilation. Crystalynn politely applauds the selection as her station requires her to do, but she is not overly enthusiastic in her celebration. While this provides some comfort to Lyosan, he still feels saddened by the news of the king.

"Now, as I said, there is a reason for our revealing Shaylynn as the top seed in our tournament. To seal the validity of this decree, he will dance with the princess this night as a symbol for the union of the princess to the winner of the tournament. And if it should happen to be Shaylynn, then this dance shall be practice for their wedding day."

The king only means to jest, which most of the crowd understands and laughs about. However, some do not find the humor in his remarks. Shaylynn and Crystalynn nervously step forward from the royal table. Sarin hides herself again. Pythyn steps away from the others and returns to his place. Lyosan folds his arms and finds a place to be alone.

As soon as Shaylynn and Crystalynn take their places in the courtyard, the king motions for the music to begin. Shaylynn politely bows to his partner, and Crystalynn curtsies to him. With a deep breath, Shaylynn extends his hand to request the princess's hand. She grants his request and places her hand in his. Shaylynn then places a hand upon her hip, and she places her other hand on his shoulder. To ease the tension, Shaylynn smiles sincerely at his friend. Her mood quickly lightens as well, and the two make the best of the awkward situation.

They move to the music as a crowd forms a circle around them. The mumbling among them reaches the dancing youths' ears, which only reforms the tension for Crystalynn. Her blossoming friendship with Sarin precludes her from even considering the possibility of marrying Shaylynn – even if some part of her desires it. He is a great man at such a young age. His deeds and accomplishments will reach far and wide. He could be a king like none other. But, for all he would do, he would not be truly happy. His heart, however much he might manage to give her, would always belong to another.

To prove his devotion, he spends most of their dance looking to her. She has managed to work her way to the front of the crowd. Crystalynn sees her first and points her out to Shaylynn. When he looks at her, the look in her eyes breaks his spirit. Seeing them together breaks hers. Without a word, she breaks away from the crowd and runs away seeking solitude.

For Shaylynn's sake, Crystalynn ends the dance abruptly. She thanks Shaylynn for his kindness and returns to the royal table. Shaylynn kisses her hand for chivalry and gratitude. Then, he fights through the crowd hoping to catch some glimpse of Sarin. By the time he's past the people, she is long gone. He considers the possibility she went home, but it doesn't seem likely. He needs some break in his bad luck to find her. Luckily, his family is about to give it to him.

Standing at the corner is Faith. She left with Sarin to keep an eye on her. Now, she intends to send Shaylynn to comfort her. "You're quite the dancer," Faith comments.

"Is now really the time for this?" Shaylynn asks.

"I only mean to calm your nerves before you speak to her," Faith replies. "You will need to be calm to settle her fears."

Shaylynn sighs. "I did not mean for this."

"None did," Faith assures him.

With that, Faith nods down the road towards the trees. Shaylynn takes off quickly. Within minutes, he spots Sarin down the road. At this rate, he will catch her in less than one minute.

Back at the feast, Lyosan has taken refuge with his family. His mood has lessened severely, and his brothers mean not to antagonize him. Even they realize how deeply this news wounds him.

"You'll have time to train," Elle says to raise his spirits.

"Not enough," Lyosan retorts. "I may be among the sixty-four, but surely I'll find myself in the lower half. And others will train. Their natural skills will take them to a place I cannot hope to reach."

"But you'll have one advantage none of the others will have," Steel says.

"What is that?" Lyosan asks.

"You'll be able to train with Shaylynn," Steel replies. "Surely, he'll be able to improve your skills."

"Some perhaps, but not enough to best him," Lyosan says.

Elle reaches over and places a hand on top of Lyosan's. "He has no desire for the throne or the princess. His heart lies with Sarin. While you may not have any desire for the throne, your desire for the princess must count for something."

"Not much," Lyosan concedes.

"As often is the case," Fallon says taking a seat next to Lyosan, "I must disagree with you, my friend. Your heart has served you well these many years. It has brought you to a kinship with the royal family which none before you had hoped to have. With but the slightest of efforts, you've exceeded your station. With even greater effort, there is no telling how high you may soar. Even the king recognizes your place amongst us. If he could not see you on the throne, you would not have been among those chosen."

Honest and sincere, the words Fallon speaks inspire hope within Lyosan's heart. He dares not think the road shall be easy, but he begins to again believe that perhaps all is not lost. With a sigh, he turns to the royal table and sees the princess conversing with some lords and ladies. Though he knows Shaylynn would not desire the princess, he must now deal with the idea she may desire Shaylynn.

"She seemed happy when they danced," Lyosan says to Fallon.

"Merely pleased she avoided contact with Pythyn," Fallon replied.

Lyosan laughs heartily. "If only it were that simple. I fear there was more to it than that."

"They are friends, as we all are," Fallon explains. "She enjoys his company as we all do."

"You think that's all there is to it?"

"If so concerned, ask her," Fallon suggests.

"That would be unwise."

"Only if you fear the answer."

Lyosan ponders the idea for a moment. He knows he can ask of her anything he desires. They've rarely kept secrets from each other. Even though their relationship continues to complicate itself, they have not passed the point of civility.

After a long drink, he rises from the table and walks to the royal table. By the time he arrives, she is alone. She seems happy he has approached her. She needs a friendly face.

"Quite the announcement, wasn't it?" she asks.

"Indeed," Lyosan replies, "it has created quite the stir."

Crystalynn's look fades away from them and into the distance. Her smile sinks away.

"I fear Sarin did not take the news well," Crystalynn admits.

"It would be hard to hear the one you love may marry another," Lyosan says understanding the feeling perfectly.

"But she must know he desires her over me," Crystalynn says.

"Aware, yes, but she also knows his sense of duty would cause him to assume the throne if required of him."

"It would be difficult for him though."

"And for you?" Lyosan asks. "How would you react to him becoming king?"

"He would make a fine king," Crystalynn admits, "but I know he would never be truly happy."

"What of your marriage to him?"

Crystalynn seems to know where this is going, but she cannot believe Lyosan would have these feelings. "What do you mean?" she asks.

Lyosan hesitates before asking. "Would you be happy if you married him?"

"He's a good man. Any woman would be lucky to have a man like him."

"But would you be happy?"

"Why do you care so much?"

Lyosan has an answer, but he does not wish to give it. This is hardly the time or place to convey his love for her. Furthermore, his admittance may become moot if he does not win the tournament.

"You are my friend," he replies. "I wish all my friends happiness."

It is not the answer Crystalynn expected or on some levels wanted. Yet, it will do for now. Cyrus interrupts the two of them and returns Crystalynn to her royal duties. Back in town, on the road to the eastern wall, Shaylynn catches up with Sarin and attempts to stop her.

"Please, talk to me," Shaylynn pleads.

"I suppose I should while I can," Sarin replies. "Someday, you shall be king and will not have time for me."

Sarin steps past him and continues on her way. Shaylynn quickly stops her by gentling grasping her arm. He then pulls her to him, but she struggles to avoid his eyes. Then, she wrestles herself away from him.

"Where are you going?" he asks.

"It matters not to you," she says. "You've more important matters to attend to."

"If you think I've anything in life more important than you, you are sorely mistaken," Shaylynn says.

Stopping, Sarin comes back to Shaylynn and slaps him across the face. Surprised, Shaylynn says nothing. Whatever the reason for her anger, he must let her express it. As Faith indicated, it is only his calm which shall alleviate her fears.

"Do not make me love you anymore, not when you know you must marry another."

Shaylynn takes her hands and looks into her eyes. "If I *must* marry, then I shall marry you and you alone."

Sarin swoons at his words solidifying the only dream she's ever held then snaps back to her perceived reality. She shakes loose of his grasp. "Why did you save me?"

"What?" Shaylynn asks.

"You heard me clearly. Why did you save me?"

"I would never watch you die while I have breath in me."

Tears form in Sarin's eyes. "It would have been better to have died in a moment than have to die slowly by watching you love another."

"Stop this!" Shaylynn cries. "Stop this at once."

He steps to her and lifts her head with one hand gently raising her chin. Then, he wipes the tears from her eyes and kisses her. She hesitates before kissing him back. She may not have these treasures for the rest of her life; she must take advantage of them while she can. A few seconds later, Shaylynn pulls his lips away and gently caresses her cheeks. She grabs his hand to keep the moment alive.

"If ever I call someone wife, you shall be the one," he vows. "You unlock a power in me that none other can. You make my heart beat, and my soul sing. I have loved you since the first moment I set eyes upon you. Now that I know you love me as well, I will devote my life to making a life for us."

"You were meant for the throne."

"I was meant for you, and you for me."

"You'll win the tournament."

"I'll forgo the spoils."

"The king will not allow it."

"I'll find a way. I'll find a way to ensure someone else takes the throne and marries the princess."

"And if they force it upon you?"

"If they try, then you and I will leave this place, and we shall make a life in another land."

He could never mean such a thing. In her heart, she knows as much. His love for family and sense of duty would never allow him to leave his home forever. Besides, she would not want to leave her family either. Yet, he says it with such conviction and sincerity that she cannot deny his vow to her. For everything this land possesses and gives to her, if it means to take him away then perhaps it would be best to forsake it.

There is too much promised in his words for her to give him a response. The love between them finally shines clear. No playful animosity between them. No quips or witty jab from one to the other. Though it will be years before they can join in legal ceremony, this night, this moment, they have pledged themselves to one another. Somehow, in some way, they shall find a way to never be parted. Either in this world or the next, they shall never be without the other's presence.

They are meant for this. They have known this day was hurtling towards them from the moment they met. They had denied it at times. They had ignored it, too. But, in the end, their destinies would always be joined. Finally, they face the moment when it occurs. It brings them peace. It brings them joy. It brings them a score of other treasures they cannot not begin to understand.

Neither will risk spoiling the moment by speaking. This goes well beyond words, and they understand this. Since they have both accepted their love within their hearts, there needn't be any word of acceptance or agreement. They feel the truth stronger than any words could bring it to them. They love each other more deeply and more passionately than they would or could ever love another. He would forsake his purpose if he did it for her. She would abandon this land if she did it for him.

As the seconds ticked away silently, the truth of the moment blooms into wonderful serenity. Her tears stop. His frustration ceases. They reach for each other and kiss deeply. If time did not have to pass on and the world did not have to spin constantly, they would have lived in this moment forever. As it is, they live in it for several moments before the outside world breaks them apart. Coming down the road is a group of Shaylynn's comrades, reveling in the prospect of becoming king. They boast of their own merits and the greatness of their potential reigns. Shaylynn reluctantly joins them. He holds Sarin's hands as he steps away from her. Just before he loses his grip, he turns to her. She smiles and nods for him to be with them. He will still be with her.

He smiles, understanding the bond between them. She slips silently into the shadows and makes her way home. He watches her as she fades into the darkness. It pains him to part from her now that so much has come to the light. Yet, he knows he never need concern himself when it comes to things which must be said. She already knows everything he would say. She knows he loves her dearly and will give himself to her as she will give herself to him.

For another day, that moment is. For now, he must play the man intended for the crown. Despite his desires for a different life, he has been given the best lot in the drawing. The highest ranking amongst his peers in a sport he greatly excels in. Even those who boast believe him to be the most likely to succeed. Still, they are allowed to dream for the moment and imagine the possibility they could ascend to the throne.

"You think you can overcome all sixty-three, Shaylynn?" Stefen asks clasping his friend's shoulder.

Shaylynn chuckles. "So long as all sixty-three do not come at me at once," he replies. "Besides, I think you shall have to defeat a couple of them yourself if you wish to meet me at the finish line."

"You certainly shall be there before any of us, Shaylynn," Darrow concurs.

"Oh, my friend!" Shaylynn replies. "Come now, you mustn't surrender to fate so easily. Nothing is written in stone. Every man here is worth the crown he may wear. And for that crown, each must be willing to give his best and his all..." Then, in jest, Shaylynn elbows Darrow lightly in the chest. "...Besides, it's not like I can't take it!"

The crowd erupts in laughter and applause. They boast the night away together even after all other townsfolk have returned to their homes. Surely, they shall pay dearly come morning when they must take up their places in the training hall, but for now, they are eager to pay the price. The day shall soon come when each must view the other with an enemies' eyes for glory, riches, and the throne of Artonia.

CHAPTER IX

With the tournament announced and the prize stipulated, the training ratchets up a few notches. The focus shifts greatly towards verti-dueling as well. More and more, the youths ascend the dueling square and spend their days learning the subtleties of the battle. Many watch Shaylynn carefully, not believing they could master his moves but hoping there is some small element of his technique which could better their own.

Shaylynn works almost exclusively with Fallon and Lyosan. Only when Jonas comes and forces the three to separate does Shaylynn acquiesce and work with other trainees. But come hell or high water, Shaylynn never trains with Pythyn. It is a feeling which Pythyn is only too happy to reciprocate. Since the announcement of the top seeding, Pythyn has looked at Shaylynn with greater disdain than ever. It does not surprise Pythyn to see Shaylynn handed the best post, but it does burn him up inside. He can barely hold in the rage and hatred he feels for Shaylynn, and only by avoiding him is he able to keep it at bay.

Another who feels a great deal of rage towards Shaylynn is Lyosan. The two have said nothing in regard to the night of the feast. Shaylynn knows Lyosan is not happy about the predicament they find themselves in, but he does not realize how angry Lyosan truly is. The dance which took place between Shaylynn and Crystalynn. The smile Shaylynn displayed and the resulting smile it garnered from the princess forced Lyosan to question whether or not Shaylynn still holds true to his word in harboring no feelings for the princess. Lyosan knows he cannot force Shaylynn to tell him the truth, so the point of conflict festers in Lyosan. His focus is off when they train. He takes every hint and piece of advice from Shaylynn with a grain of salt. He makes strides in his training, but it is not what he could fully gain were the air between them clear.

One day, about two weeks after the feast, the tension comes to a head. The three train in the dueling arena with only a few other youths around. Pythyn is not among them. Today, Shaylynn wishes to focus on sword techniques rather than the verti-dueling element. Lyosan still struggles with the balance and height, so Shaylynn wants to shore up his skill with the blade.

At the moment, Shaylynn is attempting to show Lyosan a more complex countering technique. It requires some confidence with the non-dominant hand though the blade remains in the strong hand throughout the move. As the opponent strikes from the side, Shaylynn blocks the blow with his blade. After wrapping the blade around his head and forcing the opposing blade to the ground, Shaylynn uses his off hand to club the opponent's forearm and free the blade from his hold. It leaves the opponent defenseless and forces a submission.

After showing it a few times with Fallon, Shaylynn brings Lyosan up and walks him through the move. Much to Shaylynn's chagrin, Lyosan does not keep his feet and loses his balance as they progress. Always ready to show patience with Lyosan, Shaylynn resets the move and has Lyosan try again. When he fails again, Shaylynn rebukes him to a degree, but Fallon is quick to stop him. They try the move one last time, but Lyosan fouls it up again. This time, Shaylynn cannot hold his tongue. He may not be aware why Lyosan's focus wanes, but he does realize it has lessened.

"Perhaps if you bothered to listen, you could perform the move properly," Shaylynn says.

"I think I've heard enough of you," Lyosan remarks.

Shaylynn grunts. "Yes, clearly I'm the problem."

Without another word, Lyosan lunges at Shaylynn with a wild punch. Shaylynn dodges it easily and retaliates with a sharp jab to Lyosan's nose. Lyosan drops to the ground, and Fallon jumps in between the two. Lyosan gets up, ready to fight, but Fallon will have none of it. Grabbing Lyosan by the collar, he pulls him aside while Shaylynn stands angered in the arena.

Once Fallon gets Lyosan away, he lets him go. Lyosan tries to walk away, but Fallon stops him. Lyosan doesn't want to hear it from Fallon either. Fallon and Shaylynn were friends long before Lyosan came along. Of course, Fallon will take Shaylynn's side at every opportunity.

"I am not here to serve as his whipping boy!" Lyosan grits through his teeth.

"You are no whipping boy," Fallon assures him. "You are merely a fool with a false sense of dread."

Lyosan rolls his eyes. "Ever a comfort, you are."

"If you want comfort, I suggest you run home to your mother. This is not some game where nothing is a stake. This is for the woman you love, and Shaylynn would see you win her heart."

"Would he?" Lyosan asks. "For all he says of not desiring the throne, he does precious little to avoid being put on the road to it."

"What would you have him do?" Fallon asks. "Deny the king? Rebuke his friend? You love the princess, yes, but she means something to all of us. By our life and death, we mean to serve her. It is all we have been trained for."

Still not ready to calm down, Lyosan walks away and leaves the castle. He does, as Fallon suggested, return home. Neither Steel nor Calvin are around when he arrives. All the better. He desires seclusion at the moment. He is no longer certain whom he can trust.

One who always has his trust, Elle, enters shortly after him. For Lyosan to be home so early in the day cannot be a good sign. And though she has much to do, she cannot ignore the plight of her son.

When she enters, Lyosan refuses to address her presence. She smiles to herself, remembering when the same act would take place in his younger days. The solution was easy then. She hopes it will be as easy now. From the pantry, she grabs a small cake from a jar. It has always been his favorite – ever the conversation starter between them. Taking a plate from the kitchen counter, she places the cake on it and sets the plate in front of Lyosan.

Though he wishes to eat it, he also wants to fight the tactics of his mother. In his current state, he fears the things he might say. He fears his own mother will not see his side in the matter and side with Shaylynn as everyone seems to do. Fallon does. The other youths do. He would not even want to consider how Crystalynn would react should she know the details of this conflict. Should his mother side with Shaylynn as well, Lyosan is not certain what will happen from there.

The stubborn nature which causes Lyosan to ignore his mother's offering annoys her to the bone. It is a high stakes staring match, and she will not be the one who blinks first. She never has been, and she never will be. Of course, if it seems as though she will fail, she can rely on other tactics to secure her victory.

"If a mother cannot feed her son, she must be a terrible failure," she says.

Lyosan frowns at her.

"Now you chastise me for loving you," she continues.

Finally, Lyosan cracks and takes the cake. After a bite, he sets it back on the plate though he does not look at his mother.

"Perfect as always," he says.

"And what is it this day which requires your need?" Elle asks.

Lyosan draws a deep breath and lets it out slowly before explaining. "Shaylynn will take the throne someday. I am sure of it."

"That's not what you fear him taking," Elle replies.

Lyosan sighs. "He cannot take one without taking the other."

Elle takes a seat next to Lyosan and places a hand on top of his. She wants desperately for her son to be happy, but she also realizes the happiness he seeks will be very difficult to attain. But if it comes down to encouraging him to hope for the best or discouraging him to spare ultimately his feelings, she will encourage him every day she can.

"He would rather see you take both," Elle says.

"So he says," Lyosan mutters.

Elle cannot believe her ears. "You truly think he wishes to marry the princess and become king?"

It is just as Lyosan feared would happen. His own mother believes Shaylynn just as quickly and easily as everyone else. What Lyosan believes is so foolish and stupid, it cannot be considered for even a moment.

"Why is everyone so quick to take his side?" Lyosan demands.

"Because he is on your side," Elle replies. "You seem to have forgotten that."

"He seemed to enjoy his dance with the princess the other night. She did too for that matter."

Now we get at the truth of the matter. That Shaylynn danced with the princess and appeared to enjoy himself is not the true misdeed here. Rather, it is that the princess enjoyed his company so much which bothers Lyosan. But he has been directing his anger so much as Shaylynn, he may not even realize it.

"So who are you really angry with?" Elle asks.

Lyosan pauses for a moment. He was ready to say Shaylynn at first, but with his mother looking right through him, he is not so sure.

"Why does it matter?" Lyosan asks.

"Because if you are angry with Shaylynn for something which is not his fault, you do him a great disservice." Elle explains. "Life has not been fair to you, my son. No father to raise you. Forced to work as a man when you should have been free to play as a child. And now, the one girl you love is the one who seems the furthest from your grasp. But the one fair thing life has done for you is bring Shaylynn and Fallon to you. They have shown you more than you thought you were capable of. They have given you moments of joy which I could not provide. They have been loyal to a fault, and they will surely not abandon you now."

Lyosan calms a bit, but the anger remains.

"She might love him," Lyosan says referring to Crystalynn.

"At the moment," Elle admits. "But love, true love, is not a momentary thing. It goes on for ages and ages. Maybe she loves him right now, but it does not mean she will love him tomorrow. And it does not mean she will not love you someday."

Lyosan smiles at his mother, and she smiles back. Rising from his chair, he kisses her on the cheek and leaves the house without another word. Slowly, he makes his way back up the hill to the castle. He has not been gone long. Surely, Shaylynn and Fallon will still be in the training room. Whether they wish to see him or not remains to be seen.

When he enters, the room stops. Shaylynn and Fallon had been dueling, much to the delight of the crowd, but they stop when Lyosan approaches. Some believe the fight between them will continue, and they know Lyosan will fall in a fight. However, after a few tense moments, Fallon shoes them away, so the training can continue.

Lyosan extends a hand to Shaylynn. Shaylynn lets it hang there for a moment before he takes it in his own. His face remains stern – he will not let Lyosan off the hook so easily. This betrayal of trust, however small, must be atoned for. Lyosan knows this and is prepared to make amends. It is hard, though. The admission is not one Lyosan should have ever believed to be true. But in his anger, he misplaced his emotions and let anger control him.

"When I saw you and the princess dance," Lyosan explains, "I felt more jealousy than ever in my life. Mostly because she seemed pleased to be in your arms."

Shaylynn listens to the apology and takes it in. He too feels a great deal of anger, but his comes from his own friend believing he could love someone besides Sarin.

"You know where my heart lies," Shaylynn says. "You know you are as dear to me as my own brothers. If things were different and my heart lied with the princess, I would not hesitate to tell you. But *listen* to me," Shaylynn demands. Lyosan looks up at his friend as he slowly says the words, "It does not!"

With that, all is forgiven, and the training resumes.

For another week, the city goes without knowledge of what is taking place in the North. They struggle with the absence of their loved ones, both emotionally and physically. Mothers who usually kept to the run of the house now find themselves working in the fields. Children who concerned themselves only with play and fun tend to the houses their mothers once watched over. But the greatest burden falls on those between the two realms of childhood and adulthood. The youths see their responsibilities grow even more. Groups of them are now in charge of the gates at the walls. They have to take a shift, be it during the day or at night, help around their home fronts, and many of them must train for the impending tournament. They find themselves on the brink of exhaustion, yet they cannot slow their activity in the slightest.

With their friendship renewed, Shaylynn and Lyosan begin to work in rhythm as they prepare for the tournament. Lyosan progresses with his sword play and can now set his sights on controlling his fear of heights. They continue to find themselves fortunate in that Pythyn is rarely in the training rooms when they are. Whether by fortune or design, Pythyn's assignment at the wall comes at the complete opposite as the other three. He works the wall in the morning while Shaylynn, Fallon, and Lyosan all work together in the early evening.

Even with so many uncertainties and concerns, everyone manages to find their moments of happiness. Sarin and Faith often accompany the trio to the wall during their shifts. It would be frowned upon under normal circumstances, but very little has been normal as of late. Lyosan continues to see the princess from time to time as she looks in on the training every now and then.

At times, the pinch of jealousy still hits Lyosan when he sees Crystalynn watching Shaylynn and even cheering his victories at duels. But, as he must remind himself, she cheers for Fallon, Lyosan, and several others as well. It is not a show of love for Shaylynn – merely an acknowledgement of his skill and ability. And the more Lyosan works with Shaylynn, the more Lyosan comes to appreciate that ability. When he is focused and rested, none can best him in the dueling square. Fallon can give him a good test, as can Stefen and Mitan. Most, however, fall quickly and easily to Shaylynn's steel.

Jonas cannot believe the ease with which Shaylynn can dispatch most of his peers. Even the best of the past needed months of training to set themselves apart in this manner. Here, Shaylynn has done so in mere weeks and with a great number of distractions to curb his progress. Establishing the seedings for the others in the tournament will be difficult, but setting Shaylynn at the top was the easiest decision for them to make. Days will soon come when no easy decisions exist.

As the youths train in the dueling arena, a commotion from outside stops their actions. It is not the clamor of anger and discord. Instead, it is the hurried cries for action filled with despair and fear, and so loud is the noise that Jonas abandons the room and goes to the source. Many of the youths know their place and remain where they are. Lyosan cannot bring himself to step outside his role, though he desperately wishes to know what is happening. Fortunately, Shaylynn often forgets his place, and where Shaylynn goes, Lyosan is free to follow.

Following Jonas, Shaylynn enters the main hall from whence the commotion came. Immediately, he recognizes the men as riders for Sir Erurt. They have ridden hard and desperately ask to speak with the king. Jonas, paying no attention to the youths who have followed them thus far, escorts the riders to the royal hall.

When they reach the throne room, Shaylynn is smart enough to cease his pursuit. Anxiously, they wait outside while Jonas takes the party into the king. While the wait is not too long, it feels like an eternity. Shaylynn paces back and forth, wondering what would warrant such an arrival. Whatever it is, it cannot be good, and Shaylynn is willing to bet Jorram has something to do with it.

After a few minutes, the riders exit the throne room. Jonas exits with them. His demeanor is greatly changed from when he entered. Finally, he acknowledges the three youths, but he does not do so enthusiastically.

"He wishes to see you, Shaylynn," Jonas relays. "I do not think he will mind the others coming as well."

Shaylynn, Fallon, and Lyosan enter the royal hall. When they arrive, the king sits on the throne in great despair. The boys approach slowly, uncertain what has occurred.

"My lord," Shaylynn says.

The king does not raise his head. Instead, he speaks to them in a broken, despondent voice.

"The tournament is canceled," he says. "I shall make the decree before the sun sets this day."

"If I may ask, what is the reason for this?" Fallon asks.

The king finally stands and steps down from the throne. His gait is slow and cautious. If not for the need to retain his kingly manner, he'd fall upon the floor at this moment. Finally, he faces the youths.

"I have agreed to Athorn's terms," the king explains.

Shaylynn, Fallon, and Lyosan's eyes widen in shock and terror. Never had they believed this folly of an idea would find its way to relevance again. And yet, here it is meaning to destroy their lives.

"Why would you do this?" Shaylynn demands.

The king ignores Shaylynn's tone, understanding the rage behind his voice.

"It is the best course for us to pursue," Cyrus explains.

"You cannot believe that," Shaylynn retorts.

"If I did not, then I would not have agreed to these terms."

"But you know their offer is an empty promise. They mean to enslave us!"

"You may believe you see within their heart, Shaylynn, but there is some diplomacy in them. They are men after all. Perhaps this will create some difficulties for our kingdom, but it will also keep us safe. I cannot guarantee the safety of my people with them roaming freely in the northland. I do not even know what has become of my knights. We are weak. We must find a way to strengthen our position."

"This cannot be the way. Send us with the rest of the guard to the northland. Let us find the lost knights and secure the borders of our land!"

Cyrus steps close to Shaylynn and gently touches his cheek. After all, the boy's courage is inspiring, if also slightly misplaced. The king cannot fault him for wanting to better their position, but there is no way to better it without sacrifice. While none would wish this to be that sacrifice; it will be made.

"You'd have made an excellent king, Shaylynn," Cyrus finally says. "I could wish for no better man to marry my sister..." Lyosan lowers his head in shame. Fallon clasps his shoulder to comfort him. Shaylynn remains focused on the moment. "...and I know she'd have been pleased to have you, but she has resigned herself to this. It is not just the northland that needs protecting. A force of twenty-five hundred from Jorram stands ready to ravage the southland. They've come through Daryndell and will attack through the swamps. Their assault will commence if the truce is not made in two days.

"Do you comprehend the nature of the beast we face? They've marched for at least a year and come through the swamps ready for battle. They have been at work whilst we've been dormant. I sat, fearing the disease which even now comes for me, while they planned for their attack. Because of that, we find ourselves at a severe disadvantage. We cannot hope to overcome it with brute force. We must hope diplomacy gives us the time we need to recover. Crystalynn leaves for Jorram today."

Shaylynn shakes his head and steps back from the king. The rage builds within him like a river stopped by a dam. She leaves today; perhaps, he still holds a chance.

"She has not left yet?" Shaylynn asks.

"It is too late," Cyrus warns him.

"I shall never choose to believe that," Shaylynn replies.

Without a word, Shaylynn bolts from the hall with Lyosan and Fallon in tow. He runs through the castle and out into the courtyard, but he sees no sign of the princess. Wasting no time, he runs around the castle to the main road. Faith stands waiting for him.

"Her caravan is almost at the gate," she says. "Sarin is with her, trying to stop this madness, but she will not listen."

As Faith explains, Lyosan and Fallon catch up to Shaylynn. Faith immediately goes to Fallon and wraps her arms around him. He comforts her with a kiss on the top of her head. Shaylynn looks up the road and sees the caravan progressing.

"What will you do?" Faith asks her cousin.

"Whatever I can," Shaylynn replies. "Whatever I have to."

Shaylynn takes off. Lyosan considers running with him, but he knows Shaylynn will quickly leave him behind. Furthermore, he finds his heart stumbling and legs trembling. His fear overcomes his senses and leaves him frozen in place. Even in the presence of his friends, he feels completely alone.

"He'll stop this," Fallon assures Lyosan. "If not today, then soon. She'll be among us again by the month's end."

"And he'll be on the throne a year after that," Lyosan concedes. "If he rescues her and saves the kingdom, there'll be no power in Heaven or on earth that'll keep the king from giving him the rule of the land."

"He'll deny it," Faith says confidently. "He does this for duty, but he'll not forgo his love of Sarin – even under the decree of the king."

Lyosan sighs and turns to Faith. "So, what then? He'll become an outlaw? He'll become an outcast with her at his side?"

"So long as she's at his side, he won't care what he becomes."

Lyosan sighs again as he looks down the road. He hopes Faith is correct, but his heart tells him a different truth. Forget Shaylynn and his assurance of the throne; for the first time, Lyosan begins to believe Crystalynn will become Queen of Jorram and the two nations will unite under their banner.

Their only hope lies with the youth whose conviction stands as his best asset. He cannot use his strength, his strategy, or even his magic to quell this situation. He can only hope to convince her of his point. If he fails, then the result may be what none thought possible.

Shaylynn runs at full speed, chanting a short incantation to drive his purpose further. Within a few minutes, he catches up to the caravan. Sarin, who stood alongside the princess's carriage, steps aside as he approaches. He pauses momentarily to take her hand and acknowledge her presence.

"She's convinced," Sarin warns.

"As am I," Shaylynn replies.

She kisses his cheek, then steps away. This is his fight now.

Shaylynn approaches the carriage. He can see Crystalynn, cloaked and hood raised, sitting inside. Whatever he says, he must be convincing quickly. The gate approaches.

"Princess," he calls.

She does not acknowledge him, but her demeanor changes. Her

muscles tense at the sound of his voice. She knew he'd object. Perhaps he is in the right to, but this cannot be a matter of who is right and who is wrong. This is greater than her fate. There are lives at stake.

When she says nothing, Shaylynn steps toward the carriage and hits the door. She jumps at his action, not expecting him to be so shaken. Clearly, he holds strong emotions on the matter. She must be ready to stand her ground. She looks from under the cover of her hood and gazes at him. His anger burns in his eyes. She looks away knowing her resolve must be absolute.

"You cannot deter me," she says.

"I should not have to," Shaylynn replies. "You know this must not happen!"

"I know lives must not be lost," Crystalynn retorts. "If this is the only way for it to happen, then so be it."

"This is not the only way. We have the strength to hold back this storm. Your brother can lead us to victory if only he will believe in our conviction."

"The knights have surely been taken prisoner or worse; the southland prepares for war it cannot combat. What will conviction do?"

"It will break their shield and pierce their heart if we use it. I will lead the youths into the south if I must. I will send the Jorramians to the darkness of death."

Crystalynn chuckles. "Is this it, then? Do you come here because you want to test your valor in battle? Do you seek the first in the long line of glories which will belong to Shaylynn, son of Feylynn?"

"I seek peace for our people."

"Then let me go!"

"I will not!"

At Shaylynn's outburst, the ground shakes and the caravan stops. Two royal guards circle around and draw their swords. Crystalynn commands them to cease as the caravan stops. Shaylynn keeps a hand on his sword, prepared to defend himself if he must. Crystalynn leans out of the carriage and drops her hood.

"What can I do, Shaylynn?" she asks, placing a hand on the carriage door. "My brother falters, believing we cannot weather this storm. He fears for his knights and his people. While he wishes for my happiness, he breaks under the knowledge that it must be sacrificed. So, what am I to do? Not go? Then, he must banish me and will turn over the throne anyway. At least with me on the throne of Jorram, I can fight for our kingdom."

"There are more important things than the rule of the land," Shaylynn says. "I would not sacrifice your happiness, not when I have the courage to fight."

"And if our kingdom held the same quality as you, there would be no argument. We would fight. But you are unique, special. There are none like you."

Shaylynn steps to the carriage and places a hand on top of the princess's hand. She quakes at his touch, feeling her resolve fading.

"I beg of you…reconsider," he pleads.

"Why do you fight so hard for something so simple?" she asks. She looks down the road and sees Sarin standing by. Even as Shaylynn comes for the princess, she knows his heart is for Sarin and Sarin alone.

"You have your love," Crystalynn says. "You'll bring her happiness no matter who rules you." Tears form in her eyes as she looks at Sarin. Then, she chokes up and looks down. When she collects herself, she looks at Shaylynn with great care. She had never given herself the permission to fall in love with him because of Sarin. But now, with him fighting so hard for her when no others would, she lets the thought hold some bearing. Perhaps, if he loved her, she could see the need to fight. If he was to take the throne and grant her the things he intended for Sarin, then she would stay. Even as the thought comes to mind, she curses herself for trying to steal him from the one he truly loves.

"Do I really mean so much to you?" she asks.

"You are my friend," Shaylynn replies. "Someday, you will be my queen. I would fight for you with every ounce of my strength."

"But not with your heart," Crystalynn mutters.

She says it loud enough for him to hear but not clearly enough for him to catch it. He ponders if she really said it, but he cannot be sure. Furthermore, he isn't anxious to find that answer.

"My lady," he replies.

She dares not bring the point to light. He has not given the answer she seeks, and she realizes he never will. His love for Sarin is absolute, and while he may surrender his love for the sake of the kingdom, she will not ask it of him. Instead, she leans forward, kisses his cheek, and sits back in her carriage. Without another word to him, she commands the caravan to continue.

Shaylynn stays where he is, left dazed by the turn of events. He watches as the caravan exits through the north gate and turns east on the road to Jorram. With rage building inside him, he clenches his fists and grits his teeth.

Sarin, who witnessed the kiss between him and the princess, approaches slowly. She understands the kiss means nothing to Shaylynn, but she feels uneasy at Crystalynn's actions – especially since Sarin knows Shaylynn will not let the matter rest with this. He will fight on, and he will attempt to get her back. When he does, what will the princess do then? If he is the one to rescue her, she will surely demand he take the throne. When that happens, their life together will end or their life in Artonia will end.

When she reaches him, she senses his rage. To calm him, she takes one of his hands, opens it, and firmly grasps it with her own. He squeezes back to thank her. Feeling some relief, she rests her head against his shoulder. He continues to stare into the distance for several minutes in absolute silence.

Finally, he turns away and takes her in his arms. She wishes she could forget the kiss, but it sticks in her mind. Now that he stands in the road looking for Crystalynn's return, Sarin's fear grows more.

"Do you remember when I told you I'd leave this kingdom for you?" he asks.

The suddenness of his inquiry causes her to pause. She can't fathom why he'd bring this up now. Still trying to follow his thoughts, she merely nods in reply.

"If I left, would you follow me?" he asks.

There is no joke in his voice. Only in extreme rarities does he speak so seriously, but he does so now. He's considering leaving if the king means his daughter to marry a Jorramian. He'd leave this place behind, make a new life elsewhere, and he'd ask her to come. She couldn't imagine life without her family. Perhaps she could convince them to come along, but more likely, they'd forbid her to go. She'd have to scorn their wishes and chose to be an outcast as Shaylynn would.

But at least she'd be with him. As hard as it would be to turn away from all she loved and cared for, she couldn't be without him if she could help it. If she needed one person to live with, he is that one.

"Yes," she replies, "yes, I'd follow you."

He kisses her head after her reply but says nothing else.

"Do you mean to leave?" she asks.

"I do not yet know," he replies, "but I will not live under the rule of Jorram. That, I can assure you. And until I understand his ways, I will no longer serve this king."

Sarin steps away in shock. She looks into his eyes, but they are absolute. She fears what he means. He may go on his own and attempt to save the princess. He may begin to serve his own means.

"Shaylynn, how can you say this?" she asks.

"My father would act the same," Shaylynn replies. "This is not a decision we can endorse. I keep my loyalty to this city and its people, but I will not serve in his court."

"He will send for you."

"He will not find me. I'll go into the forest and service the vow of my ancestors. I'll keep watch over the river. If you need to find me, you can. If Fallon, Lyosan, or my mother need me, you can send them to me. But I will not show myself in town until this matter has some sense to it again."

He stays with her for a while longer, but eventually Shaylynn does retreat into the forest. Sarin goes to Kandessa the next day to inform her of her son's decision. It is a good five minutes before Sarin can bring herself to enter Shaylynn's home. Normally, she would be thrilled to converse with Kandessa, whom Sarin has seen as a second mother for years. With her own mother away so often, Sarin always found a warm smile and loving hug awaiting her whenever she came upon Kandessa. She doubts this news will bring such a response.

"My lady," she says upon entering.

Kandessa immediately stops her work and welcomes Sarin into her home. Throwing her arms around the young girl and almost lifting her off her feet, Kandessa makes Sarin's news even harder to deliver. But, when Sarin does not react with her normal enthusiasm, Kandessa can already tell something is amiss.

"What has he done?" Kandessa asks.

Whenever Sarin comes to Kandessa with a problem, it seemingly always has to do with Shaylynn. Usually, it is something he has done to her, but today, it is something quite different.

"He has done nothing to me," Sarin replies.

"Then he can live another day," Kandessa says.

"But, I fear you will not like what he has done."

"That is nothing for you to worry about, child," Kandessa says sweetly. "You are not responsible for his actions. Were he wise enough to listen to you, you would not have to worry about his actions at all. Believe me, I know the sentiment." Kandessa then brings Sarin to the kitchen table and sits her down. "Alright then, out with it, what has my middle child done this time?"

For all Kandessa's sincerity, she has not completely alleviated the nerves which Sarin has lost control of. Sarin must take another minute or so before she can answer the question.

"I do not know whether you've been informed, but the king has sent the princess to Jorram to strike a peace," Sarin explains.

Kandessa has heard and does not agree with the decision. The scowl on her face says as much. "I had been told. A rash decision if you ask me. The king is acting from a place of weakness where he needs to show his strength."

"Shaylynn thought as much as well." Sarin explains. Then, after a gulp, she quickly spirts out. "That's why he has condemned the action and retreated to the forest to scorn the king's decision."

If she could, Sarin would run from the room. However, Kandessa's icy stare keeps the girl stuck to her seat. After a few tense moments, Kandessa shakes her head.

"That little fiend," she says. "He didn't even clean his room."

Kandessa's extremely tame reaction shocks Sarin. Though she is still somewhat frightened of Kandessa's reaction, she must ask, "Are you not furious with him?"

"Hmm?" Kandessa replies. "Oh, child, no! He acted as his father would…as I would for that matter. This is a drastic time, so drastic action is required. Though he is not an official knight, Shaylynn's absence will speak loudly. The king must know his decision does not speak for all his people. Shaylynn represents that now. I could not be more proud – even if I must take on his chores now."

Sarin rises from her chair and starts for Shaylynn's room. "I'll help you in his absence," she offers.

Kandessa lightly grabs Sarin's wrist and brings her back to the chair. With a light chuckle, she shakes her head. "No, no, don't you dare take on his duties. If he finds out, he'll never let you live it down."

Sarin smiles, but it is a forced smile. In truth, the inactivity is becoming too much for her to bear. Everyone around her is at work while she feels as though she is doing nothing. With her own mother in the south on a mission for the king, she has lost one person she could always turn to. Thankfully, the other is front of her now.

"I just feel like I should be doing something more," Sarin admits.

"What more can you do for now?" Kandessa asks.

"I don't know," Sarin responds, "but he is doing this for the princess, hoping she will come back. If she does, the tournament will begin and…"

Before she can say more, her voice trembles, and she cannot continue. Immediately, Kandessa sees where Sarin's true concern lies.

"He does not do this because he loves her," Kandessa tells Sarin.

Sarin has all but told Kandessa she loves her son, but she has never fully admitted as much. Hearing Kandessa say this leads her to believe Kandessa knows the two have admitted their love for one another.

"You know?" Sarin asks.

Kandessa smiles. "Maybe before either or you knew."

"But he does do it for her," Sarin says.

"As a servant of the crown, not one who wishes to wear it." Leaning forward in her seat and placing a hand on Sarin's, Kandessa smiles. "Tell me, did he ask anything of you before he chose this course of action."

He did indeed, but Sarin does not feel she should reveal it. Leaving the country to start a new life together would surely drive Kandessa over the edge.

"Yes, he did," Sarin staggers, "but…"

"Do not tell me what it was," Kandessa says to stop her. "That question was for you and you alone. What he asked of you is not important; what is important is that he asked you anything. He needed you to tell him it was okay to break free and do this. You are his strength in this course. Stay strong for him, and you will be doing more than you imagine." Sarin smiles upon hearing this. Her concerns and fears subside. She is again talking with her second mother. Before Kandessa lets her go, she gives one more piece of advice. "And prepare yourself as well. You were the one to let him go. Should this carry on too long, you will be the only one who can bring him back."

Sarin takes the words to heart and hugs Kandessa. Kandessa hugs her back and smiles that any unpleasantness is over. However, there are still some things which must be done.

"Now, you must find Faith and tell her this news. She will be able to break the news gently to Fallon. I'll not have that boy at my house every few hours to see if Shaylynn has returned."

"What of Lyosan?" Sarin asks.

"Let him know as well." Kandessa replies. "Since they are both family, they both deserve to know, but we'll say nothing more of the matter."

"What will the king do?"

"I cannot say, but I'm certain it won't be good. We must keep Shaylynn's location a secret. Merely say he is protesting – nothing else. This is for you and all the others. If the king threatens further, invoke our family's name and say you are under our protection. Since Feylynn is still the High Knight, he has certain privileges afforded him. It may only aggravate the king further, but it will keep all of you safe."

"What of you?"

"The king wouldn't dare imprison me over this," Kandessa says. "It would only further Shaylynn's cause. What's more, he'll need Shaylynn to come back eventually."

With the plan set, Sarin goes to her duty. Faith is surprised by her cousin's actions and her aunt's response, but she will not go against Kandessa's wishes and relays the news to Fallon. Neither he nor Lyosan is happy about this, but knowing their friend as well as they do, they also know they can do nothing about it. This must play out however it can.

CHAPTER X

When the king first hears of Shaylynn's desertion, he erupts in rage. Having suffered more from a child than he should, Cyrus condemns the action and demands Shaylynn's location be revealed to him. However, neither Fallon nor Lyosan will be deterred. Mostly from the fear of Kandessa's words, which does not sit well with Cyrus. His authority is being challenged by the wife a knight. For the longest time, he considers throwing Fallon, Lyosan, and anyone else who knows about Shaylynn in prison, but eventually, his anger quells. Though upset by Shaylynn's stubborn nature, Cyrus allows the protest to stand. Focusing his attention to more important matters, he leaves the matter alone.

A few days after the caravan left, Fallon and Lyosan meet in town. Neither has seen Shaylynn since he took refuge in the forest. While they wish to find him, both know he can conceal himself too easily with nature to aid him. What's worse, Lyosan has not the heart to worry about anything but the princess.

"We may never see her again," Lyosan suggests.

"Nonsense," Fallon replies.

"It is a possibility – whether you acknowledge it or not."

"Many possibilities lie before us," Fallon explains. "It is all a matter of what we choose to make happen."

"You believe we control fate so easily?"

Fallon considers the question. There are a great number of things happening now which he would not have happen. His father is gone. Shaylynn has vanished into the forest. The princess is gone. Obviously, he cannot be in control of fate entirely, but he can control his attitude towards this situation. Lyosan seems fixated on the negative outcomes. Fallon sees those ends, but he does not accept them to be his eventual reality. He has seen too much good in his life to believe everything will suddenly turn so bad. Perhaps he believes too much in his friend, especially since Shaylynn has abandoned them. He will return after all. He will come back to them and help set things right.

"Control it," Fallon finally replies. "No, I don't believe I can control fate, but I do believe we can control it when we work together."

Lyosan grunts. "In case you haven't noticed, we aren't together."

"Not now, but we will be," Fallon assures him. "And soon after that, everyone will be back together."

More than a week passes before word reaches Langerwitz of the fate of their princess. Only one returns from the caravan that left. The news is dire. Athorn has abducted the princess and means to hold her prisoner. He will not release her until the rule of Artonia belongs to him. Also, the southland has come under attack. The invading forces will continue to fight until the kingdom is turned over to Jorram.

Enraged, Cyrus comes to the house of Feylynn and demands to know where Shaylynn is hiding. At first, Kandessa means to be of little help.

"Your son," Cyrus commands.

"What of him?" Kandessa asks.

"Do not test me, woman," Cyrus warns. "I am king of this land, and you will not defy me further."

"Will you imprison me, dear king?" Kandessa asks.

"If you threaten the safety of my sister, then yes!" he barks.

Suddenly, the mood shifts. Kandessa knew nothing of the matter before the king broached the subject. Had she known, she would never have jested at the king's presence.

"Your sister," Kandessa repeats.

"She has been taken by the king of Jorram, who has no intention of bringing peace between us. He uses her as leverage over me."

In her mind, Kandessa condemns her king for his foolish actions. Under different circumstances, she would not hesitate to point out his error, but given his mood, she decides to err on the side of caution.

"Daylynn!" she calls.

In an instant, he appears.

"Go to Fallon, Lyosan, and Sarin. Bring them here in haste."

With no hesitation, he tears out of the house. Within ten minutes, he returns with the required persons right behind him.

"Find him," Kandessa orders.

"He wishes to remain hidden," Fallon replies.

"That is no longer an option," Kandessa says.

Confused, the three look to the king.

"They've kidnapped the princess," he explains. "The southland is under siege. I will send the youths into battle but not without him as captain."

With urgency prevalent, they leave the house and make for the forest. Cyrus sends his pages all over town to gather the youths and bring them to the castle. They will leave as soon as Shaylynn is prepared.

Within minutes, Sarin, Lyosan, and Fallon reach the forest. They scatter about, looking for any sign of Shaylynn. They call for him, trying to explain the situation, but he does not show himself. Either he cannot hear them or he has turned his back on the king and the land.

When they are about to give up hope, Sarin stops by the river. She can see the spot where the rocks used to stand. She remembers the night he saved her and all the things he told her. With hope in her heart, she begins to believe she can reach him somehow. Closing her eyes, she calls out to him with her heart. Fallon and Lyosan watch silently and patiently wait for him to show.

Moments pass; nothing happens.

Then, a rustling in the trees reaches their ears. Sarin opens her eyes and turns towards the noise. They still can't see him, but they know he's come.

"Shaylynn," Fallon says, "stop this! The king needs you."

"He did not need me before," a voice replies from the trees.

They search for him, but he is not showing himself. As they turn to and fro, their patience wanes.

"The princess's life is in danger," Lyosan says.

"As we knew it would be," Shaylynn replies. "That did not stop him before, why does it concern him now?"

"He made a mistake, Shaylynn," Fallon says. "We are all guilty of such things."

"Must I atone for his misgivings?" Shaylynn asks.

Fed up, Sarin stops turning and closes her eyes. This is the moment Kandessa told her she must be ready for. Shaylynn has been gone too long, and only she can bring him back. Taking a deep breath, she hardens herself and shouts at the sky. "Enough!" Lyosan and Fallon jump at her outburst. "You bring yourself to me this instant!"

A second later, he lands at her feet. Lyosan and Fallon move towards him, but she slaps him before they can get close. Her action stops them cold. Shaylynn looks at her with confusion and anger.

"Miss me?" he asks.

"I miss the man I love," she replies, "but I know not where he is."

Shaylynn rolls his eyes and places his hands on his hips.

"Forgo the king, she is your friend," Sarin chides. "She is the one your friend loves. You fought to keep her here, why would you not fight to save her?"

"Had I been listened to, this would not be necessary," Shaylynn replies.

"You are not a king," Sarin informs him. "For the weight you believe your voice should carry, it does not. You are but one voice in the ear of one who must consider all sides. You think of yourself and those close to you, but not all have that luxury."

Shaylynn thinks of how to counteract her, but she is correct in all she says. He has been selfish in this endeavor. While it served him for a while, he cannot afford it any longer. He must be the selfless man he was – like his father would be.

"You told me you'd keep your loyalty to this city and its people," Sarin reminds him. "Do you still hold to that?"

He does not have to consider her question long. "I do," he replies.

"Then do so now," she says. "The king requires a captain, and you are the best for the task."

Shaylynn gazes into Sarin's eyes. Under other circumstances, the look he gives her would melt her ambition and sweep her away. Now is not the time for silly romance and girlish swooning. As such, her look remains hard and steady.

"Have I told you how much I love you?" Shaylynn asks.

"Not nearly enough as I deserve." Sarin replies.

Shaylynn smiles. "I shall attempt to resolve that transgression in the future."

As he leans in to kiss her, she sneaks in one more remark. "See that you do."

His purpose resolved, Shaylynn returns with Fallon and Lyosan to the castle. The king waits in the great hall for Shaylynn and does not look pleased with him when he arrives.

"Hours I have had to wait for you," Cyrus scolds. "Hours wasted while you threw a petty tantrum."

Shaylynn drops to a knee, lowers his head, and presents his sword. "I have disgraced my charge, my lord. Not to mention my father and family. I surrender my sword to you. If you would demand it, I give my freedom with it. Regardless, it is yours."

Cyrus approaches Shaylynn and touches his shoulder. "I suppose if not for the foolishness of a king, you wouldn't need to sacrifice your freedom."

"The wisdom of a king cannot be understood by a mere youth."

"Bah!" Cyrus bellows as he seats himself on the throne. "Enough of your flattery, Shaylynn. The wisdom of a king holds little weight when used so lightly. What's more, I shall need something much more than a mere youth to complete the task I require."

Shaylynn smiles at the king's reply. The two are of the same mind here. They cannot worry about what has been or should have been. Much is at stake here. They must secure the southlands. They must discover what has become of the force to the north. Perhaps, most dear to Cyrus, they must rescue Crystalynn from the clutches of Jorram.

"I believe I am the youth for the task," Shaylynn says.

"You'd better be," Cyrus replies. "Much lies on your shoulders, Shaylynn Storm. Much indeed. Now, kneel, son of Feylynn."

This is certainly not the way Shaylynn expected to join the ranks of his father and brother. After standing at odds with the crown, he just as quickly finds himself honored by it. With pride beaming from his heart, he does as commanded. Cyrus raises his sword and then places it on each of Shaylynn's shoulders.

"In the name of the king and in service to our people, I, Cyrus Wuhlfies, dub thee Sir Shaylynn Storm, Knight of Langerwitz and Captain of Youth Brigade. Rise, my son."

Shaylynn stands and kisses the ring of the king. Cyrus then turns to Fallon and Lyosan. "I hope you and your comrades will not feel cheated," he says, "but your ceremony will have to be less formal. After all, war is upon us."

The king sets forth the plan with Shaylynn. He will lead a force of two-hundred and fifty from Langerwitz. Shaylynn will have total command over the youths and will be free to assign ranks as he sees fit. He immediately names Fallon his second in command and places Lyosan among the head of the troop as well. The rest he will determine in time. They will ride along the river to the southland and join with the forces of O'Lyn, Reneel, and Delreeve. Their numbers will not even the fight, but they will be able to aid a great deal if the Artonian forces can hold their own. Jorram will not have sent their best fighters, and as Artonia is not sending their best either, the battle will be impossible to predict.

What is known by all involved is there is no time to waste. Every second the youths remain in Langerwitz, the more it hastens the defeat of their countrymen. Working tirelessly to make their preparations, Shaylynn, Fallon, and Lyosan rush about the castle barking orders to the stable boys and pages. As the other youths arrive, they quickly fall into line. Even Pythyn offers no resistance when Shaylynn puts Fallon in charge of him. Pythyn only asks what he can do to help, and Shaylynn replies for Pythyn to follow orders.

Perhaps Pythyn does so because he sees a way to reach the ends he seeks, but nonetheless, he accepts his position and falls in line. He aids in prepping the youths who arrive after him. When Fallon gives commands, Pythyn replies with only the nod of his head then turns to complete the task.

Shortly thereafter, the youths are ready to march. Cyrus addresses them before they leave the castle. He speaks of the courage and bravery they must show. He assures them the hopes and prayers of all who remain in the city go with them. He orders them to follow their captain, Shaylynn, and asks for as many as possible to come home safely. Lastly, he brings them into the order of the Knights of Langerwitz.

Their orders firmly planted in their minds, the youths march out of the castle and assemble on the southern courtyard. Family, friends, and all manner of citizens stand ready to see them off. Among the crowd, five stand out. Three are the mothers of the leaders of this charge. The other two, the lovers of the captain and his first mate respectively. Shaylynn sends the others forth while he brings Lyosan and Fallon to address those who have come to see them off. As Lyosan walks towards his mother, the absence of the princess lays heavily on his heart. True, she does not love him as Sarin loves Shaylynn or as Faith loves Fallon, but he loves her the way his friends love their girls. Even if the feeling went unreciprocated, he would like to see his great love before he rides for war and perhaps death.

As it is, he embraces his mother and feels the worry in her arms. She cautions him of the dangers which lie ahead. She speaks of the pride his father would feel at this moment were he alive. Finally, she tells him not to worry. The family will go on until he returns. When Lyosan begins to question whether he will return, she stops him immediately and assures him he will return. Lyosan says nothing else.

Fallon addresses his mother first. Ellisia has little else with her husband lost in the north. Her home will be terribly lonely with Fallon gone as well.

"You have your father's honor," Ellisia tells her son. "I never wanted you to go to battle, but I wish he would be here to go with you."

"He is with me," Fallon replies. "Always and forever, his words guide my actions. They will guide me back home."

Ellisia smiles at Fallon's confidence. She knows all too well the likelihood he will not return. Her own father went out to battle and never returned. Even now, he lies buried in a foreign land. The same fate may have befallen her husband. While the exact same may not be true for Fallon, the possibility is close enough.

"If you cannot put your faith in my words," Fallon says after his mother remains silent, "then put them in him." Fallon motions to Shaylynn. "He is the greatest warrior of his age. He has far more to accomplish in this world, and he will go to hell and back to ensure I am there to see it."

Ellisia laughs. "He is a great blessing to you."

Ellisia hugs Fallon and kisses him on the cheek. As a few tears fall from her eyes, she steps away and lets Fallon move to Faith. She has already begun crying, but she tries to compose herself for Fallon.

"Your cousin will bring me home," Fallon promises.

"If he doesn't, he better fall with you," Faith replies.

Fallon smiles. "I fear for my mother while I am away."

"You needn't," Faith assures him. "I shall check on her constantly. I think it best I get to know her since I plan on becoming part of her family."

Fallon smiles again. "You've become bolder about your feelings."

"I see no reason to hide them – especially now."

Fallon reaches for Faith and kisses her. As they say their goodbyes, Shaylynn faces his own mother.

"I always believed I was meant for such things," Shaylynn says.

"You must be so anxious to see them come to light," Kandessa says.

"If there were a better way, I would…"

Kandessa waves his explanations away. "I know what you would say. It is what your father would say. He had to go off to defend our realm, and you must do the same." She hesitates before going further, but she must tell her son what she believes. She would never forgive herself otherwise. "I warned your father about a feeling I had. Something was coming to tear our family apart, I said. Now, he is gone – Beylynn with him. You prepare to ride to battle in the southlands. What will take Daylynn from me?"

"Nothing," Shaylynn replies, "and nothing will keep me from returning to you."

Kandessa touches her son's cheek and smiles. His sincerity is touching, but it holds little weight. Shaylynn leaves for dangers he has only considered and imagined. The reality will surely change his feelings on these matters.

"I wish you could stay my boy," Kandessa says.

"I am always yours," Shaylynn replies.

He kisses his mother and turns to Sarin. She tries to force a smile, but she cannot do it. Shaylynn takes her hands to try to comfort her.

"I am always yours as well," Shaylynn adds.

Sarin laughs for a moment. "Such a magician you are," she says. "Will you perform a feat of magic for me?"

"Of course," Shaylynn replies.

"Return to me?"

Shaylynn smiles and kisses her. She kisses him back, but after a minute, she wants an answer to her request.

"Will you come back?" she asks.

Shaylynn takes a deep breath before he replies. "I will do all I can."

Sarin shakes her head. "That's not good enough." She removes a necklace from her person. It is small but dear to her – given to her by her own grandmother. It is a symbol for the days when magic ruled the lands. Thus, it is even more appropriate she give it to Shaylynn now. She places it in his hands and closes his fist around it. "Promise me that you will bring this back."

Shaylynn smiles and holds the necklace tightly. "By my life, it will be done."

Sarin smiles a bit and kisses him again. Then, she turns to Kandessa.

"Is this what it's always like?" she asks.

Kandessa nods slowly. "I'm afraid so."

Then Kandessa holds her hand out to Sarin. Sarin goes to her, takes her hand, and rests her head on Kandessa's shoulder. "And sadly, my child," Kandessa continues, "there is nothing in this world which can take this pain away short of not loving those who leave."

Sarin shakes her head. "Even if I was willing to accept those terms, they would not be worth it."

Kandessa smiles in reply. "In that regard, you are right."

Shaylynn bids them farewell and returns to his steed. Lyosan and Fallon join him, and they take off towards the rest of the troop. The onlookers throw flowers on the path of the riders. Normally, this would not occur, but because the youths ride for their first battle, special circumstances apply.

Within minutes, they are out of the castle walls, and the world they knew disappears behind them. They ride hard the rest of the day before finding a place to camp for the night. Shaylynn sends out riders to forage for food while everyone else sets up tents and sparks fires. Night comes quickly, and the youths prepare for their first battle. Though they still have two days on their journey, the threat of battle is in the forefront of their minds.

They all share the same thoughts though none are willing to speak about them. Shaylynn keeps his normal disposition, but because everyone else is so quiet, he joins the silence as well. For some, it is too much for their captain to remain silent when he is so often the one to calm their fears and still their hearts. As they pace back and forth, the tension amongst the group grows and grows. When it becomes too much, Shaylynn finally speaks.

"We've two days until the battle," he announces.

After that, he says nothing. It's not exactly what everyone has come to expect from him, so they wait for him to say more. When he does not, the general unease returns. He has a point to make, but he will force them to drag it out of him. They have all this pent-up emotion which they need to release. For that reason, Shaylynn will force some kind of reaction from them. It is almost a game, but no one will play. Fallon normally would but not this time.

"We know," Stefen finally replies.

"Two days," Shaylynn repeats.

"We heard you," Darrow says.

"More than forty-eight hours…" Shaylynn begins.

"Oh, enough of it!" Pythyn cries. "Make your point."

The response amuses Shaylynn, but he holds in his laughter. It would only torment them to a degree greater than he wishes at the moment.

"You walk as though we are lambs to the slaughter," Shaylynn explains.

"We could very well die," Artimous replies.

"Yes, that is true," Shaylynn admits. Rising from the ground, he stands to address the entire group. Slowly, he walks around the fire to give his words even greater magnitude. When all eyes are upon him, he continues. "Yes, I could die. Indeed, some of us will die. And is this the manner in which you wish to face your death? Dragging it out slowly and painfully, letting it consume all of the last hours of your life? Or would you fight it with every ounce you have left and let death know it only owned you for the briefest of moments! For while death is permanent, it is also momentary. The stain of death passes, and all the world fades away to reveal what is yet to come. My brothers, our time on this good earth is precious and fleeting. Do not waste it fearing what is undeniably inevitable. Live it. Own it. Be the masters of your own destiny; do not let destiny master you!"

The words strike a chord with many of the youths sitting around the fires. This is indeed their time. Perhaps, it has come much sooner than any of them expected, but it was never for them to decide when fate would come. They have trained. They have worked. They need to face this challenge head on. It is not easy, but if they are to succeed, they need to be themselves, unfettered by their fear.

Not everything returns to normal for the youths, but the chatter among them picks up. The spring in their step returns to many of them. The magnitude of the upcoming events remains prevalent in their minds. Except now, they are willing to discuss and better prepare for the battle.

When the fires die down, the youths turn in. They rise early in the morning, have a quick breakfast, and ride out to the south. In keeping with their initial strategy, they keep to the river. Shaylynn rides out in front with Fallon and Stefen close behind him. Though they ride to war and destruction, they cannot help but be struck by the beauty of their country. The rolling green plains of the southern lands distract their minds from their cause. They encounter many villages, small family farms, and meet, if ever so briefly, some of the wonderful people who occupy those areas. It sparks a great feeling among the youths. Where they were once fearing for themselves, they now begin to concern themselves with the people they ride to protect. In the southlands, just as in this area, wonderful people are being separated from their homes and livelihoods. Sadly, some of those people are also being killed by the vultures of Jorram. Children will lose parents. Parents will lose children. The men of the area will attempt to defend their homes, but they are farmers, businessmen, and tradesmen. They have not been trained for battle, nor have they faced an opponent who means to kill them.

The latter is a sentiment shared with the youths. Their training has always been safe and supervised. Even the fiercest of rivalries has not had the chance of ending in death. For all the hostility Shaylynn and Pythyn throw at each other, the most they would do is injure lightly – not mortally. And while that thought bothered many of the youths when they left the city, they are less concerned with it as they travel. Knowing the battle in front of them cannot be avoided furthers the resolve within them. The thought of abandoning the troop and becoming deserters never enters their minds. What causes this resolve cannot be completely pinned down. Maybe it stems from their leader. Shaylynn Storm, who never shakes, even in this time of distress, rides hard and fast. When they rest, he warns them to be quick and prepare to leave as soon as they are able. He aids wherever it is needed. He gets every youth prepared for the ride and then leads the troop on their journey.

When the day ends, they find another site in which to camp for the night. Spirits remain high. The youths even train and go through their exercises to keep their abilities sharp. Though they have faced a long day, they keep their energy high knowing it is for a good cause. As he surveys the group in front of him, Shaylynn feels a swell of pride that this would be the first group he would lead into battle. That they would place their lives in his hands, for, in his position, he could ask for little more. His father always spoke to him of the times to come in which he would lead, of a time when

Shaylynn would be at the front of the pack with a legion behind him. It comes much earlier than Shaylynn expected, but he feels ready for the challenge.

As he sits, Pythyn approaches. The two have not spoken since Shaylynn spoke to the troop the previous night. Pythyn has been a model soldier up to this point. He has stayed within the ranks. When it comes time to pack up and move on, he is quick to get on the move. Regardless of what Shaylynn has done, he has not voiced his displeasure. Only now, he cannot hold his tongue. Shaylynn assumes as much when Pythyn sits across from him.

"This should be pleasant," Shaylynn groans.

Pythyn retorts, "Hear what I have to say, first. Then, decide the merits."

Shaylynn nods in agreement. This is not the two facing each other in training or squaring off on the city roads. Their relationship, however strained by their previous encounters, must be different now.

"You have not named all your lieutenants," Pythyn says.

Shaylynn nods. "And you wish to be among them?"

"I deserve to be among them," Pythyn corrects.

Shaylynn remains silent and gives Pythyn his due. Skills alone, he is at the top of the class. What Shaylynn does not know – cannot know – is whether or not he can trust Pythyn.

"I have shown in training I am better than nearly everyone here," Pythyn explains. "I do not pretend to suggest I should lead them. Though we are more equal than you would see it, none of these men would follow me were I in charge. They look to you."

"If they will not follow you, then why put you in a position of leadership?" Shaylynn interrupts.

"They will not follow me were I in charge," Pythyn repeats. "In this case, I am not in charge of my own accord. If you place me in charge – show some trust in me – and I show my willingness to follow your lead – place some trust in you – they will place their trust in me."

Shaylynn ponders the possibility. There are few among them who possess the skill to lead a charge. Shaylynn is one. Fallon is another. Someone will have to command the archers – Stefen is the best for that. Even with a small force, two lieutenants cannot perform all the duties necessary for the group. Shaylynn will need another, if not two, to serve as lieutenant. He'd hoped someone would show better quality, but really, none of them have.

From a distance, Fallon has been listening. Not to the point where Pythyn would know Fallon was listening in, but Fallon is close enough to hear everything. While it seems absurd in a sense to put Pythyn in charge of anything, Pythyn does make a good case. Besides, if Pythyn has his own command, he will not be a part of Fallon's crew.

"You are not my first lieutenant," Shaylynn finally says in reply.

Pythyn nods. "Of course not."

"Furthermore, Lyosan will be in your command," Shaylynn adds.

It is a gambit, moving Lyosan into Pythyn's troop. It is no secret Pythyn holds no good feelings toward Lyosan. If Pythyn cannot handle this move, it will prove to Shaylynn there can be no trust between them. What's more, Shaylynn will know if Pythyn goes beyond the scope of his authority. Lyosan will serve as a spy in a sense, but only if there is anything to spy.

When Shaylynn shares the news, Pythyn does not react well. A look of disdain crosses his face. The edges of his mouth curl, and his brow furls. He grits his teeth and gives Shaylynn a dirty look. On the one hand, Pythyn understands why Shaylynn wants Lyosan with Pythyn. Even though Pythyn has no intention of sabotaging Shaylynn's first campaign, he resents the implication. On the other hand, Pythyn sees Lyosan as a liability – one he cannot afford. Nevertheless, he must bear the burden in this instance.

"So be it," Pythyn says. "If you want him under my command, I'll have him."

It is a mixed message. First, it indicates Pythyn will indeed follow Shaylynn's leadership. Second, perhaps more importantly, it warns that Lyosan may be placed in a dangerous position. And with Pythyn in command, it may end up being done intentionally. He gets up to leave thinking he has had the last word. Fortunately, Shaylynn has the proper reply. Before Pythyn takes two steps, he speaks.

"You know he is close with the princess," Shaylynn responds. "As the king already regrets the loss of his sister, he will not be pleased should one of her confidants be lost because of foolish commands."

Pythyn stops at the comment and considers the ramifications. Shaylynn speaks the truth. The princess, for whatever reason, cares for Lyosan – as does the king. It will be important for Lyosan to return to Langerwitz.

Letting Shaylynn have this small victory, Pythyn walks off with no reply. Shaylynn feels no satisfaction in his remark. He still cannot tell if making Pythyn a lieutenant was the best course to take. While he sought to solve one problem, he may have created several others.

As he ponders his decision, Fallon joins him. The look on Fallon's face does not put Shaylynn at ease. For what it's worth, Fallon does not mean to make Shaylynn feel better about this.

"You question my move?" Shaylynn asks.

"I question your motives," Fallon replies.

"He's worthy."

"In some regards."

Shaylynn cannot deny the truth in Fallon's remark. It is not often Fallon finds himself able to silence Shaylynn so easily.

"Do you mean to make an ally of an enemy?" Fallon asks.

"I mean to give our campaign its best chance," Shaylynn replies.

"And he is our best?"

Shaylynn frowns at Fallon. Clearly, Pythyn is not the best in Shaylynn's eyes. Otherwise, he would not have already named Fallon and Stefen lieutenants.

"Who would you have in his place?" Shaylynn asks.

Fallon shakes his head. "Not a problem for lesser minds."

"Do not attempt modesty now," Shaylynn says. "You come to offer your opinion, so offer it."

Fallon smiles. "He is the best, after those you've already named. But while your endgame is simple and logical, I'm not sure his is."

Shaylynn nods. "I agree.

The two sit in silence for a few minutes. The fears among them are shared. The ways this could go wrong are many and dire. Pythyn will serve as lieutenant, and many will serve under him. What remains to be seen is how Pythyn will use this position should they all survive the campaign.

"We've another day," Fallon says to calm Shaylynn's nerves.

The remark does not calm Shaylynn. "A day to dread my mistakes."

Fallon chuckles. "Wasn't it you who said to master your destiny?"

Shaylynn laughs as well. "You would use my own words against me."

"Someone has to," Fallon says. "You use them against us so often."

The rest of the night, Shaylynn sleeps soundly. The decision weighs on him, but Fallon is right – he cannot let it dominate his thoughts. The next morning, he speaks to Lyosan about the decision. Lyosan is not pleased at all, but he accepts the decision for the reasons Shaylynn explains.

Once prepared, the troop rides for the day. They will arrive in the marshlands by nightfall. The next day, they come to the Hills of Carsow. Beyond those hills, the battle will be waiting for them. Just as before, the ride through the south ignites in them their desire to defend. Having followed the Lakwood River, they turn west and begin following the Reggen River towards the hills. The marshes slow their progress, but they still manage good time. Their respites are even shorter as the marshes do not provide good places to stop. The ride lasts slightly longer than expected since Shaylynn does not want to make camp in the marshes. Instead, they ride on until they reach the base of the hills. There, they make camp. Shaylynn commands the youths to get to bed early. They will rise early again, and before the sun reaches its highest point, they will be at the battle. Many are restless this night. The threat of the danger ahead lingers in the air. Their hearts beat hard and fast. Their minds race through possibilities.

When Shaylynn rises the next morning, he scans his troops who still slumber. They are too young for this, he thinks to himself. I am too young for this, he admits. But that does not matter anymore. They have come this far, and they cannot turn back. This day, they will spill their blood to protect the land they call home. Some of them will not see another day. That it has come to this is truly a disgrace.

With a heavy heart, Shaylynn begins to rouse his lieutenants. They, in turn, begin to rouse the rest of the men, and the march to battle begins. It is a quiet ride, filled with the solemnity of young minds attempting to grasp a world they do not understand. War has been a constant threat in their minds, but there it had always stayed. Now, it will become reality.

As they ride through the hills, they begin to see the remnants of the homes already attacked by Jorramians. Bodies lay dead on the ground, pierced by blades and arrows. Homes have been burned to the ground. Among the dead are children – even younger than the youths. The sight of them stirs a great anger among the riders. This has been done senselessly. The people here were innocent and trying to live a simple life. They had no warning and little chance to defend themselves. Even after Jorram kidnapped the princess and got everything they wanted, they attacked without mercy or quarter.

The anger within the youths causes them to ride harder and quells their fear for the moment. They are not sure where the battle is currently happening, but once they reach the Summit of Parvo, they will be able to scout the entire area. As they near, they see many people, ordinary citizens, either too young, too old, or responsible for others, running away from a nearby village. One of them stops Shaylynn and informs him the battle is just over the summit in the town of Delreeve. Shaylynn commands his forces to go forward towards the summit. Though the possibility of death lies over the hill, none of the troop hesitates to heed his command.

The rage of battle already within them, the youth ride for the summit. Gray smoke billows over the hills already, giving haste to their purpose. The tw0-hundred and fifty ride together as their resolve has become hardened by the sights they have already seen. Out in front rides Shaylynn, unwilling to let a moment pass wherein the people of the country may find themselves at danger's door. Atop the hill, they ride and pause to form their ranks to assess the scene below, and a harrowing scene they see. In flames, the town burns and to and fro the soldiers of Jorram ride. Bodies lay strewn about the ground. The horror of the moment grips the minds of the youths who ride with Shaylynn. Many would turn and flee for their lives if only they could muster the thoughts, but fear has returned to render them unable to move or even fathom the moment at hand.

Sensing the loss of resolve in all at arms, Shaylynn rears his horse and begins to call the troops to cause. They have come too far and risked too much to back out now. Plus, they've too much ahead that must be done. This is only the first stage of their quest. After they salvage the south, they must ride to the north and rescue the princess. If they do not succeed here, he surely will not have the means to travel to Jorram and storm the capital.

"Form ranks!" Shaylynn commands. "Archers to the left! Fallon, bring your battalion to the center flank! Pythyn, to the western edge! All others on me!"

Horses began to move without much direction from the riders. Their eyes still remain focused on the scene in front of them though on some level they are cognizant of their cause. Hope remains that they will not throw themselves into the turmoil in front of them – that their lives will not be required for this cause. Yet, each knows this hope is in vain. The moment draws near. Soon, the charge will be called. Into battle they will go. Courage will be tested. None, except their captain, feels truly ready for its call.

"Brothers!" he cries, "Stand at arms!"

For the first time, the youths tear their eyes from the scene before them and look to their leader. Even Pythyn, who would just as quickly ignore Shaylynn at any opportunity, looks to Shaylynn for hope. Shaylynn rides back and forth along the line a couple of times before he addresses his men.

"My friends, prepare yourselves! We stand on the brink of oblivion, and it is dark and full of despair and death. Only the truly brave and noble can dare to look upon it and choose to dive in. But even those who do, do not do so without feeling the fear in their hearts. Listen to me, now. None who enter this place could do so without fear in them. Not even me.

"Not feeling fear is not how you prepare yourself for what you will face. It is by controlling that fear. By remembering your fear would end the lives of the innocent and maybe even your own brothers at arms. Do not fail them now! Do not fail yourselves now! Hold to the promises you made – the vows you have taken. Serve your family, your king, and everything you hold dear. I say to you…Knights of Langerwitz…ride!"

With a loud cry, Shaylynn draws his sword and points to the battle. Fallon echoes the cry, as does Stefen, Pythyn, and the others soon join in. Even Lyosan, who feels the fear Shaylynn speaks of, raises his sword and joins in the yelling. Then, with Shaylynn at the lead, the youths ride to war and death.

The battle drags on through the day. The youths join the forces of the southern lands in defense of Delreeve. Jurl Irn is the first of the youths to be killed. He is not the last, yet many of the youths hold their own in the battle. From atop the hills, Stefen commands his archers and picks off a good deal of those in the flanks on the outskirts of town. Eventually, they must abandon their positions and join the fighting without their bows. Their effective shooting does give the Artonian forces a leg up in the battle. By taking out a good number of the Jorramian men, the Artonians have a chance to claim victory. It will still take a massive effort from the youths. Now that they fight, they do not have the constant sight of Shaylynn to keep them going.

In truth, Lyosan could use the sight of his friends to boost his morale. Along with Pythyn's troop, he rides as commanded into the heart of the town to secure the locals. With the bulk of the Jorramian force centered on Shaylynn's charge, Lyosan and his comrades are able to enter the town with ease. Pythyn puts a small group in charge of getting the townspeople clear of the fighting. Lyosan wishes he could be among them, but Pythyn does not give him the duty. Instead, Lyosan charges on with a group of seven who attempt to sneak behind the Jorramian line. They are, however, discovered quickly. In a matter of moments, Lyosan finds himself squaring off with a man for Jorram. At first, Lyosan goes wide-eyed and cannot move. The Jorramian stands tall with a wild look in his eye. He does not have the stance of trained soldier – more the look of berserker. But, he is clearly stronger and better equipped for this struggle than Lyosan.

Having enough of this stalemate, the Jorramian charges at Lyosan while letting out a mighty yell. It shocks Lyosan back to his senses but does not prepare him to defend himself. Instead, he gives ground and weakly raises his sword. Blades clash as the Jorramian strikes hard. Lyosan stumbles and must steady himself to keep himself from falling to the ground. Meanwhile, the Jorramian continues the assault. Raising the blade high again, the attacker again lets out a scream as Lyosan moves to protect himself. This time, the strike knocks Lyosan to the ground. Fearing for his life, Lyosan grabs a handful of dirt and throws it in his attacker's face. Though the distraction stops the assault, it does not end the conflict. In a moment, Lyosan will have to engage again.

In those seconds before the duel commences, a moment of calm comes to Lyosan. In that moment, he hears the voice of his friend, "Measure him," Shaylynn says in Lyosan's mind. "He is out of control – in a frenzy. Use it against him."

When the Jorramian clear his vision, an angrier scowl covers his face. Coming at Lyosan in a fury, he raises his sword and brings it down hard. Lyosan steps to the side and lets the blade come down into the ground. Using every moment he can, Lyosan strikes quick and pierces the man's arm. The Jorramian cries out in pain but also strikes Lyosan across the face with the injured arm. Lyosan stumbles back but does not fall. The Jorramian lifts sword again but measures Lyosan before making another move. Staying defensive, Lyosan refuses to make the first move. Fed up, his attacker goes to strike again. This time, he swings horizontally, causing Lyosan to jump back. He swings a second time and when he does, Lyosan moves in quickly to counter. Slashing the man's leg, Lyosan moves behind the Jorramian as he takes the upper hand. Greatly hindered by this injury, Lyosan's foe struggles to get turned around to face Lyosan. To press his advantage, Lyosan keeps moving out of the man's vision. Eventually, the Jorramian loses his temper and swings wildly. With another strike, Lyosan disarms his foe and then puts him down for good.

Having vanquished one enemy, Lyosan finds himself a little more adjusted to his setting. Finding the rest of his troop, Lyosan continues the reclaiming of the town. Not only does his troop accomplish their task, but they also meet up with Shaylynn and his battalion. Seeing his friend, alive and fighting with the ferocity of a beast ignites a fire in Lyosan as well. Before the day ends, they retake the town and drive the Jorramian force from the area.

As he surveys the aftermath, Shaylynn orders the dead be buried. Before long, Fallon finds him and all seems well.

"A fine start," Fallon says.

"I count our loses at ten," Shaylynn replies.

"There would always be some," Fallon says. "Let us be happy the number is low."

"While we mourn any number at all," Shaylynn adds.

Before they can continue, Pythyn finds them. While they would normally cringe at his arrival, they are eager for any news he may have.

"The Jorramian force is heading due west. They will reach Reneel if we give them the chance."

"Then, they will reach it," Shaylynn replies.

"It will give them a chance to make a strong stand," Pythyn argues. "If we can catch them, we can continue to have an advantage. The rest of the Jorramian force will not know we are here."

"We've duties to these people and our fallen brothers," Shaylynn responds. "We will not abandon those responsibilities."

"Give me leave to go…"

"No!" Shaylynn snaps. "Let the Jorramians know we are coming. Let the Artonians of the south know we are coming. Hope will come to those who need it while fear and despair will come to those who have earned it."

Seeing the fire in his eyes, Pythyn walks away and sees to his other duties. Fallon, standing with his hands on his hips, cannot believe what he is about to say.

"He has a point."

Shaylynn nods. "I know."

"We are still mere children in the eyes of men."

"Let that be their folly. Men have died this day – not children. We left those days behind with the first of the fallen."

As they continue with their duties, a carriage arrives bearing the mark of the Wuhlfies. Many of the knights call out its arrival, and before it comes to a stop, Shaylynn is standing in front of it.

"Are you the captain?" the driver asks.

"I am," Shaylynn replies.

The driver smirks. "Well, we are in desperate hours, ain't we?"

Shaylynn glares in disapproval. Before he can get a word out, a voice from inside the carriage calls out. "Shut up, Bevens! As usual, your tact is equal to your intellect."

The door of the carriage swings open, and a woman steps out. She has dark hair, blue eyes, pale skin, and red lips. While most have no idea who is now among them, Shaylynn recognized the voice of Lily Athimere the moment he heard it. However, he is not exactly thrilled to find Sarin's mother here.

"Milady Athimere," Shaylynn says quizzically.

"Forgive my driver, Shaylynn Storm. A lifetime of travel has dulled his manners."

Upon hearing the young captain's name, Bevens realizes his mistake in insulting the son of a great knight. "My apologies, young master," Bevens offers. "I was merely surprised is all. Now that I know who stands in front me, I am not surprised of your rank."

Shaylynn nods to Bevens as Lily steps to him.

"Have you made my daughter cry recently?" she asks.

"Yes," Shaylynn reluctantly admits, "but not for the normal reasons."

Intrigued, Lily orders a tent be set up wherein she will talk with Shaylynn privately. Bevens gets right to work, and Shaylynn offers three of his own to help. In minutes, Shaylynn and Lily sit in the tent by candlelight.

"I did not know you were in this area," Shaylynn says.

"We weren't supposed to be," Lily explains. "I was meeting with mayors near the Culson bridge. When word reached us, we figured we should offer what assistance we could. We traveled straight south first, but we did not find friendly forces until now. It has been five days. I did not know you would be in this area either."

"We were all knighted and ordered to ride south. This is the first day of battle we've seen. Tomorrow, we will ride to Reneel."

"The Jorramians have a strong presence there. You will need to be careful in your assault. The hills can be a great detriment, but if you can clear Reneel, the south will be saved."

"We will have more men with us. Some of the people in Delreeve will be able to ride."

In regards to the battle, there is not much else to discuss. Shaylynn must ride to attempt to secure the land. Lily will stay behind to perform her duties. The people will need their ambassador and her resources. Besides, Lily is more interested in other affairs despite all that is happening around them.

"So how did you make Sarin cry this time?"

Shaylynn hesitates before answering, "I told her I loved her."

The admission brings a small smile to Lily's face. Having seen her daughter tormented by Shaylynn for so long, it is about time he wised up. And since this is the only chance she has for news about her daughter, Lily wants to know everything.

"Why would this make her cry?" she asks.

"I don't think it was that news which did it," Shaylynn admits. "More to do with my being sent down here to fight."

"Understandable," Lily replies.

Lily then reaches for a glass. As she does, she sees the necklace Sarin gave to Shaylynn before he left. Recognizing it as her family's own, Lily also knows a significance in Shaylynn having it which he does not yet know.

"I take it she gave you that necklace," Lily says as she takes a drink.

"Yes, I am supposed to bring it back to her," Shaylynn explains.

Lily chuckles. "There's a bit more to it than that." Shaylynn says nothing though he is clearly intrigued. Setting the glass aside, Lily explains further. "For the past fifteen generations, only two sets of people have worn that necklace – the women in my family and the men we married. We do not know this when we are given the necklace, nor do we know it when we give it away. We are only told by our mothers once we've bestowed it on our intended." Shaylynn holds the necklace in his hand and looks at it more closely. Lily lets the silence last a bit longer. "Knowing this, do you view it any differently?"

"Only that I never wish to take it off," Shaylynn replies, "but she made me promise to give it back."

"Don't let that concern you. I think you'll find she won't take it back for quite some time. It wasn't until after we were married that I took it back from my husband. Then, I didn't want to give it to Sarin, but my mother insisted."

"Why didn't you want her to have it?"

Lily shrugs. "I always wanted her to always be free to change her mind. When or if she did give it to someone, I didn't want her locked into a path. Of course, all that became unnecessary once she met you."

Shaylynn furls his brow. "What do you mean?"

Lily gives him a playful glare. "Oh, come now, you must know she has loved you practically since she met you."

"I tend not to consider when we were younger," Shaylynn says. "I was a bit foolish in those days."

"You were a boy who didn't know it was okay to love a girl so strongly," Lily explains. "But she wasn't going to be deterred – no matter what you did."

"I fear the decision may not be up to us," Shaylynn admits.

"What do you mean?"

With that, Shaylynn explains all the details of the tournament. He tells Lily about the feast and his dance with the princess. How upset Sarin was with the whole ordeal. How much he tried to calm her afterwards. He even goes as far as telling Lily about the promise they made to each other. To her credit, Lily does not overreact when hearing about it.

"You mustn't think it will come to that?" she says when Shaylynn finishes.

"I hope it doesn't," Shaylynn replies. "But I am prepared if it does."

"Don't be so rash. It serves you well at times, but you are out of your depth for the moment. I don't believe life would thrust you two together so early only to pull you apart when you've accepted your love for each other. It is meant to guide you in your life, Shaylynn, not drive you away from it."

The words bring some peace to Shaylynn's mind, and for the rest of the evening, he can have a pleasant time with his love's mother. The next day, he must prepare to ride and fight again. Once the other knights are ready, Shaylynn goes to Lily one last time.

"I'll tell her you send her your love, shall I?" Shaylynn asks.

"You'll do no such thing!" Lily replies. "Under no circumstance is my daughter to know I was near the fighting. She has enough to worry herself as it is."

"I suppose that is right."

With Fallon next to him, Shaylynn prepares to ride. Before they leave, Lily turns her attention to Fallon.

"You will get him home, won't you?"

"I was planning on him getting me home actually," Fallon admits.

"Don't doubt your capability, Fallon Welms. Our kingdom does not have many who can measure up to you."

Fallon nods and then rides away. Shaylynn lingers for only a minute longer.

"Anything else for me?" he asks.

"Just keep the promise you made to my daughter," she replies. "I am tired of her crying over you. And I do not want to shed tears of my own."

With a smile, Shaylynn rides away and joins the rest of the knights. As they ride, they come upon a Jorramian regiment just after midday. The battle is quick, and the knights lose but one. Still, the knights find themselves proven in battle once more. Afterwards, they rest and continue closer to Reneel. They will need a night of rest before they can approach it.

After taking the night, they come to the outskirts of the town. As Pythyn predicted, the Jorramians are ready to make a stand. From noon to night, the two forces battle. The Jorramians make good work of defending themselves, but the knights will not be turned away after coming this far. Slowly, they continue to whittle away at the defenses of the Jorramians. Only the coming of night saves the invaders. Come the next day, Shaylynn believes he will see the end of this Jorramian invasion.

But Jorram will not go without a fight. Though Shaylynn penetrates their defenses early in the day, the other regiments do not have such luck. Still under Pythyn's command, Lyosan and his comrades spend most of the day separated from the main attack. Eventually, Fallon gets his troops into the town, but it is several hours before Lyosan finds himself in the town as well.

At that point, it had been many hours since he had seen Shaylynn or Fallon. He continues to fight hard and keeps his wits about him. Eventually, he relinquishes his horse and fights on the ground. With the aid of Fallon's regiment, they drive most of the Jorramians out of the town. However, as they fight, Lyosan still sees no sign of Fallon. When he can manage a moment, he turns to his comrades to ask if any have seen Shaylynn or Fallon. Few can provide even a rumor of where they might be. Of those rumors, none seem to have any truth to them at all. Still, Lyosan manages to keep alive and relatively unscathed. After several more hours pass, the day begins to darken. The longer he goes without knowledge of his friends, the greater Lyosan's concern consumes him. But he cannot let it consume him for long because the battle rages on. As Lyosan moves through the town with his comrades, he encounters more and more soldiers from Jorram. They manage to either kill or drive away the enemy soldiers. Still, the news of Shaylynn and Fallon remains next to none.

Finally, just as the battle seems won, word comes to Pythyn that Shaylynn's men are on the edge of town facing one last stand from Jorram. Lyosan wastes no time running to their aid. When he reaches the scene, he sees Shaylynn in the middle of a fight. Two soldiers from Jorram surround him. Shaylynn seems weary, but he continues to fight on. Many bodies already litter the ground around him, but the toll of the day seems to have hit Shaylynn hard. Even now, it seems the Jorramians have the upper hand. Lyosan would give anything to get to his friend, but many other soldiers are between them. As Lyosan gets ready to enter the fray, his heart sinks as Shaylynn loses his footing and falls to the ground. One of the opposing soldiers raises his sword and prepares to strike. As he brings it down, an Artonian solider, who Lyosan quickly recognizes to be Fallon, intervenes and blocks the blow. Shaylynn recovers to attack the other soldier while Fallon finishes the first. After a show of appreciation, Shaylynn gives a quick instruction, points to a nearby hill, and he and Fallon split off and continue the fight. Shaylynn goes after a small contingent who have a few of the youths surrounded. Fallon ascends a hill looking to get a sense of where the battle stands. Not long into his endeavor, a line of soldiers comes across the hill after him. Fallon calls out for help as he begins running up the hill. The line has already cut him off from any means of escape. Shaylynn sees the peril and begins to run after Fallon. Along the way, he leaps onto a horse and takes off. Fallon disappears over the hill; the line of soldiers follow – as does Shaylynn.

Not long after, the battle ends. The forces of Artonia have proven victorious. Many of the Jorramian soldiers have surrendered or perished. Now, the southern forces who remain prepare a prison to keep their prisoners in. When the time comes, they will use those who remain to trade with Jorram. They will need more than they have to get the princess back, but in truth, Shaylynn meant for other means to reacquire the princess.

Those means will become moot however, if Shaylynn cannot be found. Since Lyosan saw him last, none have seen him again. As the youths come together and count their losses, they plan their next move. Stefen and Pythyn stand as the leaders of the troop. If Shaylynn and Fallon do not show, it will be up to them to decide what to do next. That prospect does not sit well with Lyosan.

"We need to find them," Lyosan demands.

"You are in no position to command," Pythyn responds.

"But I am," Stefen replies. "And he is right, we need to try to find our captain and his first in command."

"You assume they can be found?" Pythyn asks.

"You assume they're dead?" Stefen asks.

"I assume nothing," Pythyn replies, "but I do realize we have responsibilities which extend beyond those two. Another attack could be eminent, and our depleted forces will need to regroup quickly if the attack comes. Our protocol mandates we stay with the civilians for two days while they begin the reclamation of their towns. We will help as we are needed. During that time, if Shaylynn and Fallon return, we will tend to any wounds they have and welcome them back."

As Pythyn speaks, he says little which pleases Lyosan. Wherever Shaylynn and Fallon might be, they might be wounded to the point where they cannot move. Even if one of them is okay, he might not be able to get the other moving. But, surprisingly, Pythyn adds one more stipulation to his commands.

"Whenever I can spare them, I'll spend pairs into the woods to search for any sign of Shaylynn, Fallon, and any other member of our party. If you want to head up that endeavor, Lyosan, I'll let you have it. But no one goes off on his own."

Lyosan nods in appreciation. "Agreed. As long as I'm not needed, I'll be working with them."

Either because of a small measure of kindness or because of his usual disdain for Lyosan, Pythyn gives him every opportunity to go into the woods to search for the missing boys. Most of the discoveries they make are not ones which lead to celebrations. They do, however, get to give proper burials to many of their fallen brethren.

Luckily, none of the bodies they find are Shaylynn or Fallon. And it's not all bad news. They do find some of the missing boys alive. In bringing them back to the village and getting them the proper care, Lyosan loses some of the time he'd rather spend searching. On some level, it is frustrating, but it is also completely necessary. Since the attack from Jorram seems over and done with, the primary concern can center on rebuilding the area and tending to the wounded. Some of the injuries are quite severe. Whenever the youths do leave, they will have to take the journey slowly. Too much jostling and thrashing about could only exacerbate the situation and result in furthering the extent of the injury or even killing the boys.

And as the two days tick away, the youths find no sight of their lost commander or his first officer. Though they cannot confirm either is dead, the likelihood is growing higher and higher. As the second day comes to an end, Pythyn starts to round everything up. Lyosan continues to argue for more time, but Pythyn will not have it. On one level, Pythyn does not wish to do Lyosan any more favors. On another level, he remembers the warning Shaylynn gave him about returning to Langerwitz without Lyosan with him. Even if he has to tie Lyosan up and drag him back to Langerwitz, he will get Lyosan back to the castle.

Thus, when Lyosan offers to stay behind on his own, Pythyn will hear none of it. Nor will he consider leaving any of the youths behind. It is possible the king will continue in his other plans in sending an expedition to the north to attempt a rescue of the princess.

Pythyn does not intend to champion the idea, but he will, of course, follow his king's command. They have suffered many losses during this campaign, none bigger than Shaylynn and Fallon. Some seventy youths have perished in the fight, but they could still mount a campaign if they managed to find members of the royal guard. No doubt, the youths will be unable to mount an offensive against the capital of Jorram with just their current numbers. And, at least for the foreseeable future, they cannot ask the men of the south to join them. They are needed in their own homes to recoup the losses they have suffered. It will be a hard road ahead. They are greatly fortunate the attack did not reach the harbors. The people of those towns will be able to join the rebuilding efforts.

As some of the harbor men arrive, it confirms Pythyn's decision to have the troop take their leave. Lyosan continues to lobby for more time, but Pythyn stands by his ruling and commands the soldiers to head out. Lyosan tries appealing to Stefen, but Stefen cannot disagree with Pythyn's logic. Despite the desire to try to find Shaylynn, Fallon, and any other youth who may be out there, those gathered together here and now do need to return home. Not just for the logistical reasoning of following the king's commands, but also because the families deserve to know which of the youths survived and who will not be returning home. Services need to be held. Mothers need answers – even if the answers will bring great pain.

When Lyosan hears Stefen's reasons, he stops his arguing. Just the thought of family sparks a little longing in Lyosan's own heart. He has been away from his mother for longer periods of time, but he has certainly not faced such a harrowing ordeal. It would be good to see his brothers and start to put behind him some of the sights he witnessed. He still does not wish to give up hope for his friends, but it is clear staying in the southlands and searching aimlessly will do no good. He has to hope Shaylynn and Fallon can find their own way home. Until then, it will be very difficult to bring news of their disappearance to their family and loved ones. While everyone involved will take the news hard, Lyosan fears for Faith the most. Shaylynn is her most beloved cousin, and she just started showing her love for Fallon. The loss of both of them will hit her hard.

CHAPTER XI

As the youths begin their journey back to Langerwitz, Lyosan looks desperately around one last time. He knows in his heart the futility of this act, but he cannot stop hoping his friends will show themselves. Pythyn, sick of dealing with Lyosan's disruption, leads the youths out. Lyosan waits as long as possible, but it becomes clear he will have to leave with the others and without Shaylynn and Fallon. As expected, the ride back to the castle is slow. They had two days to get to the fight. They will take twice as long getting back. Tending to the wounded and making sure they have a comfortable journey weighs on those who are well. It is a constant reminder of the terrors they went through. Although the fight lies behind them, they cannot move past it until they reach home. The longer the return journey drags on, the worse the feelings get.

When the city finally appears on the horizon, many of the youth shed tears of joy and relief. They keep their cool and ensure the wounded remain the priority. As they come closer to the city, the gates open and a welcoming party comes out to greet them. Medics come to help with the wounded. Councilors of the king come to get a full report from Pythyn and Stefen. They brief the men and get escorted to the royal chamber. Lyosan rides in with the last of the riders. Families of the youths line the streets to try to catch a glimpse of their sons or brothers or cousins or friends. Many have already found whom they sought, but others are receiving the news or coming to the realization that their loved ones are not coming back. A few minutes after entering the city, a page approaches Lyosan and tells him to go to the castle. Lyosan has not found his family or any of Shaylynn and

Fallon's family. He cannot leave them wondering. They deserve to know what's going on. Lyosan informs the page he'll ride to the castle soon, and the page tells him not to wait too long.

Lyosan rides on through the city looking for Sarin, Faith, his mother, anyone. After searching for several minutes, he finds all of them waiting together close to the castle. Steel is the first to see him and yells out Lyosan's name loudly. Lyosan dismounts and goes to his family. Calvin leaps into his brother's arm, and Steel grabs Lyosan from the side. After a quick moment, Elle gets in on the action too, and the family is reunited once again.

The moment, however, cannot last long. Kandessa, Ellisia, Sarin, Faith, and Daylynn stand nearby wondering where the other two are. As Lyosan slowly pulls himself away from his own family, he lowers his head and approaches the waiting party. When he looks up, he sees Daylynn clutching his mother's leg. Sarin and Faith are holding each other's hands while Ellisia and Kandessa try to stand strong for the others. Lyosan draws a deep breath to explain what happened, but he cannot say the words when the time comes. Instead, he chokes up and coughs a bit. Seeing how hard this is for him, Kandessa steps forward. Daylynn stays right with her.

"Are they...dead?" she asks.

At the sound of the word, Sarin and Faith both tremble. Lyosan looks into Kandessa's eyes and shrugs his shoulders.

"I don't know," Lyosan manages to say.

"What happened?"

"We were in different battalions." Lyosan explains. "I didn't see much of them during the fighting, but at the end of the last day, I caught a glimpse of them. Lyosan saved Shaylynn, and then Shaylynn turned around and did the same. Before I could get to them, they took off into the woods, and I never saw them again."

Sarin steps forward. She stumbles a bit, and Kandessa steadies her.

"Then, you didn't see them fall?" Sarin asks.

"No," Lyosan replies.

Faith can't manage a smile, but she feels a bit of hope. "Were they injured?"

"Not that I saw," Lyosan says.

"Are they coming home?" Daylynn asks.

"Of course they are," Lyosan replies.

Kandessa smiles at Lyosan's hope and kneels down to Daylynn. His eyes are red, and his lip is trembling. But his mother's words can still solve the problem.

"You know your brother promised to return," Kandessa tells him.

"Then how come he didn't come back with Lyosan?" Daylynn asks.

"He and Fallon might have some special work to complete for the king," Ellisia replies. "Your brother is very important, you know."

Daylynn smiles. "I know."

With the news relayed and everyone seemingly taking it well, Lyosan leaves to meet with the king. When he reaches the king's chamber, Stefen, Pythyn, and three other youths are already gathered around the throne. King Cyrus has been awaiting Lyosan's arrival – mostly because he knows Shaylynn will have confided in Lyosan on the way to the south. Now that the youths have returned, they need to plan the next move.

Lyosan walks in and sees concerned looks on the faces of the youths. The king is deep in thought as Lyosan approaches. Pythyn paces back and forth with his arms folded. As is normally the case, Pythyn is not pleased Lyosan is a part of these discussions.

A few feet before he reaches the throne, Lyosan goes down to a knee and bows to the king. Cyrus stands and bids Lyosan to rise. He asks if the accounts he's heard from the others are the same in Lyosan's eyes – they are. He asks if it is true Lyosan argued so often to stay in the south – it is. Cyrus is not pleased to hear that. Lyosan explains himself, but it does no good.

"I'm afraid we cannot waste time worrying about the loss of Shaylynn and Fallon," Cyrus says with a heavy heart. "We have larger concerns. The south may be safe, but we must look to the north now. The princess remains a captive of Jorram. How we will get her back, I do not know."

"Have we any news from the north?" Stefen asks.

"Pages have returned," Cyrus replies, "but they have not seen any sign of the knights or the royal guard. Citizens of the northern villages cannot be of assistance. They need to protect themselves against northern raiders. If we are to act, it will be us alone. I cannot lie – I do not see much success coming from such an endeavor."

"I agree," Pythyn quickly says. "We were lucky to bring home as many as we did. The force we faced in the south was not the best Jorram could send. They will most definitely defend their capital better. A handful of youths cannot hope to stand up to that."

"What of a covert operation?" Lyosan suggests.

"We have not the knowledge of the capital nor the training for such an ordeal," Darrow says. "Who among us could even begin to formulate the strategy for such an operation?"

The youths look around at each other. They know there is only one answer to the question, but that answer is not an option right now. With Shaylynn gone, the best chance of succeeding is gone with him.

"Then, you see the dilemma," Cyrus says. "We haven't the means or the will."

"I would go!" Lyosan declares.

A void of silence fills the air after the declaration. Though Lyosan stands tall and confident, none stand with him. He is no captain. How could he ever hope to be king?

"Your heart is inspiring, Lyosan," Cyrus commends, "but it may also be foolish. Do not let your emotions completely cloud your logic."

The talks continue for a while longer. Nothing comes of them. There will be no endeavor to the north unless something or someone else comes to their aid. As much as they cannot stand to, they must wait. Their best chance is not with the force they currently possess. It will have to come later when they have more men or a better opportunity. They know they will hear nothing from Jorram. Jorram is content to sit and wait for Cyrus to give in to their demands.

In the meantime, memorials are held for the youths who gave their lives in the south. The king holds a special service in honor of their sacrifice. Sadly, some of the youths who made the return journey have simply suffered too much and pass shortly after returning home. It is a difficult time in Langerwitz – mothers having to bury their sons. Hope seemingly dissipating with each passing day. As the mood of the city wanes, so too does the health of the king. The illness which will one day take his life hits hard while all the other despair permeates the city. Though no other bad news reaches the capital, the lack of information almost seems worse. For all they can do, the city learns nothing of the princess, the knights, the royal guard, or Shaylynn and Fallon.

Time passes. As it does, even the weather begins to turn sour. Rain pours through the lands. Cyrus will risk no further moves to the north. Most of the youths still rest from their excursion to the south. Efforts continue with great success to rebuild and remake the towns. Forces in the north look to the borders with great caution. Meanwhile, those in Langerwitz prepare for their next move, though none knows what that next move should be. While Pythyn would lead if directed, he does not believe he could successfully mount an offensive into the heart of Jorram. Though Lyosan's beliefs are quite contrary, he can offer little more than his desire to see the princess safe as his call to action. He has no plan, no course of action, no knowledge to support any action he might consider taking. As is such, he can say nothing. He can only hope some answer soon shows itself.

It has been several weeks since the youths' return from the south. No word of any other survivors is heard. Still, Kandessa refuses to hold vigil for Shaylynn, and, out of respect, Ellisia joins in as well. Even Daylynn seems in high spirits with the idea his brother will soon return. Lyosan visits him every day and revels in the way Daylynn carries on. He wishes he could be the same. The king, showing some signs of optimism, has begun discussions with the youths regarding the tournament. With Shaylynn, Fallon, and a couple other participants missing, they must decide what to do. Pythyn immediately suggests replacing the missing and dead so the tournament can continue as normal. Lyosan objects, but the king can see no other way.

One seemingly ordinary night, outside the castle wall, two riders in black approach at great speed. Guards along the southern wall cannot see the riders' approach, but they are alerted to the sound of the gates opening. One looks across the top of the wall and at the back side of the gate. The beam across the lock lifts from its perch, apparently on its own, and drops harmlessly to the ground. The guard raises the alarm to the others holding watch, all of whom draw weapons as they surround the gate.

The general alarm spreads through town and reaches the castle within minutes. Guards surround the main hall where Cyrus gathers with his council. Some ladies of the court, including Sarin and Faith, were in the main hall before the ordeal began. They shall be kept there now for safety. In a short time, Pythyn, Lyosan, and others will be summoned. For now, the guards at the gate look to hold their position.

Still, no sign of the approaching danger. The gate, unencumbered by its lock, begins to swing open. A series of guards rush the gate and attempt to keep it closed. For a moment, their efforts are successful. However, the gate swings back open quite forcefully as though a burst of energy forces them open. Several of the guards fall away from the gate. The others try in vain to push harder. Eventually, the gates open completely and pin the guards by the doors against the wall. The others form ranks under the command of the recently arrived captain.

"What's the situation?" he demands.

The guard who first became aware of the situation steps forwards and speaks quite nervously. "U-u-unknown, sir," he replies. "The beam lifted off the gate by itself. We can see no one from the watchtower. Aside from the opening of the gate, there has been no disturbance."

"Are you suggesting a gate opening by itself is not disturbing enough?"

"No, sir."

In the distance, they begin to hear the trample of horses. No more than a whisper to begin with, it rapidly increases in volume. The captain commands silence as he steps forward to assess the situation.

"It's a small troop," he declares. "No more than eight. Archers! Stand on post!"

From above, the arches draw arrows to their bows and pull the strings taught. At best, they will have one shot, and they must make it count. The others will be taken out by the guards on the ground. Still, given the weakened state of the city, they must give every precaution they can.

Moments later, the sound of the horses echoes about. Surely, the small number will be in sight in a matter of moments. As the moment of battle approaches, the adrenaline rushes faster. Hands begin to twitch. Beads of sweat form on the brows of the soldiers. None know what lies in wait, but they must realize their numbers make them the superior force. If there are only eight, they shall fall with ease. Perhaps that is why, the shock of only two gave them a moment of pause. Under normal circumstances, this pause would not be so costly, but these were not normal circumstances. For, in a flash, the two riders strode past the guards, and the horses flew into the air clearing the line with ease. A second later they were riding off towards the castle.

"Signal the castle!" the captain commands. "The riders will reach them in mere moments!"

Soldiers run to and fro, carrying out the orders. The only one who does not move is the guard who first saw the ordeal begin. Instead, he stands in awe. "How could there be only two?" he asks the captain.

Before the captain can answer, the gate closes behind them.

Alarms are raised throughout the town. The riders ride in a blur under the cover of night. Yet, they know once they reach the castle, their task shall become increasingly difficult. Proof comes to them in the sight of the castle guard coming forward in the night with torches and weapons at arms.

Within the castle, Lyosan enters the main hall. Cyrus sits on the throne. Sarin and Faith sit off to the side. Dragoon, Nycolas, and Pythyn have arrived already. They arm themselves with swords and stand around the throne.

"Lyosan," Faith cries when she sees him.

Lyosan rushes to her side and bows respectfully.

"What do you know?" she asks.

"Very little," Lyosan admits.

"Not surprising," Pythyn mutters under his breath.

"Two riders breached the southern defenses only moments ago," Lyosan continues. "It is believed they will reach the castle within mere moments."

"How is that possible?" Cyrus asks.

"They must be aided by magic of some sort," Lyosan replies. As the words leave his lips, an idea forms in his head. He does not dare bring it forward, not after all the defenses have been raised. However, if his thought is correct, the riders will not require his assistance.

"Riders from the south," Pythyn pontificates, "where many villages were sacked. Surely, these are agents of Jorram continuing their mission."

"Have they shown hostility?" Cyrus asks.

"They've breached the city," a soldier replies. "They make no effort to claim friendship; they must be enemies."

"Perhaps," Sarin interjects, for she too has had the same thought as Lyosan. Fortunately, she holds the proper place to speak her mind. "But many others were lost in the south. Perhaps they return now."

"Who?" Pythyn asks, "Who would possess the means to do this?"

"I think you know," Sarin replies.

Outside the castle, the guards take their posts and take aim at the riders. Again, adrenaline begins to rise. Fingers twitch while they keep the line pressed between themselves. The moment of battle stands before them, but they know this is no battle they have ever fought before. As the riders fast approach the wall, their courage hangs by a thread. They've already come this far – can they really be stopped?

"Archers! Volley!" the captain cries.

Without hesitation, the archers release and send a rain of arrows towards the riders. Watching with anticipation, the archers gaze to the dark sky to see the vague mass of arrows move towards the intended victims. As they drop down towards the ground, the arrows whisk in the fine, cool air. The rider in the lead raises his head towards the sky as he heard the cry for the barrage. Waiting for just the proper moment, he thrusts his hands towards the sky. Though nothing seems to come of it, the archers take note of a thin haze suddenly forming above the riders. It is little more than a blur in their vision, but the archers fear it. Before they can give it much thought, the salvo lands upon the haze and comes to a sudden stop. Moments later, the riders pass under the spot where the arrows would've landed and continue to the castle. The arrows drop harmlessly to the ground.

Rendered speechless by the sight, the archers fumble with their quivers in a futile attempt to grab another arrow. Still, the riders approach the castle walls. A battalion comes out from the castle gate with spears drawn. The riders do not slow in their progress and instead hasten their approach. Cries echo from the soldiers about holding the line and where to go and what to do. Throughout it all, the riders come closer and closer. Orders ring out, commanding the gate be closed and locked, but none move to protect the gate. Instead, the riders approach the line and again take to the air. They soar over the soldiers and land within the castle walls. At this point, the first leaps from his horse and lands a few feet from the castle door. Within moments, he is surrounded by the guards who aim the points of their spears at the intruder. The second also jumps down from his horse.

"Hold," the second says, "we mean no harm!"

"I see no sign of that!" the captain replies. "Seize them!"

Before the soldiers move, the second makes a final plea. "I cannot be responsible for what happens next."

"Nor can I," the captain replies.

With one more signal from the captain, the guards advance on the first. After a deep breath, the first draws in his hands then releases in a pushing motion. A wave of wind strikes all around him throwing the guards to the ground. Drawing his sword, he begins to flail about, striking the guards with the blunt of his blade. He makes no attempt to impale his victims or bring about their death. Rather, he takes great care in striking his advancers to cause them as little damage as possible while removing them from the fray. Within minutes, he clears enough space to reach the castle door. The second follows along while the captain calls for the archers to fire upon the riders.

As the second closes the door behind them, the arrows strike the other side of the door. The riders hope for a momentary pause in their assault to gather their wits and perhaps bring this all to an end, but the guards in the castle are quick to respond to their arrival. Again, the first wields his blade looking to stun but not kill or injure. The second also now enters the battle, but he is not so willing to test his skill with the blade. Instead, he tries his best to pin the guards to the wall to keep his companion and him moving in their purpose. After traveling far, they do not wish to be detained any further. In a matter of moments, they could achieve their goal and be in the king's main hall. However, they do not have the time nor the opportunity to explain themselves to these soldiers.

Instead, they battle through the waves of men who come after them. Using the hall to their advantage, they keep the guards from encircling them. The first deals with most of the onslaught while the second cleans up the mess and keeps the first from being blindsided. After some time passes, the first becomes irritated with their lack of progress and clears some room. After a swipe of his arm, the lights in the room go out. The guards call for new lights, but none can be made. No spark will catch for minutes. As time passes, the fear grows. They know not where the riders are, but every moment they expect them to strike. Not a single guard has realized the mercy of the riders in sparing them from serious harm and worse. They only know the castle is threatened and must be protected. So, as the lights begin to catch, they once more raise their swords and prepare for battle. The only problem is when they see the spot where the riders stood, the riders are no longer there.

Pandemonium follows. Panic reaches a new height. Through the halls runs every guard with sword in hand. Some almost impale their comrades as they come around corners and out of dark spaces.

Within the main hall, Cyrus stands on alert. No word has come to him about the progress nor has anyone broken through the door. The situation still hangs in the balance. Either good or bad can still come from this, but those inside cannot know which way the tide is turning. While Cyrus can stand tall and hope for the best, some are not so lucky. Faith, having lost so much already in family and friends, quakes in her shoes. Sarin holds her and tries to provide some comfort, but little can be done while danger still lurks. The young guardians of the citadel stand – swords drawn and ready to strike. Belief guides them that whatever comes through the door will need a swift and quick end.

Several tense-filled minutes pass with still no word. No one comes to the door, and no one signals any news through the normal means. All activity has seemingly come to a peaceful lull – the only thing which could inspire more fear than action. And when the tension reaches a level that none think they could possibly stand, a bang strikes at the door.

"They are here!" Pythyn exclaims stepping with wicked purpose towards the door.

"Be wary!" Cyrus warns. "They've come this far; they will not be dealt with easily."

"We shall see about that," Pythyn replies.

Sarin strengthens her hold on Faith who clings to her friend even more. Though Faith only acts in fear of what is coming, Sarin fears what will become of them. In her heart, she holds the hope she dares not mention aloud. Should the extreme rarity of her hope come to fruition, she fears those who protect the king will strike without thought. Pythyn's eyes show a desire for blood. Either he or those who come will die before the night has an end. The rest of the guard shows the same sentiment.

Again, a bang on the doors. Those inside begin to hear the wood crack from the assault. With the cracking of the doors, the guards' resolve strengthens. The grip on their weapons tighten, and the anger within them rises.

A third bang sounds on the doors. More cracks form in the wood. The tops of the doors begin to buckle under the stress. The locks cannot hold the force of the blows for much longer. Still, the guards cannot surrender their position should the doors fall.

On the fourth strike, the doors give out. Bursting open and almost flying off the hinges, the doors break open and a cloud of dust blocks everyone's view. At the first sign of movement, Pythyn calls for a charge and all follow. No sooner do they enter the cloud of dust than they are thrown back with great force against the wall. Stunned, they drop their weapons and writhe on the floor. The dust clears and the riders appear. The first leads the way with no weapon drawn. The second soon follows with a sword in hand. Cyrus steps down from his throne and draws his weapon.

The others around him cower away – save one.

Sarin, still hoping for her miracle, steps forward as she loosens her hold on Faith. Concerned and confused, Faith attempts to pull Sarin back, but Sarin shakes free.

"What are you doing?" Faith asks.

"Is it him?" Sarin asks with tears in her eyes.

"Who?"

Before Sarin can say more, the king steps forward.

"Stand down!" he commands.

The first does nothing but turn to the second. They say nothing in reply but hold their ground.

"I am Cyrus Wuhlfies, ruler of Langerwitz, King of Artonia," Cyrus continues. "Either stand down and make your demands known or declare yourself enemy of my lands!"

The riders consider the king's request for a moment before the first gives a reply. "Demands?" the first repeats. "What could we demand of a king?"

With the sound of his voice, Sarin begins to tremble. Faith takes her hand to keep her steady though she still does not understand. If not overcome with emotion, Sarin would explain, but she can barely draw breath to her lungs. Besides, Faith will soon see the cause for her anxiety. For as they watch, the second rider places his sword on the ground, and both riders kneel before the king.

Taken aback, the king looks to his subjects within the room. When he sees Sarin and the hope alive in her eyes, he looks back to the riders with hope of his own. Yet, he cannot give in to that hope with so much at stake. If this is what it appears, he cannot stand the nerve of these riders to perpetrate such an ordeal.

"Show yourselves!" he demands.

Lowering the cloaks over their heads, the riders raise their heads and reveal themselves. For the next few moments, stunned silence fills the air. For there, in front of them, stand Shaylynn, son of Feylynn, and Fallon, son of Degon.

Lyosan, one of the few who did not join the charge, stands in awe. He can do nothing but drop his sword to the ground. The clang of the blade echoes in the silent hall. Even those on the ground ignore their anguish in light of this revelation. The captain of the youth and his first lieutenant lost in battle now returned to them in an hour of desperation. A miracle of their greatest hopes come to fruition when all around them seemed to be lost.

But, for others, there is more than two soldiers before them. For that reason, Sarin is the first to break the silence. With a muffled cry, she races across the room. Shaylynn rises just in time to catch her in his arms. As tears fall from her cheeks, Sarin kisses Shaylynn with an impassioned relief.

Fallon steps past their reunion and looks to Faith. Once the shock of the moment wears away, she smiles and runs to him. The fear of the assault is gone, and for the first time in a long while, Faith can welcome joy back into her heart. She has her cousin back, but more importantly, she has Fallon back. And while they had kissed each other before, never had they truly done it as lovers. But now, knowing what was in their hearts was true, they reached for each other and kissed each other's lips.

But more was in play here than just these two pairs of lovers. The king and the best of his remaining guard stood disarmed both physically and mentally at the display set before them. Two men, two youths of the court, with nothing more than two horses and the blunt side of a sword breeched the castle defenses and came within feet of the king. Truly, what was the meaning of these actions?

Shaylynn, sensing the confusion in the room, reluctantly pulls away from Sarin. She holds him in her arms for a moment longer to ensure reality is not deceiving her. Shaylynn brushes a lock of her hair out of her eyes. She revels in his touch.

"I knew you were not dead," she says.

"I dared not die when I'd promised to return this to you," he replies referencing the necklace she gave him. He begins to unlock the clasp when she raises her hands and stops him.

"Keep it," she says. "If it will keep you alive, never take it off."

They smile again and share a quick kiss. Shaylynn turns to see Faith still in Fallon's arms. She reaches for her cousin, and he extends a hand to her. She grasps it firmly to say all the things she is too choked up to say. He smiles at her and kisses her hand as family does. She chokes up again and buries herself deeper in Fallon's chest.

Then, Shaylynn looks to Lyosan who has become merely a spectator in this ordeal. Shaylynn nods and places his fisted hand over his heart. Lyosan smiles and returns the gesture. If not in the presence of the king, Lyosan would speak candidly with his friends, but he realizes these theatrics are not in vain. There is reason for everything Shaylynn does, and the reason for this must be good.

Finally, Shaylynn addresses the king.

"My lord," he says with a bow.

"Enough of your propriety, Shaylynn," Cyrus replies. "What is the meaning of all this?"

"Indeed!" Pythyn, finally recovered from the ordeal, agrees. "How dare you not immediately show yourself when you arrived at the southern gate! Instead, you bring all this chaos and tomfoolery!"

"We did not know the status of the city when we arrived," Shaylynn explains. "When we were lost in the south, the battle was not in hand. For all we knew, the agents of the enemy had won the battle and continued north. It was not until we were well within the city that we understood the king was safe."

"Then why not reveal yourself then?" Pythyn demands.

Shaylynn shrugs with a coy smile. "It had become too much fun by then."

Cyrus rolls his eyes and breaks into laughter. Pythyn, still fuming, does not accept the reasoning.

"How can you…" he begins.

"Enough Pythyn," Cyrus commands. Reluctantly, Pythyn obeys and holds his tongue. Cyrus, somewhat relieved to have one of his captains back, still holds a bit of animosity for Shaylynn's youthful indiscretion.

"Foolish, young squire," Cyrus scolds. "Attempting to break the defenses of the capitol of a kingdom. Fighting hand to hand with soldiers meaning to kill. Just what gives you the gumption to brave such an endeavor?"

"Purpose, my lord," Shaylynn replies.

Intrigued, Cyrus nods and a thoughtful disposition crosses his face. As he strokes his chin, he takes the throne and turns back to Shaylynn.

"Explain yourself," Cyrus demands.

"While absent from my charge I have become convinced of two truths which have taken some time to come to terms with," Shaylynn begins. "The first is perhaps the most important – I shall lead the charge into Jorram to rescue the princess…"

Shaylynn pauses should the king attempt to change his mind. Yet he also hopes the king's desire to see his sister returned to him will overcome any doubts he holds. For the moment, that seems to be the case, as the king only replies with a question.

"And the second?"

Shaylynn pauses again for the pain of the second revelation. More than the first, this revelation was nearly impossible to accept. Upon realizing it, he had not spoken of it to anyone. Only Fallon, because of his involvement in the matter, knows what Shaylynn is about to say. And as for him, Fallon shares in this pain.

Finally, after a deep breath, Shaylynn continues. "That my father, brother, and all of the knights of your court…are dead."

He fights tears as he attempts to stand tall. Sarin immediately comes to his side and takes his hand. He squeezes her hand to show his appreciation. The king, sobered by this revelation, gives Shaylynn a moment to collect himself. However, the promise of rescuing the princess still lingers in the air. Plus, some within the court are not so willing to believe Shaylynn's claims.

"How would you know this?" Pythyn asks. "You could not have traveled to the north to learn of the knights' fate."

"Show some decency!" Sarin scolds.

Oddly, Shaylynn moves to calm Sarin's rage. "He is right to doubt me," Shaylynn says. "I'm sure he is not the only one."

Shaylynn looks to the king to confirm his suspicion. The king nods that he indeed is uncertain of the information. After asserting the loss of his family, the king will not be quick to speak out against Shaylynn's word. Furthermore, he knows Shaylynn would not bring such outrageous claims without some measure of proof. Out of respect for his possible loss, the king will give Shaylynn the opportunity to explain himself before he makes his judgment.

"It is perhaps worth noting that my abilities within the magical realm have improved since last you saw me," Shaylynn says.

"An understatement," Cyrus replies.

In this way, Shaylynn begins to recant the tale of what he and Fallon endured after the events in the southern lands. So also do come forward the trials and tribulations experienced by one who delved further into magic than any of his generation or the generation before him.

CHAPTER XII

For after Shaylynn and Fallon disappeared over the hill that day nearly a month ago, they battled a force which numbered seven. The soldiers chased Fallon for miles before he stopped to take a stand. Shaylynn followed as best he could, but he lost a step at several points along the way. When he finally found his friend again, Fallon, already having to overcome the disadvantage of being separated from his horse, tried valiantly to defend his position. Down by the river he fought and held his own, but he could not last forever. With great resolve and reckless abandon, Shaylynn entered the fray. Upon his steed, he cleared a space for Fallon and struck down two of the Jorramians. He prepared to take another when one of the attackers shot an arrow into the sternum of Shaylynn's horse. Rearing back and crying out in pain, the horse threw Shaylynn and ran for safety.

While Shaylynn lain on the ground, a Jorramian solder raced over and raised his sword above his head. As he brought his strike forward, Fallon leapt and blocked the blow with his blade. Shaylynn immediately recovered his weapon and stabbed the assaulter. Down to four opponents, the two battled on, but they incurred their own injuries. Furthermore, the battle took much out of them. Shaylynn fell unconscious from exhaustion as they finished the fight and Fallon had not the strength to bear him as a burden. Fearing for his friend's safety, Fallon would not leave Shaylynn's side, but instead tended to Shaylynn's wounds.

It would be nearly a day before Shaylynn awoke again. When he does, Fallon has a little food and some water prepared for him.

"Where are we?" Shaylynn asks.

"I know not for certain," Fallon replies.

"Are we alone?"

"Yes."

With that, Shaylynn begins to stir. Though his pain is great, he feels the need to get back to his troop. Fallon, respecting his friend's resolve, knows Shaylynn has not the strength to carry on. Before Shaylynn can get too far, Fallon gently pushes him back to the ground.

"Stay where you are," he says. "Even if you had the strength to move, I know not the way to take us back."

Shaylynn slumps back on the ground. He feels around on the ground searching for his sword. It is nowhere to be found. Rolling slightly onto his side, he sees the blade in the sand by the river. He does not believe an attack is eminent, but he knows to be prepared. What he does not know is Fallon has already taken several measures to ensure their safety. Even had he known, Shaylynn would most likely still stir. The situation before him causes great concern. He knows not if the knights of Langerwitz have defeated the forces or Jorram or if they continue to roam free. In any event, the forces will be moving soon whether for Artonia or Jorram. Neither will linger long with the journey ahead of them. Should Fallon and Shaylynn not recover quickly and find their party, the worst will be assumed.

But the strength is not within him. Shaylynn cannot continue along this way. He must rest especially if they cannot make it to the troops before they depart. The more times passes, the more the possibility becomes reality.

For his part, Fallon attempts to continue on as though nothing has changed. He understands the situation but also feels fortunate to have survived this long. He too fears for the safety of his comrades and ponders their fate. More than that however, he ponders the situation he is now in with Shaylynn. Surely some attempts will be made to find their way back home, but he cannot figure out what can be done. The paths that might lead them back to the village have been trampled and never has he journeyed through these lands before. They are in the wild for certain. They cannot expect help to come to them; they must help themselves. Given their circumstances, that means but one thing – follow the river. It will be a long journey since they will have to travel south before they reach Lakwood, but they have few options. Despite the extra time the river will add, it will inevitably lead them home. But what dangers lurk along the river are truly unknown and with but the two of them, what chances do they stand?

Then, there is the wild card of his company. If he was to be stranded with only one companion, there is no doubt he would choose Shaylynn. In matters such as these, Shaylynn has shown his ability to come out on the better end. But, he is wounded. Even now, he can barely keep himself awake. Can he recover enough to use his abilities to guide them? Is there any part of his abilities that would be of help? Fallon has seen him advance in battle and athletic prowess, but what about this situation? Even if he would want to use his magic, could it find the troops if they were already on their way? If not, could it alert them to the oncoming presence of the Jorramians? Too many questions, Fallon realizes. Too many questions to consider when the first aspect of their condition is clear – they must get well enough to travel.

Two days by the river, they stay. During the first, Shaylynn begins to rise to his feet. He stands for a few minutes, gains his balance, and by the end of the day, he can walk about. When he tries, he cannot lift the sword to defend himself. Clearly, he's risked too much in the battles prior. He's gone too far beyond his body's capability despite the amount he managed to accomplish. Caution is required. He must understand the limits of his being, as much as he might want to ignore them. Thus, he waits by the river as Fallon goes after lunch. It is not difficult to find food this deep in the wild. Fallon returns with a couple rabbits and a bag of berries. They eat quickly, and soon into the afternoon, Shaylynn begins to test his limits again. He fares better, but he is still not ready to travel. Nonetheless, he forages for food that night with Fallon. Even in his weakened state, he manages almost as good as his friend. They eat and sleep that night. In the morning, Shaylynn rises first and goes for breakfast on his own. He struggles along at times, but he succeeds in his endeavor.

This is enough proof to him he will be ready to move in the afternoon. Fallon assures him they can wait longer. Surely, the youths, if they proved victorious, have moved on. If they have fallen, the time away from the invading forces will give them a better chance at surprise. Yet Shaylynn cannot deny the need to move on. He knows one way or the other, they must move along. Their time of rest has passed; their time of battle is just beginning.

Traveling light and quick, they follow the river to the south and the east. A good deal of the way they travel in the open. People are few and far between. What's more, neither Shaylynn nor Fallon plans to rest until nightfall. The more they go, the more Shaylynn's strength returns to him. His gait seems easier and unencumbered. Fallon smiles the more he sees it. Given Shaylynn's state the first day, Fallon did not think they'd be on their way this soon. With their current pace, they may be within the castle walls within the week. That night, they find a place to rest in the wild. Again, they forage and find themselves sustenance. Before they rest for the night, they speak of their fears for their friends.

"Do you know anything?" Fallon questions.

Shaylynn hesitates. "There is some discomfort in me."

"But you know not why," Fallon assumes.

"It is unclear at this point. I sense all is not well, but I cannot find the source of the disturbance."

Fallon frowns and sighs deeply. "Have you any inclination as to the state of Langerwitz?"

Shaylynn hears the need for news within his friend's voice, but he will not lie to him. There would be no comfort in such a lie. "I cannot say with certainty or honesty," Shaylynn replies. "But I have no cause to say it has fallen."

There is little comfort in such a response. Uncertainty is its own fear that goes beyond the responsibility of knowing. Fallon searches for answers with only his eyes or ears to bring him answers. Shaylynn searches with something more yet yields the same results. And in that lack, there is a world of possibility. How can they find rest with such a world before them?

"I fear for them," Fallon finally admits.

"Them?" Shaylynn inquires.

"My mother, my aunt and uncles, cousins…Faith." Fallon pauses a moment to let this sink in with Shaylynn. They've rarely discussed the matter of Fallon's feelings for Faith, and when they did, they did so lightly. Being away from her this long has solidified the feeling in Fallon's heart. He does not wish to hide from it any longer. "I love her, Shaylynn."

Fallon knows not what reaction to expect from Shaylynn. At this moment, he does not care what reaction might be given. He's denied this truth far too long.

"It's not exactly a secret," Shaylynn finally replies.

"Do you approve?" Fallon asks.

Shaylynn is in shock. "What?"

"Were I to marry her someday, would you give it your blessing?"

"My blessing," Shaylynn repeats. "As though it holds some weight." Shaylynn pauses to consider. Fallon cannot wait for a reply. He must know now.

"Would you?" he prods.

"That a man I already call brother should enter my family through marriage," Shaylynn explains. "Yes, yes, I would approve of that. In truth, if you do not take her hand, then I will have some complaint with you."

Fallon rests easier with that information – not enough to get a completely restful slumber but enough to help get some rest. He rises early with Shaylynn, and they continue on their path. After a day and a half's travel they come upon Forleen Forest. This provides them two benefits: the first being Forleen will give them a place to rest for the night, the second that after pooling in the DaReen Lake, the river will flow to the Lakwood and put them on the proper route to Langerwitz. However, there is, to some, a significant danger in traveling through this forest. As has been written over the past century, something lurks within the forest. Many have come; few have survived. The stories range from beast and bird to men of unusual strength and ability. Some even claimed the men of these woods were as large as a full-grown bear. They supposedly moved with the grace and speed of jungle cats.

But these are merely stories to most – folk tales told to frighten children made all the more potent by the sight of the forest. The trees lurch before those who prepare to enter. The collection of them is so dense it is hard for light to penetrate the borders. It is heavy with animals, so sound pervades the air with every breath one takes. Still, the advantage it provides dwarfs any childhood fears of the land. Hence, Shaylynn and Fallon do not linger long before entering the forest.

"It's bigger than I thought it would be," Fallon remarks.

Shaylynn scowls. "It's a forest. How do you underestimate the size of a forest?"

Fallon, toying with Shaylynn more than anything, smiles as he steps towards the trees. "I don't know," Fallon replies, "but something about the stories made it seem much more compact than it actually is."

Shaylynn shakes his head. "Maybe I don't want you in my family."

Upon entering the forest, they find their pace greatly slowed by the foliage in the woods. The river begins to snake unexpectedly and thick plant coverage makes it nearly impossible to follow the river directly. Instead, they must circle around quite often in order to find the river again.

Though they have no encounters with animals of any kind, they can hear them all around them as they travel. From time to time, they think the shadows move out of place. However, these sights are nothing more than misinterpreted images from the corners of their eyes. In the moment, the movements are forgotten, ignored, or disregarded. In time, they will see the error of their shortsightedness.

"How long do you think we've traveled?" Shaylynn asks.

"Not nearly the distance we'd expect for the time we've traveled," Fallon replies.

"At this pace, our journey will be lengthened by a day at least."

Shaylynn slices through some of the tree limbs in front of him to create a path. Helping to clear the way, Fallon hacks through some of the tall reeds so they can see the river's progress. They have just managed to find it again and appear to have some luck in that it straightens out for a bit.

"Perhaps we can make up some ground," Fallon says hopefully. "We appear to have a clear path for a while."

"I can only hope," Shaylynn replies. "I assume the day is almost done. Perhaps this will give us a place to rest."

"It certainly looks better than any place we've seen thus far."

"We just need to find some food nearby."

They begin to set up camp and hunt for their dinner. This proves to be much more difficult than previous days. For though they've heard the cries of many a forest animal, they can find no true trace of their existence. Before, when they meant to merely pass through the forest, they did not notice this absence of evidence, but now, it is all too clear to them. Despite the sounds around them, there are no animals nearby. With this revelation, Shaylynn begins to revisit those moments when the shadows seemed to move with distinct purpose. When they appeared to stretch beyond their simple means and take on a different life. The stories, he still tells himself, cannot be true, but perhaps some element of the truth lies within them. Something may still protect this forest, be it magic of some variety or some unseen force. If he plans to uncover the mystery, he must act with extreme caution. For he has already begun to sense it – death has taken place in this forest. And not death by natural means.

Quietly, without speaking, he relays his plan to Fallon. They will gather what they can to provide some manner of dinner. Then, under the guise of preserving energy, they will turn in for the night. A force that lingers in the shadow will surely attack when night falls. When it does, Fallon and Shaylynn will only have one chance to strike back.

They gather what they can – mostly fruits from trees and bushes. They replenish their canteens and divide what little they've kept along the way. While they eat, Shaylynn gauges the area around him. He dares not look suspiciously. Instead, he scans with his mind. This skill is still relatively new to him; thus, he cannot detect much. It is much like the unease he feels for home – only here, in the woods, it is stronger. Fallon nervously follows Shaylynn's example. He cannot detect even the slightest disturbance, so he constantly looks to Shaylynn to ensure they're safe for the moment. Once they've eaten, they clear a spot on the ground and lay down for the night. Shaylynn throws an extra log on the fire but feels they will not be around long enough for it to burn out.

They both feign sleep though sleep comes for them quickly. Fallon keeps one eye open while Shaylynn continues to see with closed eyes. Yet after the long day of travel, both are weary. They still need rest though they cannot necessarily afford to let their guard down. In his mind, Shaylynn begins to question the wisdom of entering this forest. Surely, they could have circled around the border and still found the river on the other side. It would have added days to their journey, but at least they would've been safe.

As they lay in wait, the shadows begin to stir. Coming together, they prepare to enact their attack. Not beasts, nor creatures of the dark, but men begin to show themselves. Men with the cunning and stealth only achieved through a close connection to nature. On the ground, the grass barely bends when they walk by. Those in the trees do not rustle the branches more than a subtle breeze. But Shaylynn knows there is no breeze tonight. Even their gentle rustle gives them away. They are coming for the two knights who've entered the forest. They suspect they have an easy mark, but they overestimate their hand.

As the knights lay on the ground, the men creep slowly towards the two intruders. Without a sound, they draw their weapons and prepare to strike. The one in the lead turns to signal to the others to encircle their prey. He turns his head for but one second, and when he comes back, Shaylynn is standing in front of him with the point of his sword at the man's throat.

"Yield," Shaylynn commands.

"I think not," the man replies.

The rest of the attackers step up and point their swords at Shaylynn. More in the shadows, unseen until now, draw the strings of their bows and take aim. Fallon, also on his feet, stands back-to-back with Shaylynn and tries to find one opponent to focus on. Shaylynn's eyes remain fixed.

"Yield," Shaylynn says again.

The man laughs. "Do you really think you stand a chance? You were barely able to detect our presence."

"There are seven of you surrounding us at this moment. Two are relatively competent, three are somewhat nervous, and the two at your flank are shaking in their boots. You have a dozen archers in the trees, none of them at a proper firing angle. In order for them to be effective, you've got to move us into an open position. However, you've encircled us, so we cannot be in an open position. Furthermore, the darkness provides little opportunity for a successful shot. Seven of the archers have the confidence to shoot, four have the ability to hit consistently, but only two can hit from the trees. Assuming I disarm you, keep the circle of your men around us, it'll take roughly five minutes with minimal opportunity for damage to properly disarm the rest. Then, we take to the shadows and deal with your archers one by one."

The man, somewhat impressed by Shaylynn's assessment of the situation, still smiles as he eyes the point of Shaylynn's sword. "You assume all we have is weapons," he says coyly.

Though the remark takes Shaylynn off guard for a moment, it also plays into his hand. For, while the man has been listening to Shaylynn's commentary, Shaylynn has been pooling a small amount of magic in his off hand. He will not be able to do much, but it will give him all the time he needs to enact his actual plan.

"So do you," Shaylynn retorts.

With a swipe of his hand, Shaylynn throws a wall of energy in front of him. The leader of the group goes flying backwards. The two men behind him fall as well. Ripples of the energy reach the trees and stagger four of the archers. They manage to stay in the trees, but the arrows drop out of their bows and fall harmlessly to ground. Shaylynn then hooks arms with Fallon, and Fallon whips Shaylynn around. Fallon swings wild to make the men fall back. Shaylynn swings as well coming from the opposite direction creating a twin blade circle to create a barrier for a moment. Once his feet hit the ground again, Shaylynn throws another ripple of energy towards the trees. Two arrows, already on their way, change direction as a result of the ripples. It is not nearly enough to knock them from the sky, but they do miss Fallon and Shaylynn by inches. Again, it rattles the archers in the trees.

A second later, Shaylynn feels a pull that jerks him to the ground. He hears the whistle of three arrows pass just over his head. One of the arrows hits one of their adversaries in the leg. Then, Shaylynn turns to see Fallon has pulled him to the ground.

"You owe me one," Fallon remarks.

"Suddenly you wish to keep count," Shaylynn replies.

"So long as I'm in the lead."

Shaylynn rolls his eyes as he rolls away from the swing of a sword which lands in the spot he'd been laying in. Two men square off with Shaylynn while Fallon deals with his own attacker. At this time, the leader of the troop regains his senses and gets to his feet. Propping himself up with his sword, he gazes angrily at the knights making quick work of his soldiers.

Raising his arms high, he motions to his forces in the trees to hold their fire. As he holds his sword high above his head, a small flame begins to wrap itself around the blade. While it snakes around, it grows in intensity, eventually turning into a blazing fire on the sword.

Embroiled in their fight, neither Shaylynn nor Fallon notice the event taking place behind them. However, Shaylynn can sense the magic building around him. Had he the time or opportunity, he might attempt to find the source of the disturbance. But now four men surround him. He must maintain full focus if he has the slightest hope of keeping them at bay.

In his mind, he races through the strategies he needs to utilize. Only one of the attackers is coming at him fully. The others keep him in check. Every now and then, one of the others attempts to sneak in a shot from Shaylynn's blindside. Within those moments, Shaylynn finds his best chance to attack. For now, they mean to keep him encircled and wear him out. Then, suddenly, they back away and Shaylynn is exposed.

A second later, the leader swings his sword forward. The flame shoots from the blade directly at Shaylynn. He cannot react in time, and the flame strikes him in the chest. Shaylynn then drops to the ground. The flame peters out, but Shaylynn is left unconscious. Fallon, having seen the flame, fears the moment he sees Shaylynn drop. Within that distraction, one of the men strikes Fallon in the head with the blunt of his sword. Fallon falls but still tries to reach Shaylynn. He is grabbed before he gets too far.

"What have you done?" Fallon demands.

The leader steps forward and examines Shaylynn.

"He's not dead," he says, somewhat impressed.

"You are men of this country," Fallon accuses, "and you attack your own!"

"My own," the leader repeats. "Aside from my presence in this country, what really makes you think I am your own?"

Fallon fears the worst. "You serve Jorram?"

The leader shakes his head. "No, I serve the earth, not some fool who declares himself king."

This man then commands his followers to bring Shaylynn. Those with a hold of Fallon begin to drag him along with the rest of the caravan. As they make their way through the woods, Fallon cannot help but be concerned for Shaylynn. He still has not moved since struck by the flame.

"He should be dead," the leader says to Fallon. "Perhaps his gifts are more than I assumed they'd be."

"You meant to kill him," Fallon assumes. "Did he scare you that much?"

The leader does not respond at first. He laughs to himself. As they move through the forest, Fallon gets a better look at the man. He must be thirty years of age. He is extremely rugged, a shaggy beard on his face. His eyes are cold and unforgiving.

"You are clearly men of the king's court," the leader finally says. "You fight well, dress well. Yet he knows ways we've been told were long forgotten."

"He is special," Fallon admits. "Not many can do what he can."

"Clearly, else you would've aided him in the fight."

They travel for hours through the night. Morning must be coming soon, but Fallon cannot know for sure. He can get no bearing on their current location, and Shaylynn remains unconscious. It has been some time since Fallon heard from the leader; his curiosity cannot be ignored any longer.

"What do you mean to do with us?" Fallon asks.

"You have intruded in our home," the leader responds. "Your fate will be decided by our elders. Some are killed; other's minds are wiped. It is a matter of the severity of your transgressions."

"We've made no transgressions," Fallon states.

"I must disagree!" a voice calls out from before them.

Fallon takes note of their surroundings. They've reached DaReen Lake where more of the people apparently involved in this gang have gathered. One sits at the head of the lake in a throne hewn from wood from the forest. He is old, probably around the age of eighty. His white beard hangs well down his chest. His white hair hangs scraggily around his head. One of his long-nailed hands grips the arm rest of the throne. The other hand holds on to a long wooden staff. A gaggle of others sits around him on the ground, at the top of a small ridge from behind the lake. The lake reflects the moonlight Fallon had seen not sign of until now. Again, thick trees cut off most of the view. Fallon can only see a few feet beyond the edge of the lake. Along with Shaylynn, he is brought before the man on the throne and tossed to the ground. The drop somewhat seems to jar Shaylynn back awake. Still, he remains face down.

"You have committed crimes against the Forest of Forleen," the man on the throne explains. "How do you plead?"

"We have committed no crimes," Fallon replies.

"Your ignorance will not save you," the man scolds. "For the better part of a day, we watched as you and your compatriot hacked through the trees of our forest. You laid waste to bushes, grasses, and meant to slaughter animals for your food…"

Fallon cannot help but plead his case. "We merely meant to pass through."

"Silence!" the man calls and stamps his staff on the ground. A wave of energy reverberates from the staff. It knocks Fallon back and jolts Shaylynn even more. Very queasily, he lifts himself off the ground. Eyes still closed, he grabs his chest and takes a deep breath. After a cough, a trail of smoke passes through his lips and into the night air.

"I don't know what that was," Shaylynn remarks, his voice scratchy from the attack, "but I will have to be better prepared for it in the future."

At that time, Shaylynn opens his eyes and gazes at the figures before him. He has to strain his eyes to bring everything into focus. When he finally sees the men surrounding him, he furls his brow.

"Who are you?" Shaylynn asks.

"That is of no consequence to you," the man replies. "All that matters is your plea."

"Plea?" Shaylynn repeats. "I see no court to judge me."

The men begin to grumble over Shaylynn's disrespect. Finally, the bearded man raises a hand to silence them and faces Shaylynn. "We shall judge you!"

"Are you so appointed by the king?" Shaylynn asks.

"We do not recognize whoever now sits upon the throne in Langerwitz."

"Indeed you do not, for you have placed yourself upon a throne."

"I have been placed in the role; I did not claim it as a birthright!"

Shaylynn can tell he is getting under this man's skin, and given their predicament, he does not care at this point. He cannot look weak or willing to please this man. He must appear an adversary if he is to have any hope.

"Hmm," Shaylynn replies, "and how many of these men placed you upon that throne? Or were they just led to believe that those who came before them did?"

"Do not question their loyalty to me!" the man says slowly.

"I do not question their loyalty, and I'm sure you do not either. I merely suggest maybe they should question their loyalty to you."

The men continue to stir and grumble while Shaylynn smiles arrogantly at their leader. The leader sits forward in his chair and studies Shaylynn. He cannot believe someone so young could be so brash. Never has a man come before them and been so secure in his surroundings. Even his comrade falters when he sets eyes on the scene. But not this boy.

Shaylynn looks at the men behind the throne. They are poorly situated, totally unprepared for a strike. Should he be able to draw enough magic to him, he could give one burst good enough to break him and Fallon free. They are clustered together enough to make his shot fairly easy. However, the trees give little chance of a fluid escape. Furthermore, these men seem to know the forest very well. They managed to surround Shaylynn and Fallon in the darkness. Who knows what else they are capable of?

Still, he will not risk staying here. He need only distract the man on the throne for a little longer before he has what he needs. Then, he can strike and take his chances. The longer they are here, the more danger lurks for Langerwitz and his friends. He must get to them without hesitation.

The fear in Shaylynn's eyes shows to the leader. Furthermore, he senses something is amiss with this boy. Something troubles him and causes him great distress. While he cannot find the source of Shaylynn's fears, he knows enough to tell his concerns are for others, not himself. For someone so supremely confident to be concerned with another is truly admirable. If not for his disrespect, the leader would admit this boy possesses some special quality. He must test him to be sure.

"And who are you to question us?" the leader asks.

"You ask my name after refusing to give me yours," Shaylynn replies. "Why should I provide a better example of civility than a man who sits on a throne?"

The men grumble, but the leader quickly quiets them. "A show of good faith," the leader replies. "Proof that our capture of you is unjustified."

Shaylynn considers this response. He did not consider this to come his way. His focus dwindles a bit, and the magic begins to falter in his hand. It would be easy to answer this man – perhaps even provide him a better opportunity to collect his wits. Or maybe, something else is at play here.

"I am Shaylynn Storm," Shaylynn finally responds, "son of Feylynn Storm, of the high court of Langerwitz. My friend, Fallon Welms, son of Degon Welms, also of the high court of Langerwitz."

"Tell me, Shaylynn, son of Feylynn, what is your purpose here?"

The leader does not admit the name rings familiar to him. Something from his past. Something that his father taught him when he was just boy. At that time, even Feylynn's father was just a babe. It was the family which was well-known. A truth about them which gives him cause to pause.

"We are making our way back to our city," Shaylynn explains. "We were separated from our party some days ago. I fear for the safety of my friends and all those who dwell in the city. So we follow the river to bring us back to Langerwitz."

"Would it not be quicker to cross over field and plain?" the leader asks. "Rather than follow the turns and twists of the river?"

"We must be able to survive the journey," Fallon responds. "Our provisions are few, and we clearly cannot rely on the kindness of strangers."

The remark, though honest and for the moment true, again sends a wave of disapproval through the onlookers. Some begin to call for the intruders to be punished for their crimes and now for their insolence. But their leader gives no indication he is ready to hand down a sentence or that he has decided their fate. Instead, a scowl on his face from Fallon's remark, he turns away from the offenders and ponders the circumstance.

"And why should your journey to Langerwitz be of any consequence to us?" the leader asks.

Fallon opens his mouth to answer, but Shaylynn raises a hand to ask his friend to remain silent. Though Fallon cannot follow Shaylynn's current train of thought, he concedes and gives Shaylynn the floor.

"We have answered your questions," Shaylynn replies. "Now, it is time for a show of good faith on your part. Your name, good sir?"

The leader considers this request for a long while. With each passing moment, the crowd behind him stirs louder. Shaylynn's face tightens under the strain of this exercise. He has much larger things to consider. He should not be wasting his time with this. Yet, he cannot risk any action at this moment. While he has gathered a considerable amount of magic, it is not what he'll require to guarantee an escape.

"I am called Darek," the leader says. "I lead the Order of the Grey Eagle."

Shaylynn shudders at the name – not of the man but of the order. For as long as he can remember, his father has told him stories of this group. They are magical – devoutly so. Since their inception some three hundred years ago, they have forsaken their place among the kingdom to live as outcasts. They despise the monarchy and everything it has granted the so-called king. The current order of the country offends the manner in which they believe a man should live – at one with nature and therefore building a strong connection with the magical arts.

Shaylynn would have considered them a threat if he had not been led to believe the order had ceased to exist some one hundred and fifty years ago. A lost relic – that was how his father described them. A pillar which stood when magic was strong, but now lost to the world which turned to a different source of belief.

"I know of you," Shaylynn admits.

"I am not surprised," Darek replies. "Surely, the names of my forefathers emblazoned themselves in the memories of your forefathers. The last true wizards of this realm, and the only ones whose opposition of the throne brought division among the land. Perhaps, with just a little more power, they would have kept Cyrus's ancestors from controlling the lands."

Shaylynn chuckles at the remark. "You make it seem as though the Wuhlfies had to fight for the loyalty the people gave them. They sought refuge from Jorram, and the Wuhlfies could provide as much. Furthermore, my father would not let your description of yourself as a true wizard stand," Shaylynn remarks. "From what I hear tell, you and your clan can do little more than parlor tricks and fancy displays of showmanship..."

Darek quickly interjects his rebuttal. "We did enough to almost bring about your death, young knight. Would you call that a parlor trick?"

The crowd begins to chuckle as a smile glows on the face of the man who struck Shaylynn down. Shaylynn, for his own part, reflects the smile out of derision. He has only begun to play his game.

"Perhaps not," Shaylynn replies, "but I would call it the action of a coward and a fiend."

Immediately, the laughter ceases and is replaced with angered shouts for swift action against the boy. The man steps toward Shaylynn with a hand reaching for his sword. Shaylynn turns towards him and grabs for his as well. Not wanting the situation to get out of hand, Darek again thumps his staff on the ground. The shake of the ground causes everyone to go silent. The man reluctantly stands down despite his desire to show Shaylynn the error of his beliefs. Shaylynn continues to smile and eye the man. Fallon carefully eyes the two of them.

He has seen enough of this banter and stands ready for any action Shaylynn would be willing to take. Given the situation, he fears he will not be able to provide much assistance. After seeing Shaylynn go down by the strike of these men, Fallon understands the danger of the situation. The fact Shaylynn flaunts himself so confidently with no regard for their safety only deepens Fallon's concerns. He continues to trust, as he always has, Shaylynn can get them out of this predicament when the time comes. For now, that trust wavers in the face of such outrageous odds. Perhaps there is some way out of this situation, but Fallon cannot begin to see it.

"You mean to antagonize us," Darek accuses.

"As you have already villainized me, it seems only appropriate," Shaylynn replies. "Why bother to play another part when one has already been cast?"

For much longer than usual, Darek does not speak. Instead, he studies the boy before him. Shaylynn's answers to these inquires confuse Darek. They are not the answers of a boy, nor are they the answers of a prisoner.

The fear which Darek observed just minutes ago has suddenly vanished or been hidden. There is no indication from this child that he understands any moment might be his last. Truly, this Shaylynn Storm does not understand how close to death he came – he was but a moment from falling from this world and joining his ancestors. He counts himself as neither blessed nor fortunate for being able to stare into the eyes of death and come out the better for it. Something stirs in this boy which Darek has not seen for a lifetime. Something that could be exactly what he has been looking for.

He must be sure. There must be proof Shaylynn can go beyond the normal means of the men Darek has already assembled for himself. Great men he has chosen. Men like Samwen, who brought the intruders to him this night. Men who could lead an army into battle and death, without fear or remorse. Men who could delve into the magical arts with skill and be able to perform astounding feats. Yet, Darek needs a man with sight beyond any of them. He needs a special talent which is rarer than one in a million but is indeed one in an eternity. Without realizing it, Shaylynn is about to give Darek the sign he needed to begin to believe.

"Or do you mean to test me?" Shaylynn asks. "Perhaps that is it?" Shaylynn begins to walk freely among his captors. He gazes at the men who surround them and a thought begins to form in his mind. "Many men have come to these woods," Shaylynn muses. "Stories would say those men never came out of the woods and died from men, monsters, or some other entity. Those stories are only half truths, aren't they?"

The accusation astounds Fallon. When they entered this forest a day ago, Shaylynn scoffed at the stories. Now he uses them to levy charges against these men. Perhaps more surprising, the men make no move to defend themselves. If anything, they seem surprised someone has figured out the truth. A truth Shaylynn does not hesitate to expound upon.

"The men you have before you," Shaylynn continues, "they are the men who came to these woods over the years. They possessed something you cherished. They harbored some small gift for the arts your clan desperately tries to hold to. Did you draw them here, Darek?"

Shaylynn pauses to give Darek some time to answer. When it becomes apparent Darek has no intention of answering, Shaylynn assumes the silence to be admittance on some level.

"You drew them here, tempted them with a life bent on harnessing their abilities to your needs. Those who met your expectations were allowed to stay. Those who didn't were sent on their way to spread the tales of the things that go bump in the night in the forest of Forleen. Most likely, you forced the new recruits to wipe the minds of those who fell short. Of course, some did die which allowed the mystery of the land to retain some of its fearful reputation…"

At this revelation, Darek interrupts Shaylynn's recanting of their history to pose his own question. "I will not call us innocent," Darek admits, "but does it surprise you Shaylynn that you know so much about a people you thought extinct only minutes ago?"

Shaylynn does wonder but has not the time to consider it. If this is a test, he must pass it at all costs. "You all tell the story with your eyes," Shaylynn responds. "The truth of it shines on their faces."

With that, the two sides come to an impasse. Darek must decide if Shaylynn possesses the potential needed to complete the task at hand. All his life, Darek has been prepared for this possibility, but he never believed the moment would be in front of him. Nor did he believe the potential boy would be a Knight of Langerwitz. But, he cannot allow his own prejudice to cloud the rationale of his mind. If Shaylynn is to be the boy of prophecy, then so be it. As long as the task is completed.

Shaylynn and Fallon will not allow this clan to stand in judgment of them. Fallon realizes Shaylynn holds them in contempt. Through his own means, he has learned the past of this party, and darkness clouds them all. Their fate still hangs in the balance, but clearly, there is some chance of survival here. But, they will not barter their lives for their dignity.

Silently, secretly, the Order of the Grey Eagle begin to converse with each other. Shaylynn can tell the communication is taking place, but he cannot begin to break into their thoughts. No doubt, one of the first trainings these men received when they came to the forest was how to protect their minds. Still, he can gauge quite a bit from their body language.

"What are they saying?" Fallon whispers.

"Darek is giving some instruction…or a decree, I suppose."

"What is it?"

"I cannot tell completely, but I know for certain many of the men here do not agree with it."

Fallon spends a few seconds gazing at the Order. Indeed, he can tell many have become more distressed in the last few seconds. Given their reaction to his and Shaylynn's presence, Fallon sees their dissention as a good sign. The Order, however uncivilized, clearly lives and dies by the rule of Darek. Even if they don't like the idea of letting them go, the Order will let it happen if so ordered.

And yet, they are still no closer to leaving. Shaylynn continues to monitor the situation, but he gives no indication of his plan. Or if he even has one. All the while, thoughts of Faith and Langerwitz dance in Fallon's head.

"How do we get out of here, then?" Fallon inquires.

"I'm not sure we do," Shaylynn replies. "At least not for a while anyway. Something's afoot here. Something which could change the course of events."

"But we need to return home."

"Agreed, but there may be something we need from this place to make our return more triumphant. And if the city is in distress, it may be more necessary than I realize."

The ground begins to rumble beneath them. It is not enough to knock them off their feet, but it makes it clear that distress is close at hand. Shaylynn begins to feel waves of anger radiating through the forest. Darek must have made his decree and made it clear that none may challenge his decision. The only question which remains is whether or not they will accept the decision within their commitment to the Order.

In his mind, Shaylynn feels a threat growing by the moment. Darek means him no harm, but that is not the case for all present. Perhaps this feeling can be contained, but Shaylynn senses not everyone is committed to the cause. One will mean to take matters into his own hands, and he will do so soon.

"We will do you no harm," Darek promises, "if you commit yourself to learning our ways."

"Why should we join with murderers and thieves?" Shaylynn asks.

"Because you sense the power we possess," Darek replies. "You know our intentions and our purpose. You know you are meant to possess this power yourself." For the first time in Shaylynn and Fallon's presence, Darek rises from his chair with his staff to support him. He takes one step forward, then speaks again. "Most importantly, you know your family holds the Order in high esteem."

Fallon would question Shaylynn immediately if the situation did not call for Shaylynn to speak. But he feels the question will soon be answered anyway.

"At one time, they held the Order in high esteem," Shaylynn corrects. "Some time ago, when the Order meant to continue the ways of olden times and support those who would govern, yes, my family held the Order in esteem. Clearly, that is not the purpose of the Order anymore."

"We did not mean to serve a tyrant," Darek says. "The corruption of our magic within the power of a throne would not mesh together. We warned the council of elders when the time came; they would not listen. Their desire to be governed under the rule of one man overcame their senses."

"So why do you want him?" Fallon asks.

Shaylynn turns unsurely to his friend. "They said both of us," Shaylynn corrects.

"I am no fool," Fallon replies. "You are the one who possesses what they seek. It is merely chance that I am here."

"I do not mean to insult him, but he is right, Shaylynn," Darek confirms. "We require only your talents, not his. He is, of course, under our protection should you decide to stay within the forest and learn our ways."

"To what end?" Shaylynn asks.

"To reclaim our place within the kingdom, to close the rift within the magic powers, and restore what once was. To do something that never would've been believed possible," Darek replies.

Shaylynn, intrigued by Darek's words, suddenly feels the moment of action is upon him. Indeed, from among the crowd, a man rises with bow in hand. Pulling an arrow from his quiver, he cries out.

"He is not the one! He is not one of the Order!"

Without a moment's hesitation, he fires the arrow at Shaylynn. None have the time to react to the shot, except Shaylynn. Raising an arm, he shoots out a beam of magic which collides with the arrow and deflects it harmlessly into the trees. The archer fires again. Now that he has more time to react, Shaylynn can handle the assault easier. He continues to deflect the arrows one after the other. When the archer comes to his last arrow, Shaylynn freezes the arrow in its flight. The deflections were impressive to all those who saw them. This move is awe-inspiring.

Slowly, Shaylynn rotates the arrow, so it faces the man who fired it. With a quick flick of the finger, Shaylynn sends it back at the attacker. However, he does not mean to kill the attacker – only disarm him. The arrow hits the archer's bow and shatters it. The arrow also breaks into slivers and splinters. The archer, somewhat relieved to still be alive, can only stare at Shaylynn in shock. Everyone there holds the same expression on his face – save one. Darek, still standing with the help of his staff, smiles big and lightly chuckles to himself.

"He may not be of the Order now," Darek says to himself, "but he will be soon."

The hostilities between Shaylynn, Fallon, and the Order cease. Though they do not completely trust the Order yet, Shaylynn and Fallon accept the sudden hospitality they are given. Darek orders a tent be set up for Shaylynn and Fallon. The boys are taken to a small encampment deep in the forest. Both offer to help with food or any other task the Order might need. The Order accepts their aid as fair compensation for their boarding. At this encampment, they will eat and sleep, but Shaylynn's training will be in all places within the forest. For the next few weeks, Shaylynn trains with men of the Order. He takes on physically demanding tasks with Samwen tutoring him. He sharpens his mind with Darek.

The physical tasks are more than anything Shaylynn experienced with his training in Langerwitz. In truth, they are more in keeping with the tasks his father had him complete when he was younger. Only, the tasks from his father were few and far between because Feylynn knew how taxing they were. Samwen is not so kind. He keeps the training intense and the tasks coming one right after the other. The archer who intended to kill Shaylynn becomes one of the members whom Shaylynn works with more often. It is an uneasy partnership between them, but Shaylynn cannot deny this man can teach him a great deal. The archer, named Cophen Truk, pushes Shaylynn's limits and does not hesitate to inflict pain whenever he can. There is more to this than some petty grievance between the two. Along with learning the extent of his physical skills, Shaylynn also learns the magical arts of healing. Those in the forest can cure the most severe of injuries. Many who knocked on death's door were brought back with only the smallest scar to show for their near-death experience. In those instances, the healer was not also the injured. Shaylynn is learning he can heal quite a large number of the injuries he incurs. In many ways, those lessons are more draining than those which go for hours on end. Healing injuries requires a great amount of energy, and for a person already injured, expending a great deal of energy can be a risky venture. But with time comes experience and wisdom. Shaylynn learns how to control his energy levels and even learns some simple concoctions which can raise his energy levels for a short time. These potions will not be easy to come by – many of the ingredients are rare and hard to find. Others, which are far less potent, will be easy to generate.

As much as he enjoys the lessons with Samwen, it is the sessions with Darek he looks forward to the most. These are the times when Shaylynn feels the power within him growing. Though they are little more than periods of meditation and deep thought, they seem like so much more. Shaylynn learns to step outside the physical realm and make contact with the spiritual world around him. He sees fallen souls who still roam the earth. He follows the journeys of energies in the world – plant, animal, nothing is off limits to him. After a few sessions with Darek, he even learns to focus his thoughts and transport himself, spiritually anyway, to other places in the world to see the people he cannot be with. He visits Langerwitz, sees his mother, brother, Sarin, and many others. He cannot see much and gets no indication about what is going on in the city. In his heart, he can feel the general sadness and despair among the people. It makes him worry the venture to the south was unsuccessful. When he begins to feel more confident in his ability, he even ventures into Jorram. It is remarkably difficult to travel to a place he has never actually seen himself. Darek is leery to even let him try. The reason is not clear – Darek does hide some things from Shaylynn. Some truths which the Order are not even aware of are for Darek and Darek alone. One secret he does share with Shaylynn is the one Shaylynn revealed to the king – the death of his own father, Feylynn Storm. To Shaylynn's great surprise, Feylynn knew Darek – more spiritually than physically, but they did encounter one another. Now, Shaylynn can connect with his father in this manner. In the time he spends with his father, Shaylynn learns of the truth behind his father's death. The assault from Jorram, being surprised on the road to the north. The loss of his brother Beylynn and Fallon's father are not easy things to hear, but they were things Shaylynn prepared himself for.

Though Shaylynn knows he must return to Langerwitz, the longer he stays in the forest, the more he wishes to remain with the Order. He is growing stronger every day, both physically and magically. Since he is safe, he can return home whenever he chooses. He could even let Fallon return home, so his family would know he was okay. The challenges he faces here are so much greater than what he faces in Langerwitz. There is little pressure here. No one wishes to make him king or tries to make him something he does not want to be. There are definite drawbacks of course. Sarin is not here. He looks in on her from time to time to make sure she is all right. He can see her face more clearly than anyone else's. While she is getting through her days, she is not happy. The sparkle in her eye is somewhat diminished. Whether this is because the forces of Jorram now pervade the city or because she merely misses Shaylynn, he cannot tell. She waits for the day when Shaylynn will return to her, and while he awaits the day as well, he does not feel like it is yet time for him to return. The truth Darek told him – that he was destined to learn this power – sticks in Shaylynn's mind. He is learning, but he does not have full control of it. He will need to stay in the forest to hone his ability and learn to fully control it. Fallon cannot believe it when they speak of returning and Shaylynn says they must stay longer. Fallon wishes to get back to his family and to Faith. Knowing Shaylynn approves only increases his desire to be with Faith. They need not hide their feelings. They can be free. Why Shaylynn denies himself the opportunity to return home confuses Fallon. In his own mind, he assumes it has something to do with being able to connect with Feylynn. Shaylynn loves his father dearly, in life and now in death. To be able to converse with him again, to hear his father's voice, is a hard gift to pass up.

While that is indeed part of the truth, the other stems from Shaylynn's difficulty in seeing into Jorram. He has caught glimpses of the country – brief flickers of sights he cannot completely understand. He assumes the princess is still there, but he would like to have a clear sight of her before he leaves the forest. If he can find her in his mind, it will be easier to plan a rescue. But, something keeps getting in the way and making the image fuzzy. Shaylynn can always get so close before he loses control and things become a fog. Whenever he asks Darek about this, Darek only remarks it takes time to craft one's abilities, but he never offers any solutions. Though Shaylynn suspects a great deal more, he knows Darek will hold these secrets hard to his chest. Then, on one seemingly ordinary day, Shaylynn makes it into the castle of Belvik. He scours the rooms searching for any sign of the princess. Many of the rooms are closed to Shaylynn, and he worries she resides in one of them. After going through several floors, he manages to find her. The sight of her ignites a flurry of action in his mind and jars him from his meditation.

Darek open his eyes as well and sees Shaylynn standing. Per usual, the two are at the bank of the DaReen Lake.

"I have lingered too long," Shaylynn says.

Darek shakes his head in disagreement. "You have increased your skills and abilities. You cannot consider that a waste of time."

"No, but I have forgotten my duty," Shaylynn replies as he heads back to the encampment. "And seeing the princess has told me as much. I know what I must do."

"You still believe you owe the king your allegiance?" Darek asks.

Shaylynn stops for a moment. It remains a point of contention between Shaylynn and all of the Order. Shaylynn will not forsake his post in Langerwitz despite the draw of the forest. He holds to his loyalties and oaths.

"Despite what you believe, he has given me a great deal," Shaylynn explains.

"And only asks for your life in return."

"No!" Shaylynn barks back. "Not my life. My life is my own. I choose to serve."

While Darek believes Shaylynn's priorities to be misguided, he cannot deny he admires the ferocity with which he sticks to them. However, Darek believes the truth in Shaylynn's loyalties lies somewhere beyond the throne. For all Shaylynn has told him, Darek knows Shaylynn is one many consider next to rule the land. Darek would rather Shaylynn not be king, but he doesn't like the other alternative Shaylynn chooses for himself.

"I know who you serve," Darek says, "and as I have said, she will hold you back."

Shaylynn will not entertain a debate about Sarin. Once, and only once, did the two argue about her. It did not end well – for either party. Shaylynn will not go back to that place again.

"Do not bring her into this," Shaylynn warns. "Else, I will never again consider being a part of the Order."

"So long as you tie yourself to her, you can never truly be a member of the Order," Darek reminds him. "The commitment you would give her would interfere with your duties to our cause."

"Then know your own words have ended my chances, not mine."

Shaylynn ends the conversation there and goes to the encampment. He finds Fallon quickly and tells him to pack.

"We are leaving?" Fallon says with a lift in his spirit.

"Yes," Shaylynn replies.

Samwen, who was working with Fallon on a chore, stops when Shaylynn replies. The news of Shaylynn's leaving is troublesome for him. Though no one has told Shaylynn, his time to join the Order was fast approaching.

"Do you really mean to leave?" Samwen asks.

"I do," Shaylynn replies.

"Why?" Samwen asks.

"Because I know the princess can be rescued," Shaylynn explains. "And I know I am the one to do it."

"Delusions of grandeur?" Samwen says. "This is what draws you away from us?"

"I was never going to stay," Shaylynn clarifies. "We all knew as much. I've a life, a family, and someone I love dearly."

Samwen says nothing else while Shaylynn gathers his belongings. Darek demands two horses be brought for Shaylynn and Fallon. Shaylynn thanks Darek for the horses and everything else the Order has given them. Darek, while displeased with Shaylynn's decision, knows their time together is not over. Shaylynn will return to the forest – Darek only questions the manner in which he will return.

"There is a great deal of power in you, Shaylynn, son of Feylynn," Darek says. "But you are not invincible. Because you are so young, your power is out of control. Those who can control their ability will have the advantage over you until you complete your training."

Shaylynn takes the words seriously. For all he has seen in his time in the forest, he knows there is much which he remains blind to. But circumstance will not allow him to sit back and wait for those things to reveal themselves. He must charge on and hope his abilities will serve him well.

"Can you tell me anything about Langerwitz?" Shaylynn asks before they depart.

"Nothing that will serve you," Darek replies. "We have turned our backs on it so often, we cannot see it now. You must approach it carefully. Assume nothing until you are absolutely sure."

With that, Shaylynn and Fallon ride away from Forleen Forest and back to Langerwitz. For the next two days, they ride hard, taking only brief rests to eat and sleep. The closer they come to the capital, the more they look for signs of its current condition. They see no sign of Jorram, but Darek's warning keeps them on their toes. As such, it becomes the reason Shaylynn and Fallon decide to lay siege to the castle and try to make it to the king's chamber.

CHAPTER XIII

Having relayed the entire account of their travels, Shaylynn returns to his larger point. "What say you then, my liege?" Shaylynn asks. "Will you allow me to lead the campaign to rescue your sister and our princess?"

Cyrus considers the idea for a minute longer. Shaylynn has proven much by returning from the southern battles and surviving Forleen Forest for several weeks. And yet, no other knight besides Fallon and Lyosan have come to his side. He cannot trust Lyosan's motives completely knowing of the emotions he harbors for Crystalynn. Fallon, however, is a different matter. He is tragically loyal to Shaylynn, especially since Shaylynn was so pivotal in helping him survive the ordeal in Forleen. But Cyrus knows how vital Fallon is to the continuation of the kingdom. He was, after all, named second among the pool of candidates competing to assume the throne. If he is truly willing to charge into Jorram, with only Shaylynn to guide him, perhaps that says all Cyrus needs to know. Fallon, along with Shaylynn, has recently lost family. Neither of these two would allow revenge to cloud their judgment in this manner. Neither has said much about their respective father aside from the fact that each is dead.

Furthermore, this is all for Crystalynn. They want to save her from the bondage she currently suffers. As it is Cyrus's fault which has thrown Crystalynn into this situation, he cannot deter those who look to right his wrong. In different circumstances, he would abandon the throne to go after his sister himself. His advisors would never allow it. The kingdom lies in great disarray after the attacks in the south and the threat to the north. He cannot run off to captain a campaign even if it is for his own sister.

Someone must rescue her, and these men are willing and able.

"I will give my consent," Cyrus finally says.

A bright smile breaks across Lyosan's face. The news he's been waiting to hear for months has finally reached his ears. He looks to Fallon and Shaylynn, but there is no joy upon their faces. It is a determined look of resolution to the task ahead of them. They knew they would undergo this operation with the king's consent or not. However, with Cyrus's blessing, the campaign will be unencumbered by conflict.

And yet, there is more to be done. They cannot travel just the three of them. Even if no one else goes with them into Jorram, they will need a group on the other side of the border to await their return or provide assistance if needed. The only question is where shall they come from? Who shall it be? Stefen, Brynnal, and Nycolas will surely come now that Shaylynn is leading the endeavor. They might be able to get a few more to come to the border, but they cannot trust any to cross with them. Then, there is the problem of Pythyn.

Lyosan looks to him to see the disgust on his face. That anyone would risk such an endeavor goes beyond the sense of duty Pythyn holds. He does not expect diplomacy to provide any finality to the situation, but he also does not expect a small group of youths to be able to journey into Jorram, storm a castle, and leave with the princess safe and sound.

"So you sanction this?" Pythyn asks with surprise.

"I do," Cyrus replies. "Furthermore, I call upon you and your fellow youths to ride with Shaylynn, Fallon, and Lyosan to the border of Jorram."

The decree shocks Pythyn and Lyosan. To some extent, Shaylynn and Fallon appear to be surprised by the order as well. On some level, Shaylynn would probably prefer Pythyn not accompany them.

"You want us among those who travel in Jorram?" Pythyn asks.

"I will not force any member of my court to travel to a foreign land without his consent," Cyrus explains. "However, I can send a caravan to the edges of our borders and expect them to follow my orders."

"Agreed my liege," Pythyn quickly says. "However, many of the youth are injured and would not be much help in this matter."

"What's more my lord, I do not think it wise to send a large number," Shaylynn says. "If it becomes too obvious what we are doing, our campaign will suddenly see more obstacles than if we try a subtler approach."

Cyrus follows Shaylynn's plan. "How many would you take?"

"No more than twelve," Shaylynn says.

"Find however many you need," Cyrus agrees.

The next day, Shaylynn goes throughout the city gathering his forces. He gives the decree as the king gave it. He informs the youths they are not required to join Fallon, Lyosan, and him in their expedition into Jorram. Within the day, he has twelve preparing to ride out the following day. Stefen, Brynnal, and Nycolas have agreed to go as Shaylynn expected. Darrow, Shawl, Dragoon, Mitan, Artimous, and Athen round out the troop. Shaylynn instructs them to gather at the north gate just after sunrise. Once all are accounted for, they will ride for the border.

Shaylynn, Lyosan, and Fallon sleep early that day. Knowing the trials that await them, they gather what rest they can. Lyosan and Fallon believe they will need to convince some of the youths to enter Jorram with them. Shaylynn remains firm in his confidence that the three of them could complete the task if necessary. Still, it is wise to bring more help just in case something should go wrong.

Well before sunrise, the three leaders of the charge rise. Each carries out the normal chores for his family, then rides for the gate. They bring their weapons, shields, attire, and other supplies with them. They will need to ride light and fast. Most of the food they will require can be found as they ride. There are a few towns they will be able to stop in on the way. Mostly, they will rely on their abilities to forage in the wild. It will be their greatest aid in this journey.

When they arrive at the gate, two are waiting for them. Surprisingly, they are not members of the troop going to Jorram. Instead, it is Sarin and Faith. Faith goes to Fallon and helps him prepare for the journey. Sarin stands by Shaylynn and tries to draw his attention, but he will not be deterred.

"I would have a word with you," she says.

Shaylynn goes about his business. "Speak your mind then," Shaylynn encourages. "I am happy to discuss while I work."

"I'd rather you stopped for a moment."

Shaylynn shrugs. "It is awfully difficult to stand still when the world is sprinting ahead of you."

"Speak your riddles to everyone else but not with me," Sarin chides. "Others might think them clever, but they only worry me."

Shaylynn drops the items in his arms and lets them crash to the ground. Sarin jumps at the sound. "Things are in motion, Sarin," Shaylynn explains. "Dangerous things I cannot hope to control. But I can't see it all; I can only see bits and pieces, ideas, and concepts. I don't know how they all fit together or even if they do…" The words he speaks bring fear to Sarin's heart. She begins to worry he sees his own end. That he will die if things do not go well. As Shaylynn turns to face her, he sees that fear on her face. "…I know I will survive if I just play my part, but there is much else in play I cannot see happening. There are so many lives at play and so much more when I consider the consequences that might ensue. The future cannot be ignored, yet I cannot do anything to change it."

Sarin gives a soft smile and slowly approaches Shaylynn. His hard exterior keeps up as she comes near which is hard for him to keep up. Warmly, she wraps her arms around him. In time, he drops his guard and reciprocates.

"Just come home to me," she whispers in his ear. "So long as you do that, everything will work out in the end."

Shaylynn sighs deeply and kisses Sarin on the cheek. She quickly grabs him behind the neck and kisses his lips. It surprises Shaylynn for a moment, but then he finds himself and kisses her back.

"Did you really think you'd get away that easy?" Sarin asks when they pull apart.

"You know I never want to leave you," Shaylynn replies.

"Just come back," Sarin says with a tear in her eye. She believes Shaylynn when he says he'll survive, but given the moment, she cannot trust anything until he is back in her arms. The journey is just beginning and so is the worry.

From a few yards away, Fallon and Faith see them kiss. They were not eavesdropping, but they caught them at the right moment. Faith has not spoken to Fallon about his leaving yet, but it is on her mind.

"She's worried about him," Faith says.

"If I weren't going, I'd be worried about him too," Fallon replies.

"So your going is some sort of protection for him?" Faith asks.

"No," Fallon responds, "I just have myself to worry about first."

Faith reaches for his hand. Fallon gives it to her. For a moment, they stand in silence as they attempt to subdue the emotion rising within them. Fallon is the first to calm himself enough to speak.

"I take great comfort with him at my side," he says.

"I still worry for you," Faith admits. "Even more than him. Even though he's family, you're the one I fear for. You must come back to me, regardless of what happens to the rest. And I hate myself for feeling that way, but I do."

"You merely believe Shaylynn will return before any of us," Fallon says. "We all feel the same way – that if we are to lose someone, it'll be one of them before Shaylynn. We would all perish ten times over before he even gets a scratch."

"Why do we all feel that way?" Faith asks. "That he is indestructible, and the rest of us so expendable?"

"Because we've seen what he can do. We've seen what he's capable of and how we fall short of his abilities. In that way, we know it will take something big to take him down. And if he falls, the rest of us don't stand a chance against it."

The sobering truth washes over them. As does the unspoken truth of their love for one another. Through this honesty comes another feeling – peace. Now that they've revealed their truth, they believe Shaylynn will guide Fallon through this crisis and bring him back safe and sound. As he is family to Faith, she feels it in her heart. As he is a captain to Fallon, he knows it in his mind.

Within ten minutes, five more of the troop arrive and begin prepping for the journey. Sarin and Faith take their leave. Shaylynn begins debriefing about the route they will take, the stops they will make, and the duration this should last. He gives each member a special task to perform while they travel. Darrow, he puts in charge of the map. Nycolas is given the duty of rationing out the supplies. Artimous will be the scout. Athen will track the time. Shawl will keep an eye on the battle supplies to make sure none are lost along the way.

By the time the rest of the troop arrives, Shaylynn, Fallon, and Lyosan are ready to leave. They aid their team members in whatever way they can while bringing them up to speed on the details of the mission and giving them a command chain to follow. As leader, Shaylynn obviously takes the top spot. He names Fallon and Lyosan as his seconds in command. When Dragoon hears this, he questions Shaylynn a second time as far as who is second in command. Shaylynn merely repeats his original statement and walks away. Though Shaylynn means them to be at the same level, most agree they will report to Fallon before Lyosan. Beyond those three,

Shaylynn lists Stefen as third and Darrow as fourth. Beyond them, the troop is small enough for it not to matter. Once everything stands clear among the troop, they continue preparations for departure. Everything seems on schedule and ready to begin when something rather unexpected occurs.

As the gates opens and Shaylynn takes his place at the head of the party, one more rider comes from the city. As a member of the knights, he of course has standing to participate in this campaign, but everyone believed he was sitting this one out. Many of them, Shaylynn, Fallon, and Lyosan among them, preferred it when he was sitting it out. Nonetheless, as Pythyn approaches, he clearly stands ready to travel. Though his tardiness creates some animosity, he has at least come ready to leave at moment's notice. As further evidence of his compliance with the mission, he rides to Shaylynn and salutes him. Shaylynn, however, is in no mood to be cooperative.

"What are you doing here?" Shaylynn asks.

"Well that's just typical, isn't it?" Pythyn replies. "Here I am, ready for the mission, and all you do is complain."

"I don't recall you volunteering to accompany us," Fallon says.

"I don't recall you asking," Pythyn retorts. "I do, however, remember the king asking all youths to come on the mission."

"I asked for twelve," Shaylynn reminds him.

"One more will not matter."

"Not superstitious I see," Fallon remarks.

Pythyn ignores the comment and focuses on the mission. True, he does bring the company to thirteen, which the king himself would frown upon. What's worse, in being the thirteenth to arrive, Pythyn bears much of the bad luck himself. In time, this may not benefit him, but for now, it is a mere inconvenience.

"I assume I hold the same rank as the southern campaign," Pythyn says. "I will then take my place with you, and we can proceed."

Pythyn points his horse in the direction of Lyosan's. Given his place, it is Lyosan who will have to step aside. However, Shaylynn moves in the way before Pythyn can get too far. The look on Pythyn's face, sheer insult and confusion, brings a smile to Fallon's face. Lyosan feels relief wash over him knowing he will not be humiliated by having to cede his spot.

"You assume wrong, Pythyn," Shaylynn explains. "Perhaps, if you had made your intentions clearer, sooner, and if you had arrived with the punctuality of the rest of your peers, then I could grant your *request* to take your traditional spot. But as I have already given orders on this mission and established clear pathways of communication, you will have to take the bottom spot."

The indignation of such a demotion offends Pythyn down to his very being. For a few seconds, he cannot even reply to this command. The others around him smirk and snicker under their breath. Finally, Pythyn finds the right words.

"Just insert me into the command. It will not be difficult to change the protocol before we depart," Pythyn suggests.

"The gates are open," Shaylynn says. "We have embarked already. You are late. Take your post, soldier."

Shaylynn rides off saying nothing more. As Fallon passes Pythyn, he gives a different option.

"You could always stay home."

Pythyn scowls as each of the youths rides past him. When the last one passes, Pythyn begrudgingly takes his place at the end of the line and follows the caravan out of the gates.

Riding hard through the afternoon the caravan makes good progress to the border. As they journey, they see many people out and about living their daily lives. Farmers plow the fields, plant the seeds, and water the grounds. Children play in nearby creeks and ponds. Some older children train with wooden swords while young maidens look on. When they spot the knights coming, some stop their actions and watch them go. A few call out and wave to them. Shaylynn waves back but does not slow his progress. Oddly, only the children bother to acknowledge the knights. The adults do glance at them from time to time, but mostly they force themselves to focus on their tasks. Athen sees their reaction. He is puzzled by this. Normally, a troop from the capital would be received with warm hospitality. The townspeople would be clamoring for the knights to stop for a while and take some of the bounty of the town.

Instead, the knights ride on, uninterrupted. Over the valleys and hills of the land, the knights see the majesty of their country. Despite the troubles its people face, the land keeps its beauty. For the knights, it is a moment of joy to see all they are fighting for laid out before them. The glory of nature restores the warmth in the hearts of its inhabitants.

As the sun begins to set over the horizon, the knights find a place among the wild to camp for the night. Shaylynn, Shawl, and Dragoon hunt for food while the others prepare a fire and campsite. There are no towns for miles around, thus the knights will not have to be overly cautious while they rest. Still, two will stand on guard in shifts for the night. The hunt succeeds. Shaylynn, Shawl, and Dragoon bring in two small fawns. Fallon has built the fire and prepared a spit for roasting. Within the hour, the youths have a food to eat. They sit and tell stories by the campfire for a long while. Throughout the discussion, Athen remains silent. For a while, this goes unnoticed by the group, but eventually, Shaylynn picks up on it. He wishes not to call attention to it, believing it possible something important lies on Athen's mind, but when Athen fails to respond to a direct address, the matter comes forward.

"Is something wrong, Athen?" Nycolas asks.

It takes a moment for Athen to respond, and when he does, he is none too convincing. "I'm fine," he says weakly.

"Don't seem like it," Darrow replies.

Athen opens his mouth to speak, but nothing comes out. He averts his eyes momentarily. His discomfort becomes apparent. While most are willing to give him space, Pythyn is not so kind.

"Speak your mind already," he demands.

"It is nothing," Athen assures them.

"Correction," Shaylynn says, "it could have been nothing if you'd only revealed it sooner."

Athen pauses and sighs for a moment. Then, he sets his plate down and leans forward in his seat. "When we rode through the towns today, the people barely acknowledged our presence. I'd always been told stories by my father of the welcomes he and the other knights would receive while traveling through the land. Sometimes, he even brought home gifts he was given by the townspeople. Today, when we went through, there was none of that. They looked upon us as one would a prisoner sentenced to death…"

"That is how they see us," Shaylynn informs him.

All the knights turn towards Shaylynn. His remark concerns them greatly. Each knew death would be a possibility, but the idea that it is expected presents a new concern. Furthermore, the categorization as prisoners goes beyond their normal understanding of their purpose. Before they can question him, Shaylynn explains his reasoning.

"We all know the dangers of this mission," Shaylynn says. "That is why the king did not command all of us to enter Jorram. He's already sent the best the land has to offer, and they have been killed. When you think about it, what chance would youths such as ourselves stand against a force who slaughtered our fathers? These people have seen death; they fear more of it will occur."

"And you wonder why we scoff at the opportunity before us," Pythyn snorts.

"Is it truly that dangerous?" Athen asks ignoring Pythyn comment.

"We travel into enemy lands," Shaylynn replies with a shrug. "Surely, there can be few things which rival such danger."

Now others begin to feel the concern Athen feels. "And you would go on anyway?" Brynnal asks.

"Without question."

Many mutter under their breath and shake their heads in dismay. "How can you be so certain?" Artimous asks.

"It is the oath I swore," Shaylynn replies. "The princess, my future queen, lies in foreign lands in wicked hands. For the purpose of peace, she lost the freedom each of us now holds. Men of disreputable quality and conviction made promises in good faith which they then broke in violent and deadly means. Darkness dwells over the land. When these times are upon us, the people look to the crown to bring them light.

"I am an agent of the crown. It bids me bring back her who was taken from us in such callous fashion. For such evil cannot be allowed to triumph..." Shaylynn pauses for a moment as he looks to the sky. Some follow his gaze to the stars. "...and with the intercession of a higher power, it never shall. Such a power will see our better days restored. In the depths of my heart, it lets me know our princess shall walk these lands again in happiness and safety. That is how I am certain."

For a while, none speak. The words are cutting and deep. They expose a cowardice in many of them they wish not to acknowledge. If the task were now immediately ahead of them, perhaps all would enter into the fray. But, something within Shaylynn's message creates more tension. When posed, the question restores all concerns that once lingered.

"You say the princess shall walk the lands again," Darrow repeats. "What of us? What of those who enter the land of Jorram? Would we walk these lands again?"

Shaylynn does not answer right away as a stern look covers his face. His silence speaks more than his eventual reply does. "It is uncertain," he says quietly.

Shock sweeps over all the knights, save Shaylynn, Fallon, and Lyosan. The three of them are already committed to the cause. As these three scan their comrades, they see a look that longs for home. None can be certain, but it seems many would leave now if they had the opportunity.

"So you would ask us to risk our lives?" Stefen asks.

"As if we have not done so before?" Fallon replies with insult in his voice. He stands and steps towards the fire to be at the center of the troop. "When we journeyed to the southern lands, we knew death would come for some of us. We did not hide. We did not run from it. We ran into the very mouth of hell knowing that perhaps it would feed upon us…"

Mitan interrupts him. "There were many of us then."

"It matters not how many stand among you when death comes. If he is meant to take you, he will take you!"

"And if we go looking for him, it'll be easier for him to find us," Dragoon says.

"We cannot hide," Shaylynn replies from his spot. "Nor will death stop his search, but he will not take you until your time has come. Until then, we should do everything we can to make this world a better place. That is why we accepted the task given to us. We believe we can make a difference. We know wrongs must be righted. In front of us stands a wrong. I will make it right. Search your heart to see if you will do the same."

Shaylynn says nothing more, and the conversation dies. Fallon walks away in a huff with Lyosan in tow. Shaylynn volunteers to take the first shift. Mitan agrees to the first shift as well. A few hours later, Lyosan rises from his slumber and comes to relieve the first watch.

"Who else should I wake?" Lyosan asks.

"No one," Shaylynn replies. "I'll maintain my watch."

"You should rest," Mitan insists. "We will reach the border by tomorrow's nightfall. You'll need to be ready for the task."

"Your concern is noted," Shaylynn says. "But as you may not enter with me, it will not be your concern."

Rather than risk an argument, Mitan throws up his hands and moves to his bedroll. Shaylynn keeps an eye on the fire as Lyosan sits down next to him. For a while, they sit in silence and watch the flames envelop the wood on the pile. In his mind, Lyosan does wish Shaylynn would rest for the night. Knowing they will enter Jorramian land in less than a day, Lyosan still believes Shaylynn will bring him home safely. However, he also believes it will be no easy task. At the same time, he does not question Shaylynn's preparation for this mission.

"We are on our own," Shaylynn finally says.

The suddenness of the remark takes Lyosan by surprise. For a moment, he questions whether Shaylynn means just the two of them, but he quickly realizes he would never leave Fallon out. Perhaps, he is commenting on the fact they are so far removed from the castle, and the troop stands alone. Either way, Shaylynn continues his thought before Lyosan can question it.

Shaylynn turns his eyes to Lyosan. "None of the troop will join us. We will enter Jorram on our own."

"Nothing is yet decided, nor does it need to be," Lyosan says to keep Shaylynn's spirits up. Indeed, no decision is final. They are not before the border now. Perhaps some will change their minds.

"Enough has been said," Shaylynn says. "Fear will take them soon. It will wash over them and burn away their resolve. When the time comes, they will ask to go home rather than enter Jorram. Perhaps I should let them."

"We will need them when we come back," Lyosan reminds him. "They will come to the border no matter what fears they have about entering Jorram."

Shaylynn drops his eye line. "They fear death so much..."

"Besides you, who doesn't?"

"You don't."

Lyosan scoffs. "Of course I do." Lyosan pauses for a moment before adding, "and if you think Fallon doesn't, you are wrong. Both of us fear dying in Jorram. We fear not completing the mission. I fear failing the princess."

Shaylynn rustles uncomfortably on the ground for a moment. There is much Shaylynn would like to say at this point, but he cannot reveal too much. He does not want to give false hope, nor does he want to overstate the importance of their endeavor. Clearly, much rests on Lyosan's mind already. Much is on Shaylynn's mind as well. Knowing the other youths will leave them soon brings trepidation to Shaylynn's resolve. He needs to calm himself. It will be important for the next day.

In the calm of the night, he begins to find peace. A full moon sits overhead. Stars flick on to speck the dark sky. Meandering through the trees, a gentle breeze drifts across the sky. The limbs and leaves gently brush together in the peaceful whispers that night brings. All the worries of the world shrink away beneath its beauty.

In his mind, Shaylynn hears Sarin's voice whispering to him. *Everything will be okay. Soon, you'll be home and in my arms. Just follow your heart.* Comfort finds him, and if he could, he'd drift off to sleep. The mission does not allow it, however. He needs to keep watch. At some point, he'll need to draw upon his abilities. What is more important now is keeping Lyosan and Fallon ready to do their part. As much as he believes he'll rescue Crystalynn, he knows he will not be able to do it alone.

"Why would you think you'll fail?" Shaylynn asks.

Lyosan laughs with derision. "We enter Jorram, just the three of us according to you, and will have to break into their king's castle, rescue the princess, and leave without getting her injured. Only in doing those things do we succeed. Otherwise, we fail."

Shaylynn waits for a moment before saying, "So do you think you'll fail?"

Lyosan laughs again, this time with joy. Shaylynn smiles at hearing a pure laughter in such a situation.

"How will we do it, Shaylynn?" Lyosan asks. "How will be break into a king's castle without causing a row?"

"We may have to create a row," Shaylynn replies. "After all, I entered Langerwitz despite creating a great row."

"But you didn't escape."

"I didn't try."

Lyosan rolls his eyes, but his smile remains. He takes a few small twigs and throws them into the fire one at a time. Shaylynn's confidence seems restored. If only Lyosan's would return so easily.

Again, they sit in silence for a while. Shaylynn senses the concern on Lyosan's mind, but he will not draw attention to it until Lyosan does. If he is truly going to be of help, he must wait until Lyosan asks for it. Lyosan must be ready to hear what Shaylynn will say if the words are going to hit their mark.

"Can you promise I'll come back?" Lyosan finally asks. It is not the question Shaylynn anticipated, but it is one he would have to answer sooner or later.

"If you fight as though you won't," Shaylynn replies.

"But she'll come back?" Lyosan asks.

"If you fight as though she won't."

"You said you saw her walking these lands again," Lyosan says beginning to feel lied to. "You couldn't guarantee our return, but you could hers!"

"I do see her walking these lands again," Shaylynn explains, "but I also see you and Fallon playing a vital role."

"You said nothing of this before."

"It did not matter before. I did not doubt you would be able to perform admirably when the time came. However, if you act as though you are not in danger, danger will take you. I guarantee nothing but that you will face trials like you never have before."

"You've seen this?"

"I've seen nothing," Shaylynn replies. "I merely know where we are headed."

"And that is why I fear failing."

"You heart will guide you if you let it. Your love for her will play its role as well."

They talk for a while longer though the conversation lightens. They speak of home and the comings and goings of family. No doubt everyone within the city monitors the crops closely since they have just been planted. This makes for long days and fretful hopes for less rain. They joke whether Shaylynn could stop the rain from so far away. He imagines he could try, but they would never truly know if he caused it or not. Besides, they both have larger concerns on their minds. Thinking of home merely passes the time. Soon, a critical moment will be at hand.

Later in the night, Darrow and Stefen stir and replace Lyosan and Shaylynn. Shaylynn is happy to give up his post this time. Now that his mind is calm again, he can take his normal rest and be ready when dawn comes.

When dawn peaks over the horizon, Shaylynn rises with ease. Fallon and Lyosan also rise and wake the rest of the troops. They make a quick meal for breakfast then take off for the border. Along the way, the knights speak of home and ask what will happen when they reach the border. Shaylynn informs them they will need to keep a small camp by the river and be ready to attack from the other side of the border to provide cover. To provide the best opportunity for concealment, the troop must cross to the eastern side of Lakwood once they reach the Mountains of Grailtin. There, they can continue to follow the river until they find themselves at Belvik's backdoor.

As they travel, they come upon a distressing sight. It will be only a short time before they must deviate from the normal means into Jorram and sneak across the river as Shaylynn has instructed. It is in this area where the attacks on the princess and the royal guard must have occurred. The first evidence they find is the carriage of the princess. Shaylynn remembers it well from the day he came to it and tried to convince her to stay in Langerwitz. Together, the youths pause and repair it. Shaylynn assures them they will need it to bring the princess home which raises their spirits. It is hard work and takes some time to repair it. Shawl and Mitan lash their houses to the carriage and prepare to drive it. Before they leave, Shaylynn suggests they rest and eat lunch.

While eating, Shaylynn begins to feel something odd. They are very close to the border, but something stirs in the air. As they are ahead of schedule, Shaylynn believes he has time to explore this occurrence. As he rises from his place, the other knights become confused.

"Where are you going?" Pythyn demands.

Shaylynn waves a hand at him and continues.

"Hey!" Pythyn cries when Shaylynn ignores him. "We cannot delay in this way."

"We've plenty of time," Shaylynn replies. "Something feels odd about this place."

"Odd how?" Nycolas asks thinking perhaps an ambush is about. He grabs his sword just in case. When he does, the others do as well.

"I cannot explain it," Shaylynn says. "I sense something is special about this place or at least someplace nearby."

Shaylynn continues to wander off. The others soon follow. Without word or warning, Shaylynn takes off into the wild crashing through trees and over rocks. The others work to keep up with him, but it is nearly impossible for them to do so. They call to each other trying to stay as one group. Each asks if Shaylynn is nearby, but none see him. At times, they fear they have lost him, and consequently, their way back to camp. Fallon eventually takes the lead, believing he can follow Shaylynn's tracks.

He wanders about for a while. Those with him begin to feel he doesn't know where his is going. There is talk about splitting up or just trying to find their way out of the wild. Fallon carries on with Lyosan right behind him. As the others have nothing better to do, they continue to follow Fallon. Slowly, Fallon finds more evidence he is on the right track. Finally, after crashing through a row of trees, Fallon finds himself at the base of a valley. There, a few yards away, stands Shaylynn. The others soon spill out of the woods. When they find him, Shaylynn is standing before a patch of earth overturned and piled high.

"What is the meaning of this!" Pythyn exclaims. "You, who have been named captain of this troop, race away from it on a whim. You ask for our bravery, then you run away like a coward!"

Shaylynn does not turn to acknowledge their presence. He keeps his eyes focused on the earth in front of him. Pythyn steps towards him, but Fallon raises his blade to stop him. Reluctantly, Pythyn stops and puts up his hands to indicate he will stand down. When the matter resolves itself, Fallon walks up to Shaylynn slowly. Lyosan is not far behind. Shaylynn still does nothing but stare at the ground.

"Shaylynn," Fallon whispers.

Still nothing.

"Shaylynn," Fallon says a little louder.

He goes to touch Shaylynn's shoulder when Shaylynn takes a deep breath and waves him away. For a few more moments, they stand in silence. The others grow restless behind them. The longer they delay, the more they risk the mission. As Fallon prepares to move Shaylynn along, he finally speaks.

"Do you know where we are?" Shaylynn asks.

Fallon looks around the area, but he sees nothing which recalls any memories. His attention then turns to the ground in front of him. It is strange for it to be overturned in this fashion even though it brings no thoughts to his mind.

"I have no idea," Fallon finally replies.

"This is where they fell, Fallon," Shaylynn says solemnly.

Fallon looks closer at the mound on the ground. A shallow, mass grave perhaps. All the members of the royal guard gathered together in their final resting place. It is possible that underneath this dirt, their fathers lie together as close as Shaylynn and Fallon stand now.

The reality of the situation hits in a matter of moments. Fallon cannot know for certain this is the place, but he knows Shaylynn's senses enough to accept it as the truth. Months they wondered, weeks ago they learned the truth, and now they have come to the place.

There are many things Fallon would wish to say at this point. In his heart, he would attempt to fight this truth. He would demand to know how Shaylynn knows this or what has convinced him of this truth. Shaylynn, ever his friend, knows doubt lies in his friend's mind. And yet, there is so little he can do to convince him of the truth.

"The main road is but a few minutes from here," Shaylynn explains. "The Jorramian soldiers lay in wait in the trees. When the caravan came, they descended upon it. Our fathers ordered the men to bear arms. They struck my father, first. Their attack was so precise and well-concealed that he could not mount a proper defense.

"The fight went on with the royal guard fighting from a place of weakness. A second wave came from nowhere and attacked from above. Arrows rained down on them. Some managed to last for a few more minutes, but the fight was over.

"Rather than leave evidence of their attack, the men on the front dug a mass grave while the officers stole from the dead. They put the bodies in the hole they'd dug and left them here. I saw this very spot from the Forest of Forleen. My father called to me from here, where he now rests. Yours rests here as well." Then turns to the rest of the troop. "As do many of theirs."

Lyosan brings the rest of the knights over and informs them of what Shaylynn has found. Among the rumblings, the youths question whether Shaylynn is right or not, how he could possibly know this is the spot, and whether or not proof can be found. Those whose fathers are buried also wonder if they should move the grave back to Langerwitz and give them a proper burial. Furthermore, their families would want to know the truth.

"What do we do with them?" Darrow finally asks, as his father is one of the deceased.

"Let them rest," Shaylynn replies, "while remembering what it was they gave their lives for. We honor our fathers now as we were born to do."

"And if we should join them?" Darrow asks.

"Then they will welcome us with open arms."

Shaylynn turns away from the scene and begins to walk back to the campsite. The others linger for a while longer, mostly those whose fathers rest in this place. They memorize the sight, feel, and sounds of this place. They lock it away forever within their hearts so they will always remember what they have seen this day. When they feel they cannot bear anymore, they turn away and rejoin the troop.

By the time they return, Shaylynn has his horse prepped and ready to ride. Fallon, Lyosan, and most of the others prepare to leave as well. Only Pythyn hesitates.

"Would you be kind enough to explain what that was?" Pythyn asks.

"I believe I've answered that question," Shaylynn replies.

"You claim it is the burial pace for close to fifty of the best knights of our kingdom, but you refuse to prove yourself."

Shaylynn stops and stares into Pythyn's eyes. "I will not disturb their final resting place."

"If that's what it is," Pythyn retorts.

Shaylynn turns away from Pythyn and mounts his horse. As Pythyn moves to get in his way, Fallon rides up on his horse and gets between them.

"It is," Fallon confirms. "I felt it in my heart."

"Leave it to you to believe Shaylynn without thought or merit," Pythyn scolds. "You'd say the crown jewels lie under that dirt if he directed you to."

Fallon brushes his horse against Pythyn to voice his displeasure. Pythyn jumps back and scowls. "Just because I go beyond the limits of your intelligence and capabilities does not mean I merely believe what I am told," Fallon says. "Of course, you'd need a heart to feel something in."

Pythyn rolls his eyes and gets back to his business.

"It still does not explain why you went there," Pythyn says.

Shaylynn stops his horse and turns to face Pythyn.

"We do not know if we will be in this place again. Perhaps, this is the only time we'll be able to look upon their resting place. Most likely, our families will never see it. We are the witnesses who must give them a legacy to hold. Before I enter that desolate country of Jorram, I would know what they did with my father. That way I'll know what to do with them if they attempt to stop me."

Shaylynn rides off, and the others quickly follow. Pythyn mounts his horse quickly and manages to keep pace. They ride the rest of the day, and as evening comes, they find themselves at Lakwood River. Here, they must cross and enter the kingdom of Daryndell. They will find no quarrel from the people here. In fact, they find no people at all. They merely ride, seemingly with greater speed and energy than before. Almost as if aided by some unseen force, they find themselves at their destination faster than they could have imagined. They are just beyond the Mountains of Grailtin, and a great forest lies to the north. When he sees it, Shaylynn feels a small part of him yearning to venture there, but he will not be deterred. Instead, he stays by the river. For on the other side lies the land of Jorram. Within that land dwells their princess, wrongly taken by the men who rule the kingdom. Soon, Shaylynn, Lyosan, and Fallon will enter Jorram without concern for self-preservation. The only question which remains is whether they will enter alone.

"Begin crafting a raft," Shaylynn instructs.

"For how many, captain?" Dragoon asks.

Shaylynn smiles, knowing the answer and feeling the inevitability of their withdrawal. After everything they've seen and heard, they still will not be swayed. Most of them do not even realize this yet. They will be shocked by their own refusal as though it came from nowhere.

"I suppose we must answer that question now," Shaylynn says turning to them. "You know the king's command. He will not send you into the foreign land, but he asks that you go.

"Those of you who stay will be expected to prepare for the return of those who go. We will have two days to enter Jorram, make our way to Belvik, and recover the princess. Those who come will need to travel light and fast. We do not have time to dawdle. Mainly, because if we are discovered, we will be captured, tortured, or worse. There will be no rescue for us."

As he says these words, he feels the courage of many falter. He cannot lie to them about what they face. Perhaps, they were not meant to come. He believes he is meant to carry out this purpose; perhaps, he is meant to do it alone. Yet Fallon and Lyosan will still come with him. In his mind, Shaylynn considers the possibility of leaving them behind as well. Let him carry the burden of the rescue he so desperately wants to carry out.

And yet, he knows they would never let him get far. Fallon believes in loyalty more than anything. If Shaylynn moves to leave, Fallon will be right behind him. Should Shaylynn attempt to leave Lyosan, Lyosan would charge into Jorram on his own for love of Crystalynn. Shaylynn, as disappointed as he may be, still does not stand alone. Though they may be few, they will count for much in the end.

"Make it for four," Shaylynn commands without taking note of the other knights, "three going over, four coming back." Indeed, none of the others had their hands raised to go, but Shaylynn would not have counted them anyway.

"Are you sure, Shaylynn?" Dragoon asks, a question meant to devise if Shaylynn means to go on with this task at all.

Shaylynn walks away without a word. Immediately, work on the craft begins. Within the hour, the raft is ready. All the youths are needed to get it in the water. Once afloat, the knights place supplies on the raft, enough to give them a day's ration. Enough to get them to the castle. They will need little but luck and speed to make the return trip.

Once the preparations are made, Lyosan and Fallon climb aboard the raft and await Shaylynn. He must give the final commands to the remaining youth before going into Jorram.

"Move a few leagues into the trees," Shaylynn instructs. "There, build a campsite for yourselves and keep the princess's carriage well-maintained. Work in small shifts to find food and water. Never return to this river. There are smaller and less dangerous streams within the wood. If soldiers patrol the border – as I imagine they do – your very presence may give us away.

"We shall cross the river tonight, leave the raft tied to a tree. I will cast an enchantment to make it invisible to all eyes but us three. From that point, we will have two days to finish our quest and return to you. Though the castle is not far from the river, we will have to move slowly to ensure safe passage. If all goes well, we will reach the castle by tomorrow's nightfall. If we have not made ourselves known to you by the third day, return to Langerwitz and alert the king of our failure. With any luck, you will not have to do so."

"Should we not at least attempt a rescue?" Stefen asks.

"You are not brave enough to come with me now," Shaylynn replies. "You shall not be brave enough to succeed where we have failed."

The knights acknowledge his commands then watch him climb aboard the raft and sail to the Jorramian side of the border. Once there, Shaylynn pauses for a few moments to say the enchantment, and then the three take off into the woods. The youths linger a while, perhaps longer than they should, then eventually fall back into the woods to build their camp as commanded.

The trio of knights works their way through the Jorramian forest with stealth and silence. Shaylynn takes the lead, Lyosan follows close behind, and Fallon watches their back to ensure their safety. As they go, they also scout places where it might be safe enough to camp for the night. They will not want to enter the castle until darkness falls the next day. That gives them close to twenty-seven hours to spend within the Jorramian borders all the while trying to make their way to the castle undetected. At most, it will take four hours to get to the castle. Surely, they will need to rest. They can work in shifts, or Shaylynn can keep watch all night. Most likely, the others will not allow such a thing to occur. To ensure he is at his best, Fallon and Lyosan will demand he take some rest during the night. The true danger will come the next day. For the time being, they have the shadows to keep them hidden. Shaylynn can cloak them and keep them out of the sight of any Jorramian who might cross their path. It is harder during the day not to mention when there are more people to worry about. There may be a stray hunter or two young lovers out and about, but outside of that, there will be nothing but the animals of the night.

As they walk, they come across a small cottage. Shaylynn signals to the others that it lies ahead. Immediately, they drop low to the ground and cease movement. Shaylynn studies the cottage for a long while. It is quaint, a simple structure put together with some skill. Some of the logs seem a bit out of place or non-centered by some small margin. They are at the back of the property from what Shaylynn can tell. They see one window and a very simple door – not the type expected to welcome visitors. Smoke rises from the chimney. A stack of recently chopped wood lies about fifty feet in front of them. The axe used to perform the deed is left with its blade buried in a stump.

After a few minutes of resting, Lyosan makes it clear he wishes to proceed, but Shaylynn is not so convinced. He feels four people present in the cottage. Something is about to happen which will require them to be still for a few more moments at the least. They sit among the tall grass. Lyosan waits for a few more seconds, but then he grows impatient and starts to move. Fallon attempts to stop him, but Lyosan is out of reach and Fallon will not sacrifice his position.

A moment later, a small child bursts through the door and runs into the backyard. Lyosan trips over his own feet and collapses with a thud. The noise attracts the child's attention. Shaylynn casts an enchantment to cloak the three of them, but he cannot be certain it will work. For a few tense moments, the child stares straight at them. Shaylynn now sees the child is a young girl, probably no older than Daylynn.

"Merienna!" a voice calls from inside the house, "come inside this moment!"

The cry knocks Merienna out of her trance. "No!" she cries. "I'm not coming back in. I'm running away!"

The first voice had to be Merienna's mother. Another voice comes from the house, this one must be her father. "Oh, let her go!" he says. "She'll run around for a while, get tired, then come inside."

"This is your answer to everything that goes wrong with her!" the mother protests. "You never want to solve the problem."

"Her brother was picking on her," the father explains. "It happens a lot with children. You'd know that if you weren't an only child."

As the parents continue to argue, Merienna's attention goes back to the spot where she heard the noise. Shaylynn, Lyosan, and Fallon have not moved from their spot. The cloak appears to be working as the child has not said anything about them. Clearly though, she has heard the noise and wishes to know what caused it. Slowly, she makes her way towards the tree line.

Lyosan glances over to Shaylynn and asks with his hands if they should move. Shaylynn shakes his head. The cloak will hide them from being seen, but it will not mask their movements or silence their steps. Fallon agrees and quietly taps Lyosan on the shoulder. When Lyosan looks at him, Fallon motions for him to stay still and keep low.

About a minute later, Merienna stands a few feet away from the trio. She still has not said anything about seeing someone, but she carefully examines the area where she heard the noise come from. Peering over the edges of the grass, she looks for but cannot find the source. As she looks, her face mirrors the frustration she feels. Shaylynn begins to suspect she saw them for a split second before the cloak kicked in. If that's the case, the only thing that may satisfy her curiosity is another look at what she saw.

"Is someone there?" she whispers. Then, she waits a few seconds to see if there's a reply. When none comes, she whispers again. "I promise I won't tell on you," she swears. "I just thought I saw someone and wanted to make sure I was right."

It would be a calculated risk to show themselves right now. Though it is obvious the child knows something is out there, there is no telling if the parents will come get her soon. Or perhaps her brother will come outside, forced by the parents to apologize for whatever indiscretion he's perpetrated.

Merienna sits down on the ground a few feet from the tall grass. She continues to look into the trees, and a tear falls down her cheek. "I really just want someone to talk to," she says. "No one in my family cares what I have to say. So, if someone else was going to run away, maybe I could come with you."

The tragedy of the moment becomes too much for Shaylynn. Knowing the difficulties of the youngest child, he will not sit idly by and let the child suffer. He motions to Fallon and Lyosan that he's going to reveal himself. Neither of his comrades is fond of the idea, but they cannot stop him.

Merienna gazes with wonder as a figure steps out from the shadow and materializes in front of her. Shaylynn then sits down next to her as excitement overcomes her.

"I knew someone was there!" she exclaims.

Shaylynn quickly covers her mouth and places a finger over his mouth. She quickly nods in agreement and places a finger over her mouth – actually over Shaylynn's hand – to consent to his terms.

"I'm sorry," Merienna whispers.

"It's okay," Shaylynn replies with a warm smile.

"Are you running away from home, too?"

Shaylynn shakes his head. "Actually, I'm here to make sure you don't run away from your home."

Merienna starts to back away from Shaylynn. She is not going to alert anyone to his presence, but she's not sure she wants to play with him anymore. Despite the assurances from her father that she would come back inside when she was tired, Merienna truly means to leave home this time. She just wants someone to go with her so she isn't so lonely.

"Why would you care if I leave or not?" she asks.

"Because," Shaylynn replies, "I have a family I don't get to see that much these days."

Merienna rolls her eyes as she pulls her knees to her chest. Then, she sighs and puts her head down turning away from Shaylynn. "Yeah, but I bet you have a nice family – not anything like my family. They're mean."

"Well, I do have a good family, but we don't always get along that well."

Merienna wasn't expecting this answer. She turns to face Shaylynn but keeps her distance from him. On some level, this is still probably just a trick to get her to stay. She won't be convinced so easily.

"Do you yell at each other?" Merienna asks.

"Sometimes," Shaylynn confesses.

"And not talk to each other for days and days?"

"Yes."

"Does your brother throw things at you?"

"Well, I have two. My older brother does – well, he did. He's a bit old for that now. And my younger brother has thrown things at me, but I have to admit I threw things at him first. Plus, the two of us threw things at our oldest brother." Shaylynn smiles a bit as he tells Merienna this. She laughs with him – imagining having someone to team up with and pick on the bigger sibling. But then she remembers something Shaylynn said earlier.

"Why did you throw things at your younger brother?"

Shaylynn shrugs. "I can't really remember anymore. I'm sure I was mad at him for something not important. Or I just wanted to do something and didn't think of anything better to do."

"That's not very nice," Merienna chides.

"No, it wasn't," Shaylynn agrees. "That's why, after a while, I stopped doing it."

Merienna grunts. "I wish you were my brother."

"And I'd love to have you as a sister," Shaylynn says, "but I bet your brother likes having you for his sister. If you're his only one, I'd hate to take you away from him."

"He wouldn't even realize I was gone," Merienna replies with a tear forming in her eye. "My parents wouldn't either."

A few more tears form in Merienna's eyes. She tries to choke them back, but it's apparent to Shaylynn she's crying. He reaches over and places a hand on her back. No sooner does she feel his hand does Merienna bury her face in his side. Shaylynn wraps his arm around her and holds her for a few minutes.

"Now don't say that," Shaylynn says. "Of course they would realize you'd gone. Then, they'd move heaven and earth trying to find you. Even if your brother doesn't show it right now, he loves you too. In time, you will see the love they have for you."

"You really think they'd come after me?" Merienna asks.

Shaylynn pulls away from her and raises her chin with his thumb and forefinger. After wiping away a couple tears, he looks in her eyes and says, "There is no force in this world that would stop them."

Merienna hugs Shaylynn tightly for a more minutes. After a while, she raises her head and looks at her home. She glances at Shaylynn for a moment then walks back to her house. Before opening the door, she turns back one last time.

"What's your name?" she asks.

"Shay."

"I shall always remember that."

"And I shall always remember you, Merienna."

She goes back into the house and closes the door. Shaylynn returns to the tall grass with Lyosan and Fallon. Neither man has moved since Shaylynn left the safety of their cloak. For a few moments, neither speaks to him as they wait to see if anything else will come of this experience. The house stays calm and eventually the lights turn out. Once that happens, the three assume they are in the clear.

"You risk too much," Lyosan complains when they start moving again.

"I agree," Fallon agrees.

Shaylynn grunts. "I expect as much from you, Fallon, but you, Lyosan, having siblings of your own, I expected more."

"We are in enemy territory," Lyosan says. "Evil is all around us."

"And yet innocence still exists," Shaylynn replies. "I will not dare come to the place where I cannot recognize it."

"It is not the child who concerns us," Fallon explains. "We can know nothing of her family. Had she alerted them to our presence, our mission may have failed."

"You underestimate me then," Shaylynn says.

Though Fallon and Lyosan both would say more, they drop the subject and continue through Jorram. They find a place to camp and sleep in shifts. They light no fire and eat only what the trees can provide.

Shaylynn does not sleep much despite the complaints of Fallon. To appease him, Shaylynn rests his eyes, but sleep does not come to him. Being in this land is unsettling for Shaylynn. He cannot completely put his finger on the reason why, but something is afoot here he cannot yet see.

Moreover, he longs for home. Having talked with Merienna only reminds him of everything he's left in Artonia. He wishes to be with his family; he wishes to be in his own bed; he wishes to be with Sarin.

And yet, he is captivated by the child whom he met a few hours ago. She intrigues him in ways he cannot comprehend. She seemed so certain of her family and their lack of bonding. The honesty within her went beyond the mere discussion of the moment. It spoke to something more. For a brief moment, Shaylynn regrets telling her to return home. He only wishes to be in his own home, he realizes.

When morning comes, Shaylynn rises and finds breakfast before Fallon or Lyosan rise. He lights a small fire and gets the meal ready. With his mind, he breaks the smoke before it rises too high into the sky. Still when Fallon smells the smoke, he wakes with a start.

"What are you doing?" he asks.

"We need a good meal to keep us prepared for the task at hand," Shaylynn replies.

"I take it you're dealing with the smoke?"

"Of course."

Fallon wakes Lyosan and starts searching the area. It takes Lyosan a few moments to realize what is afoot, but once he sees the fire, he joins Fallon in securing the area. Unlike Fallon, Lyosan is unaware of Shaylynn's talent for dealing with the smoke which, under normal circumstances, might alert someone to their presence.

"You are growing reckless at a poor moment," Lyosan says once convinced all is well.

Shaylynn laughs softly. "You continue to underestimate me," he says. "There has been little more than a coyote's step in the past four hours."

"It would not take a coyote to see the smoke of your fire," Lyosan retorts.

"The smoke barely clears the trees," Shaylynn says. "I'd not let it go any further than that."

"You control the smoke now do you?"

"This smoke I do, yes," Shaylynn replies.

To prove his point, Shaylynn blows over the top of the fire. The smoke drifts away from the fire and begins to surround Lyosan. It swirls around him continuously in a taunting fashion. For a few seconds, Lyosan tolerates the playful teasing, but when Shaylynn persists, Lyosan swipes at the smoke to break it up. Shaylynn chuckles to himself as Lyosan steps away from the vapors.

Lyosan sits down on the ground near the fire and begrudgingly accepts the plate Shaylynn has prepared for him. Fallon joins them shortly, and the three eat their meal.

"I hope your skills go beyond pure nuisance," Lyosan comments.

"They do," Shaylynn says with a smile. "They most certainly do."

The remark reminds Fallon of the times spent in Forleen Forest. Ever since they have entered the borders of Jorram, Fallon has forgotten the sights which took place there. This seems much more dangerous than any other task they've undertaken. When in the forest, they were all, eventually, on the same side. When they fought in the south, they had a legion of soldiers with them. Now, they are alone.

While Fallon would believe Shaylynn could accomplish any feat placed before him, he knows not even Shaylynn has dealt with the forces of Jorram in such large numbers. They are still young after all. Despite the minor skirmishes they've fought, time has not aged them any further than normal. They still attempt to right where their fathers were wronged. They face a nation which means to plunge them into darkness and death. And yet, Fallon and Lyosan stand in good company because Shaylynn is at their side.

CHAPTER XIV

Once finished with breakfast, they clean their campsite to leave no trace of their presence. Moving silently through the forest, they encounter little in the way of resistance. In the few instances in which they cross paths with another person or persons, Shaylynn sees them coming with enough time to move their path out of the way or to climb the trees and find cover. Shortly after lunch, the castle comes into view. When it does, the trio goes on high alert. They meticulously maneuver through the forest, sometimes keeping still for up to ten minutes at a time. Though this greatly slows their progress, it keeps them safe. As the sun descends, they quicken their pace a bit. Lyosan's steps quicken as the castle grows in his eye. Fallon keeps his head and ensures the safety of the troop. Shaylynn constantly keeps his focus on the area surrounding them. In his mind, he sees the forests for miles beyond the normal sight of his comrades. Keeping his eye on so much, he consistently needs to refocus his attention on smaller locations. At times, multiple targets enter his sights. In those moments, they all come to a stop.

Still, by nightfall, they are within throwing distance of the castle wall. For a full hour, they remain amongst the reeds to ensure their presence will go unnoticed. Looking for patterns in the guard patrol and any weakness the castle may possess, they monitor continually with the mindset of a predator. Quietly and calmly, they discuss what they've witnessed and begin to see a plan forming which will bring them inside the castle walls.

With Fallon and Lyosan at his side, Shaylynn crawls to the edge of the grass. He dares not breach the line knowing the Jorramians would be on watch. Instead, he places a single palm flat on the ground and closes his eyes. Fallon signals Lyosan to watch behind them. As for Fallon, he keeps a close eye on their forward position. Lyosan wishes for things to progress quickly, yet he understands their need for caution. Furthermore, the method Shaylynn utilizes is not an easy one to master.

Using small pulses of energy, he sends out feelers in all directions. With them, he will be able to detect all around them. Given the nature of the pulses, he cannot reach far with a single pulse. He also has to use caution for if he sends too much forward, the ground will billow and give them away. As the pulses run out, Shaylynn begins to take in the landscape around him. The trees, they know, protrude to the south and the east. The river cuts forth in the north. In those places, he feels not just the trees and the running water, but also the creatures who inhabit the woods. He feels squirrels, owls, and even a wolf or two. They are far away and not likely to interrupt their path, so he pays them no mind.

Instead, he fears what lies to the west. Beyond the cover of this high grass, the castle of Belvik lies in darkness. There dwells the king and their imprisoned friend. Even if storming the castle would be an easy feat, navigating its unknown corridors will not be. True, once inside, Shaylynn could attempt to map the boundaries with just the touch of a wall, but he'll need time and he cannot guarantee himself that. He assumes Crystalynn's prison will be well-guarded, so violence would be necessary. The more his pulses race along the ground, the more certain he becomes that violence will come sooner than that.

For on the ground alone, he feels five heartbeats of men along the nearest wall of the castle. He cannot be certain, but he believes each to be heavily armed. As he moves his way up the wall, he trembles at the thought of how many more lie in wait. And yet, he knows that just minutes from now, he will storm the castle with Lyosan and Fallon at his side.

Indeed, Shaylynn has seemed driven by purpose since the moment he returned to Langerwitz. Fallon has noticed it greatly. Ever the joker and clown, some of Shaylynn's humor has diminished. Even when he spoke to the king, it was not in the same manner. Whatever had happened to him during those days they spent in the forest, they have changed him greatly. Having seen the ways in which he's grown, Fallon takes great pride in knowing what glories lie ahead of them.

For Lyosan, the changes bring fear. He's always known the greatness

Shaylynn is capable of. He's always known Shaylynn would be the best of his age, but this is quite different. This is beyond the call of chivalry and duty; this is beyond the normal scope of men. And Lyosan does not know if he has the strength to be a part of it.

As they wait in the brush, Lyosan's heart begins to race. Several minutes they've stayed under cover with no sight or sound to report, and the silence worries him.

"Perhaps we should move," Lyosan whispers.

"It is not time," Shaylynn replies, slightly irritated.

"When will be the time?" Lyosan asks.

"I will know it if I have the silence to recognize it," Shaylynn explains.

"That doesn't make any sense," Lyosan replies.

"To you," Shaylynn retorts.

"Nor I," Fallon adds. "They do not know we are coming. They cannot be ready for us. You are being so careful in your attack, but surely you have the means to aide us."

"What means do you suggest?" Shaylynn inquires.

Fallon shrugs. "Surely you could shroud us in darkness which would hide us?"

Shaylynn shakes his head. "I could hide our forms but not our steps. Someone would see our movements and worse, hear our progress once we took to the wall."

"What of flight?" Lyosan suggests. "Could we not fly to the top of the wall?"

"I could myself perhaps, but it would be difficult to guide the both of you," Shaylynn admits. "We would have to be cloaked the entire time as well. Another drain which I would need time to recover from. Forleen fed my power. I am not receiving the same boost here."

"Could we walk through the wall in some manner?" Fallon asks, recalling something he'd seen in the forest.

Shaylynn understands where Fallon is coming from, but it would not work here. There is something at work they know nothing about. He's chosen to hide it from them until the absolute moment of their need. That moment, it seems, is at time.

"Another force is at work here," Shaylynn explains. "Some power, not too strong but strong enough, protects the walls in some regard. I can slip past it without detection, but I dare not prod it into awakening."

"You said nothing of this before," Fallon says. Suddenly, he feels a pit of fear growing in his stomach. Shaylynn can handle magic well, but he has not yet been tested against it. Now, with so much at stake, is not the time for the test to take place.

"I was not certain of it before, but now that I am here, I cannot deny it. I did not want to worry you unnecessarily."

"Instead, I'll worry twice as much now," Fallon comments under his breath.

Lyosan has been silent for a while. He fears the presence of magic, same as Fallon, but he does not want anything to deter him in his crusade to rescue the princess. He is ready to give his life, as Shaylynn has warned him might be necessary, and he is not about to waver now.

"Distraction, then," Fallon remarks. "We need some form of distraction."

"I cannot think of one that would suffice," Shaylynn says.

"Perhaps a fire," Lyosan finally says.

Shaylynn shakes his head again. "I'd thought of that, but they'd see the place from which I conjured it. They'd be on us in a moment's time."

"Too bad you can't bring fire from the sky," Fallon jests.

A jab at him indeed, but there is some validity to the suggestion, Shaylynn realizes. Not fire exactly, but something to cause fire. The men of the wood told him it is possible, but he fears he lacks the control needed. The danger would be great should he miss his mark. The results, a disaster if he cannot bring about the right spell. And yet, it seems the only way. For, not only could he provide the distraction needed, but he could also rattle the courage of the men in front of them. Perhaps not enough to make them disperse but enough to give them cover for a few moments.

As he looks to the sky, Fallon sees the worry come over him. While it is uncommon to see such concern on his friend's face, Fallon takes some comfort in it. It shows Shaylynn will be focused; he will be on his game should he decide to go along with this idea. Fallon still knows not the manner in which Shaylynn would enact his suggestion, but he feels assured something would happen and happen soon.

"What's your thought?" Fallon asks.

"I can bring fire from the sky," Shaylynn admits.

"Then do it!" Lyosan exclaims.

"It is not as easy as that," Shaylynn says. "There's a certain amount of precision to this. I'm not certain I'm capable of."

"You needn't be too accurate," Fallon says. "You just need to be sure not to bring it to you."

"I am not certain I can do that."

"You've got to try!" Lyosan barks.

His outburst surprises both Fallon and Shaylynn. Never have they heard Lyosan speak with such passion or purpose. They understand the reason for his desire shining through. Indeed, if Crystalynn were not involved, it is possible, if not likely, he would not have come. As it is, he is determined to provide assistance in any form he can. This mission, by his will alone, will have a successful conclusion.

From this, Shaylynn can draw strength. It is the moment he has been looking for – the moment when Lyosan would show something he'd been afraid to draw from his entire life. This is not when he would defer and allow his preferences to drop to the side. This is not the moment to stand aside and let the river run by. This is the moment to take the river full force and deal with the consequences of his courage. Through this display, Shaylynn can have assurances his efforts will not be in vain. The plan, as he designed it, will follow through without fail.

Drawing closer to the grass's edge, Shaylynn gazes to the sky with respectful caution. Clouds cover the moon, providing the opportunity needed to bring forth lightning. For sure, he can conjure but one bolt to the ground and have the strength to ascend the castle wall. Lyosan and Fallon must be quick in their movements. Their window will be small.

"When I say, take the lead," Shaylynn says to them both. "I'll be close at hand."

"Try not to get us singed," Fallon says.

Shaylynn lowers his eyes and begins calling to the clouds with his mind. Softly and politely, he beckons forth a bolt from the clouds. In his communion with them, he feels the charge begin to build. In his last moments of conjuring, he directs it towards his intended target. He looks for a place just in front of the castle wall. He wishes to kill none of the guards but perhaps injure them to remove them from the spot in which they stand.

From forth the darkened sky, a bolt of lightning flashes. For the moment, day returns whilst the bolt protrudes the air. A moment later, it lands and collides with the top of eastern castle wall. Stone erupts and becomes a shower of boulders in the air. Then, the blare of thunder pierces the ears of all around. Sadly, they have not the time to react as the debris rains down upon those below. Whilst the heaviest of the fragments land closer to the guards, some small pebbles reach the spot where Shaylynn, Fallon, and Lyosan lay.

For their part, Lyosan and Fallon are in awe. Never have they seen such a display. Never would they have suspected Shaylynn could cause such a sight. Meanwhile, Shaylynn quakes a bit in fear. He wished not to disturb the castle at all. In his foolish aim, he may have triggered the magic that lies within. His presence, which he hoped to hide until the end, might have been detected with the blast.

In any event, their moment is now spoiled. It will take time and men to clear the space. The distraction will draw people to the wall, not away from it. He needs something better than this. And yet, he's been so sure that in this moment, he would have all he needed to storm this castle and complete the task at hand. It seems unlikely he has that now.

"Medic!" a voice cries from near the wall. "We need a medic here!"

Shaylynn peers out over the scene. The debris from the blast landed on two of the posted guards. Another seems to have fallen from atop the wall. They all appear alive though one is in much direr straits than the other two. In his heart, Shaylynn prays for the safety of them all. He'd hoped to escape the night without death, but he knew the chance was small.

"Our moment may yet be at hand," Fallon whispers.

"Let's hope the price was not too high," Shaylynn replies.

Shortly thereafter, a cluster of men come from the castle to bring the wounded inside. As reports ring out of the events which took place, Shaylynn, Fallon, and Lyosan wait for the scene to clear. It is doubtful they have the men ready to take the injured soldiers' place. The wall may be vulnerable for some time.

Within a short time, the scene has cleared. Shaylynn sends out pulses again to gauge what lay before them. Two guards still patrol the wall, but none walk the grounds. If they can reach the wall undetected, they will have the perfect chance to get inside the castle. The crevice in the wall dips low and provides an entryway without detection. They need only to pass through without disturbing what remains standing.

For several minutes, Shaylynn studies the wall looking for the guards to take their measure of the scene. And yet, through it all, none look over the wall. Either they are aware of his presence and look to capture him once he moves, or they fear another strike will come to the wall and wish to avoid it at all costs. Shaylynn fears the former more than he expects the latter. Thus, his hesitation lasts longer than Lyosan and Fallon hope. They understand and appreciate his desire to keep them safe, but they wish for action. Longer than two hours now they've waited in the grass as the night nipped at their skin.

"We should go," Fallon prods.

"Perhaps," Shaylynn replies.

"Then why do we wait?" Lyosan demands.

"To ensure our safety," Shaylynn explains.

"It is not my safety that concerns me," Lyosan admits.

"Well, one of us must look out for it then," Shaylynn says. "It appears it must be me."

He examines the wall for a while longer with an aim towards storming it. He senses the tension rising among his comrades and wishes to avail their concerns. Still, he will not risk their safety when caution can be afforded. To test the waters, he skips a stone into the grass. It is not loud enough to cause a scene. Rather, it sounds as one trying to silently maneuver through the grass. If the guards lay in wait, it might be enough to arouse their suspicions.

For several moments after his ruse, Shaylynn watches the wall. Still, no one comes to the wall. He still feels his movements might be rash, but he is convinced they have to move or forfeit the night. With a nod to his fellow men, he beckons them into the clearing. Without hesitation or apprehension, they bolt towards the wall. Emboldened by their earnest desire, Shaylynn takes off after them. He overtakes them before they reach their destination and holds flat against it while he waits for them to reach him. As soon as they do, he begins to climb the wall.

He moves silently and quickly with the dexterity of a spider. He lurches forwards with his arms, then pulls himself onward with great grace and ease. Fallon has drawn his bow and pulls back the string with the nock of the arrow resting comfortably in its place. He has a bad line of sight against the wall, but he could at least startle any who discover them. Perhaps Shaylynn could aid his arrow with a little magic to guide it to its mark successfully. Hopefully, his skills will not be needed yet.

Shaylynn reaches the crevice in the wall, leaps over the edge, and rests himself in the wall's wake. A moment later, a line of rope leaps from the wall and tumbles to the ground. Fallon catches the tip to keep it from making a sound. After a tug to ensure Shaylynn has bound the rope to something fixed, Fallon starts up the rope. Lyosan comes quickly after, and within minutes, both reach the rift. Fallon climbs over the edge and takes a defensive position to protect against anyone coming. Lyosan reaches the edge as well, but as he comes over the edge, he is stunned to find Shaylynn has held the rope the entire journey up the wall. The shock on his face catches Shaylynn's attention, who wishes Lyosan would hurry along.

"You cannot have borne both our weights," Lyosan whispers.

"It does get harder the longer I have to do it!" Shaylynn admits.

In haste, Lyosan climbs over the wall and joins Fallon in defense. Shaylynn pulls the rope up and then joins his friends. Fallon notices Shaylynn tenses his hands as though in pain.

"Too much for you?" Fallon asks.

"Not in the slightest," Shaylynn replies. "Give me but a moment, and we'll be on our way."

After stretching his fingers a few times, Shaylynn rubs them together fiercely. Lyosan hears Shaylynn chanting under his breath. He cannot make out the words, but a few seconds later, Shaylynn stops and shakes his hands out.

"Let's go," he says.

"Where to?" Fallon asks.

"I haven't the faintest idea," Shaylynn admits. "I'm just hoping the damage will keep others from coming this way."

They move through the halls of the castle silently. They keep to darkness as much as they are able. Several times, Shaylynn puts out a flame from a lighted torch to give them safe passage. They do not come across many people, which Lyosan and Fallon take great comfort in, but Shaylynn seems only to worry. Their ease in avoiding detection might be proof of a larger problem. Again, a trap may be set for their coming.

After a few minutes of wandering, Shaylynn settles in a dark hallway. Fallon and Lyosan take watch. They've gone several minutes without even the hint of another person. Shaylynn assumes he now has the opportunity to map the castle's floors. Placing one hand on the wall, he sends out feelers again. He does not have to be as careful with these as stone is less likely to break. However, if a presence with powers like his is sensitive enough to feel his pulse, a great danger may await them.

Out he stretches his reach and more and more the labyrinth before him begins to clear and materialize. He begins to see the path he should follow and the people who stand guard. And yet, his discomfort does not pass; his concerns are not availed. Something still troubles him about their passage, and the more he studies the layout, the more he understands why. The great hall, the king's parlor, lay but two stories down. Gathered there is a great mass of people, and every path seems to take them there. Whether by design or chance, he is being led to those who lie in wait. There is no getting around it; there is no other avenue to take. He will have to present himself to Athorn in the great hall.

"I don't think we need worry about our route," Shaylynn admits. "They are waiting for us to come."

"How can that be?" Lyosan asks.

"I fear the blame is mine," Shaylynn replies.

"We are none of us without blame," Fallon corrects. "We've brought it all upon ourselves."

"Perhaps they were waiting for us anyway," Shaylynn suggests, "or perhaps they felt our presence when lightning struck the castle. In any event, they mean to draw us out."

"And we must go to them?" Fallon asks.

"We must," Lyosan immediately barks.

"Indeed, we must," Shaylynn concurs before adding. "Or at least, I must."

"You cannot survive alone," Fallon says.

"Not alone," Shaylynn replies. "Merely separated. I will guide you to the hall where you might not be seen. There you can cover me from above."

"How many wait in the room for you?" Fallon asks.

"I figure twenty," he replies.

"Twenty!" Lyosan repeats. "We cannot handle twenty even with surprise on our side!"

Shaylynn's coy smile returns for the first time since they embarked on their trip. It is a most welcomed sight. "You forget," he says, "the princess in undoubtedly one of them. I can take ten on my own. That leaves five for Fallon and four for you, Lyosan. Surely, if you cannot handle but four, I should not have brought you in the first place."

Lyosan rolls his eyes and draws a deep breath. Fallon laughs quietly to himself. His resolve is strengthened once again.

The Great Hall of Belvik has stood for three centuries. Designed by the great King Amon, it holds six hundred at capacity. The stone is pure marble, a mark of the splendor and glory of a lost time. Large pillars create elaborate archways in the ceiling. Along each archway is an elaborately designed work of art. While it creates a great scene in the daylight, it gives wonderful cover at night. One cannot be certain whether or not the figures casting shadows belong to the craft or an intruder. In those scenes, one sees great battles from times of old. Swords were drawn; shields clashed; men raised their arms in victory while others floundered in defeat. Such a sight is the hall's ceiling where torches are placed all about to give light to the scenes at night.

On the floor of the hall, the pillars create a great path from the chamber doors to the throne where sits Athorn. To his right sits his son, Dreilon. To Dreilon's right sits the princess. The throne is carved of pure gold. A lush red fabric drapes over the seat and the back of the throne. It all sits upon a stage, raised from the floor by three small steps. A luscious red carpet fringed with gold tassels stretches from the throne across the floor to the chamber doors. The doors are thick mahogany, painted black as night. They are closed at the moment, but two guards stand near the handles of the door. In between the pillars, closest to the carpet, stand two guards in each opening. As Fallon and Lyosan quickly find out, Shaylynn has greatly missed the mark with his guess of twenty guards. Surely, there are closer to forty.

Nonetheless, he will not be deterred which both brightens and darkens Lyosan and Fallon's moods. Darkened because they feel the task's chances greatly lessened by the number of guards. Brightened, because Shaylynn carries on in his typical fashion. His mood, though rarely dampened by such challenges, seems to raise higher when he sees the numbers they faced. Still, he leaves them at two vantage points which gave them sight upon the king.

Lyosan quakes as he watches the princess nervously sitting by the prince. She seems healthy, though her demeanor is definitely that of a prisoner. She says nothing, looks quickly and sharply but never to anyone in particular. When the prince leans over and speaks in her ear, she lowers her head and tightly shuts her eyes. In these moments, a rage builds within Lyosan. He boils inside at the thought of Dreilon's mind embracing

Crystalynn as his wife and queen. If he had not the sense, he would leap from his spot and charge the crown prince to tear him from the pedestal on which he sits. But the plan is enacted; he cannot risk the chance.

Indeed, the plan quickly comes into focus as Shaylynn broaches the chamber doors and steps into the great hall. Immediately, the guards at the doors draw upon him. Shaylynn unleashes his sword and disarms the guards in moments. More fly as panic reaches the room. Far more than guards fill the hall – civilians too. Innocents who are no doubt the lords and ladies of the kingdom. How prepared were they for Shaylynn's arrival that they could make a spectacle of it? How long had they known of his coming?

After disarming five, the guards stop coming for Shaylynn. Instead, they encircle him with spears at the ready. Shaylynn poses himself and draws a dagger from its sheath. If they wish to merely fight, he could finish them himself. However, the king rises from his throne and raises his hand.

"Enough!" he commands.

The room stands in awe that the king would relent when clearly the advantage is becoming his. All turn to see his purpose, and soon they understand. For the king motions to his guards to lead Shaylynn to the throne. Slowly, they do. Slowly, Shaylynn follows. He drops his arms and walks with ease – an insult directed towards his host. Many around speak of his bravado in whispers and murmurs.

As he approaches the throne, Shaylynn takes stock of the princess. Concern is on her face as he seems ready for slaughter. She opens her mouth as if to speak, but Dreilon clasps her arm to silence her. Shaylynn twitches with anger.

"Indeed, your highness," Shaylynn directs to Athorn. "This is enough! Give me my princess, and nothing more will be lost!"

"Your princess?" Athorn repeats. "So you are indeed Shaylynn, the would-be-king of Artonia."

The hall gasps in shock. News of his deeds have reached them. Shaylynn is actually impressed.

"I am no king," Shaylynn responds. "I leave such things to better men than I. But, as I am a son of Langerwitz, I stand loyal to the crown of Cyrus, King of Artonia. His sister, whom you have abducted, is my princess, and I will see her returned."

"You say she is your princess," Athorn replies. "Yet, I say she is my daughter-in-law, betrothed to Dreilon, crown prince of Jorram. In that instance, I need not return her to anyone. She is home."

The crowd laughs and mocks Shaylynn at the king's decree. Surely this boy, this mere child, would not dare stand up to a king. Surely, he would not question his mighty word. And if he truly is foolish enough to do so, then he must know death will come to him.

"Having seen the devastation to our southern lands, I say the bargain which granted your son her hand is broken."

"Do you speak for your king?" Athorn asks.

"I do," Shaylynn replies.

"And has the king decided the fate of his sister if she does not go to my son?"

"To some extent," Shaylynn admits.

"Please, tell."

Shaylynn does not wish to trade barbs with this man. And yet, a king of men, the ruler of Jorram says please to a boy just recently granted knighthood. This display of respect goes beyond the venomous nature of the king. It is not for enemies but for respected kinsmen. When he asks, he does not ask with malice or in jest. He genuinely wishes for the answer. He wishes to converse with the boy.

Silence prevails for moments while thoughts race in Shaylynn's head. In one hand, he counts the people around him and takes note of their placement. In the other, he calculates the purpose for the king's diplomacy. Perhaps he stalls to trigger a trap. Perhaps he knows of Fallon and Lyosan and has sent guards to capture them. Perhaps he has something far more sinister in mind.

"A tournament shall be held," Shaylynn finally answers. "A tournament to determine the next in line for the throne. I, along with sixty-three of my peers, shall participate in this tournament."

The king paces back and forth for a moment stroking his beard. Deep in thought, he is clearly carefully picking his next words.

"So, you will participate in the tournament," Athorn says, "yet you are certain you will not be king."

"Yes," Shaylynn replies slowly.

"I was led to believe you are the best of your age," Athorn says.

"Perhaps," Shaylynn says.

"Then who shall defeat you?"

"He who should be king."

In his mind, Shaylynn thinks of Lyosan though he will not speak his name. Should Athorn believe Lyosan the next king, he would undoubtedly believe Lyosan came with Shaylynn to rescue the princess. Athorn notes this absence of information and marks Shaylynn's cleverness. With a smile, he drops his hands and turns to the boy.

"Should not you be king?" he asks.

Shaylynn shrugs. "I am not so certain of such things," he says.

Athorn turns towards Crystalynn. "She would have you as her king," he says.

Shaylynn's eyes widen, and his muscles tense. Because of the acoustics of the hall, the sound surely carries to Lyosan and Fallon in the rafters. This admittance, true or otherwise, will stir certain emotions in Lyosan. Because of this, Shaylynn refuses to make eye contact with Crystalynn. The last thing he wants is to discover the king's words are true, and with but a look upon her face, he would be able to detect as much.

In the rafters, Fallon quickly gazes from his perch to where Lyosan lay. Though ready with an arrow, Lyosan's pull on the string has lessened. His attention clearly diverted, Lyosan looks from their spot to the princess sitting in the chair next to the prince. Her visage does indeed betray her feelings. Red flushes her cheeks, and tears fill her eyes. In some regard, she seeks Shaylynn's gaze, but he will not let her find it. In those few, silent moments before Shaylynn speaks again, Lyosan turns to despair. Again, the thing he seeks seems out of reach. Both the distance to her now and the distance to the crown expands in the silence of his heart.

Fallon fears Lyosan is no longer focused on the task at hand. Though he would reach over and knock some sense into him, he is too far and Fallon cannot risk any noise. Still, he fidgets in his spot, wishing again for action to come. All this night, worries built when bodies were at rest. In the moment when things are in motion, they worry for nothing but the success of the mission. Now, everyone's thoughts seem to slip to the future – a future they will not have if they fail. Their trio of warriors seem weaned down to two as Lyosan falls from the moment into his thoughts. Hopefully, there will be no price to pay for their loss.

"I do not believe that to be true," Shaylynn says as firmly as he can.

"Indeed, you do not," the king replies, "for you *know* it to be true! You came to her carriage the day she left your city. You saw the look in her eyes; you heard the love in her voice, but you chose to ignore it."

The memory of the day stings Shaylynn even now. He'd not caught it in the moment. Even if he had, he'd have ignored it, but he could not deny the hope Crystalynn had for the chance he would pledge himself to her. But he had not; he could not. And she knew why.

Yet, a greater concern lies before them. True, Shaylynn was at the carriage that day, but Athorn was not. Surely, Crystalynn did not give this information willingly. If they forced it out of her, by what means did they acquire the details.

"How could you know this?" Shaylynn asks.

"Do you deny it?" Athorn asks.

"I do not deny it, but how do you know this?"

Athorn laughs wickedly. "Come now, Shaylynn. You must know magic lurks in every crevice of this castle. Surely, it cannot be a surprise to you that we would have the means to read her thoughts and see her memories."

The thought had come to Shaylynn, but he hoped it would not be the case. He has not been guarding his own mind since entering the castle. Perhaps someone is trying to get in.

Shaylynn starts searching the crowd for the reader who must be among them. If Athorn knew Shaylynn was coming, he would be wise to protect himself with his own mages. As Athorn watches fear grip Shaylynn, he smiles.

"You needn't concern yourself," Athorn finally promises. "You know we are not that powerful...yet."

"And yet you attack our lands, kidnap our princess, and threaten my life."

"You've invaded my lands. What else am I to do?" The king steps forward and glares at Shaylynn. "Back to the matter, Shaylynn. Why do you deny your place as king?"

"Of what concern is that of yours?" Shaylynn asks.

"No concern," Athorn admits. "Merely a means to an end. You wish to have your princess back. She wishes for you to take the throne and be at your side. Vow to me, on your honor as a son of Langerwitz, that you will take the throne, and I shall release her!"

"Tis a joke!" Shaylynn cries.

"Tis the only way we shall have peace," Athorn warns. "As you may have noticed, I do not fear your king! I will attack his lands; I will kill his people; I will steal his goods! He is a fool and a mockery of his crown. A lesser descendant of greater men!" Athorn then turns and faces Shaylynn. "But you!" he says, pointing at Shaylynn. "You, Shaylynn, son of Feylynn, master of the magic arts, are a worthy king. Forsake the tournament. The princess can bear witness. Deny your king and take your place upon the throne!"

"You wish to create unrest?" Shaylynn asks. "Deny my king? I see your game, Athorn, and it shall not come to be. I stand with Cyrus, not against him. His sister does the same. She will not turn against him."

"So you may think, but we have seen her thoughts. On that day, Shaylynn, she would have stayed. Yes, she would have denied her brother if only you had given your love to her. What say you now?"

Shaylynn hesitates while the thought comes to him. He's known in his heart the full measure of that moment in time. In those days when he'd abandoned his post and lived in the trees, he replayed those moments in his mind and indeed, the thoughts came to him that if he had decided to give his love to her then she would have stayed. And yet this he could not do. He had already given his love to another, and another would have it or none.

"She longed for her home, not for me," Shaylynn says.

"Lies!" Athorn curses. "You know full-well she longed for you. She longed for the strength and power which dwells in your blood. She knew the love you could afford her would bring her happiness and joy. Still, you deny it and then claim to be a son of Langerwitz. You care nothing for the lands you claim loyalty to!"

He merely means to incite anger now. Shaylynn can see through his words enough to see that. Athorn means to divide Artonia between those loyal to the king and those who would be loyal to Shaylynn and Crystalynn. Then, the vulnerability would be enough to conquer the land with ease. Athorn would take Artonia for his own and lay waste to its people.

"Harsh words by a harsh man," Shaylynn remarks. "But they are hollow since they come from a man who would not honor his own word. I've heard your pleas, answered your questions, and nothing has come of it. Now return the princess to me or risk death or worse."

"Take the throne, Shaylynn," Athorn commands. "Take the throne or worse."

With a gesture from his father's hand, Dreilon grabs the princess's arm and pulls her to her feet. Drawing a dagger from his hand, he holds the blade against the skin of her neck. Above the scene, Lyosan snaps back to attention. In fact, he means to send an arrow towards the prince right away. Only his promise to Shaylynn steadies his hand.

When Fallon sees Lyosan is not going to fire, he exhales. From the moment Dreilon drew the knife, Fallon silently pleaded with Lyosan to maintain his composure. Their moment is close at hand. They cannot have a break in their resolve now.

As for Shaylynn, he raises a hand to ask for a hold. He does not doubt the king will dispatch the princess without a moment's thought. The chaos which would follow would be unyielding. Furthermore, Shaylynn would never be able to return to his homeland. Having failed on his mission, he would be disgraced. Fallon and Lyosan as well would be banished with him; although, the death of the princess would probably be followed shortly by Lyosan's demise. His rage would not yield until the perpetrators perished or he did. If Shaylynn were not ready at a moment's notice, Lyosan would fall.

"Your grace," Shaylynn pleads, "there are elements at play which would make a catastrophe of a misunderstanding. You do not understand what will be set in motion by this act."

He signals to Dreilon, who keeps the blade close. Crystalynn's breathing quickens as she feels the steel against her skin. Athorn looks to his son then to Shaylynn. He seems quite pleased with how the situation is going.

"Another way then," Athorn suggests. "You needn't lose your princess tonight, Shaylynn. In fact, you needn't lose her at all. I would not have my son wed this wretch, but I would have her power for my own. Again, declare your love for her. I shall make you my servant. You shall rule over Artonia and ensure its well-being. You shall have all you desire and more."

"You cannot expect me to take such a foolish offer," Shaylynn replies.

Athorn motions to Dreilon. He pushes the blade against Crystalynn's neck. She gasps and tilts away from him, but he draws a trickle of blood. Shaylynn, though angered by this disrespect, smiles in devious pleasure.

"It is your only chance, Shaylynn," Athorn warns.

Shaylynn holds up his palms for a moment, then places them politely behind his back. He bows to the king, then rises and says, "I disagree."

Before the king can respond, Shaylynn pulls two daggers from his belt and throws one towards the prince. So quick is his motion and so great his strength, the blade pieces Dreilon's hand before he can react. In pain and agony, he drops the dagger and falls to the floor. Crystalynn breaks his hold and runs for Shaylynn.

"Kill them!" Athorn commands.

Shaylynn throws the second dagger behind him, striking a guard in the leg. Before the guard hits the floor, arrows rain from the rafters. One by one, guards fall as more point to the ceiling looking for the assailants. Shaylynn draws his sword and moves towards the princess. Two guards move to capture her, but he quickly does away with them.

Chaos ensues. The lords and ladies in the hall disperse quickly. More and more men fill the hall making for Shaylynn. He returns to the center of the hall with sword in hand and the princess at his side.

Two ropes fall from the ceiling, and seconds later he is joined by his comrades. When she sees Lyosan, Crystalynn runs for him and throws her arms around him. He basks in her embrace for a brief moment, then sees to his duty. A good number, fifteen at least, surround them. Surely, they mean to end this now.

"Stand close together," Shaylynn commands.

"One of your tricks?" Fallon asks.

"I don't think it's a trick if it saves our lives," Shaylynn replies.

The four of them stand back-to-back as tightly as they can. Shaylynn extends his arms and circles them as far as he can behind his back. Fallon, Lyosan, and Crystalynn note a strip of the air in front of them begins to blur. All around the group of them, it circles until it meets Shaylynn's other hand. The blur seems a burning blaze but without a source. No flame to speak of. Only the blur hanging in the air. Shaylynn bends his knees and stands in a braced stance. The guards in front of him note Shaylynn's own eyes began to blur, but in them, they see the flame. Their courage begins to waver; they consider running from their posts. Before they can move, Shaylynn swings his arms forward. The blur races out in all directions. As it strikes the guards, it knocks them into the air and sends them crashing to the ground.

As Shaylynn surveys his work, he sees a man step forward. He is old, ancient almost, and cloaked in black with a beard wispy and white. His eyes are clouded and grey. A smile sits on his face – a smile which unnerves Shaylynn greatly. Before Shaylynn can even raise the slightest defense, he feels a needle in his head. Sharply and deeply, it burrows into his brain. Try as he might, he cannot remove it from his mind. Instead, his sword drops to the ground. The clang of it against the floor troubles his friends. Crystalynn turns and upon seeing Shaylynn drop to the ground, she comes to his aid. Fallon takes note of the scene, but his thoughts quickly turn. Now, they are at a great disadvantage. While he fears for his friend, he fears for their chances more.

Lyosan steps toward the king. Now that they are uncovered, his courage comes to life.

"What are you doing?" Lyosan demands.

"Me?" Athorn replies innocently. "I do nothing."

Lyosan raises his sword and steps towards the throne. Shaylynn cries out in pain as he raises his gaze to the stranger in black.

"He's telling the truth," Shaylynn painfully squeaks out.

Lyosan stops and turns to Shaylynn. Shaylynn, hands clasped around his head, stares through the crowd to the man still lurching forward. Lyosan steps towards him. Shaylynn quickly stops him.

"No!" he cries through the pain. "Leave it be!"

Lyosan looks to Shaylynn, then yields. Shaylynn struggles to get to his feet, but he finally rises. He tries to stand firm, but his legs buckle beneath him. As he wavers, he works through his spells to find the correct one. Surely something in his arsenal can avail him of this pain.

"What's the matter, Shaylynn, son of Feylynn?" the man croaks. His voice is cold and ill-mannered. He speaks as demons of the night speak. He is a nightmare incarnate. "Do you not recognize the source of my arts?"

"Those who dwell in darkness are often hard to find," Shaylynn replies.

"There is your weakness," the man explains. "You know not what I do thus you cannot protect yourself. All the time you spent with the Order in the forest has come to nothing! So simple is my act too. Even the simpleminded could learn it. In but a minute, your friends could know it, and so soon they will too!"

"Never!" Shaylynn cries.

"Then pledge your allegiance to me, Shaylynn!" Athorn commands. "End your stubbornness, and I shall end your pain."

"My pain is mine to bear; it will be mine to end!" Shaylynn replies.

"Then suffer pain that never ends!" Dreilon cries.

With dagger in hand, Dreilon flies towards the princess with arm raised and ready to strike. Shaylynn turns to see him come but has not the strength to react. Crystalynn turns too late as well. He comes upon her in a flash, and she braces herself for the cold touch of death.

And yet, it does not come to her. For while others do nothing, Lyosan raises his blade and catches Dreilon where he lands. Run through by his own haste, Dreilon drops the dagger and grabs for the blade. Having felt the blade in his skin, Dreilon realizes death is coming for him.

With a gasp, he chuckles, thinking this all a bad joke. Yet, he knows it is not. Back he steps and falls against the steps to the throne. As he does, the cry of the king echoes in the hall. The sound distracts the man tormenting Shaylynn, and Shaylynn responds by knocking him to the ground with a flick of his hand. Thus, the scene turns. Athorn goes to his son, who draws his last few breaths. None who are armed stand on guard. Swords and spears clang to the ground. Silence captures the air except for the cries of the king. Shaylynn steps forward but keeps a respectful distance. He did not know this would happen, but he knew something of the like would occur. He did not want this, and he wished it could be avoided. But the stubbornness of men does not always yield when it should.

Time stands still while the king mourns and cries for his lost son. None move against Shaylynn, Fallon, Lyosan, or Crystalynn. They fear their king's power. They fear his recourse. His only son and heir is lost. The only reminder of his deceased wife gone in a moment's notice. Though he was slain, it was of his own accord. He moved against another, and a man came to a woman's defense. It is not honorable, but it is understood.

After a period of time, Fallon moves to Shaylynn. He is willing to respect the dead, but he also knows the danger in staying. The king's sorrow will turn to wrath. When it does, it makes sense it would be directed at Lyosan.

"We should go," Fallon says.

Shaylynn turns to the others in his company. They are ready to go as well. Crystalynn gazes in horror at the scene in front of them. She clings to Lyosan who has lowered his blade – a blade still stained with the prince's blood. The king kneels at the foot of his thrown, hands clutching the corpse of his fallen heir. While this loss does not belong to Shaylynn or any of his party, they do not belong for reasons greater than this. They, despite their just cause, were perpetrators of this event. Through the hands of Lyosan this came to pass. They could not mourn when their cause had won the day.

They should withdraw, not just for the tactical reason put forth by Fallon, but for the respect for a fallen adversary. Shaylynn understands this as well as he does the other reason. With a nod, he motions for them to go. Crystalynn turns immediately to leave. Lyosan, still comforting her, goes with her. Fallon guards their passage. Only Shaylynn hesitates. Something still seems out of place. Something seems too simple, too easy for the moment to pass without incident. So little rage has come from such violence and action. So little bloodshed when all is said and done. One life lost is more than he wanted to see, but not nearly what he had expected. Then, considering the life lost, for them to remove themselves from the scene does not seem likely. And so, like a wolf poised to strike, he hesitates in the hall. Had he a coat of fur, it would have risen on the back of his neck. From the depths of his heart, a growl would have formed, built like a storm, and rumbled through his chest before bursting from his mouth. Indeed, something is genuinely amiss. Yet, he cannot see it. Somewhere, it lies in front of him, either just out of sight or just beyond his vision, almost like it taunts him.

Despite his unease, he has no time. Already, he lingers too long. Fallon nudges him to hurry him along. "We must go!" he says forcefully.

Shaylynn turns but holds his ground. Fallon's words break the veil over the room. The king looks up from his perch and releases the body of his son. Shaylynn considers for a moment that perhaps his fears have cost his troop.

"Go!" the king commands.

"You cannot mean this!" the old man replies.

Shaylynn turns to the cloaked man, who moves quickly to the king's side. If Shaylynn is not mistaken, he moves as a shadow along the ground.

"Sire, they killed your son," the man hisses. "They must be punished for their insolence!"

"And what of my own?" Athorn asks. "I've ravaged their lands, tormented their people, kidnapped their princess; my son moved against her thus his life was ended. How is his death not some comment on my actions?"

"Stay the course, my lord," the man pleads. "We stand on the precipice of achieving our ultimate goal."

"Our goal!" the king roars. He rises from his place causing the man to cower away in fear. "My son lies dead in his own blood, and you speak of some goal as though we might accomplish some victory. You are as foolish as I to have trusted you."

With malice in his eyes, the old man turns away. He looks one last time upon Shaylynn, then fights through the crowd looking to exit the chamber. Shaylynn follows the man's progress as long as he can before finally the man vanishes from Shaylynn's sight and is gone forever. As quickly as he is gone, the threat which had grown in Shaylynn's mind diminishes, and peace enters his soul again.

He turns back to his friends. Lyosan and Crystalynn stand hand-in-hand. Hope restores itself in Shaylynn that perhaps their union would come to pass. Seeing them, he longs for Sarin. He wishes to see her and touch her and kiss her once again. More than anything, he wishes for home. Normalcy seems ready to restore itself to life. They have only to journey home to make it so.

"I will not say it again, Shaylynn, son of Feylynn," Athorn commands, "Go!"

Shaylynn bows respectfully to Athorn, King of Jorram, as do the others present. Without a word of remorse or condolence, for none need to be spoken, they turn and remove themselves from the room. Though many scowl at them and show a clear desire to cause them harm, none approach them. Shaylynn leads the way with Crystalynn behind him. Fallon and Lyosan flank the princess from behind. As they make their way to the path back to their company, Shaylynn inspects the castle wall where the lightning struck. Though he does not regret his action in bringing down the wall, he wonders if his powers have drawn unwanted attention. Clearly, the king has made deals with dangerous fellows. Once he has the opportunity, Shaylynn will need to report these findings to Darek and the rest of the Order. Surely, they know some information which will be helpful.

During the walk back to border, the party is quiet. Shaylynn remains deep in his thoughts regarding the king and the magician within his employ. The very thought of a power growing outside the kingdom brings Shaylynn back to the discussions he shared with Darek. The echoes of a rarely mentioned prophecy ring in his ears. He begins to see the pieces coming together. He fears greatly the next step in the process if indeed this is the way of progress.

Fallon keeps a steady watch on the path behind them. Given all he has seen this night, he will not dare to presume safety until he finds himself back home. Even Shaylynn struggled with the opponents they saw this night. If that is the case, and greater dangers lurk around them, he must be on guard if he is to be any help at all.

Lyosan feigns interest in helping Fallon keep watch. In truth, he would comfort Crystalynn if he could. She has been captive of Jorram for near two months. While she seems in good condition, the duration of her stay must weigh heavily on her. From the moment he killed to save her, the reality of it seems to have truly struck her. A boy, however guilty in his own right, having barely known the pleasures of life, lies dead by Lyosan's hand. He would not change his action given the opportunity, but he would wish she had not been present for the blow. He would have her look upon him as she did prior to this ordeal. The change cannot be undone. He will have to move her past this moment if there is to be resolution to the matter.

For Crystalynn, the harsh reality hangs above her as they travel. There was always the chance death would accompany this matter, but she had believed a peaceful alternative was possible. Now, she sees the naivety of her thoughts. This matter went far beyond the limits of her understanding. It delved into a world she did not want to exist. Though they came to rescue her, she cannot look at her liberators in the way she did before. Shaylynn, who seemed a mystery and unshakeable, now seems undone by the mystic in Jorram. Fallon, who was always sincere and kind, turned callous when faced with the death of the crown prince. Lyosan, innocent as the sunrise, is now forever darkened by his act.

It is dark in the forest as they make their way to the rendezvous, almost as though the land grieves the loss Jorram has suffered. They encounter no one in their travels and yet, they feel the presence of ill will all around them. Nature seems to follow them with unseen eyes and condemn their actions in this land. If it could, it would make their passing less pleasant.

Still, they press on. When they reach the river, they find relief they are almost out of Jorram. Crystalynn feels the relief the most. A wave of comfort and joy washes over her. The thoughts and fears of just a few moments ago fade away almost as if they never existed. Shaylynn finds the barge he left tied up for their crossing. None have found it. As they prepare to make the crossing, they see the first rays of sun for a new day rising over the horizon. Warmth returns to them, and the coldness in their hearts begins to melt away. For the first time since the events in the castle, a sense of normalcy finds them. Their friendship, though not fully recovered, begins to replenish itself in the presence of a new day. Fallon and Shaylynn prepare to load the barge. Lyosan leads Crystalynn onto the barge. Again, silence finds them once they are on their way.

Shaylynn and Fallon steer the barge over the river. Lyosan sits across from Crystalynn with a worried eye. She sits with arms folded and eyes staring intently at the opposite side of the river. She longs for home and to be in her brother's arms once again. More than anything, she wants for the ordeal to be completely behind her so she can continue her life as it was. For now, every second she spends in Jorram reminds her of the harrowing experience she has been put through. Comfort will not find her until she stands on home ground and feels the comfort of a familiar place.

Slowly, the barge floats across the river. The current does not deter their progress in any way. It, like most of the elements surrounding them, casts aspersions upon them – silently judging their actions in Jorram. As Shaylynn and Fallon quietly paddle the barge over to the Daryndell side, the paddles make small ripples in the water. A hush pervades the scene as finally, the barge glides into the bank and comes to a peaceful stop.

Shaylynn jumps off the barge and ties it to a nearby tree. As he does this, Fallon helps the princess to her feet and leads her onto solid ground. Lyosan, still upset by Crystalynn's demeanor, steps off the barge as well. In no time, Shaylynn begins leading the group through the woods to the rendezvous point. The spirits of the company lift slightly as they find themselves on more friendly ground. Though none of them has visited this placed before, there is something about the air and the trees around them which already reminds them of home despite the fact they remain in a foreign land.

Along the way, tensions ease. Guards begin to come down once again. Fallon begins to speak fondly of returning home. Shaylynn teases Fallon for merely wanting to see Faith again. Crystalynn smiles for the first time, though there is little joy in her smile. Lyosan even finds it difficult to suppress a smile. They make no mention of the dangers they encountered while in Jorram. Though each seems to be putting the matter behind him or her in some way, they are not yet prepared to discuss it openly.

Shortly, they reach the rendezvous. Ten small tents stand in a circle. The remnants of a fire rest in the middle – some of the embers still smoldering from the latest fire. Darrow and Stefen, standing guard in the trees above the tents, are the first to see their approach. They bark out the news as they drop from their posts.

"They have returned!" Darrow yells.

Stefen adds. "They have the princess!"

Brynnal, Athen, and Dragoon had been eating breakfast by their tents. When mention of the princess reaches their ears, they drop their plates and immediately come running. They speak in hurried voices proclaiming their amazement and disbelief.

Artimous, Mitan, Shawl, and Nycolas next come stumbling out of their tents. With the rest, they crowd around the new arrivals with questions aplenty. They reach for and violently shake the hands of Shaylynn, Fallon, and Lyosan. None have the gall to touch the princess though each bows and wishes her a welcome home. She smiles at their excitement and finally basks in the warmth of her rescue.

"How did you do it?" Athen asks.

"Are their soldiers chasing you?" Nycolas asks.

"Are any of you injured?" Shawl asks.

"Do you see King Athorn?" Brynnal asks.

"Did anyone die?" Artimous asks.

At the question, Crystalynn shies away reminded of the unpleasant memories. Shaylynn, Fallon, and Lyosan notice her discomfort.

"Enough," Shaylynn commands. "We are back. That is all that counts."

From the back of the crowd, a voice begins to call out, "Move! Let me through! Let me through!"

Eventually, shoving the rest out of his way, Pythyn steps forward to see Shaylynn returned with the princess complete safe. Astonished at the sight, he stares openly at the four of them. He says nothing for the longest time, muted by his shame and cowardice.

"I don't believe it," Pythyn finally squeaks.

"I'm not surprised," Shaylynn retorts as he walks past him, "it takes character to brave the impossible."

"Gather your belongings," Fallon commands. "We ride for Langerwitz and home!"

The others cheer, save Pythyn, who stands in awe. He'd truly seen himself as Shaylynn's equal until this moment. To brave the castle Belvik, face a king, and come away unscathed has truly shown another side of his quality. A side Pythyn cannot dare to aspire to. A side which gives Pythyn reason to fear Shaylynn and put serious doubts on Pythyn's quest for the crown. Somehow, he realizes, he must close the gap between them or find some way to circumvent it.

CHAPTER XV

By noon, the caravan is ready to travel. Shaylynn, Fallon, Darrow, and Stefen ride out front leading the way. Stefen and Darrow demand an account of the events which transpired in Belvik. Shaylynn is not quick to regale them with the tale, but Fallon eventually volunteers and tells the story.

Athen, Darrow, Nycolas, Shawl and Pythyn ride next, giving cover to the carriage, which holds the princess. Among them, they tease Pythyn for his unwillingness to travel with Shaylynn and achieve true glory. With each remark, Pythyn grows more embittered and furthers his desire for the crown.

At the rear, behind the carriage, ride Lyosan, Artimous, Brynnal, and Mitan. Shaylynn and Fallon attempted to have Lyosan ride with them, but he preferred to stay close to the carriage. He doubts the princess will require him, yet he will stand at the ready should the time come. Besides, he feels diminished after the ride from Jorram – not in a physical capacity. This was truly the first time he'd been around the princess when she did not converse with him openly. She shares with the group but says nothing to him. This change concerns him. He'd thought with certainty his coming to her rescue would elevate him in her eyes. It appears to have done the opposite.

His spirits lessen further when the princess calls for Artimous. Surprised, Artimous rides to her side, speaks with her a moment, then races on ahead. Lyosan can only assume the princess wishes to converse with Shaylynn – a further fall from grace in his eyes.

Indeed, Artimous rides past the next group of riders and reaches the lead party. Fallon is in the middle of his description of Shaylynn bringing lightning from the sky when Artimous approaches.

"...Before he summoned it, there had not been a cloud in the sky. Then, with a wave of his hand, he beckons it forth. In a flash, the wall of the castle turns to rubble giving us a clear entrance to walk through..."

Shaylynn interrupts. "You exaggerate the facts, Fallon."

"As you are guilty of on plenty of occasions," Fallon jests.

"Perhaps," Shaylynn concedes, "but I cannot let this stand..."

Shaylynn prepares to set the record straight, but Artimous interrupts the discussion. "I do apologize, my brothers," he says, "but the princess has requested your presence, Shaylynn."

Shaylynn looks at Fallon, who shrugs with uncertainty. Both are aware of how silent she was during the journey from Jorram. They had assumed she'd speak with Lyosan once she had the opportunity. Yet, she turns to Shaylynn. He will not deny her request – even if he fears the intent.

Turning his horse around, Shaylynn directs his stead back to the carriage. Crystalynn sits near the door looking for Shaylynn to come. When he comes into view, she smiles meekly at him. It is uncommon for a princess to do so in the presence of one of her servants. In her eyes, however, Shaylynn is not a mere peasant.

As he brings his horse up to speed with the carriage, Shaylynn looks to Lyosan. His eyes show concern. If Shaylynn could, he would alleviate those concerns, but he knows not what this is about. When the time comes, he looks through the window. The princess, now averting her eyes from him, takes a few deep breaths.

"My lady?" Shaylynn says.

Crystalynn smiles again and draws one more breath. Then, she looks for Shaylynn. When she sees him, the sight of his face hastens her heartbeat. She should not feel this way; she knows it is wrong. Still, she cannot help it and above all, she must overcome it.

"I realize I was not very appreciative of your efforts to rescue me," Crystalynn says.

"I only perform my duty," Shaylynn replies.

"You go further than any other would dare," Crystalynn says.

"I was not alone when I rescued you," Shaylynn points out.

"But you were leading the charge."

Shaylynn feels where the conversation would turn if the princess were left to her own devices. For that reason, he sighs and turns away from the carriage for a moment. He scans the trees briefly before he nods and accepts the praise being given.

"Perhaps," he concedes, "but I do what is best for the kingdom."

Crystalynn sighs now as the rumble of the road drowns out her displeasure. Shaylynn understands where they stand. He knows what his charge into Jorram means. The tournament will take place. Despite what he said in Jorram, he still holds the best chance of winning. He will be expected to participate – the city will demand it when they see his triumphant return. Unless he throws the tournament, he will be in line for the throne. There will be great unrest if he cedes the throne to another – especially Lyosan. He was diplomatic when it served him; what will he be when diplomacy betrays him?

Perhaps they are too close to the event still. After all, Crystalynn has not spoken to Lyosan since they left. Shaylynn has much on his mind. Plaguing him with this dilemma may be unfair considering his endeavor to save her. For now, she must bask in the moment and merely be satisfied with her reclaimed freedom. She would give anything to return to normalcy even if she must surrender this cause for some time.

"Well, I merely mean to thank you for rescuing me," Crystalynn reiterates to change the tone of the conversation.

"I am your servant, my lady," Shaylynn replies.

As his position dictates, Shaylynn cannot leave until excused. However, the princess says nothing more. Shaylynn waits patiently believing she will either dismiss him or continue with a discussion of a different topic. After a good while, it becomes apparent she has a conversation in mind. Her brow furrows, and she fidgets with her hands. Shaylynn cannot be rude, but he will attempt to ease her discomfort.

"Is there something else, princess?" he asks.

She turns, somewhat startled he broached the subject, and looks at him with nervous eyes. But when she looks at him, she gets caught in the kindness of his eyes. They are as she remembered them from before. He is the boy she saw playing in the courtyard, fighting in the training sessions, and chasing after Sarin. When she thinks of Sarin, Crystalynn feels some guilt in her heart. She remembers the love between them, and again, she tries to come between them. She must accept the truth and that begins now.

"I feel different," Crystalynn admits.

"In what regard?" Shaylynn inquires.

Crystalynn takes a deep breath before continuing. "I am among my dearest and closest friends, yet I feel displaced. I was always aware of the training you and your peers underwent with a respect for the dealings you would eventually face in life. But to be present for them and see the rage and wrath in your eyes has shown me something I'd rather not see."

"I do not deny our business can be an unpleasant one," Shaylynn replies. "But that side is but one face of a die." Shaylynn looks at Crystalynn, but his remark does not seem to have brought her comfort. With a smile, he adds, "And it does not come up often."

The truth in the statement causes Crystalynn to smile as well. It is not enough to completely alleviate her distress, but she can find some comfort in the remark. Furthermore, it makes it easier to openly discuss the situation since Shaylynn is aware of the nature of their battle state.

"It is just so...concerning that the three of you can enter such a mindset and become so callous," Crystalynn explains. "That Fallon, who cares so much for the welfare of others, could ignore the loss of a life when faced with the prospect of escape. That you could view this event with optimism for the future..."

Shaylynn interrupts on instinct. "I never said such a..."

Crystalynn quickly explains herself. "It was on your face," she says. "You saw that moment as an opportunity for the tensions between our two countries to cease, if only for the time being."

Shaylynn cannot dispute this as the truth, but he must rebuke the thought that he was pleased with the action which caused the ceasefire.

"If there were any other way to gain the peace we so desperately need, I would have preferred it," Shaylynn explains.

"I know as much," Crystalynn admits. "Still, in the moment, it was not a pleasing notion." Crystalynn pauses as a worried expression crosses her face. She's not sure how to broach the subject, nor does she want to say anything out of turn. "Then there's Lyosan," she finally says. "Even amongst you all he seemed out of place – against all the violence, wishing for a calmer life. It was endearing to see one so removed from the hustle and bustle of the political realm. Then, there he was, standing between me and Dreilon plunging a sword into his stomach..."

Crystalynn's voice trails off as the memory comes to her. She stares at the front of the carriage for a while. A chill seems to trickle up her spine as she sits. It takes all her wherewithal to fight it down.

Shaylynn sees her discomfort and the opportunity to begin to remedy the situation.

"If it were not you in that position, I doubt he could've brought himself to doing it," Shaylynn says. "We fought in the southern lands for a few days. He took part, but he was not in his natural state."

"He certainly seemed in a natural state before."

Shaylynn shrugs. "He was acting in your defense. Giving his life for you is natural for him."

Crystalynn smiles at the notion. Though she'd rather hear Shaylynn say something of the like of himself. On some level, it is true of him. As a knight of the royal court, he would give his life in service of the crown, but he does not mean the same for Lyosan. Lyosan would act from a place of love not a place of duty. The only person who Shaylynn would give his life for in that manner would be Sarin. And again, Crystalynn finds herself ashamed of her jealous inclinations.

Once she gets past those however, she finds warmth in her heart from the notion Lyosan values her so much. She always knew of the feelings he bore for her, yet she did not feel he would ever express these feelings in any way. He had always been so conscious of his station and so hesitant to assert himself as a person. Suddenly, when she needs him most, he saves her life without hesitation. Though the image of him impaling another person causes her distress, the intent of the act cannot be overlooked. His love, if she can call it that, shows clearly. Shaylynn, as if sensing the moment of realization is upon her, furthers Lyosan's cause.

"I've been told he attempted to mount offensives to retrieve you from the moment he returned from the southern lands."

"And he had not the troops to follow him," Crystalynn says.

Shaylynn replies. "We are not always able to show the path to those who choose not to see it."

"Is that meant for my brother?"

"It is meant for all of us," Shaylynn corrects. "Even I would not have been able to make this siege work without accepting my own limits."

Crystalynn stands in awe. Never has Shaylynn been this honest or vulnerable in her presence. When his father was alive and within the city, he stood forever in his shadow. When his father left, he could do nothing but stand strong for his mother and younger brother. Now he speaks so candidly and with great wisdom and regard for himself and others.

"What has happened to you, Shaylynn Storm?" she asks without considering the phrasing of the question.

Shaylynn smiles, understanding the difference in his demeanor. "I've seen much," he explains. "I've been pushed to limits which were so far beyond what I'd imagined before it has changed my understanding of my place in this scheme.

"I am not meant for the throne. I'd always known my heart belonged to Sarin, and for the longest time, that was enough to keep me from attempting to claim it. But now I understand the throne is not my place. I cannot rule; I cannot live with the purpose of guiding an entire people."

Crystalynn cannot believe these words. "If you are not meant for the throne then I cannot believe any of your like are."

"There are plenty who would serve as king with great honor and better reference than I."

"Like who?"

Shaylynn assumes Crystalynn expects him to volunteer Lyosan to serve as king. He always attempts to speak for Lyosan where Lyosan is too meek to do so. Even before this topic came up, he was attempting to restore Lyosan's place in Crystalynn's eyes. The truth is however that Shaylynn does not believe Lyosan is ready for such a responsibility. In fact, all who ride with him now are too young, too naïve to take the throne right now. Much must be proven in the times ahead. Great strides must be made if any is to make a run through the tournament and win the prize.

That being said, Lyosan possesses many qualities which would make him a good king. He does have the respect and reverence for life Crystalynn spoke of. Never does he speak solely for himself or act in a manner which would be beneficial for himself. But he is not assertive enough nor willing to stand strong for the things he believes in. Even now he rides meekly at the back of the troop willing to accept his assumed place among the rest. Despite his actions in Belvik, he will not rise up to take his place with Shaylynn and Fallon. When they return home, Cyrus will throw a ceremony for them and award them for their valor.

At that time, Lyosan will present himself before the king in front of the members of the cabinet and the royal court. Whether justified or not, each member will decide the validity of Lyosan's position within the court.

As captain of the legion, Shaylynn will already have proven himself to any who would question him. Though Shaylynn has given his approval to Fallon and Lyosan both, Fallon has the advantage of surviving the journey from the southern campaign and being rated the second of the youth in the impending tournament.

Lyosan must use this opportunity to show he belongs. Until such time as he can stand up for himself, Shaylynn knows he cannot put more on his friend than Lyosan is willing to accept.

"Perhaps the right candidate does not yet exist," Shaylynn finally says in reply.

"I can admit that is not what I expected you to say," Crystalynn replies. "Then again I rarely hear what I...expect from you." The pause is short but noticeable. Shaylynn would question it if he anticipated a pleasant exchange. She says *expect*, but Shaylynn assumes she means *want*. Rarely does he say the things she wants him to say. Better to leave it. She changed her mind after all.

"You think I favor Lyosan too much," Shaylynn says instead.

"I think you wish him happiness," Crystalynn replies.

"I do," Shaylynn admits with a nod. "At the same time, I do not dare assume what will result in happiness for others."

"He is a good man," Crystalynn says ignoring Shaylynn's comment.

"Indeed."

"And yet, he does not appear to have the quality within him to lead."

"Indeed," Shaylynn says again, with a more somber tone.

"You admit as much?" Crystalynn asks.

"I do," Shaylynn replies. "Never has he shown to me he would make a competent leader...let alone an exceptional one."

Again, the candid nature of Shaylynn's conversation surprises Crystalynn. Not only does he forgo attempting to raise Lyosan in her eyes, but he also uses the opportunity to point out a great flaw in Lyosan's character. Truly, he is not the boy who broke the stone in the river just a few months ago. But this is not an attack of Lyosan, nor does she believe Shaylynn does not care for Lyosan any longer. He merely assesses the situation with honesty and integrity. So why does he believe so strongly when he clearly sees the flaws at hand?

"Then why do you support him so?" she finally inquires.

"Because there is something there," Shaylynn explains, "something that inspires and removes doubt from my mind. Whether that is enough to lead a people, I do not yet know, but I will do all I can to find out."

"I know what you mean," Crystalynn admits reluctantly, "if you can follow my intent. He does have a quality within him which only a chosen few have. He makes me happy and removes grief or sorrow from my life."

Upon hearing her belief in Lyosan, Shaylynn can only ask, "Then why do you not believe in him more?"

She swallows hard before answering. It is difficult to admit this of someone she cares for so deeply. "It is hard to believe in someone who fails to believe in himself. To rely on the word of others when better evidence lies before your own eyes."

"It is hard to argue with your logic," Shaylynn replies.

A few minutes later Crystalynn dismisses Shaylynn, and he returns to the front of the caravan. They ride the rest of the day before they begin searching for a town to rest in for the night. Artimous finds lodging at the Crescent Moon in the town of Vilrill. Shaylynn and Fallon ride into town upon Artimous's return and secure the premises for the princess. Word travels fast throughout the town that the princess has returned to Artonia. When the caravan enters the town, despite the darkness, most of the town stands on the main road with torches and candles lit. They cheer the knights who have procured her return. Pythyn, smug as always, raises his hand in appreciation as though he took part in the rescue.

Darrow, Brynnal, Athen, and Lyosan ride close to the carriage to ensure the safety of the princess. Spectators come close to the carriage but not close enough to alert the knights. Those on the ground merely want a look at their future monarch. Though it is dark and they catch a glimpse at best, the lift to their spirits is unimaginable. Within an hour, Shaylynn and the others get the princess safely inside the Crescent Moon. They also set up a perimeter around the lodge and convince the citizens to return to their homes.

Each of the rooms in the inn hold four people easily. Shaylynn rooms with Fallon, Lyosan, and Stefen. Darrow, Shawl, Mitan, and Artimous share a room as well. Nycolas, Dragoon, Brynnal, and Athen take another. As none can truly stand Pythyn that much, they agree to let him room alone. At first, he requests the room closest to the princess to ensure her safety, but Shaylynn will not allow it. Instead, he places Pythyn the furthest from Crystalynn's room and tells him to serve as a decoy should something go wrong. He protests greatly at first, but when none come to his defense, he charges into his room and doesn't come out the rest of the evening. The rest of the knights couldn't be happier.

The owner of the inn opens the kitchen for the use of the knights. Most are too tired from the day's ride, but Shaylynn, Fallon, Lyosan, Shawl, and Mitan stay up for dinner. Together, they sit around a table by the fire and recant the tale of their journey into Jorram. Fallon begins to understand this story will be told several times within the next week. Even after everyone has heard it once, they will want to hear it again. It's not every day a trio of youths manages to infiltrate a foreign castle, rescue a damsel in distress, and escape without a mark to show for it. Now that Fallon thinks about it and reflects on the journey, he cannot believe they were able to accomplish what they did.

Thus, as he tells the story, there is a vigor in his voice. A sort of disbelief that maybe he doesn't believe the story himself. In that manner, the telling of the story becomes elevated in a way. Lyosan sits on the edge of his seat just like the others. Shaylynn reclines in his chair, foot on the edge of the table, but laughs with the telling of the story. Seeing Fallon invigorated in such a manner is truly entertaining. Especially with the part of the story he's about to tell.

"…then Shaylynn went into this kind of trance," Fallon says. "All around you could feel a tingle going through your body. Around and around it danced, and you could feel it as though it had a mind of its own. From the clouds, you heard a low rumble, then for a split second you saw a flash and then…. BOOM!"

Fallon slams his fists onto the table. Everyone, save Shaylynn, jumps then erupts in guffaws of laughter.

"The wall explodes with the strike of the bolt, and rock rains from the sky!" Fallon concludes.

Taking a break, Fallon drops to his seat, grabs his drink, and takes a long swig. The others do as well. Shaylynn watches as his comrades boast and enjoy the night. Mitan throws an arm around Fallon and the two smile. Then, Fallon looks past Shaylynn to the hall. Suddenly, his demeanor changes. Not in a drastic, frightening manner, but a manner which definitely shows a more somber tone. Shaylynn looks to the rest at the table and sees the same. Rising to his feet, Shaylynn turns and sees Crystalynn standing behind him. The sound of chairs scraping along the floor suggests the others follow Shaylynn's example.

"We are sorry for disturbing you, my lady," Shawl says.

"Think nothing of it," Crystalynn replies. "To think I would've missed such a recanting of the events makes the disturbance a welcome one."

Fallon, mildly embarrassed, smiles and takes a drink to hide his face. The others chuckle under their breath. For a minute, the princess stands before the table in silence. The knights stand waiting for her to either leave or make a request.

"Do you need something of us?" Shaylynn finally asks.

"No," Crystalynn replies, "I wouldn't want to disturb you. I was hoping I could get something to eat. It's been quite some time since I've had a good meal."

Shaylynn calls for the owner, who appears in a flash. He diligently takes the order from the princess then scurries off to begin cooking the meal. Again, Shawl and Mitan find themselves in an uncomfortable situation. Even Fallon remains quiet despite his familiarity with the princess.

"Would you care to join us, my lady?" Shaylynn asks.

The princess quickly shakes her head. "Oh, no, I wouldn't want to interrupt your fun."

Shaylynn, sitting next to Lyosan, reaches over with his foot and slides his chair back away from Lyosan to make room. Lyosan reacts to the movement and jumps a bit. A second later, he composes himself.

"But Fallon is at the best part of the story," Shaylynn remarks.

The princess smiles and steps towards them. "I could use some good company after my ordeal."

Lyosan grabs another chair and brings it to the table. He helps the princess into the chair then takes his place next to her.

"Shall I start from the beginning?" Fallon inquires.

"No, that's quite alright," she replies. "I heard everything from my room already."

Fallon continues with the story of their entrance into the castle and the battle between them and the Jorramians. Shaylynn interjects once or twice to keep the truth of the story intact. When it comes to the fight in the king's hall, Fallon chooses his words carefully. He's noticed, as have the others, that the princess wishes to avoid that subject as much as possible.

Yet, as the same time, Mitan and Shawl have not heard the story before and wish to get the full effect of the tale. Thus, while Fallon works to omit certain parts of the story, they continuously hound him for the details he chooses to leave out.

"...Shaylynn devised a plan wherein he would enter the chamber while Lyosan and I ascended the stairs to the rafters above. While he distracted the guards below, we took positions to be in the best possible firing line..."

Fallon slows his speech when he comes to the point. He gazes slightly toward the princess. She holds her hands in her lap and refuses eye contact with anyone at the table. Lyosan contemplates saying something to her and begins moving a hand to comfort her. Instead, he withdraws and returns his attention to the conversation.

In her mind the images from Belvik already replay. She sees Shaylynn approaching and remembers the fear she felt regarding his quick demise. She begins to feel the animosity she felt for Dreilon, who held the blade to her neck. The memory of the cold steel against her skin returns. All this anger and fear will soon be replaced with pity once Lyosan steps forward with his own blade. The scene will turn, and she has no way of preventing it.

"...from there," Fallon continues, "the fighting began to blur together, and it became too difficult to really tell what was happening..."

Mitan quickly disagrees. "Darrow spoke quite candidly about the fact you could recall the events clearly. Do not hold out on us, brother. Tell us the tale!"

"Yes!" Shawl agrees. "We heard mention of the death of the prince! You've not told us about that yet."

Unsure if he should bring such memories forward in mixed company, Fallon looks to Shaylynn. Lyosan attempts to draw Fallon's eye to demand Fallon keep his silence, but the silent debate goes on between the other two. Shaylynn will not condemn or condone the telling of the attack. Like so many things that people come to regret, it is done and cannot be undone. Even if they could, there is no telling whether replaying this event would turn out for the better.

In truth, they might wish again to change the course of time should one of them or, heaven forbid, the princess be lost to them. The chasm that would form between them should Crystalynn be lost may never come to a close. While they may not wish to relive these moments too often, they must accept them as fact and live with them.

"It was the work of Lyosan," Fallon admits. "We had made our way to the princess and been surrounded by palace guards. The prince moved against the princess with dagger in hand. In a flash, faster than Shaylynn or I could hope to act, Lyosan stepped forward and caught the prince upon his blade."

Mitan and Shawl sit shocked as they slowly turn to look to the unsung hero. For truth, Lyosan has not boasted of his own accomplishment – if the slaying of a prince could be called as such. Furthermore, he knows the princess does not wish for these matters to be discussed. They need a distraction or diversion of some sort to steer the conversation. Before they could go further, they get one.

The owner of the inn steps out of the kitchen with a large plate in hand. "Here we are!" he proclaims. "I'll admit, there is quite a bit. Give me a few moments, and I'll bring it all out! Of course, if I had a few extra hands, I'd have the meal out quicker."

Seeing the ploy for help, Mitan, Fallon, and Shawl attend to the owner. He thanks them for their help and assures them it isn't at all necessary. They continue to help without a word of trouble. While they work, Lyosan checks on the princess. She still has said nothing in quite a while and holds her hands tightly.

"They should not have discussed such a thing," Lyosan says.

Crystalynn raises her head and shakes in disagreement. "It is fine," she assures him. "The memory is not pleasant, but it is just a memory."

"Only if we can let go of it," Shaylynn injects with a coy smile.

They both turn to him – Crystalynn with interest, Lyosan with anger. If she says she's fine, then they should both be willing to accept that. Drudging up the memory will only make matters worse. He also doesn't have to have that smile on his face while he says it. Yet he sits there, reclining as though everything is at peace, as though he doesn't have a care in the world. He knows better. He knows those around him have been drastically changed by the events which took place.

Still, he must have a reason for what he's doing. At least Lyosan hopes he does. It's at these moments Lyosan despises the friendship he has with Shaylynn. Shaylynn sees things so differently Lyosan can't even begin to follow where Shaylynn's mind takes him. Even if he is that clever, he doesn't have to be so proud of it.

"It is a memory," Shaylynn agrees. "But some memories have a way of becoming more than that. In one simple moment, everything changes from what it once was. Our eyes see things differently as everything we were taught, we believe, we understand, is coded differently by that one event. We change, not through any manner of choice, but because we fear what we have seen."

"But you say you are different because of what you have seen," Crystalynn remarks, recalling their earlier conversation.

"Not just because of what I've seen, but because of what I've done. There is more to the world than seeing and believing. Sometimes, we must put ourselves upon the moment of experience before we can change the manner of our beliefs. Would you believe the world different if you could bring lightning from the sky?"

Crystalynn nods. "I would say so."

"And what if you traveled over land and field over distances no other person could dare travel before? Would the world be different then?"

"Absolutely."

"I've done those things. I've done so much more I wouldn't dare be able to explain it all to you if I tried. And while all those things have happened and changed my perceptions, there are still certain elements of my life which have not changed – which will never change."

"Such as?" Crystalynn asks.

Shaylynn takes his foot off the table and straightens himself in his chair. Solemnity covers his face now though the smile remains. It is different as he is different in this moment.

"I am far from home, as I have been so often lately," Shaylynn explains. "Yet in my heart there is a tug. There is an image in my mind which keeps me forever at home. There is a voice in my mind which calls my name..."

"Sarin?" Crystalynn guesses.

"Sarin," Shaylynn confirms. "She keeps this world the same for me. She lets me know that despite all the change, things are really just the same as they always have been."

Crystalynn smiles. She's never smiled like this before when Shaylynn talked about Sarin. She'd always somewhat toyed with the idea of turning Shaylynn towards her. She knows, of course, that would never happen. Now, looking at his face, she knows she doesn't want it to happen. That kind of happiness cannot be touched nor should it be questioned.

"Have you ever told her that?" Crystalynn asks.

"What?" Shaylynn replies, suddenly returning to his old form. "Of course not, I'd never hear the end of it if I did."

For the first time since the events of Belvik, Crystalynn laughs. Immediately, it calms Lyosan down. With the princess's smile, he forgets all his concerns of just a moment ago and allows the moment to pass. As he does this, the others return with the food and place it upon the table. Despite the late hour, the owner shows he treats royalty with great regard hoping to earn their patronage if ever they should be back in Vilrill again. A great feast of roasted pig, tomatoes, boiled potatoes, fruits of a great variety, breads, and cider to drink.

"I do not think I can handle this on my own," the princess says once she sees the enormity of the buffet. "Would you all be willing to assist me?"

Shawl grabs his goblet and raises it high. "If it be thy will, we shall follow!"

The table erupts with laughter as the owner places plates in front of them.

"Some missions definitely tax your loyalty," Fallon says jokingly.

For several hours into the night, the six of them eat and drink merrily. They are still nowhere near finished with the feast when they have finally had their fill. They advise the owner to leave the food for their comrades who shall be up in a few short hours. Before turning in, they also make it clear they do not wish to be disturbed. After the feast they have shared, they will not be rising with the sun's first light.

CHAPTER XVI

Indeed, no one wakes at morning's break. The sun has already been up for several hours when the first of the knights begins to awaken. Nycolas, Dragoon, Brynnal, and Athen stumble from their room and become concerned when they see the sun high in air. Surely, they were supposed to be gone by now. Shaylynn was supposed to lead the charge in the morning, yet he is nowhere to be seen and his room remains locked. Artimous and Darrow come from their room complaining that Shawl and Mitan refuse to rise from their beds. As they gather in the common hall, they see the feast from the night prior. Much remains, but they still revel in the food which was clearly part of a feast to begin with.

Pythyn eventually bursts from his room demanding to know why he has not been woken already. None answer him. For one, they do not know themselves. For another, they are too hungry to concern themselves with him. As Pythyn becomes privy to the source of the distraction, the owner comes out and tells the troop of the night prior.

"I'm afraid they were up rather late eating and celebrating the princess's return," he explains. "They suggested you have a good breakfast and be ready to ride after lunch."

He motions to the food on the table. Pythyn steps towards it and places his hand on the food.

"It's cold!" he complains.

"Yes, well," the owner stammers, "it has been out for a few hours now. I would make you something else, but I've rather exhausted my supply until the other shops open for the day."

"This is insanity!" Pythyn proclaims.

Stomping off to Shaylynn's room, Pythyn loudly cries out for Shaylynn to get up. When he reaches the door, he pounds on it vigorously.

"Shaylynn!" he cries. "Show yourself at once!"

"Shut up, Pythyn!" Fallon calls groggily from inside the room.

"This is none of your business, Fallon!" Pythyn replies.

"When an imbecile rouses a tired man from his slumber for no good reason, I'd have to disagree," Shaylynn retorts.

"Rise this instant or I shall return to Langerwitz without you!"

"At least we shall have a pleasant journey home," Fallon comments.

"I shall take the princess with me!"

"I doubt that entirely," Shaylynn explains. "If you would dare awaken her in this manner, you would find her of the same mind as us. I would also think the consequences would be much more severe. Perhaps a few days in the dungeon."

"Wake her, Pythyn! Wake her!" Fallon teases.

Pythyn stands at the door for a few moments unsure how to proceed. Given his history with Shaylynn and Fallon, he cannot take them at their word. At the same time, he does not know if it would be worthwhile to test their sincerity. He must be part of the party when they ride into Langerwitz. Should he upset the princess in this way, she may not let him be part of the caravan. Someone will need to ride ahead to Langerwitz to alert the castle of their arrival. Pythyn will not allow that individual to be him if he can help it.

To that point, a subdued anger swells in his face. His brow furls tightly, and his eye lids pinch close together. The other knights watch as Pythyn clinches his fists, which begin to shake slightly. When he's finally had enough, he points a finger at the door and gives one final decree to Shaylynn.

"We leave at noon!"

"Well, it's not noon now!" Shaylynn replies.

Eventually, Pythyn leaves the door and sits down at the table where the food sits. The others grab some food as well and then step outside. The rest of the morning they sit and lounge until Shaylynn, Fallon, and Lyosan begin to stir. Stefen steps out of the room first. Pythyn still sits at the table with his arms folded.

"What's your excuse?" Pythyn asks.

Stefen shrugs. "Apparently, I needed the rest."

The other three slowly come out of their room. They are not in full dress, but they are properly covered. As soon as Pythyn sees them, he begins to shake his head in derision. Unaware of him, perhaps by choice, Shaylynn, Fallon, and Lyosan stretch and beckon themselves to the waking world as they step to the table and grab some of the remaining scraps of food. Pythyn continues to stare them down, and they continue to ignore him. Finally, when he's had enough of their inattentiveness, he stands up and steps in front of Shaylynn.

"Are you well rested?" he asks.

"Save for your idiocy," Shaylynn replies. "With the sun already up, I feared I wouldn't be able to go back to sleep."

"I had no problem," Fallon says.

"Nor I," Lyosan adds.

"Your bed did not face the window," Shaylynn reminds them.

"True," Lyosan says.

"Perhaps you should have taken the light in your eyes as a sign to rise for the day," Pythyn suggests.

"'Tis foolishness," Shaylynn replies. "As if the sun could control our days so easily."

Shaylynn grabs a chair and flops down with a plate of food. Fallon and Lyosan grab a couple drinks and sit across from him. Stefen, who's been enjoying the repartee, smiles as he approaches the table. Pythyn walks away in a fury. Lyosan and Fallon laugh to each other as he does.

"Do you think he's waited for us to rise?" Stefen asks.

"Most assuredly," Shaylynn replies. "I'm sure he wanted us to see him storm off."

"It was quite a performance," Lyosan comments.

Stefen joins them at the table. For a while, they sit in silence and enjoy their breakfast. Eventually, the other knights wander in from outside once they realize Shaylynn is up and Pythyn is gone.

"What is the plan now?" Brynnal asks.

"The princess will awaken soon," Shaylynn replies. "We are a few hours from the Langerwitz walls. One rider will take off before us and ride hard for the city. The king will want a welcoming party. The three of us will most likely receive our accommodation and the rest of you will be praised for accompanying us."

"What of the tournament?" Nycolas asks.

"What of it?" Shaylynn asks.

The knights pause for a moment and exchange looks for a while. Knowing his feelings for Sarin to be absolute, they do not wish to broach the subject with him. But, the discussion has come up in the hours of this morning, and they wish to know what Shaylynn will do should their situation come to fruition.

"Do you believe the tournament will still occur?" Darrow asks.

Before Shaylynn can respond, Lyosan steps up to interject. "Why would it not?"

Again, they hesitate. When Shaylynn looks up from his plate, Dragoon jumps and quickly begins to explain. "This was your campaign," he says. "The king may believe the tournament a farce and proclaim you king. He already called the tournament off when the princess left."

Fallon drops his fork against his plate. He has heard enough of this discussion and cannot believe they would bring this subject forward now. They have returned from a taxing endeavor only to be taxed further.

"The king will not go against his word," Fallon says. "He said the tournament would take place to find a king within our land. We are back to that predicament again, so there will be a tournament!"

"Perhaps," a voice calls from just beyond the room. Everyone turns to see Pythyn walking back to the table, "for when the king realized the princess was kidnapped, he did put the tournament back in place. However, you two were removed from consideration because of your absence."

"And you think the king will not simply put us back in our spot?" Shaylynn asks.

"He cannot," Pythyn replies. "Replacements were put in your stead. They have been trained and given their spot in the tournament. The king cannot expand the field because of his original decree, and if he were to remove the new participants, they would have claim to the throne once the tournament ended. You are out!"

Lyosan seems to fear the logic Pythyn presents. Though Lyosan's ultimate goal is to win the crown himself, he despises the idea of Pythyn gaining an advantage in any way. Not having Shaylynn or Fallon in the tournament definitely aids his odds. For their part, Shaylynn and Fallon are not worried in the slightest. No one speaks of the issue again. Shaylynn goes to Crystalynn's room. She is already awake and preparing to leave.

They bring their supplies outside and make the horses ready for travel. The owner of the hotel comes out, as do many of the townsfolk, to speak to her and see her one last time.

She is very regal and carries herself well as she interacts with her subjects. Lyosan and Mitan stand on guard. Shaylynn chooses Darrow to ride ahead being one of the better riders among them. On a scroll, Shaylynn writes a message for the king to give validity to his news. The paper also gives news of what happened in Jorram and the death of prince Dreilon. Once fully prepared for the journey, Darrow mounts his ride and takes off for Langerwitz.

About half an hour later, the caravan is ready to depart as well. The admiration of the townsfolk delays the departure longer than some would like. Yet the princess will not insult these kindhearted people who merely wish for a moment of her time. When it becomes clear their arrival in Langerwitz will be greatly delayed, Shaylynn gently prods the princess into leaving. She agrees despite the wishes of those still around her. Quickly, she says her last goodbyes.

As she does, Lyosan watches her. To this moment, he'd been on guard making sure nothing happened to endanger the princess. Only now does he simply watch her interact with the people. It is with great ease she endears herself to them. Her smile wins them over with a single look. Her laughter entrances them with a joy they've rarely felt before. When she speaks to them, they hang upon her every word. It reminds him of all the moments he has shared with her and brings back the love he feels for her. He'd been concerned their relationship would never be the same, but he affirms he will always love her. How anyone could not love her, he cannot begin to understand.

"She is rather lovely," Shaylynn says.

Lyosan snaps from the moment and looks at Shaylynn with slight alarm. Lyosan's supposed to be vigilant in his duty. He's been far from it in the last seconds.

"She's a princess after all," Fallon adds.

"Do not tease me," Lyosan begs.

"I merely assert my opinion on the matter," Shaylynn remarks.

"And yet you would not have her as your wife," Lyosan says.

"Indeed," Shaylynn agrees, "for she is lovely, but that does not mean I love her in such a manner."

"'Tis a fine line to walk," Fallon says.

"She does not look at me the same," Lyosan says.

"She sees nothing the same for now," Shaylynn says. "Give her time. All will restore itself in the end."

The princess enters her carriage, and the caravan prepares to depart. Lyosan joins the front of the caravan for this journey. Pythyn prepares to move forward from his previous spot in the order. Shaylynn stops their preparations when he sees Pythyn.

"What are you doing?" Shaylynn asks.

"I ride with the first group," Pythyn replies. "As I am honored as the best of the knights in the tournament."

"That holds no bearing here," Shaylynn explains. "You refused to join the expedition to Jorram, so you will ride with all those who stayed behind."

"The king..." Pythyn begins.

"The king named me captain of this campaign," Shaylynn interrupts. "As such, my orders take precedence in the matter. If you wish to question them, you may do so once you've ridden into the city. Or, if you so desire, take your complaints to the princess and further delay our departure."

With a huff, Pythyn moves to the back of the caravan. He forces Shawl from his spot so he is closer to the front. Satisfied, Shaylynn gives the command for the caravan to head out. They keep good time on the journey home. Fortunately, there are no delays to speak of. Shaylynn stops them only once – when they can first see the castle walls.

"Move us to the side," Shaylynn commands.

The caravan pulls off the road. The carriage sits with the windows facing north and south. Shaylynn rides back to the carriage.

"My lady," he says.

Crystalynn moves the curtain to one side and peers out curiously. She looks to the front and back of the caravan looking for the problem that has stopped them. When she sees the riders on their horses all ready to continue, she becomes confused and looks at Shaylynn quizzically.

"What is the problem?" she asks.

"No problem, my lady," he replies. "I thought maybe you'd like your first look at home."

Realizing where they are, Crystalynn looks around Shaylynn and sees the city glimmering in the distance. For a moment, her heart stops in seeing the safety and comfort of a home she once thought she'd never see again.

As it sits there, just upon the horizon, a beacon of hope shining in her heart, she feels awakened from a nightmare. Now, more than ever, she is restored mind, body, and soul. The horrid ordeal of Jorram truly rests behind them. Her life will continue, and she will prosper. All the events of her life will play out just as her father promised her they would.

The moment is almost too much for her – to be so close to home and not yet be able to touch it. Tears begin to form in her eyes. Fallon and Lyosan stand in awe for a moment as they reflect on their accomplishment. The other youths, though they did not face the same danger, feel relieved to be home as well. There had always been fear that some of them would never come home given their task. Yet they all had returned from the journey. Mostly, because Shaylynn took the burden on himself and ventured into Jorram with only two of his friends.

A few minutes later Shaylynn continues the return home. The closer they get to the castle, the more joy enters their hearts. All the cracks and crevices of the walls begin to materialize in front of them. They can see the main gate beckoning them home. Cries reach them from within the walls. Lookouts have seen their approach and begun the celebration of their arrival. Slowly, the gates swing open, and a throng of people show themselves. Each man looks for a familiar face, but amongst the crowd, it is nearly impossible to distinguish one person from another. The mass of cheering citizens calls out to them. Some call Shaylynn by name. A few call for Fallon and Lyosan as well. As the horses begin to cross into the city limits, the people drop flowers onto the road. Throughout the remainder of the journey, the road turns into a flowery path to bring their quest to its successful conclusion.

The effect on the knights is staggering. Never have they been the center of such excitement. They can each remember witnessing such an event from the crowd, but they never imagined what it would be like to receive such a reception. Shaylynn holds himself well. He waves gracefully at the crowd and smiles warmly. Fallon and Lyosan, a bit more unnerved by the attention, nod from time to time to acknowledge the people. Pythyn waves to the crowd as well. The look on his face is one of superiority even though he had nothing to do with the actual rescue. He still basks in the glory which is not his own. The rest of the youths revels in the attention. Smiles gleam on their faces. They look at each other with shock. They can say nothing in reply to the outpouring of love and admiration. Yet each knows the true rewards lie in wait for Shaylynn, Lyosan, and Fallon.

As they approach the castle, Shaylynn, Fallon, and Lyosan begin to see familiar faces. The king stands in front of the castle gate surrounded by his royal cabinet. To the right are Kandessa, Daylynn, Ellisia, Elle, Steel, and Calvin standing proudly. Sarin and Faith are nearby as well. To the left stands Jonas holding a very official looking box. The king raises a hand to bring the caravan to a stop. Shaylynn happily halts their progress. Guards lead the other knights to the side. Shaylynn, Fallon, and Lyosan step down from their horses and away from the door of the carriage. Two royal guards process from the king's side and approach the carriage. One stands on guard while the second opens the door. As the princess steps out of the carriage, a wave of relief rushes over the crowd. Nowhere is it more apparent than on the king's face. Though normally unwavering in his resolve, the king's expression breaks as a trembling smile crosses his face. The princess smiles as well and fights away a tear in her eye. Cyrus opens his arms and beckons his sister to him. Gladly, she leaves the guards and rushes to her brother. The two embrace as the crowd looks on in pleasure. Shaylynn, Fallon, and Lyosan look to each other with proud smiles, for they have played the critical roles in making this scene possible.

After a long embrace, the king lets Crystalynn go and she takes her place by his side. "This is a gift greater than any king deserves," Cyrus says to the masses. "As everyone in the kingdom knows, when word reached us of the kidnapping of my sister, things could not be worse among my people. Though, in many ways, this occurred because of my lack of faith in my own kingdom, these three knights have proven themselves in ways I could not ask of all my subjects. For their bravery, valor, and unwavering commitment to their king, they shall be commended in the highest regard."

Cyrus looks to Jonas and gives a slight nod. Jonas acknowledges the order and steps forward with the box in hand. The king waits as Jonas steps towards him. Shaylynn turns to his comrades and whispers to them.

"This is our moment," he says. "All the kingdom looks upon us. We must show we are worthy of this honor. We must prove to our fellow citizens our actions are not limited to the battlefield."

Fallon nods in agreement. Lyosan begins to look around at the crowd with worry about to fill his senses. He did not want all of this. He merely wished to see Crystalynn returned to her brother. If given the opportunity, Lyosan would step away from the ceremony and return home.

"My friend," Cyrus says to Jonas, "you have trained the knights of this kingdom for several decades now. You have brought forth many fine knights who take a great place among our ranks. In all that time, only a select few have been chosen to receive the honor you hold in your hands. The Golden Phoenix has been bestowed upon six knights in the history of our land. You have now selected three knights to receive this accommodation for action beyond the scope of any expectation. Do you still honor that consideration?"

Jonas nods without hesitation. "I do my king."

Cyrus then turns to the princess. "My sister, do you believe these three knights to be worthy of this honor?"

Crystalynn turns to them and smiles. "I do, brother."

With great pride, Cyrus turns to Shaylynn, Fallon, and Lyosan.

"We may never know such glory," Shaylynn says to his friends. "Nor may we be together to have such an opportunity."

"Relish it, my brothers," Fallon adds.

Still, Lyosan is speechless. He can say nothing about what he is feeling or how honored he is to receive this recognition. He still wishes to walk away from it all and return to his normal life. Yet, how can things become normal when he has done so much? At this moment, the totality of his actions and their repercussions become apparent to him. He has taken more than a life. He has crippled the kingdom of Jorram for generations to come. He has killed the crown prince in duty to his king and princess. Even if he never sits upon the throne, he is a marked man. Everyone will know he is the man who killed Dreilon.

"Step forward Shaylynn, son of Feylynn; Fallon, son of Degon; and Lyosan, son of Armous," the king commands.

Shaylynn begins to advance with Fallon at his side. Lyosan hesitates for just a second then follows more on instinct than understanding. Together, the three of them approach the king stopping just before him. The king bids them to kneel, which they immediately do.

"I have watched each of you grow from an infant to the fine young men you have become," the king begins. "Never would I have thought you would have to deliver my sister from certain death and despair, but I always believed you were capable of such greatness…"

Lyosan cannot help but notice the king looks at Shaylynn as he says these words. Only a couple times does he acknowledge Fallon, but he never looks at Lyosan. In fact, as Lyosan scans the crowd, he sees almost every eye looking at Shaylynn. Only his family looks at him. Lyosan looks over at Crystalynn, but she is listening to her brother speak. Lyosan does at least find some comfort in the fact she is not obsessively staring at Shaylynn.

"...Now we begin to see that greatness fulfilled," Cyrus continues. "Journeying from the only home they've ever known into a hostile land to face a hostile force, they risked their lives to rescue the princess when none other would dare partake. They do their fallen fathers proud. They begin to restore the glory of Langerwitz and make it clear a bright future awaits our kingdom."

Cyrus motions for Jonas to step forward with the case. He lifts the lid off the box and takes the first medal from its place. It is a golden emblem containing the mythical bird with flames surrounding it. A blue and green ribbon holds the medal. Stepping to Lyosan, Cyrus holds the ribbon with both hands and drapes it over Lyosan's head. The ribbon comes to a rest around Lyosan's neck, and Lyosan sees the metal shining in the sunlight.

For a moment, unimaginable joy fills his heart. He thinks of everything he has done to make his family proud. Finally, he has found the proper way to accomplish his goal. Though he would wish for a different means of invoking that pride, he will take whatever he can at this point.

Lyosan then looks to watch the king approach Fallon. Again, he takes a medal from the box and places it around Fallon's neck. Some cheers ring out from the crowd behind him. Lyosan had not noticed if there were cheers when he received his medal. Suddenly, he begins to doubt that there were. He can only imagine what will happen when Shaylynn receives his medal. To be feeling this way, now, brings great conflict to Lyosan. On the one hand, he feels joy for himself and his friends, that they are here in this place being honored in such a way. And yet, he feels isolated at this moment. As though he does not belong and is only a part of this because Shaylynn made a place for him on the team. True, Shaylynn would not have let any other knight take Lyosan's place knowing how much Lyosan loves the princess. But no one else, save Fallon, would have chosen Lyosan for such a mission. It matters not that Lyosan fulfilled his duty by protecting the princess and killing the prince.

Cyrus goes back to the box for the last medal. Lyosan watches as the king approaches Shaylynn with the medal in hand. The cheers begin when the king is three steps away from Shaylynn. Lyosan is now certain there were no cheers when he received his medal. The low rumble quickly turns into a roar of applause and cheers. Even a chant starts among them. At first, Lyosan can't tell what they're saying. He can tell it doesn't make Shaylynn happy though. He sees a look of frustration overcome Shaylynn. Shaylynn, remembering his place in front of the king, does his best to mask the emotion swimming over him. It remains apparent to Lyosan however that this chant bothers him greatly. As he looks over to Sarin, he sees her disturbance from the chant as well. Suddenly, it strikes Lyosan the chant has something to do with Shaylynn becoming king. With this in mind, Lyosan strains to hear the chant.

"Mallee beka kay! Mallee beka kay!"

Shaylynn does nothing and waits as the ribbon comes to rest on his neck. Once the king has the medals awarded, he steps aside. Crystalynn comes forward and kisses each of the knights on the forehead. Lyosan cringes when the cheers elevate as the princess kisses Shaylynn.

The king bids the knights to rise before him. They then turn to the crowd. The king raises his hands to ask for silence of the crowd. Once they are quiet enough, he finishes the ceremony.

"My subjects," he says. "I present to you, the most honored Knights of Langerwitz!"

The cheers resound again. Shaylynn, Fallon, and Lyosan wave to the crowd as they honor them. The royal guard steps up to the three of them and guides them towards the castle. Unbeknownst to them, there is to be a feast in their honor. They are more pleased with the opportunity to talk to one another again.

"What were they saying?" Lyosan asks.

Shaylynn ignores the question. Fallon understands why, but he does not wish to discuss the subject within earshot of Shaylynn. Instead, he slows his pace and hopes Lyosan will follow. When Lyosan continues after Shaylynn, Fallon attempts to garner Lyosan's attention.

"What do you mean?" he asks.

Lyosan stops looking at Shaylynn and turns to Fallon. Shaylynn hurries ahead as he sees Sarin already in the dining hall.

"The crowd," Lyosan continues. "They were chanting something when Shaylynn received his medal. It continued when the princess kissed him."

Fallon makes sure Shaylynn is far enough ahead before he responds to the question. "It goes back to olden times," Fallon explains. "There is no exact translation for the phrase, but the closest we've come to is 'our future king'."

Lyosan immediately understands the significance of the chant.

"It was reserved for the presentation of the crown prince," Fallon continues. "In the untimely event of the crown prince's death, the phrase would be repeated when a suitable replacement was found. My father told me the last time the chant occurred was when Cyrus was born."

"Do you think the king had anything to do with the chant occurring?"

"It is doubtful, but he knows the significance of the chant – especially when it comes from the people. They are making it clear they want the next king to be Shaylynn. And you know Shaylynn will not have that!"

As they enter the hall, they see Shaylynn speaking with Sarin. There is a beleaguered look upon her face. Shaylynn holds her hands and speaks with great passion and conviction, but it seems to do nothing to quell her concerns.

"They do not make my fate," Shaylynn tells her.

"They will hate me if you refuse the crown for me," she says. "I'll never be able to walk the city without feeling their shame."

"I do not care," Shaylynn replies. "We've spoken of leaving before. If that is what we must do to ensure our happiness, then I will gladly do it."

She smiles a bit when she hears him say that, but a tear still trickles down from her eye.

"You say it with such ease," she says, "but I never want to test your commitment to such an idea."

"It is not an idea," Shaylynn assures her. "It is a promise – a vow. If this land will not provide the happiness I seek, then I shall never call it home again."

Sarin reaches for and kisses Shaylynn's lips. She holds the moment as though it may be one of the last she will ever have with him. Fallon and Lyosan approach slowly, not wanting to interject themselves where they don't belong. Luckily, Fallon gets distracted when Faith comes looking for him.

"Happy to be home?" she asks.

"Happy to be wherever you are," he replies.

Upon hearing the talk behind them, Sarin and Shaylynn break apart. Until now, they had not been able to enjoy the return of the knights and the princess. With the unpleasantness behind them, the attention can return to the glory of the knights in accomplishing a feat beyond the imagination of most. The fear, the concern, and the anxious uncertainty that filled their minds are gone for the time being. They must enjoy the time they now have together.

"We were quite worried you would not return," Sarin admits.

Shaylynn grabs the necklace Sarin gave him.

"With my protection, how could I fail?" Shaylynn asks.

Sarin smiles again and kisses Shaylynn on the cheek. "You should be so lucky to be so protected so easily."

"It is only because of your zeal it works so well," Faith comments. "Your love for him is rather strong."

"Do not speak out of turn," Sarin says.

"How do you mean?" Faith asks.

"Who are you to comment on my *love* of Shaylynn?"

"Do you deny your love for me?" Shaylynn asks.

"You've never been so forward with me," Sarin notes.

"Shall I tell her what you said to me?" Crystalynn asks.

They turn to see the princess coming towards them. They bow respectfully as she approaches. Sarin lightens at the idea Shaylynn has spoken of her in such a manner. He seems slightly embarrassed by the notion.

"I'd rather you didn't," Shaylynn admits.

"I must disagree with your sentiment," Sarin says as she turns to the princess. "If you are in the telling mood, I am certainly willing to listen."

Crystalynn smiles at Shaylynn before she says anything more. The stern look on his face furthers the idea he wishes his sentiments to remain somewhat private. This proves to be one of many times when being a princess has its perks. For even though Shaylynn wishes for secrecy, Crystalynn knows he will do nothing should she decide to broach the subject. Given Shaylynn's sense of propriety, he will hold to his duty and remain silent on her word.

"We were merely having a discussion regarding the changes we've been through," Crystalynn begins.

As she speaks, Shaylynn rolls his eyes and takes a step away from the group. Fallon and Faith squeeze each other's hand, giddy over his embarrassment. Lyosan chuckles to himself as he takes a drink. Before

Shaylynn can take another step, Sarin grabs his hand and holds him in place.

"Going somewhere?" she asks.

"I thought I could use another drink," he replies.

"Wait a moment and I'll go with you."

Crystalynn continues as Shaylynn reluctantly turns to hear the rest of the discussion. "I must admit," she says, "I felt as though things would never be the same for me again. All that I had seen changed me so. That's when Shaylynn told me of the – what was it? – tug in your heart…?" The princess pauses and looks at Shaylynn who averts his eyes and shakes his head. When Crystalynn turns to Sarin, tears begin to fill Sarin's eyes. "He said it was something that brings him home and keeps him grounded to this place. Something that, as the rest of the world changes, never does and retains some sense of normalcy for him. He said that was you."

Crystalynn stops to let Sarin respond, but she cannot. Overcome with emotion, she can do little else but smile and squeeze Shaylynn's hand. After a moment, she wipes the tears away and turns to face Shaylynn. A tempered smile is on his face. In a rare moment of vulnerability, his usual swagger is unnoticeable. He is just a boy hopelessly and completely in love with a girl.

"You have never told me this before," Sarin finally says.

"Technically, I still haven't," Shaylynn jests.

"Why would you hide this?" Sarin asks. "Are you ashamed to say it?"

Shaylynn's look straightens. A serious change in mood comes over him. "Never have I hidden this from you," he says. "Perhaps I have not expressed it in words, but I have always looked to you to be my strength…" He reaches for the necklace she gave him and shows it to her. "This hangs over my heart," he says, "because it would do me no good anywhere else. I love you in a way I cannot explain. That is why I've never spoken of it. With all other things, I can say what I mean, express myself truly and without fail. In describing the love I bear thee, I would falter. Never with words could I say what I feel in my heart. It is too much for mere words. Too much for this world."

Sarin reaches for him and kisses him. As she pulls away, she whispers in his ear, "In the future, you should at least try with your words."

Cyrus then enters the hall and takes his seat at the head table. Calling for Crystalynn to join him, he asks everyone to take a seat so the feast can begin. As the food is brought out by the servants of the castle, Cyrus addresses the people once again.

"I thank you all for joining me this evening," Cyrus begins. "We honor these knights who served our kingdom so well. What they have done for me, I cannot overstate just how important it is. They have restored hope for the kingdom. They are truly the men who should be leading our kingdom when I have gone…" The serious nature of the speech takes everyone by surprise. None expected Cyrus to speak so candidly, nor do they understand where he is going with this conversation. For his part, Lyosan seems touched to be spoken of so highly. However, he soon expects the conversation will turn to Shaylynn and his exploits rather than his own. "…All three of these young men were, at one point, part of the tournament which will decide our next king…" The idea starts to come to everyone in the room. Shaylynn looks cautiously around him while Sarin grabs his hand. Fallon and Faith look at both of them. Lyosan feels a deep sigh welling up in his chest. Pythyn, on the other side of the room, shifts in his chair as anger overcomes him. "…Lyosan holds his spot which he so clearly deserves and could in fact be raised from his current position. However, Shaylynn and Fallon both have lost their spots after leading a campaign to our southern lands and struggling against all odds to return home. When they did, they said nothing of their place in the tournament. They merely wished to lead another campaign to Jorram to rescue my sister. Thus, I believe that we would be remiss if we did not correct this error!"

Cheers erupt from the hall. All seem pleased with the notion except for a few notable dissenters. Obviously, Shaylynn, Fallon, and Lyosan do nothing. Sarin and Faith cheer but only to keep from creating a scene. Pythyn festers in his spot while one member of the royal court stands. He is Ferdin Mouldin, whose son took one of the spots vacated by Shaylynn and Fallon.

"My good king," Ferdin says as the crowd calms. "How exactly would you enter these two in the tournament? By royal decree, you cannot raise the participants in the tournament nor can you remove a participant without legal cause. While I cannot speak for young Olin, I can say quite confidently my son has done nothing to warrant removal."

"My friend, I would agree with your argument," Cyrus quickly says, "and I would never think of removing a worthy participant from the tournament. Your son has worked valiantly to secure his place in this competition; he will have it." This explanation appeases Ferdin for the moment, and he takes his seat again. So there is not any further confusion,

Cyrus continues his explanation. "Rather than insert these two into the tournament, I will leave them as alternates should a young man be unable to fulfill his duty. Also, should there be no need for them to replace another youth, each shall have the opportunity to challenge the winner should they feel the need to do so."

It takes a moment for the scope of the king's statement to be fully understood. It was one thing for the king to give these two the opportunity to challenge for the throne without participation in the tournament. It is something else entirely to add they could only challenge if they felt the need to.

When it becomes too much for the crowd to bear, one member of the cabinet rises and speaks for them all. "My lord, it is interesting you suggest this accommodation for these two, and I must say I feel it is justified, but I cannot understand this notion that they would not challenge for the throne."

"Indeed," another says joining in the conversation, "why would two youths of our land suddenly decide to abandon a campaign for the throne when they have done so much to ensure your line's continuation?"

The answer seems unfathomable for most. It is quite an offer to refuse. For men who have trained their entire lives to serve the crown and have learned all the knowledge to aid in the ruling of a kingdom, the idea of ruling that kingdom himself has to be enticing in an undeniable way. And yet, both men are ready to forgo the opportunity. Those who know them understand why they would scorn the chance. Having seen the love they bear for Sarin and Faith respectively, many know a kingdom to rule is not a prize if they cannot be with the one they love.

This love is the only thing which brings solace to Pythyn. Anger has boiled over since hearing the news Shaylynn and Fallon would possess the right to challenge the winner of the tournament. Surely, this obstacle will prove too much should he win it. For either of them to forgo the love they have to merely prevent him from earning the throne would be a great sacrifice, and perhaps, it would be a sacrifice too much for them to consider.

Pythyn rises from his seat with an idea already in his mind. It may backfire, but it may be the push he needs to finally rid himself of these two. He still needs a minute to compose himself before he speaks. It's still a nerve wracking moment before he poses his question to Shaylynn. If he does not receive the answer he anticipates, it will prove most disastrous.

"My liege," Pythyn says, "I too find it curious you think they would need to challenge the winner of such a prestigious tournament. Furthermore, my lords, as to your inquiry about what would cause Shaylynn and Fallon to forgo the opportunity to claim the throne, I must say the answer is right before us." Pythyn steps over to Shaylynn and Fallon's table and motions to Sarin and Faith. "Those of us who have traveled with these two know of their feelings towards certain ladies of the court. To ask them to spurn love in such a way would almost be cruel."

The first member who spoke gives a little laugh. "This is something else entirely, my dear boy. This is a life of luxury and a calling which goes beyond the needs and wants of one life. Furthermore, a life married to the princess would surely make up for any unrequited love."

The king says nothing to this reply. Pythyn feels fortunate the idea came forward. It was not what he initially intended, but it brings up an interesting notion to consider. Moreover, it reinvigorates the discussion. Pythyn has the moment he has been looking for with this topic.

"What say you, Shaylynn?" Pythyn asks. "Since we speak of you and Fallon, perhaps we should turn our attention to your intentions. The king grants you a generous privilege when it comes to your ability to challenge the winner of the tournament, but would you assert that privilege?"

Pythyn circles the table in an attempt to bait Shaylynn into the trap. Within the next few moments, he could have a guarantee from Shaylynn that he would not surrender a life with Sarin – even for the kingdom. While many would call his decision foolish, he would have made his decision in a very public situation. All the nobles of the city currently reside within the castle walls and will have heard Shaylynn vow to live a life with Sarin rather than be king. Even if Shaylynn would change his mind, the stress upon him would be severe.

Shaylynn senses the trap but cannot see the trigger. Pythyn rarely does anything publicly without having ulterior motives for his actions. He understands it has something to do with Sarin. In truth, it is wise to use Sarin to create a chasm between Shaylynn and his political beliefs. Though Pythyn would not have knowledge of Shaylynn's pledge to leave Artonia to create a life with Sarin, he would probably assume it to be a truth. So what if Shaylynn stood up and said in front of all these people he would challenge for rule if he desired? So what if he said he'd let go his love of

Sarin in order to protect the throne?

She would know better.

And yet, the strain upon her would be immense. Through the entirety of the tournament, she would have to live with the idea that perhaps Shaylynn would challenge the winner. True, it would most likely only occur if Pythyn won the tournament, but he would have to be the one to make the claim. Fallon would try, but perhaps not win the battle. Furthermore, Fallon would not want to be king. Instead, he would surrender the throne to Shaylynn when Shaylynn took his opportunity to challenge for the throne. Fallon, no matter what happens, will end up with Faith. Shaylynn, on the other hand, may have to sacrifice the one thing he has counted on for his entire life. When that happens, who knows what the results will be?

Slowly, Shaylynn rises from his chair. His answer must be calculated and above all must not directly answer the question. "It is too far from the end to say," Shaylynn admits. Then he turns to Sarin. "You speak true, Pythyn, when you speak of the love I have for another." They smile at each other as Shaylynn turns to address the rest of the crowd. "And yet, as a knight of Langerwitz, I must do what is best for the kingdom. Perhaps, for the moment, I cannot foresee a circumstance wherein a need would arise to challenge for the throne, but perhaps, in time, it will become necessary. I will not pray for it – for the throne of Langerwitz to fall into distress. I will have faith that the winner of the tournament will be honorable, wise, and kingly." Shaylynn stops for a moment and looks at Lyosan. Lyosan's face reddens at the attention. "For the moment, I will accept the honor bestowed upon me and enjoy the life I live. I will love the ones I love. But time shows all of us things we do not wish to see. Should the time come, I will face it, but I've stronger convictions in a higher power."

Shaylynn bows respectfully to the king then sits back down. While many must decode the cryptic message behind his words, Sarin reaches for him and offers him her hand. He gladly takes it and kisses it. Unfortunately, Pythyn does not have the answer he is looking for and will not stop until he does.

"Forgive me, Shaylynn," Pythyn says, "but I did not hear a clear answer in your speech. Perhaps you could just speak plainly – do you intend to challenge the winner of the tournament for the throne."

"When I know, you'll know," Shaylynn replies.

The crowd erupts in laughter, and the king rises from his seat.

"I believe we have heard enough on the matter for the time being," Cyrus says. "Let us return to the joyous purpose of this feast and reward our heroes in the manner they deserve."

All raise a drink and cheer for Shaylynn, Fallon, and Lyosan. After that, there is no more mention of the tournament, Shaylynn's place in the race for the throne, or his potential marriage to the princess. The youths revel in the night. The adults take solace in the peace of the moment knowing it will not last forever.

With those events over, Shaylynn, Fallon, and Lyosan finally take time to be with their families. Mothers kiss their sons on the cheek. Siblings hug their brothers and their friends, happy to have them back. Stories are told, and memories shared. There are some moments of sorrow in the realization fathers and brothers will not be coming home. Though Ellisia and Kandessa have long accepted their husbands have moved on and Kandessa has accepted the loss of her eldest son, they have not openly discussed the matter with their families. When the truth finally hits, it is hard to accept.

They are fortunate to be able to share their grief with family and friends. Given the nature of the campaigns Fallon and Shaylynn have undertaken lately, they can find comfort in the return of some loved ones. They can also find joy in the revelation of love between Shaylynn and Sarin and Fallon and Faith. They have believed for years the couples would always end up together, but to see them accept this so young shows a maturity which brings great comfort. What's more, they are very pleased with the relationships their children have formed.

When the feast ends, it is long into the night. Kandessa convinces Shaylynn to walk her home. Some part of him wishes to escort Sarin, but he realizes he has spent too much time away from family to decline his mother's request. Besides, they do have to plan for remembrances for Feylynn and Beylynn. Daylynn also takes the opportunity to reconnect with Shaylynn after his time away. While Kandessa meant for their walk together to be a different sort of reconnecting, she is happy to see Daylynn smile again. When they reach home, she puts Daylynn to bed while keeping Shaylynn up for a while longer.

"I hope I do not ask too much of a tired body," Kandessa says.

"So long as you require me, I shall not be tired," Shaylynn replies. "After being gone so long, I'm sure the fatigue you feel rivals my own."

Kandessa laughs a bit. "It has been difficult around here, but our friends have managed to help us out." She pauses for a moment before getting to the heart of the matter. "I meant to talk to you of your place within this tournament."

Shaylynn frowns at the subject. He wishes it could fade away for just a few moments of his life. Yet, he will not scorn his mother's wish.

"Please, do not think I am going to try to advise you in any way," Kandessa says.

Shaylynn frowns again, only this time in confusion.

"I know it is surprising to you that you would not be receiving advice, but I know this is not a decision I can make," Kandessa explains. "This is a path you must take. So long as you wish this path, then I shall support you in doing this." She pauses for a time to let the moment sink it. Then, she asks the question Shaylynn has never considered until this moment. "Are you sure this is the decision you want to make?"

If it were anyone else posing the question, Shaylynn would immediately respond he was certain of his course. He would go on and on about the love he has for Sarin and how he would leave the throne to other men. However, he knows he can be completely candid with his mother and not have it go any further than this table. For weeks now, he has been running around the country with everyone looking to him for safety and security. He had to be the one to know the plan and carry it out with absolute certainty.

Here, he does not have such a burden. He is still just a child in front of his mother who carried him in her arms for the first years of his life. For the first time in a long time, he can be vulnerable and open. He can speak his mind and have a conversation no one else would dare have with him. For that reason, he is calm when he speaks.

"I could be king," Shaylynn says.

Kandessa nods. "Yes, I believe you could."

"I never saw myself as king," Shaylynn continues.

"Nor I, but I always believed you were capable of great things. This is just one of those things."

"No, this is something more. This is ruling where other men would not dare. This is a prize sought by every heart in the kingdom..."

"Well, nearly every heart," Kandessa interjects. "It does not seem to be the object of your desire. You seem to have settled on something else...or should I say someone else."

Shaylynn blushes slightly. It is one thing to declare his love in a room full of people. It is something else entirely to admit that love to the other woman he's loved so completely in his life.

"I have," Shaylynn admits with a smile.

"You love her?"

"I do."

"Then why do you question yourself?"

"Because this is the throne of Artonia. This is the rule of the kingdom and the chance to elevate our family to a new stratum. I think of all I can do now, all that I have done, and I think of how much more I must be able to do. I think of how my friends look to me and ask me to solve their problems, and how I will do so for the rest of my life."

"Do you need to sit on the throne to accomplish this?"

Shaylynn considers this. "I suppose not."

"You will attain whatever greatness you were meant for," Kandessa explains, "and it matters not where you rest your head to accomplish those feats. No matter where you go or what you do, your friends look to you because of the heart you give to your friends. They do not look to you because they see you as their king; they look to you because they know you will fight at their side. They have seen the nature of your heart. It is the same reason Sarin wants you as her husband. If you feel you need her to keep your heart pure, then you cannot let her go."

In hearing everything he wants to hear, Shaylynn fears everything is coming too easy. The decision, though presented to him simply, cannot be this easy to decide. He cannot simply pass over this opportunity without a second thought. Though his mother can offer her support, there is one who cannot.

"What of father?" Shaylynn asks. "Would he advise me the same way?"

Kandessa places a hand over Shaylynn's and speaks with absolute confidence. "Absolutely, he would."

A tear forms in Shaylynn's eye. "He spoke so often of honor and loyalty to the crown."

"But he knew family was more important," Kandessa counters. "And he knew family only came from following your heart. If your heart is leading you to Sarin, then you cannot ignore it now. Your heart is what has drawn people to you, and if you start to ignore it, it will turn them away from you."

The words bring comfort to Shaylynn's heart even if they do not completely avail him of his concerns. In many ways, he wishes he were back in the forest with Darek and the Order. Perhaps, in magic, he could find the answer which eludes him presently, but the forest is not home. If he is to gain peace, it will only come to him here. As he has always suspected, family is what brings peace to him.

Family also brings comfort to Lyosan. Across the way, Lyosan has made his way home with his mother and brothers in tow. Calvin goes with ease as he drapes his arms over Lyosan and rides on his back. Steel runs out in front going from side to side as they walk. Elle keeps an arm around Lyosan's arm reveling in having him home once again.

"So brother," Calvin says, "what was it like being on the road with the princess for so long?"

"I wasn't exactly with her exclusively," Lyosan explains. "I had twelve other knights with me at the time. Furthermore, she rode in her own carriage away from the rest of us."

"Yes, but you saved her!" Steel exclaims. "Surely that warrants some special treatment for you!"

"Steel, keep your voice down," Elle chides. "Some people are trying to sleep."

"Sorry, mother," Steel says sincerely. Then, he goes back to his point. "You stabbed the man who tried to kill the princess," he continues. "You risked life and limb to go after her. You acted when Shaylynn of all people could not. Surely, you didn't ride back as though you were part of the company?"

"Well, of course I did," Lyosan replies.

Steel moans in disappointment. "Oh, you have to be kidding!" he groans loud enough for Elle to slap his shoulder. Steel quiets himself again but goes on with his complaints. "How can you expect to catch her eye when you insist on hiding in the shadows? What you have done only comes along once in a hundred lifetimes, and when that moment comes to you, you take advantage of it by saving her life only to shirk the glory which comes with it."

"I received the Phoenix, which virtually no other knight has," Lyosan reminds him.

"And yet you did something no one else did," Steel responds. "You saved her life and ensured the continuation of our country. In doing something no one else has done, you deserve something no one else should get."

They arrive at the house, so Lyosan lets the subject drop. Steel immediately goes to his room and shuts the door. Calvin drops off Lyosan's shoulders and gives his brother a big hug.

"Don't let him bother you," Calvin says. "He only wishes he could do the things you do. I know you're great just as you are!"

Lyosan chuckles to himself. "You, above everything else, are the reason I am happy to be home again."

Elle sends Calvin to bed while Lyosan takes a seat at the kitchen table.

"Can I get you something?" Elle asks.

"Perhaps just something to drink," Lyosan replies.

Lyosan rests his head on the table for a moment, picking it back up when he hears a mug thud on the table. Snapping back up, he grabs the drink and takes a long sip. Out of the corner of his eye, he notices the fidgeting of his mother's hands. This vexes him greatly as she seemed worry free just a moment ago. Wanting to solve the problem, Lyosan cuts his drink off and sets the mug down.

Perhaps, he would have been better served to continue uninterrupted. Though he waits for Elle to speak, she is clearly not prepared to say her piece. Waiting for the words to form in her mind, she collects herself for a few more moments. Yet, every time she glances at her son, her mouth tremors, and she cannot get the words to come out. But, every time she pauses, his concern grows. She can see it in his eyes. She has to say what she has to say and let the chips fall where they may.

"Your brother is not wrong," Elle says.

Lyosan ponders a moment which brother she is speaking of. He hopes it is one but suspects it's the other. "Calvin?" Lyosan asks.

"No," Elle replies, then she remembers what Calvin said. "Well, yes, but his words are not what I am concerned with. I speak of Steel."

For this to come up now is less than opportune. After struggling with what he had done all the way home, he finds himself faced with another angle of the same situation. It is not enough he took a life; now, he must take advantage of its happening.

"Did you talk of this with him already or did he just happen to suggest it earlier by chance?" Lyosan asks.

"He knew nothing of my thoughts," Elle replies. "In fact, I had not given much thought to it until he broached the subject." Lyosan rolls his eyes to indicate his unwillingness to discuss the matter. Elle sees this and continues on her own accord. "You rescued the princess from the hand of death. Surely, that warrants more accommodation than you've received. Shaylynn and Fallon earned the opportunity to challenge the winner at the end of the tournament..."

Lyosan interrupts, "They were part of the tournament, and now they are not."

"Please, the king wishes Shaylynn to succeed him," Elle interjects. "If Shaylynn gave the slightest indication he wanted the throne, Cyrus would end all this tournament talk and hand it over to him."

"And Shaylynn would make a good king."

"But he does not want it. He wants a life with Sarin in servitude of the crown. I applaud his loyalty and honor, but it does nothing to help you win Crystalynn's heart."

Lyosan's face solidifies in an emotionless glare. He does not want to betray his love for Crystalynn, for he knows it will become the best weapon in Elle's arsenal. She smiles warmly and places a hand on his.

"I know you love her," Elle says. "You have ever since you were a child. As much as you dream of being with her, it will only happen if you win this tournament. If nothing else, you should use this event to get yourself a better seed for the tournament."

"It matters not where I lie in the tournament," Lyosan counters. "I will have to fight my way to the end. If it is meant to be, then it doesn't matter what is in my way. I will overcome."

"And I believe you shall," Elle says, "but I do not believe there is any harm in trying to elevate yourself in the eyes of your opponents."

"Only one thing can elevate me in their eyes and that is beating them," Lyosan says. "Those who will face me have known me long enough to know what I am capable of. This will not change their minds. I am merely another bump in their road to success. I reside in the shadows of greater men like Shaylynn and Fallon. They do not fear me, and even if I win, they will wonder how it happened."

This is a moment of revelation for Elle. She's known for a long time Lyosan does not see himself on the same level as Shaylynn or Fallon, but now she realizes he sees himself as below all others around him. He truly does not realize what he has accomplished nor what he is capable of. If he does not believe himself capable of winning the throne, and thereby the princess's hand, he will never be able to realize his full potential.

"Perhaps they are not scared of you," Elle corrects, "but they do respect you." Lyosan rolls his eyes in disbelief. "They do!" Elle quickly reiterates. "Even if you are not the best fighter or the smartest strategist, they know you can be counted on. They know you have a good heart and will use it to protect your friends."

"Is that all it takes to be king?" Lyosan asks.

"It is a good start. All else can be proven in time."

CHAPTER XVII

Given the events Langerwitz has seen, time will not be wasted anymore. Cyrus would see a winner of the tournament crowned soon. With the decree standing that Shaylynn and Fallon can challenge the winner of the tournament if they desire, everyone knows the youths will need to be at the top of their game. The normal air of invincibility which surrounds Shaylynn only grows with the recanting of his deeds in Jorram. The entire city knows he played a key role in the rescue, but they know nothing of his exploits which got them into the castle. His development into something of a sorcerer certainly strengthens his position as the best of the youths. As is normally the case with him, he cares nothing for what the people say of him. Instead, he tries to ready the one whom he believes will be best for the throne.

Being awarded the Golden Phoenix has increased Lyosan's confidence a great deal. He will not place himself in the company of Shaylynn or Fallon, but he does begin to believe he can rival any of the other youths. He is more willing to accept challenges from other dueling partners. When Shaylynn and Fallon are needed elsewhere, Lyosan does not feel the jealously he felt before. Instead, he focuses on the task at hand – knowing he will need everything he has to achieve his goal.

His newfound confidence does not go unnoticed. Pythyn sees it and, while it is not enough for him to seriously fear Lyosan, it does draw his eye. The way the bracket currently stands, Pythyn and Lyosan would not fight until the final round. Before, Pythyn would've never considered the possibility of Lyosan being the one he would face for the crown. Now, he realizes the possibility is stronger. Pythyn still expects Stefen or Nycolas or Darrow to be his greatest competition of those in the bracket. He knows his greatest challenge comes from outside the bracket. Sadly, for Pythyn, he can do nothing about those challenges.

The other who notices Lyosan's change – perhaps the more important – is the princess. Since her return from Jorram, she has taken a greater interest in the tournament which will decide her husband. Knowing it will begin soon brings a whirlwind of emotions to the forefront of her mind. Having escaped the terror that would've been a marriage to Dreilon Grepportorn, her fate again moves out of her hands. She hopes her marriage will be to someone she cares for. She has known so few of her suitors intimately. There are only a handful she would detest being married to. Unfortunately, one of them stands high in the bracket since Shaylynn lost his spot.

She can bank on the notion, however, that Shaylynn would never let Pythyn become the king of Artonia. Though he would choose Sarin if he had the chance, his sense of duty would win out if the situation turned dire. For that reason, Crystalynn cannot fight the small part of her which sees Pythyn winning the tournament as a terrible means to a wondrous end. She would never intend to come between Shaylynn and Sarin, but should fate intervene, as it does in every other aspect of her life, she may not mind this time. It is a terrible thought. She knows this, but at the same time, she must be honest with herself.

She must also be honest when she admits she feels a growing appreciation of Lyosan's devotion. As she told Shaylynn before, it is difficult for her to believe in Lyosan because he fails to believe in himself. Since they returned, this has not been the case. The more he believes in himself, the more he appears to be a true knight of Artonia. The confidence he carries within himself gives off a different view of the boy she once knew. She begins to think she sees what Shaylynn sees in Lyosan.

Unfortunately, it all goes away when Shaylynn is near. The two have said little about what Athorn revealed to Shaylynn when they stood in the great hall. Everything he said was true. Given that Shaylynn did not refute the statements strongly, Crystalynn suspects he knows the truth behind the revelations.

It is a normal day of training when Shaylynn and the princess run into each other. At first, they act as decorum dictates. Quickly, however, the mood turns, and these two who have become friends in recent months could not feel more uncomfortable around each other.

"I'm sorry to stop you," Crystalynn says. "You must be in a hurry."

"Not at all," Shaylynn replies. "I was just speaking with your brother. He had some matters to discuss regarding the tournament."

Mention of the tournament does not make the mood any better for the princess. Feigning joy, she replies, "Ah, yes, it approaches, doesn't it?"

Indeed, it does. Little more than a month separates them from the first round of duels. Shaylynn has still said very little about whether or not he will challenge the winner of the tournament. Publicly, he turns away from the question whenever posed. Privately, he hopes the choice will be rendered moot by the result of the tournament. But, as he has broached the subject with the princess, he cannot dodge the topic now. They are alone, so whatever is said will remain between them and them only. And yet, the conversation could turn quite serious in a moment.

"It must be a very…conflicting time for you," Shaylynn finally says.

Crystalynn smiles. "Yes, it is." There is a great deal she would say if she knew the truth would not complicate matters, but it would. The mere thought of her marrying Shaylynn would raise the tension between them a hundredfold. At the same time, having to hold all this in has been remarkably difficult. Her greatest confidants lie at the center of this debacle. She has not been able to speak freely on the matter since it began. She will not do so now. "But you have matters to attend to. I won't stop you."

She motions for Shaylynn to move on, but he hesitates. Though he stands on the opposite side of this matter, he can understand the difficulty the princess faces. He saw the look on her face when they stood in the castle. He remembers the words she spoke when he tried to prevent her from leaving Langerwitz. And though he does not know what help he can be, it is in his nature to at least try.

"My lady, if you need an ear to bend, you always have mine," Shaylynn offers.

Crystalynn lowers her arm and studies Shaylynn for a moment. She cannot decide how genuine his offer is. A knight of his caliber would of course offer his services, but he may be hoping she appreciates the offer without taking him up on it. The latter seems the more likely.

"I've created too much drama for you," she says. "I needn't make more."

She begins to walk away, but Shaylynn continues.

"You cannot speak to Lyosan about this," he says. Crystalynn stops. When Shaylynn sees she is listening, he adds, "You certainly would not trouble your brother with the matter. And I wouldn't have you going to Sarin or Faith with this, so please, lay your burdens on me."

Crystalynn turns and looks at the boy again. If only things could be simpler, she thinks to herself. If only they'd known a boy from the city would be needed to be king. They could've groomed him from the beginning. He wouldn't have had the chance to fall in love with Sarin. But she wouldn't wish that on him.

"I fear there's a great deal to be said," Crystalynn admits.

Shaylynn nods. "I would assume so. You've kept so much to yourself. You've dealt with so much. You deserve the chance to vent."

Right as always. She did speak briefly with Shaylynn on the return journey to Langerwitz. She was so happy to be free of Jorram, she didn't get to tell of the things she endured while held prisoner. Of course, many of those complaints would seem small coming from a princess. The life of luxury she lived in Langerwitz being denied to her for a small fraction of her life would not warrant much sympathy from a boy who toiled all his life. True, Shaylynn's life has been much easier than most, but he understands hardship much better than her.

He also knows some of the secrets of her mind. That she would have him as her king. That she would've stayed had he given himself to her. It is not fair for him to possess this knowledge. That she must deny her awareness of his awareness does anger her quite severely.

But it is this anger she wishes to address at the moment. Shaylynn has asked about the tournament, and the tournament stirs up its own set of problems. True, they stem from what happened in Jorram, but they are something else entirely. Since Shaylynn seems sincere, Crystalynn will have this talk with him.

"When I first arrived in Jorram, I assumed it wouldn't be for long," she explains. "Brother will send the cavalry after me, I said. But after a while, I realized the cavalry was with me. They had been defeated, and I was a prisoner because the best we had had been beaten. When that sunk in, I didn't know how, but I still believed Cyrus would rescue me somehow.

"Weeks went by, and nothing happened. Every so often, Athorn would bring me to the throne room to tell me of the damage he was causing in Artonia. He promised me it would all end if I agreed to marry Dreilon. I refused of course – thinking my rescue was imminent. At first, I was defiant in my denial, and Athorn only laughed at me. 'You've no idea how little control you have in the matter,' he would say to me.

"And he was right."

The princess pauses for a moment as the emotions she felt then begin to seep out. She collects herself and continues.

"I understood that the longer I stayed in Jorram," she says. "I was at the mercy of my captors. After a while, they stopped being merciful. The old man, the sorcerer who attacked you, started visiting me." Shaylynn would ask a million questions if he could, but he promised to listen – not talk. Besides, the mention of him seems to trouble Crystalynn greatly. "He frightened me from the moment I saw him. He seemed to like how much he scared me.

"Whenever he came, Athorn was always there. The first thing the old man did was prod my mind. He entered my thoughts and was suddenly a part of every memory I had. It was nightmarish. I couldn't get away from him – not in my thoughts and certainly not in reality." Tears begin to roll down her cheeks as she pauses again. She turns to Shaylynn to ask a question of him. "Can you do such a thing?" she asks.

Were he to say yes, it would seemingly break her heart. That Shaylynn, son of Feylynn, captain of the youths, winner of the Golden Phoenix, could be so monstrous would destroy her very image of him. And yet, he cannot lie to her – not now.

"I possess the skill," Shaylynn replies, "but I could never invade someone in such a way, no."

The princess smiles through her tears. "Of course you wouldn't," she says. "You are a light in this world – meant to protect people from such darkness."

Shaylynn considers ending this talk, but the princess continues before he can say no more.

"I lost hope after that," she says. "I gave myself over to the thought I would marry Dreilon and become queen of Jorram. I assumed I'd rarely, if ever, see my brother, my friends…my home. I resigned myself to a terrible life and began to think how I would merely make it through my days. Then, word reached the castle. The campaign in the south failed. Shaylynn, son of Feylynn, led a group of youths to victory over the Jorramian force. A spark of hope flickered in me. You were coming for me, I told myself. With the south secure, you would come to the north and somehow rescue me from this place.

"It was a hope quickly dashed. News also came you were lost and perhaps dead. The old man was not convinced. He warned the king you would not be stopped so easily. The only speck of hope I had heard in weeks, and it was coming from the greatest source of fear I knew. But weeks went by, and you didn't come.

"The old man continued to warn the king, but the king didn't listen. He only planned my wedding. Dreilon started coming around more. He was so detestable. He knew I would come to love him, he said. I shouldn't expect much from him, he said, but that distance he put up would only draw me to him. I was fortunate he never laid a hand on me – not until he knew you were coming anyway. He was deathly afraid of you. The old man told tales of what magicians and sorcerers used to be able to do. Though I knew you were not a magician or a sorcerer, I tried to frighten him into thinking you were. One day, after I went on too long, he slapped me across the face. Once he did it, he wasn't afraid to do it again…"

Shaylynn cannot sit and listen anymore. The princess never mentioned Dreilon had assaulted her in such a way. True, Dreilon died before Shaylynn would have had a chance to exact revenge, but she needn't keep this secret to herself.

"You never told me this," Shaylynn says.

"I told no one," Crystalynn admits.

"Why?" Shaylynn demands.

Though Shaylynn shows anger, Crystalynn cannot. The matter has passed her by.

"What would it matter?" she asks. "He's dead. I'm not damaged anymore."

It matters a great deal to Shaylynn. That someone – some lowly degenerate – would abuse his princess cannot stand. But it is clear to Shaylynn that Crystalynn wishes to discuss this matter further, so he lets her continue.

"Then, you were there. After shattering a castle wall and sneaking into the throne room, you appeared like a hero from a fairy tale. With Lyosan and Fallon, you rescued me like I'd hoped you would but had given up believing could happen. You took me from the nightmare and brought me home. And now, I fear the nightmare may return…"

The princess stops speaking and begins to cry. Shaylynn cannot understand where this is coming from. The prince of Jorram is dead. Athorn would not be foolish enough to try to reach Crystalynn here. To comfort her, Shaylynn takes her hand which she squeezes tightly. Quickly, she becomes embarrassed by her loss of control.

"How can you think such a thing?" Shaylynn asks. "You are home. We are all here to protect you, now."

"But you cannot protect me from what must happen," she replies. "My husband will be decided by this tournament. I will marry whoever wins. And since you have been removed from the tournament, it makes Pythyn the odds-on favorite to win. I know he is not Dreilon, but when I see Pythyn, I am reminded so much of the Jorramian Prince. I see a lifetime of unhappiness with him as my king. You would marry Sarin. Fallon would marry Faith. Lyosan would take a wife as well. Though Pythyn would never banish any of you from the castle, he would make it difficult for us to spend time together. He would use the power afforded him to distance us. He would imprison me just as Athorn did – just as Dreilon would have."

"You assume so quickly he will win," Shaylynn says. "There are sixty-four participants in the tournament – sixty-six with Fallon and myself granted the honor to challenge the winner."

"Perhaps, in your eyes, it seems as much," Crystalynn explains. "But I have only ever seriously considered two possibilities – either you or he will claim the prize. Now that you have your out, I only see him."

Shaylynn would make a promise to her right now – a reckless promise, but one he would hold to. In truth, he would rather raise her spirits in another fashion. If he can get her to see the situation with a bit more optimism, perhaps he can avoid the promise.

"There are several more youths able to defeat him," Shaylynn says with a little more pep in his voice. "Honestly, why you choose to see me as your only way out…"

Before he can finish the thought, she interrupts with the one topic they both wish to avoid. "You know why. Athorn told you as much. I love you."

Silence takes them both. Shaylynn knew the conversation would turn this way. Why he finds himself so speechless is beyond him. For her part, Crystalynn would say a great deal more, but she knows it would only lead to her despair. He will not, cannot, say the words she wishes to hear.

Now, they both look at the hand they use to hold the other's. They consider what it means, what it could mean, and what they want it to mean. For Shaylynn, there is not much difference between reality and desire. It is the action of a friend meant for the showing of friendship – nothing more. For Crystalynn, the difference could not be greater. She knows what it really means and knows it could never really mean anything else. When it comes to what she wants it to mean, she is not going to hide it. She wants it to be a sign of love and devotion – not a consoling effort.

Before things turn too awkward, Shaylynn tries to salvage the situation. "I assumed Athorn was merely trying to rile me up."

Crystalynn cannot fight the truth. "No, you didn't," she says calmly but firmly. "The words surprised you only because you realized the truth behind them. If I truly had my pick – if you did not so devotedly love another – I would make you king." She stops looking down for a moment and looks at Shaylynn's eyes. He meets her gaze, but the emotion in his eyes does not match hers. "I would appeal to Cyrus," she continues. "Tell him to hell with the tournament and demand you be named the successor."

Her candor is catching Shaylynn off guard. After side-stepping the issue for so long, facing it head on is more complicated than he assumed it'd be. Her last statement is troubling to him. She could make such a demand. It is well within her rights. Given all he has done, Shaylynn is well-accepted by most of the kingdom. Some would oppose the decree – mainly those who prepare to fight in the tournament. The king could calm their concerns in a number of ways. As long as the next king was decided, Cyrus would offer any service to quell the outrage.

"You could make such an appeal," Shaylynn states, "but you don't."

His intent is to point to her inaction as a sign that she doesn't feel as strongly about him as she claims. He will admit to being aware of some admiration – even a small infatuation – but this notion that she loves him? He cannot see it. He is himself blinded by his own love for Sarin and his loyalty to Lyosan.

"Of course I don't" the princess replies. "I don't want you to resent me for our entire life. I don't want my husband looking at another woman with more love than when he looks at me. I want you to be happy; I just wish your happiness could be with me. Because then I wouldn't have anything to fear."

"Pythyn will not be king," Shaylynn replies. This was the issue which caused her concern. Perhaps, he can solve this discomfort by alleviating it.

"You are so sure," Crystalynn retorts cynically.

"I am!"

"Will you promise me as much?" she asks. She takes his other hand in hers and faces him. "Will you promise me that should Pythyn win the tournament, you will take the luxury afforded you and face him?"

He could've done so minutes ago. It might have prevented some of the revelations coming to light. But he knows the truth now. A truth he cannot speak of to Lyosan or Sarin. He would not even bring it to Fallon. It is a truth between the princess and him. There is already so much between them. He can hold on to one more.

"Yes," Shaylynn finally replies, "I promise to you that should Pythyn win the tournament, I will step in and face him."

A smile comes to the princess's face.

"It is not a guarantee I will beat him," Shaylynn adds.

"It's more than I can hope for," Crystalynn admits.

Shaylynn feels a terrible guilt in promising this. He cannot tell if Crystalynn now hopes for Pythyn to win so he will have to enter the fray or if she is merely content knowing a safety is in place. In any event, he has not made a declaration of love, but she looks as though he has. While she may love him, he cannot see himself worthy of such devotion.

"I wish you did not love me," he admits.

Without another word, Crystalynn reaches for Shaylynn and kisses him. Shaylynn does not match her fervor, but he does not pull away either. For a few seconds, the princess remains pressed against Shaylynn. When she pulls away, Shaylynn quickly hides his shock.

"I am sorry," she replies, "but I do."

Shaylynn returns to the training arena, obviously affected by the exchange. Fallon and Lyosan stand in the center of the room going over a particularly challenging dueling strategy. Shaylynn approaches but says nothing as he sits down and watches the two go through the steps. Lyosan's focus is unquestioned, but he cannot yet go through the motions of the whole move. Fallon stops the training for a moment and begins to explain the steps again. As Lyosan follows his instructor, Shaylynn begins, for the first time, to question whether Lyosan can accomplish the task Shaylynn has set out for him. Though he still believes Lyosan capable of winning the tournament, he wonders if he can draw the performance out of him.

More importantly, he wonders if Lyosan can rise to the challenge. Even now, he misses a step, carries his sword low, and does not smoothly make his movements. He will advance in the tournament – there is no doubt in that. The first few rounds will not offer enough challenge to knock Lyosan down early. But can he defeat Pythyn? Can he defeat someone like Darrow on his way to the finals? Much will need to change in order for the answer to become yes.

Now, Shaylynn places more than his faith in Lyosan. He places his future in Lyosan's hands. The marriage he seeks may become a mere dream should Lyosan fail in his endeavor and Pythyn win the tournament. It is a truth Shaylynn has known in his heart – if Pythyn wins, Shaylynn will challenge him. If the kingdom rests in the hands of a deviant, he will take the place so many believe is already his. He will not leave the princess and the kingdom in a difficult spot; he will sacrifice his own happiness. The life he imagined with Sarin will retreat to the recesses of his mind, and he will think of it no more.

It is not what he wants of course. It is only what he is willing to do. It is perhaps because of that reason he watches Lyosan with a more critical eye. As Fallon takes him through the motions, Shaylynn sees every error and every mistake magnified a hundred times in his eyes. When it becomes too much for him to handle, he rises from the ground and lashes out at Lyosan.

"Are you the slightest bit focused?" Shaylynn demands.

He steps forward and pulls the blade from Lyosan's hands. Waving Fallon aside, he steps in front of Lyosan and goes through the motions. As he does, he barks out the moves and puts Lyosan on the defensive. When he finishes, he tosses the blade back to Lyosan and demands he repeat his actions.

Fallon cannot understand where this sudden outburst has stemmed from. This is an advanced progression of their training which Lyosan has only seen a few times. When Shaylynn first showed him the steps, he admitted it would take time for Lyosan to get it all. Now, he snaps after watching Lyosan perform the stunt one time.

"Is this a new training technique?" Fallon asks.

"We showed him the moves two days ago," Shaylynn replies.

"I mean where you embarrass him into performing better," Fallon clarifies.

Shaylynn is not in the mood. "We have coddled him too much as of late."

"Coddled him?" Fallon repeats. He cannot agree with this notion. Lyosan has been pushing himself too hard if anything. From dawn to dusk Lyosan puts himself in the training room. He only stops to eat and complete the small chores he needs to do at his house. "He has tripled his efforts since we returned."

"You think that is enough to challenge the others?" Shaylynn asks.

Shaylynn leaves Fallon and goes back to working with Lyosan. He corrects a few elements in Lyosan's form then steps back. Fallon approaches him again.

"Why do you doubt him suddenly?" Fallon asks.

"I do not doubt him," Shaylynn replies. "But there is a great deal riding on him. He is competing to be king, and if he cannot meet the challenge, then it may fall to me."

"This is not just your burden. It is mine as well," Fallon reminds him. Shaylynn laughs at the remark which Fallon does not appreciate. "Do you doubt my loyalty to our cause?" he asks.

Shaylynn shakes his head as he replies, "We both have the privilege, but we both know I will be the one expected to exercise it."

Fallon sees now the concerns which trouble Shaylynn so dearly. The tournament is a chance for Lyosan. It is also a threat to Shaylynn's plans. That has always been the case. Why would now be so different? He never thought to doubt Lyosan before. Now, after a few mistakes, he loses his trust.

"Has something happened?" Fallon asks.

Shaylynn thinks carefully before he replies. He cannot say anything which would betray the princess's trust. What's more, he does not want Fallon to have to share in this burden as well.

"I've faced a truth I wished to deny," Shaylynn replies. "It hit harder than I expected."

"Something you need to discuss?"

"No, my friend, I need quite the opposite. I need to keep this one to myself."

"As you like."

Though Shaylynn admits no fault, he sees the error in his tactics.

Lyosan is indeed trying his hardest – the routine is simply too new to him. In time, he makes progress to the point where he can perform the moves from start to finish, but they are still lacking a certain rhythm and flow.

From afar, the princess watches his progress. She keeps herself hidden, knowing the situation with Shaylynn will only generate tension. In the weeks to come, she keeps her distance from him. When she can, she steals a moment with Lyosan, but his training has become so intense, he rarely is without Shaylynn and Fallon.

It cannot be avoided forever, however. Eventually, Shaylynn and Crystalynn do come together. They say nothing of what had transpired between them. They do everything they can to hide any discomfort they might feel around one another. Instead, the princess focuses on Lyosan. As his confidence in his skill has grown, he has not been shy about his desire to win the tournament. He will not completely come to the point wherein he says it is because he loves the princess, but the obviousness of it cannot be denied. As Crystalynn watches him, she deepens her understanding of her appreciation of him. What he did for her, saving her life, comes full circle in her mind. Originally, she looked at Shaylynn as her savior, but in truth, Lyosan slayed the prince. While Dreilon came at her, Shaylynn was incapacitated. Lyosan stepped forward and protected her.

His loyalty to her has never been in question. She just never fully realized where his loyalty stemmed from. It is not because she is a princess, and he is her subject. It is more than that. It transcends the bounds of social decorum or mere loyalty to the crown. He does not look upon her as a princess but rather a person. Crystalynn believes she would be happy married to Shaylynn. She begins to understand Lyosan would always try to make her happy. He always has in the past. Given the opportunity, he would always try in the future. When she thinks about it, he has always been able to succeed in that endeavor. Why would she now think he would fail in the future?

For that reason, at least in part, she begins to look beyond Shaylynn and to Lyosan, among others. It would be a happy life, she realizes. Even if he is not fully trained now, Lyosan will always guide with a steady mind and a good heart. On the throne, he will defend his own and protect the lands. With Shaylynn and Fallon at his side, Lyosan will have good counsel. As he has always trusted them before, so will he trust them in the future.

The training goes on as the time for the tournament approaches. With about a week before the opening round, Shaylynn, Fallon, and Lyosan find themselves in the training room as usual. Jonas's role in their development has lessened as of late. He does not instruct as much as he offers his advice and gives help when asked.

Thus, it is of no consequence when Sarin and Faith enter the training room without provocation. At first, Shaylynn and Fallon do not notice them, but they quickly make their presence known.

"What are you doing here?" Shaylynn asks.

Sarin grunts, then replies. "Perhaps if you could be found elsewhere, I would not need to come here."

Shaylynn rolls his eyes. "We have little time left before the tournament."

"Don't give me excuses. I've seen very little of you as of late. It needs to be remedied."

Shaylynn smiles. He always likes to know he's appreciated.

"How can I do that?" he asks.

"This evening, when the sun goes down, you may take us to the river," Sarin replies.

"Are we to have another episode like before?" Fallon asks.

Faith jabs him in the ribs. "Don't be crass," she replies. "Of course nothing like last time will happen again."

Sarin smirks. "I make no promises."

Shaylynn smirks back. "So be it. Just remember, the necklace which gives such wondrous protection is around my neck – not yours."

"Then I shall stay close to you."

The night sounds promising, but it leaves Lyosan out of the mix. He does not mind in all honesty. He's not seen much of his family. A night in with them would be nice before the pressures of the tournament hit with full force.

His plans, however, quickly go out the window when Sarin spots the princess nearby. In the confines of the castle, Shaylynn has not shown the slightest bit of discomfort being around the princess, but outside of these walls, even if just the six of them are together, those emotions might change. Still, he has not the time to stop Sarin before she goes to the princess.

The exchange between them is brief. Shortly after the question is posed, Crystalynn turns to Shaylynn. They exchange a brief look of uncertainty before the princess turns back and replies to Sarin. Sarin curtsies respectfully, then returns to the others.

"She'd love to come," Sarin says.

"Wonderful," Shaylynn replies with his typical fervor.

Lyosan, knowing he was too passive on their previous encounter, decides to up the stakes a bit. Leaving the others behind, he approaches the princess as well. She smiles as he approaches.

"You'll be joining us," he says quite pleased.

Crystalynn gives Shaylynn one more look before replying, "Yes, I certainly will. To think what I might miss given what happened last time."

Lyosan reflects on the incidents when Shaylynn dove into the river, rescued Sarin, and blew up solid rock. They all have changed so much since that night. They've fought in mortal combat. Shaylynn and Fallon have been presumed dead. They've led a covert mission into enemy territory. Lyosan has killed many men.

To think it was only a few months ago. At the time, he wouldn't dare consider acknowledging out loud the feelings he holds for the princess. The mere notion of revealing them would cause his heart to race and his face to flush.

Now, he realizes the silliness in those actions. He does not mean to yell his feelings from the rooftops, but he certainly cannot hide them anymore. They have guided him this far. If he is to become king, he must let them guide him on that journey as well.

"Well, I think things will be much different this time," Lyosan says.

"Oh, how so?" Crystalynn asks.

"The emotions between Shaylynn and Sarin and Fallon and Faith have certainly grown," he replies. The mention of Shaylynn and Sarin brings a small frown to the princess's face. Lyosan sees it but does not understand what it means. Instead, he continues his thought. "They will not show off as they did before."

"I suppose you're right. I guess it may whittle down to just you and me."

"I would be most pleased if it did."

"Why? Do we not spend enough time together?"

"Whatever time we have together is not enough for me."

This is more forward than Lyosan has ever been in the past. It does not go unnoticed by the princess. For a moment, she cannot think of anything to say. Instead, she smiles and moves away. After a few steps, she pauses and looks back at Lyosan. The smile remains, and Lyosan smiles back. When Crystalynn turns away, Lyosan is certain he catches her giggling to herself.

He must not have been the only one because the others quickly gather around him. They watched the entire encounter from afar, but now that the princess has left, they must know what transpired between them.

"She seemed happy," Fallon notes.

"I wonder what raised her spirits," Sarin says.

With the moment now past him, Lyosan's typical nervousness reclaims his demeanor. The confidence and surety which coursed through his veins dissipates when surrounded by Shaylynn and the others. He has just worked himself up to being able to act in this manner; he cannot see himself bragging about it so quickly.

"I'm sure I don't know," Lyosan says trying to skirt the question.

As he turns to walk away, Faith quickly stops him. He turns another direction, but Shaylynn is there to stop him. It's a family effort.

"Should we guess for you?" Faith asks.

Shaylynn adds, "In all honesty, we did not hear everything, so we may not be able to give a good answer, but…"

"We certainly have some thoughts," Faith says.

With a roll of his eyes, Lyosan puts his hands on his hips and accepts his defeat. Rather than try to escape the ensuing onslaught, he gives in and tells what he did. All four of his friends show great happiness in his boldness. None is happier than Shaylynn. Not only because it might remove him from the existing predicament, but it might also mean Crystalynn is opening herself up to the possibility of being with Lyosan. The dream which Lyosan sought for so long may be coming to fruition.

The rest of the day, the youths train hard, but they do so with a small amount of levity. When Lyosan makes an error, they laugh it off and continue in their training. Fallon even manages to sneak out a victory against Shaylynn in a duel. The win is met with a large celebration at Shaylynn's expense. Fallon drops his blade and takes a victory lap around the room. Stefen and Artimous cease their duel and lift Fallon up on their shoulders. Chants, cheers, and jeers fly across the room as Shaylynn is forced to sit and watch. Without a word of discouragement, Shaylynn stands with his arms folded and lets the fools have their moment.

Eventually, Fallon stops the celebration, and they return to their training.

From a corner of the room, Pythyn watches the celebration with a careful eye and great disdain. Believing Shaylynn will at some point stand between Pythyn and the throne, Pythyn now looks for any weakness he may be able to exploit. Even though Fallon has managed a victory in a duel with Shaylynn, he has not exposed any flaw in Shaylynn's method. If anything, it was just a matter of familiarity and repetition. If Pythyn had a few hundred times to face Shaylynn, he could easily earn a victory. But he will not have all those chances, he will only have one. Thus comes the disdain. Because of who he is, Pythyn has been excluded. He is one of the top seeds in the tournament, but he feels there are many more who have a better chance to become king. Those who flock around Shaylynn. Those whom he has no objection to. They have some advantage Pythyn could never be party to.

Jonas, as though he works in consort with Sarin and Faith, ends the training session early and closes the doors to the room. He says they have trained too hard and need to give themselves some time away from the castle.

In truth, and the princess is well aware of this fact, the king's illness has come on very strongly. In his current state, his advisors believe it best for the castle to be cleared for the night. The king needs to rest and attempt to recover his strength. He will be visible for the entirety of the tournament. If he is any less than his best, the people will spend more time with their eyes on him than on the duels. That cannot be allowed. The next king of Artonia will be determined through this tournament. It needs to be given the reverence such an event deserves. Though, at this time, the disease has not reached its fatal stages, it could be some time before the king is healthy again.

So, it comes as no surprise that the princess can easily leave the castle at night. The guards do not follow. As she explains, with the three knights who earned the Golden Phoenix, she is in the best hands the city can provide. Though her normal guard feels the move is reckless and would be looked down on by the king, they allow her to go. They realize referencing the king, given his state, will only upset the princess.

As the six friends walk along the road, they talk of light affairs. None mention the tournament. None mention the king. Shaylynn and Crystalynn stand away from each other – each occupied with another's company. They run into many people who are on their way home for the evening. A few make brash comments about the tournament and ask Shaylynn on his plans to become king. The others shield him from the remarks, and they move on without acknowledging the commenters. Most, however, simply acknowledge the princess and merely stop to say hello. Always the regal type, the princess stops to have a word with many of them as well. As a result, the journey to the woods takes far longer than expected.

When they do escape the city, they quickly move into the cover of the trees. Shaylynn, knowing the woods better than any of them, leads the way. He did stay in these trees for a good number of days at one time. Sarin follows immediately behind him with one hand in his. Her other hand is clasped onto Faith's who also holds one of Fallon's. Continuing the chain, Fallon holds on to one of the princess's hands, and she holds tightly to Lyosan's hand. After several minutes, Shaylynn stops his movements and brings the company to a halt in a small, open area. With Fallon and Lyosan's aid, he builds a small fire, and they all sit around it for a while in complete silence.

Each seems to appreciate the rarity before them. Though Shaylynn, Fallon, and Lyosan have always been close, and Sarin and Faith sought Shaylynn and Fallon respectively, the friendships they have built among all of them are truly special. While some actions might fracture their friendship, those who guard their bond will not sacrifice their relationships by bringing them to light. In this way, it is a selfless and selfish act. Shaylynn says nothing to Sarin of the kiss the princess gave him. He does not admit his awareness of her affections towards him. At the same time, the princess does not look to drive a wedge between them by telling Sarin what she has done. It was not an innocent act, but it can be handled innocently. They can move past it, so long as the other never references it again. As the last few weeks have shown, each means to do so. But the rarity of this situation does not lie in the loyalty each person would show to the other, but rather, it lies in the fact that they share this moment together. Nothing from the outside world can cause them distress here. Nothing can bother them. Crystalynn is not a princess at the moment. Shaylynn is not the highest knight in the city. They are merely the best of friends, reveling in each other's company.

As such, they must take this moment for all it may be worth. Rather than squander it worrying about small grievances or mistakes which cannot be undone, they take in the moment for all it can give. Sarin, as one might assume, is the first to decide the silence has carried on for too long.

"Do you remember when last we were here together?" she asks. "Or does it seem like some fantasy from a dream?"

"I do remember it," Crystalynn replies, "and it does seem like a dream."

"So long ago," Fallon adds.

"And yet not," Faith says. "It only seems so long ago because of all which has transpired."

"Perhaps that is the deception of time," Shaylynn theorizes. "That not so long ago we fancied ourselves children, and the world so quickly and suddenly showed us otherwise."

"How could it have done this?" Faith asks.

Shaylynn shakes his head. "We did this," he replies.

"How so, cousin?"

"We took on the responsibilities our parents knew." Shaylynn explains. "We stopped our games and our follies. Some more drastically than others." He leans into Sarin as he says this. She blushes a bit but smiles.

"I do not regret my actions," she says.

"Nor I," Shaylynn adds. "I only wish I had been able to stop them from being necessary." The group shares a laugh before Shaylynn continues, "But we did this nonetheless. We sought love, duty, honor, and all the things our parents promised us. We traveled to distant lands and fought, not to show our merit, but to bring death to those who opposed us." As he speaks, the looks on everyone's faces begin to turn – not to sorrow but to acknowledgement. What they have seen, experienced, and felt has changed them most profoundly. "But," Shaylynn concludes, "we have not come here to measure our progress, I think."

"Indeed!" Fallon calls out. "We have come to regress even if in the smallest measure! We are not the adults Shaylynn claims we have become. We are mere children again."

"Wiser children than we were before," Faith adds looking at Sarin. Faith certainly does not want a repeat of the previous venture. "But children all the same."

With that, they engage in some childish behavior. They play childish games, take on childish dares, and engage in meaningless discussion. Sarin does taunt and tease Shaylynn but not over the river as she did before.

When he can, Shaylynn amazes with small feats of magic – little bursts of lights sparkling like fireworks in the night. As he delights, the rest take a moment to sit back and wonder. Sarin stays at his side, arms wrapped around his waist. Faith and Fallon sit in the grass – hand in hand. Though the princess does catch herself from time to time looking longingly at Shaylynn, she spends more time focused on the spectacle he creates.

With the others occupied, Lyosan takes a chance to get closer to Crystalynn. Asking to join her, he sits down, once granted his request, and watches Shaylynn's show with her. For a few minutes, they sit in silence. Crystalynn wonders if he means to converse with her in the manner he did earlier in the day. Lyosan wonders if he is capable of doing so. This is much more off the cuff. He cannot plan out what to say as he did before. If things go awry, he'll not be able to slink away. The others will be privy to his failure instantly.

"He never would've done something like this before," Crystalynn comments.

Lyosan is thinking so much about what to say, he can't make out her meaning.

"Shaylynn," Crystalynn finally clarifies. "He wouldn't have used his abilities in this fashion."

"He might not have thought himself capable of doing it," Lyosan suggests. "We all must learn about ourselves before we discover our limits."

"I have seen your training," she comments with a smile. "You certainly are learning more about yourself."

Lyosan smiles as well. "Yes, I suppose so."

"You train too hard, or I should say, you let Shaylynn and Fallon train you too hard."

"It is no more than I ask for," Lyosan says. "They would not push me so hard if I did not ask for it."

Knowing Shaylynn's desire to avoid the throne, Crystalynn believes there is a different motivation for Lyosan's training regimen. From the way he is talking, Lyosan seems completely unaware of the possibility. Now that she has the chance, she might as well inquire about it.

"You really think that's why they push so strongly?"

Lyosan looks at her with confusion. "What other reason could there be?"

"I must admit, Lyosan, you never struck me as one who sought the crown so strongly."

"It is not the crown which I desire."

The comment hangs in the air and washes over Crystalynn like a cool breeze. It also stops her in her thoughts. Her inquiry into Shaylynn's motives suddenly becomes moot. Lyosan stands on the verge of telling her he loves her. How can she think of anything else when he stands ready to reveal his heart?

"I don't know what you mean," the princess says to see how far he means to take this.

"It is certainly foolish to think this way," Lyosan explains. "That the crown and the throne are mere side notes in the matter. I know serving as king would require a great deal of training and work. It would be years before I could even begin to see myself as a king. But when it comes right down to it, I do not train because I would see myself earn the wealth and power."

He pauses, a sign of uncertainty – should he open himself completely or let things be as they stand? Were this another time, he would certainly not venture any further. Nor would he have said anything to begin with. But now, with the matter almost revealed, what reason does he have to hide? As the silence continues, Crystalynn reaches over and places a hand on his.

"Why do you train?" she asks.

It is the confirmation Lyosan needs. The sign he should empty his heart and reveal all secrets he holds so tightly.

"Because I love you," Lyosan replies, "as I have since we met. And if the only way I may achieve a life with you is by fighting off sixty-three other challengers, I will take that challenge every day."

That he could be so sincere does not surprise her. That he would be so honest does. She does not know how to respond. If these were words from Shaylynn, she would kiss him immediately. But this is Lyosan – the closest confidant she has ever had. The friend she used to play with and get into trouble with. The quiet, humble boy who always knew his place and tried to stay out of the way of people he deemed more important. Now, he has changed so much. This revelation is only the final verification of his change.

Could she love him as he claims to love her? Would a marriage to him truly bring her happiness? She knows he would always try to make her happy. Could he succeed?

After what he has said, she considers finding out. With hope in her heart, she leans towards him. Lyosan, feeling his heart about to burst through his chest, leans forward as well. As they reach for each other, all the world falls away behind them. Silence surrounds them. The night blots out everything but the two of them.

And just as their lips are about to touch, the neigh of a horse breaks through the silence and the world returns. Three knights from the castle ride with great purpose and come to a stop just at the road.

"My lady!" one of them yells. "My lady, the king summons you!"

With his illness in full swing, Crystalynn cannot risk wasting any time. She gives Lyosan a sad look but then turns and runs towards the soldiers. In a minute's time, she is gone, and Lyosan remains at the place where they sat.

Their minds suddenly stricken with worry, the others decide to end their night. With Lyosan, they walk home. Shaylynn and Fallon attempt to keep his spirits up. Though none of them know what was said, they did see Crystalynn and Lyosan almost kiss. For his part, Lyosan cannot share in the joy they all see in this development. Yes, they almost kissed, but when it comes down to it, they did not.

Fortunately, the mixed company allows the female perspective to come to light. Sarin and Faith, to Shaylynn and Fallon's eternal gratefulness, assure Lyosan the princess will not so easily and quickly forget the events of this night. Though they were unable to finish what they started, Lyosan and Crystalynn will surely have another chance for the moment to repeat. When it does, Lyosan will see the fruits of his labors.

For now, he will have to settle for the fact he revealed his true emotions to her, and on some level, they seemed to be met with a favorable reception. Crystalynn may not be ready to declare outright a love for Lyosan, but she can begin to see a future where the two are married.

Lyosan's mind also comes to an ease the next day when he learns the king's health begins to climb. The illness hit the king hard the night before – harder than it ever had. Though the doctors did not believe the king's life at stake, he wanted his sister at his side should things turn dire. Now that they have not, the city can look forward to the tournament in a few short days' time.

CHAPTER XVIII

The training continues. Lyosan goes hard day in, day out. He would work himself to exhaustion if not for the careful eye of his trainers. He also keeps an eye out for the princess. Given their last conversation, he would like to have some matters resolved. Shaylynn and Fallon continue to show him everything they can while keeping themselves sharp as well. They hope their abilities will not be tested, but they must be ready. Since the king may insert them into the tournament to replace a participant unable to heed the call, they cannot even begin to imagine whom they might face or when they might face him.

As the days end and the tournament draws near, Jonas gives the youths less time in the training room. He wants them rested for what lies ahead, so he sends them home earlier and earlier each time. The day before the tournament, no training is allowed. Each youth is instructed to stay home and be with family.

Lyosan spends most of the day with Steel and Calvin. They tend to some chores around the house, but mostly, they engage in shenanigans and wrestle around as they used to when they were more carefree – Lyosan anyway. When they grow tired, they retreat to the house where Elle waits for them. Steel and Calvin go to their rooms for the time being, and Lyosan sits with his mother at the dinner table.

"Are you rested?" she asks.

Lyosan nods. "I believe so."

"I don't see how you could be," Elle replies. "You've pushed yourself so hard this past month."

"I need the work."

"You need the belief. The belief Shaylynn has in you. The belief Fallon has in you. You say yourself they are the two best your group has to offer, but they turn to you in this matter."

Lyosan does not believe the matter to be so simple. Shaylynn and Fallon are the best yes, but they do not turn to Lyosan because they believe he is better than them. There have much different matters on their minds.

"They turn to me because of how I feel for the princess," Lyosan replies. "And because they do not feel that way. Their feelings lie with others."

"I know whom they love," Elle says with a laugh. "It's not as though they try to conceal their emotions from the world. But do you truly believe you are the only boy they could find who loves the princess? It is not so uncommon – to desire a beautiful woman of wealth and power. They could throw a stone and find a boy who would marry her. They choose you because of what you may become."

So often, Elle has spoken to Lyosan of what he may become. She has reminded him of all he has accomplished, the things he never thought himself capable of, and she has tried, whenever possible, to instill the confidence in him he needs to succeed at the task ahead.

Lyosan has always thought she did so simply because she was his mother and believed in him as a mother always does. Yet, there seems to be something more as of late. Perhaps, his latest escapades have exceeded the expectations Elle had for him. His fighting in the south, his rescue operation, his training may all be proving to his mother something she always believed but now has tangible proof of. The words, however nice they had been to hear in the past, might finally have the backing Lyosan could never see.

But as Lyosan told the princess, he is not ready to be a king. He only wishes to be her husband. One cannot come without the other. The pressure he would find himself under starts to become a concern for him. He knows Shaylynn and Fallon will always be at his side, but they will have their own responsibilities within the castle. They will not be able to make decisions for him.

"How could I, of all people, become a king?" he asks.

It is a serious question – one which Elle cannot gloss over. It is a difficult position – especially for one who has no training in kingly affairs.

With few exceptions, none of the boys in this tournament could truly be considered king material. For that reason, it is not entirely a bad thing Lyosan might enter into this world he knows so little of. He is a smart boy who means well. He will have advisors and councilors to guide him in his early days. King Cyrus will not die tomorrow. Lyosan will study under Cyrus's tutelage for a number of years. Best of all, he will have the princess at his side. She will come to love him and will always have his best interests in mind. Having grown up together, he knows he can trust her, and since she has been raised in this world, she will give him the best advantage possible.

With all this in mind, Elle feels confident in answering her son's question. "Every kingdom, big or small, old or new, has begun the same way – with someone who had not been a king. While they may have aspired to a throne, until they fought or earned the position, they were ordinary people like the rest of us. They only became kings when people looked at them as such. And though you may not believe it, the people of this kingdom will accept you as their king if you become the champion. You have already proven yourself afield. You will do so again when you win this tournament."

Lyosan's spirits return. He feels better about what lies in front of him. As the day rolls on, he finds peace within himself. When Sarin, Shaylynn, Fallon, and Faith come find him, he is eager to join them in their revelry. Sarin is the one who suggests a venture to the castle to call upon the princess. Since the king has been fighting his illness, Crystalynn has been locked up in the castle and might need the company. As a side thought, Sarin would also see if Lyosan can pick up where he left off in the woods a few days ago.

Crystalynn will not leave the castle this time, but she is happy to have her friends around her. The week has indeed been taxing for her with her brother's illness and all the preparations for the tournament. To have some time with her friends to walk about and ease her concerns will be most appreciated.

They walk along the highest wall of the northern edge of the castle. Only the flames from the torches illuminate the night. Above them, the stars shine brightly in the sky. Though Shaylynn, Sarin, Fallon, Faith, and Crystalynn are in bright moods, Lyosan's mood has lessened a bit. A small part of him remains disturbed by his training. He does not feel he is at the place where he will need to be if he is to win the tournament. Furthermore, with Shaylynn and Fallon possibly entering the tournament should a youth be unable to perform, he knows he will not be able to win unless Shaylynn or Fallon agrees to throw the match. Should such an event take place, all of the city will realize the conspiracy which led to his victory. Lyosan will need to make great strides if his place is to be assured.

Crystalynn can sense the trepidation in Lyosan. She wishes she could calm him and assure him all will end well. The concept of their marriage begins to bring her great joy though a part of her still wishes Shaylynn would claim his place as king. Yet she accepts more and more as each day goes by, Shaylynn will never be what she wants him to be. Lyosan, on the other hand, will dedicate himself to making her happy. For that, she can dedicate herself to him.

"Is something wrong?" she asks placing a hand on his.

Lyosan trembles at her touch. It jolts him back to the moment at hand. "No, I am…I am fine," he says none too convincingly.

Shaylynn realizes the cause of Lyosan's distress. "You needn't worry about your training," he says. "You are progressing much better than you realize. You cannot expect to master such a skill in so short a time."

"You exaggerate my progress," Lyosan says. "The tournament is not even a full day away. I may not be able to reach the finals at my current skill level, let alone win them."

"You must believe," Faith says. "Your commitment to the task goes far beyond any of the other combatants. They fight in the hope of attaining glory. You have a higher calling and much more important purpose. Those who dare face you will come to realize the futility in their fight."

"Will I?" a voice asks from behind them.

They turn and see Pythyn approaching from the open door. He holds his sword in his hand. He looks as though he has just come from training.

"Will I fall to someone with a higher purpose?" Pythyn asks. "Is that what you are relying on, Lyosan? Are you hoping your silly infatuation with the princess will win you the prize you seek?"

Lyosan does not answer. Fallon steps forward.

"Do not be foolish enough to believe you will gain that prize," Fallon warns. "Remember the honor granted to Shaylynn and myself. Both of us could bring your downfall with but the flick of our wrists."

"Yes, I'm sure you could," Pythyn replies sardonically. "But if such a scenario were to present itself, then one of you would have to abandon the life you've worked so desperately to create for yourselves. Will you surrender Faith so easily, Fallon?" Pythyn asks standing toe to toe with him. When Fallon does not respond immediately, Pythyn looks at Shaylynn. "What of you, Shaylynn? Will you abandon a life with Sarin to keep me from the throne?"

"You know I would," Shaylynn replies through his teeth.

For the first time, Sarin brings her feelings on the matter to life. "And I would gladly see it happen," she adds.

It is truly a comment on this one happenstance. If she had to live under Pythyn's rule or see Shaylynn on the throne, she'd choose the latter. If anyone else claims the throne, they may have it, so she may keep Shaylynn for herself. But if this pathetic slime is to be next in line, she will give what she must to ensure it doesn't happen.

Pythyn snarls at her comment. "Don't be so sure he means what he says. So many times now, he has been granted the opportunity to claim the throne for his own, but he refuses it. And all for his love of you." Pythyn circles Sarin as he speaks. "When all the world knows he should be the rightful king after Cyrus, he rebukes the hand which grants him all the treasures such a kingdom could offer. The people he claims to protect practically beg for him to take the throne, but he won't even consider it because he cares solely for you."

"I know why he does what he does," Sarin replies. "But he knows, given the circumstance, he would be king to save the throne from you."

"Such a man does not deserve to be king," Pythyn exclaims. Shaylynn moves in front of Sarin to protect her. Pythyn steps away and moves towards the princess. "This is what none of you understands," he continues. "He is not fit to be king. He knows this and professes it freely. Yet you look to him almost as though he is superhuman. Well, he is not! Even if he could defeat me, he is still just a man. A man who loves a woman and will not give her up for anything. The same goes for you, Fallon.

"So all I have to concern myself with is you, Lyosan. Given your performance in training lately, I would say I don't have much to worry about…"

"He is twice the man you will ever be!" Crystalynn cries.

"He is a coward and a simpleton!" Pythyn responds turning away.

"True, he is all high and mighty when Shaylynn is around to protect him, but when he is on his own, when he has only himself to rely on, he whimpers away like a frightened dog. And yet, you would have him over me?"

"Without question," Crystalynn replies.

What happens next is uncertain. The princess takes a step closer to Pythyn when she says her piece. As Pythyn moves to respond, he makes a motion with his hand. From their vantage point, it seems to Shaylynn, Fallon, Sarin, Lyosan, and Faith that he strikes the princess across the face. She stumbles away, and a look crosses Pythyn's face. Shaylynn moves quickly and draws his sword.

"You cur!" Shaylynn yells.

"I did not mean to strike her," Pythyn claims.

"You are a disgrace to our order," Fallon says coming to the princess's side.

Lyosan, who has been quiet through most of these events, does little more than move to the princess's side as well.

"We settle this now!" Shaylynn yells.

"No!" Pythyn replies. "Not you!" With the tip of his sword, Pythyn points to Lyosan. "You!" he says. "Face me now, Lyosan. Face me and put this matter to rest! Beat me now, and I shall step aside. Shaylynn can have my place, and the two of you can conspire to take the throne."

Shaylynn scowls at the idea they would collude to give Lyosan the throne. Shaylynn knows in his heart Lyosan will be able to win the throne on his own if he only steps forth and believes he can.

Lyosan says nothing to Pythyn's proposition. He is far too concerned with the princess to consider any challenge. Whether by intent or accident, Pythyn has drawn blood in striking her. Tears are in her eyes. A horrific flash back to her days being at the mercy of Dreilon Grepportorn floods her mind. Sarin and Faith work quickly to calm her, but the damage has been done.

Shaylynn waits for Lyosan to answer the call, but he does nothing. With each second, Pythyn grows confident he will have nothing to fear when it comes to Lyosan and his claim to the throne. Much more rides on this moment than Lyosan will give thought to. If he will not realize the moment, Shaylynn must realize it for him.

"Enough of this!" Shaylynn exclaims.

He jumps onto the castle wall with blade drawn. The action stops for a moment as everyone takes in his challenge. Pythyn feels the cold grip of fear rise in his spine. He will not face Shaylynn here. He will only face Lyosan.

"I have no qualm with you," Pythyn says.

"But I with you," Shaylynn replies. "So face me, Pythyn if you have the courage. The same bargain – for your place in the tournament!"

There is a gasp from the onlookers. To have Shaylynn out of the way would create a sizable advantage for Pythyn. Then, he would only truly have to concern himself with Fallon. But what if he were to lose? He cannot risk his place in the tournament.

Understanding the scope of Shaylynn's intentions, Sarin tries to talk him out of this challenge without usurping his place. She realizes how much is at stake and how dangerous the moment has become. Shaylynn cannot lose this duel. He cannot leave the throne entirely to Pythyn's will. There must be a better way.

"The princess is injured!" Sarin says to Shaylynn.

"Take her inside," Shaylynn replies. "All of you. There is nothing here she should see anyway!"

A cruel smile forms on Pythyn's face. Shaylynn notices but ignores it. He cannot remove himself from this path now. He has committed too much. Though the risk is high, the reward is unimaginable.

Pythyn, upon hearing Shaylynn send his friends away, steps up onto the wall and presents his sword for dueling.

"How will we be sure of the winner?" Fallon asks knowing Pythyn's deceptions would be easy in this manner.

"The winner shall claim the loser's sword," Shaylynn replies. "Until then, the duel shall continue."

"And if your sword should fall off the wall?" Pythyn asks.

"I would not concern myself with such matters!" Shaylynn replies.

"So be it then," Pythyn says coldly.

Quickly helping the princess inside, the others leave Shaylynn and Pythyn to their duel. Once they are out of sight, Pythyn steps to the middle of the wall. Shaylynn joins him. A plan is entering Pythyn's mind. It is of the darkest kind, but it will surely cement his place on the throne if he enacts it. However, he cannot bring himself to commit to it.

Not now, Pythyn tells himself, *it may not be necessary. If I can beat him, then I will be beat him.*

The combatants raise their swords to their faces in respect. Then, they brandish and retreat to their sides. Shaylynn takes on a bleak look as the duel begins. This is not the way he wants this to happen. Lyosan should be ready to defeat Pythyn, but he is not. Because of that, Shaylynn feels he has failed.

Before he can finish the thought, Pythyn charges and swings low. Shaylynn leans away from the blade and goes on the defensive. Pythyn swings over the top which Shaylynn easily blocks. Pythyn then spins around and attacks low, but Shaylynn blocks that as well. Finally, Shaylynn bumps up against a pillar. Pythyn comes down on Shaylynn, and Shaylynn again deflects the blow.

"What's the matter, Shaylynn?" Pythyn asks. "Not up to the challenge?"

Shaylynn shoves Pythyn away with ease and rises from the pillar. With a determined look coming into his eyes, he advances. Pythyn swings high again, but Shaylynn ducks and deflects the attack with much more force than before. Pythyn loses his balance a bit but recovers as Shaylynn begins to strike to the right, then to the left, and back to the right. Each time, Pythyn defends himself, but each time, he is a bit slower than before. It is clear to him he must do something to turn the tide, else this duel will end quickly.

Immediately after one of Shaylynn's strikes, Pythyn lunges forwards and puts a shoulder into Shaylynn's chest. It does not knock Shaylynn to the ground, but it pauses his assault for a moment. Unfortunately, Pythyn needs a moment to recover as well. Running into Shaylynn was like hitting a brick wall.

"Using some of your magic to help you?" Pythyn asks.

"I only use what I need to defeat you," Shaylynn replies. "Believe me, I need no magic for that."

Pythyn raises his blade and charges with a scream. Shaylynn leaps over him and lands on the other side. Anticipating this, Pythyn swings wildly and scratches Shaylynn's chest. Shaylynn falls back in surprise, but upon realizing it is merely a scratch, he raises his blade and advances.

Moving quickly, Shaylynn parries and thrusts with a mixture of kicks and strikes with his opposite hand. The pattern is so elaborate Pythyn cannot figure it out and guesses to defend himself. For a brief while, it holds Shaylynn at bay. However, after a sweep kick Pythyn must jump to avoid, Shaylynn drives the hilt of his sword into Pythyn's chest and drops him to the ground.

Before Pythyn can react, Shaylynn grabs the sword from his hand and places his own blade against Pythyn's neck. The duel is over. Pythyn has lost, but he is not defeated!

"It is over," Shaylynn says. "You have fallen. You will not participate in the tournament. On the word of the princess, it shall be known what you swore this night and that you lost the wager! You are finished, Pythyn!"

Shaylynn stands and turns his back to Pythyn. All the hatred Pythyn can muster fills his heart as he realizes the loss he has suffered. But Shaylynn is wrong when he says all will come to know of it. None shall know but the two of them, and only one shall live to tell the tale!

Pythyn rises to his feet in a flash and charges Shaylynn. Shaylynn sees Pythyn coming out of the corner of his eye but has not the time to react. With one shove, Pythyn sends Shaylynn over the wall towards the ground below. Shaylynn does not cry out in grief or fear, but a scream does penetrate the air.

Sarin has come back to see the results of the duel. She sees neither Pythyn nor Shaylynn, but she feels in her heart what has happened. As she rushes to the wall and looks over the edge, she sees the body of Shaylynn crash into the ground below.

Without a thought, she rushes through the castle. Fallon, Faith, and Lyosan see the despair on her face and take up pursuit. They try to calm her and figure out what has happened, but she will not respond to them. Through the entire castle, they run. Sarin bursts through the castle entrance and sees the spot where Shaylynn has fallen. A group of soldiers have discovered him and stand over him. Their faces reflect the dire situation they find themselves in.

"NO!" Sarin yells as she rushes to Shaylynn's side.

Fallon, Faith, and Lyosan begin to understand what has happened. Faith breaks down and cries on the spot. Fallon grabs his sword and begins a futile search for Pythyn. He knows his friend would not fail but Pythyn would resort to this. Lyosan stands in horror with a small realization that perhaps this would have been him. It should have been him. How much that would have solved if it had been him! Slowly, he walks over to where Shaylynn lays. Amazingly, he still draws breath though his time is close at hand. As Lyosan looks him over, he sees the point of a dagger protruding through Shaylynn's stomach.

"No, my love," Sarin pleads. "Do not leave me!"

"I am sorry, my love," Shaylynn replies weakly. "I'm afraid I've overused the protection of your necklace."

"You cannot die!" Sarin cries. "I've lost you too many times; I will not lose you again!"

Before Shaylynn can attempt to comfort her, Fallon bursts in. "Where is he?" he demands. "Where is the coward who did this to you?"

"Safe at home, by now," Shaylynn supposes.

"There will be no safety for him when I find him!" Fallon says.

"No!" Shaylynn cries which takes much of his remaining strength. "No! You mustn't."

"After what he has done, you would have him live?" Fallon asks.

"What proof have we?" Shaylynn asks. "You did not see it. I shall not live long enough to tell the tale. He will deny everything, and if you kill him, your life will be forfeit."

"So be it," Fallon replies.

"No!" Shaylynn cries again. In his anguish, he coughs deeply and harshly. It stops Fallon and brings him to Shaylynn's side.

"Save yourself," Fallon says. "As I have seen you do before. Save yourself!"

"I cannot," Shaylynn says. "This must be."

"Why!" Fallon demands.

"My friend," Shaylynn replies. "Do not think to understand the workings of this world. They are a mystery to us all. Merely trust in good and let it guide you. Your place in this kingdom will be great and cannot be lost."

"And what of yours?"

Shaylynn does not answer, feeling his time is short. Instead, he calls over Faith. She is at his side in an instant.

"Cousin," she says.

"My Faith," Shaylynn replies. "Do you remember when I used to call you that...my Faith?"

Tears well in her eyes as she chokes out a reply. "Of course I do."

"You were, you know," Shaylynn says. "You were my faith and my hope. So you will need to be for Fallon and the rest of our family." Faith nods quickly as more tears fall. She cannot lose a single word he says, for they will be the last she hears from him. "Tell my mother I love her. Daylynn too. Tell them not to worry. I shall be in the company of my father and brother soon. They shall greet me with opens arms."

"I will tell her," Faith manages to say.

Shaylynn raises his head a bit and kisses Faith on the forehead. She responds in kind, holding his head for a few moments longer. She wishes to keep him alive if she can, but she knows she cannot. When she lets him go, she moves into Fallon's arms. More knights and people from the castle come out, including Crystalynn.

"Lyosan," Shaylynn calls with a raised hand. Lyosan comes to Shaylynn's side. "You must claim the throne," Shaylynn says. "I have known this longer than almost anything. The throne must be yours."

"Why do you tell me this now…as you die?" Lyosan asks.

"Because you know everything else," Shaylynn says. "You know I love you as a brother, as I do Fallon. You know we've had the best of times. You know the stories of us will be of legend. But tell them from the throne."

The princess joins them. Shaylynn turns to her.

"I have failed you, my lady," Shaylynn says.

"Never," Crystalynn replies. "never before and not now. You rescued me. You saved me. You've done everything I could, in good conscience, ask of you. There is none better than you."

"There is one," Shaylynn replies. "He does not know it yet, but he is. He is better than me. Soon, very soon, he will show you."

Shaylynn coughs again as his strength leaves him. Lyosan and Crystalynn move away. Fallon steps forward again.

"Please," he begs.

"I cannot," Shaylynn replies. "This is the path I must take."

"But I was supposed to be at your side wherever you went," Fallon says.

"And you will be," Shaylynn assures him. "I take you with me, as I take all whom I love."

Fallon nods, places a hand gently upon Shaylynn's heart and moves away. Once again, there is only Sarin.

"We should have run away together," Shaylynn tells her.

"There's still time," Sarin replies. "Get up and let's go."

Shaylynn shakes his head. "No, my love. I've not the strength for the journey. I need to rest."

"You are weak, then?" Sarin jests, trying to keep him going.

"Only when I cannot make you smile," Shaylynn replies. "Only when I did not have your love."

"You have always had my love."

Shaylynn smiles and chuckles a bit to himself. "I knew I'd get you sooner or later."

Sarin stops, as the pain is too much for her to bear. She starts to move away when Shaylynn reaches out and grabs her hand. She stops and places her other hand on top of his. Looking into his eyes one last time, she strokes his hair and kisses him. As she pulls away, Shaylynn stops her, raises his head, and whispers something in her ear. He then smiles, takes a final breath, and closes his eyes to enter the sleep of death.

That night, Cyrus decrees a postponement of the tournament. The city will be rattled by this loss and certain inquires need to be made. Kandessa and Daylynn are brought to the castle. They claim the body and take it home. Faith stays with them that night. When the morning comes, Kandessa returns to the castle and demands justice for her son. Cyrus, still weakened by his bout with his disease, agrees but cannot find any means to further the investigation. Lyosan and the others have said all they can on the matter. Pythyn seems the culprit but claims Shaylynn slipped off the ledge. To the enragement of Fallon, Pythyn even claims he tried to grab Shaylynn and save him from the fall. With the matter coming down to Pythyn's word against Fallon's, no finality can be brought to the situation. Crystalynn tries for all she is worth to get the king to see reason, but either by fault of his condition or his own mourning at the loss of Shaylynn, he cannot bring himself to place punishment on Pythyn.

Outrage runs rampant through the city. Fallon tells anyone who will listen what he knows to be true. The princess, though not speaking publicly on the matter, still condemns Pythyn for his actions. The youths of the tournament know Pythyn to be capable of such treachery, and with one of their own championing the cause, they turn on Pythyn as well. Yet, for the all the outrage and anger, it does not change the fact that Shaylynn is dead. He will not take any part in the tournament, nor will the world benefit from the life he would have led.

Two days after the tragedy, Kandessa holds the memorial for

Shaylynn. It is held in the small church near their home. Cyrus would have held the service at the castle, but since he will not rule on the matter, Kandessa turns his offers away. As a result, the church is overflowing with mourners. In the front sits Kandessa with Daylynn at her side. He never relinquishes his grasp on her. Sarin sits in the same row with Kandessa. Though they were never truly married, Sarin still feels a part of Shaylynn's family. Kandessa feels the same. Fallon and Faith sit with her – each holding on to the other for strength. The only time they part is when Fallon rises to speak on Shaylynn's behalf. While Kandessa may have refused the king's hospitality, she certainly will not refuse his presence. With Crystalynn at his side, the king sits with the family. He too will eulogize the fallen. At Crystalynn's behest, Lyosan sits with her. All of the boys who served under Shaylynn, save Pythyn, come to the service as well. Since Feylynn and Beylynn never received a proper burial, this service, in a small way, is for them as well. Thus, all who remain of the royal guard, the highest dignitaries of the city, even dignitaries from the south, where Shaylynn fought his only campaign, come to the service.

When the time comes, Fallon leaves Faith in Sarin's care and approaches the podium. Shaylynn lay in a casket shrouded by a white cloak. It is the way of the Knights of Langerwitz. For several moments, Fallon cannot bring himself to speak. Cries of anguish and the falling tears stifle his resolve. After gathering himself, he takes a deep breath and begins to speak:

"I first met Shaylynn when I was only a babe. I remember nothing of the encounter of course, but my mother tells me we were friends from the moment we were together. That once we were brought together, nothing could separate us." A small round of laughter goes through the chamber. They all know this to be true. "And as I grew up, I believed this would be the case forever. Even when I first served this city as a knight, I followed his lead. When we were lost in the Forleen Forest, he was with me. And when he, Lyosan, and I snuck into Jorram to rescue the princess, we did so together. He would be my captain, and I would serve him proudly. That is what I felt.

"I never had a brother in my family, but I had a brother in him. He cared for me, raised me up, and made me feel I was worth something. Whenever something seemed too difficult, he assured me I was capable. If I doubted him further, he showed me how easy it was by doing it himself..."

another guffaw of laughter, "…It was his way – to show off when he could. To use his skills and powers to amaze and delight. He loved a crowd.

"But there were others he loved even more: his mother, Kandessa, who brought purpose to his life; Daylynn, who made his brother proud every day; Sarin, who captured his heart so completely; Faith, who was by far his favorite cousin; Lyosan, who was also like a brother to him. And yet, for all those he loved, he loved this country even more. Many of the people here now would have been pleased to see Shaylynn serve as the next king of Artonia. His plans were far simpler. But I say this – if he had become king, there is no man better deserving of the honor. And by my life or my death, I would've followed him to the end."

Fallon approaches the casket and places a hand on the coffin's edge. He speaks a few words to his friend – words meant only for them. Then, he returns to his seat, and Cyrus takes the podium.

After speaking of the losses the Storm family has suffered and the extreme sorrow he feels for Kandessa, Cyrus turns to the matter of Shaylynn. He describes in vivid detail the amazing quality of the boy whom they have come to honor. He echoes Fallon's sentiment that Shaylynn would have made a fine king and would have served the country well. Cyrus also does well to acknowledge the love Shaylynn had for Sarin. When the time comes for Cyrus to discuss his death, the mood starts to turn.

What had been a group of mourners turns to an angry mob. They remain as calm as they can out of respect for the family, but the anger which every one of them feels when hearing the assumed guilty party would not be punished festers in their hearts. When the king says it is a terrible tragedy, cries ring out saying the truth is far different. The king says he wishes something could be done to atone for this misfortune, and many cry out the answer is obvious. They call for Pythyn to be removed from the tournament, to be banished from the city, and some call for his death. Knowing this is far from the time and place, Cyrus holds his tongue on the matter though the insolence of the crowd angers him greatly. As the anger in the room rises, it seems the funeral is about to get out of hand. Fortunately, Kandessa rises and demands the crowd calm themselves.

"It is so easy for us," she says, "to cast aspersions and claim the matter so simple to resolve. No resolution will bring my son back. If you are here for any reason than to mourn him, then please remove yourself from this service. I have lost more than any of you in this matter. I will not have this taken from me as well."

Though they are at odds for the moment, the king and Kandessa can still respect one another to make this work. Larger issues are at play. The citizens only view this as a loss of their would-be-king. They did not know the man for who he truly was.

When the service ends, Fallon, Sarin, Faith, Lyosan, and Crystalynn gather together outside the church. They can say so little to one another when before they could've said everything.

"It is not right," Crystalynn says. "There is no justice here."

"It is all we can be afforded given the circumstances," Sarin replies.

"I do not understand this," Crystalynn says. "Of all, I figured you would be the angriest."

"Believe me," Sarin says, "I've rage to pummel that weakling for days, but Shaylynn would not have me act in such a way. What more can I do now but honor him?"

"He deserves better," Lyosan agrees. "And to think that wretch could still be king…"

"It is not something we will allow," Faith interrupts. "I know Fallon will step up to do what Shaylynn would've."

She turns to him, but he is not looking at the others now. Instead, he stares, intensely, at the ground below him. He rests an elbow on his other arm, and brings his hand to his lower lip. When he says nothing in response to Faith's last remark – a remark which jeopardizes their future together – the others surely do notice.

"What is wrong?" Faith asks.

Still, he seems to not notice them.

"My love," Faith says placing a hand on his shoulder. He turns towards her at her touch, but he still says nothing. "What troubles you?"

Finally realizing he has missed out on something, Fallon lowers his arms and clears his throat. He does not know what he has missed, but he knows he would rather not discuss his thoughts.

"I am sorry," he says. "I was…my thoughts were elsewhere."

"What were you thinking?" Sarin asks.

Fallon waves them off. "Another time," he replies. "Another time."

"Please," Crystalynn says. "Whatever it is, perhaps we can help."

After a moment's thought, Fallon reluctantly explains himself.

"When we were in Forleen," he begins, "I witnessed many miraculous sights. None more profound than the time when Shaylynn healed his own wounds. Blades that pierced him, falls he took, arrows that hit him – they were nothing. He was right as rain in less than an hour. But then to see him fail, to not even try, to save himself, I cannot reconcile it."

Faith steps to Fallon and wraps her arms around him. She brings his head to her shoulders and quiets him for a minute.

"We cannot understand his ways," she says. "He belonged to a time much different than ours. Someday, we may very well come to understand it, but for now, we must believe he did all he could."

"I am not so sure," Fallon replies.

The two pull away from each other slightly, but they remain in the embrace.

"Then believe me," Faith says. "He would do anything he could to remain with us. If fate would not allow it, then it simply could not be."

At this, Fallon begins to cry, and Faith consoles him. Sarin stands alone, still coming to terms with the matter herself. Crystalynn stands nearby, watching the events unfold. As the grief becomes too much for her, she reaches over to Lyosan and takes his hand. He holds hers gently but firmly. For several minutes, the group stands together, in silence – save the cries of the grief stricken – and mourns the loss of their friend.

CHAPTER XIX

Two more days pass, and the tournament is set to begin. After a day of nothing, Fallon comes to find Lyosan to give him some last-minute tips. Fallon knows he is not the instructor Shaylynn would be, but he knows he is the best Lyosan has at his side.

In his first duel, Lyosan faces Refgen. Though Refgen is a good youth with many quality characteristics to his name, he is a terrible verti-dueler. Much like Lyosan, he is frightened of heights. However, where Lyosan has worked to master his fear, Refgen remains at the mercy of his. It can be seen plain as day as the two approach the dueling construct. Several have been built so many duels can be held at the same time. One stands out among the rest – the center dueling stage. It is where the final duel will be held, and until then, it will serve as the watch post for the king. As it is, Lyosan does not duel in the center position for his first round. It upsets him somewhat, knowing the princess will not see him fight, but he must ignore the disappointment and focus on the matter at hand.

Fallon walks with Lyosan to the ladder. Refgen and his father do the same on the opposing side. As the official announces the particulars of the match, Fallon takes one last opportunity to instruct his friend.

"You know Refgen will not handle the height well," he says. "Use it to your advantage. Press early and make him worry about you as well as the elevation. The more time he has to acclimate to the environment, the better chance he has of sneaking out a victory."

"Which moves will work best here?" Lyosan asks.

"Don't worry about your moves," Fallon replies. "This is not about using tactics to earn a strategic advantage. You have a weaker opponent with a debilitating failing. Use this duel to make a statement. Come at him wild and frenzied and put him down early. Let all who see this know Lyosan is coming for them, and he will not be deterred."

Lyosan ascends the ladder and stands across from Refgen. Refgen is doing his best to stay focused on Lyosan, but everyone watching can tell it is taking all Refgen has to avert his eyes from the ground below. With all Fallon has told him fresh in his mind, Lyosan waits for the official to give the sign to begin.

At the wave of the official's arm, Lyosan races along the beam and leaps to a side. Refgen, not yet comfortable with his footing, moves slowly to try to prepare himself. Lyosan runs down the side beam and leaps onto Refgen's before Refgen can get to a defensive position. The crowd begins to cheer as the battle ensues. With barely his blade up, Refgen goes on the defensive as Lyosan uses his sword to hammer down on his opponent. Refgen manages to back up and gets a shield up to help defend.

However, after a few more swings, Lyosan knocks Refgen to his back and sends the shield flying to the side. Refgen throws a few weak strikes with his blade, but Lyosan evades them with ease and presses his advantage. After a few more moments, Refgen calls out that he yields and the duel comes to an end. As the crowd cheers the victor, Lyosan extends a hand to Refgen and helps him to his feet. With respect, Refgen raises Lyosan's hand as the winner, and the crowd cheers the sportsmanship.

"You fought well," Refgen says to Lyosan.

"And you..."

Before Lyosan can finish his thought, Refgen stops him. "You have beaten me soundly," Refgen says. "Give me some dignity by not lying to me."

The two smile before descending the ladder and finding their coaches. Refgen's father is not pleased, but he is happy his son in okay. Fallon seems very pleased with Lyosan's performance.

"That didn't last long," Lyosan remarks.

"That's good," Fallon assures him. "These preliminary rounds are mere formalities anyway. The best are meant to shine in the simplest manner possible. You need to look unbeatable before you meet the real competition in the final rounds. And that's what you looked like up there."

A chorus of boos echo from nearby. Knowing it must be Pythyn,

Fallon and Lyosan stop talking and head in the direction of the row. It does not take them long to find it. The duel is already over. One of the youths who served in the south lies in the straw below the dueling square. Pythyn makes his way down the ladder without acknowledging the crowd in any way. Nycolas stands nearby – he has also won his first duel.

"Did you see it?" Fallon asks.

Nycolas nods. "It wasn't much," he explains. "Pythyn banged shields with him for a few moments, then side stepped him and used the blunt of his blade to smack him off balance."

"That's why they boo," Fallon realizes.

It is a cheap trick – using the blunt of one's blade. But, as Pythyn has already resorted to murder, it does not surprise the boys in the slightest that he would turn to this tactic as well.

"As soon as the hit occurred, Pythyn pounced and knocked him off," Nycolas finishes. "Used a boot to the gut to do it. I wouldn't stoop so low, but it was impressive."

As Pythyn reaches the ground, the boos continue. Everyone can tell he would say a great deal to them if he could. But as he is not king yet, he will let the matter rest. He turns to see Fallon and Lyosan watching him. When he does, he turns the other way and fights his way through the crowd.

Nycolas grunts as Pythyn disappears. Believing wholeheartedly in Pythyn's guilt regarding Shaylynn's death, Nycolas was hoping he'd see Pythyn fall. But the poetic justice has not come so soon. It may still happen, but he and the others must wait for another day. Perhaps Lyosan will bring that day, but Nycolas finds that hard to believe.

"He cannot look you in the eye," Nycolas remarks to Lyosan. "But not because he is intimidated by you – more because of the company you keep."

"I don't care if I intimidate him," Lyosan says. "Either way, I will bring his downfall if given the opportunity."

Words are cheap – Nycolas knows this. Still, these are words Lyosan would have never spoken in the past. Even with Shaylynn's absence, Lyosan acts in the manner he would with Shaylynn at his side. The training and time he has put into his skills have advanced far more than his natural abilities. Now, the death of Shaylynn may have pushed him over the edge into a place where nothing can stop him.

"I would hope so," Nycolas says. "But you realize, if we both continue to win, we will face each other before you get to him."

Lyosan lets out a deep breath. "I do."

"And I know you want to avenge Shaylynn, but there is more happening here than the two of you."

"I am aware."

"Good, because I don't intend to hold back."

Saying nothing more, Nycolas walks away and leaves Fallon and Lyosan to ponder over his words. There is a ring of truth to them. If Lyosan focuses too much on facing Pythyn, his other opponents will get to him first. In these early rounds, he will be able to get away with it, but soon, he will have to really focus on the boy in front of him.

After discussing the matter with Fallon, Lyosan turns his focus to his next opponent. The two youths who could face him will be dueling in an hour. Until then, the two can watch other duels and get the lay of the land. In the first few hours of the tournament, none of the higher seeds lose. Aside from Pythyn and Lyosan finishing their duel quickly, Stefen also wins his duel within a minute's time. Brynnal wins quickly as well. A couple of the youths, Artimous and Athen, need more time and do at one point find themselves on the verge of losing, but they rebound quickly and end up winning with ease. All the competitors arrive at the tournament ready to participate, so at least in the first day, there is no need for Fallon to enter the tournament.

Faith finds Fallon and Lyosan as they walk around. Sarin has decided to stay away from the tournament – at least for the first day. Even for Faith, it is difficult to walk around, see all the festivities, and not think of Shaylynn. Fortunately, she has Fallon by her side. While Fallon and Lyosan would try to keep Sarin's spirits up, they could not accomplish such a feat. As difficult as it is for Faith, it is better than remaining home. Very little has been happening since the tragic events of Shaylynn's death, and she can only dwell on thoughts of him when stuck at home.

Here, she can somewhat escape her thoughts with Fallon to talk to. She can also concern herself with keeping Lyosan focused on his tasks and offer encouragement to keep his confidence up.

Fallon is happy she arrived when she did. Faith did not have to see Pythyn fight or at all. With his match completed, he surely will retreat to his own home. The crowd would hound him relentlessly if he stayed. No doubt, Faith would confront him too. This way, the focus stays on the tournament, and Faith can keep her emotions more in check.

"Was it a difficult match?" Faith asks, meaning Lyosan's opening duel.

"Not at all," Fallon replies. "I think he won in twenty seconds – if not less."

Faith is impressed. Lyosan does not like the boasting, but it does keep his confidence high.

"At that rate, you'll be king in under two minutes," Faith jests.

"I seriously doubt the rest of the competition will go so easily," Lyosan says.

"Think positively," Fallon says. "If you keep the same mindset, they can seem just as simple regardless of how long they take."

They continue to make their way from duel to duel, catching whatever they can. Fallon points out small elements of weakness he sees in each duelist, but Lyosan concerns himself with the strengths. He sees the speed, agility, and veracity in the attacks, and he wonders if he can hold off those attacks. Refgen did not give Lyosan a chance to test his defensive skills, and if he must be honest, Lyosan's defense is his larger weakness. Knowing his concern would be growing, Fallon keeps Lyosan focused on the larger picture. Most of the duels they are witnessing will not affect him in the slightest. Several of these duels are from the other side of the bracket, so they will have to face Pythyn before they get to Lyosan. Others are in line to face Stefen who Fallon assumes will be the one to get to the final four of the tournament.

Even the ones who will face Lyosan give him concerns. True, this is for further down the line, but Lyosan cannot entirely put it all beyond him. When they walk past the main dueling square, Lyosan does get a slight reprieve from his worries. Crystalynn sits in a chair to the right of her brother. She watches the duels going on at the time, but after a minute, she turns and sees Lyosan looking back at her. She smiles at him, and he smiles back. She would join the three of them as they walk around the tournament, but she must keep up appearances at the king's side.

Still, for a moment she holds his attention and makes his hardships seem less so. They look at each other, not quite as lovers would, but not as simply as friends do. There is more to their relationship now – something which may have been there all along, but only now do they acknowledge its existence. Lyosan has been aware of his feelings all along, but he never considered Crystalynn's feelings for him. With this possibility becoming more and more conceivable, Lyosan's emotions begin to churn within him. What was once a fantasy beyond the furthest reaches of conception is slowly moving towards the reality which will fill Lyosan's life. As he comes to terms with this, Lyosan begins to wonder if he could make the princess happy should they marry. It was one thing when the two were merely friends enjoying each other's company, but should it evolve to a lifetime together, he will find himself in a world he never approached previously.

Yet, when weighing the possibilities, he would rather risk the world he knows than stand aside and give Pythyn the throne. Shaylynn died believing Lyosan would become king of Artonia. He would not give his faith so easily. As his mother so often told him, Shaylynn put his faith in Lyosan because Shaylynn knew Lyosan would make a good king.

Crystalynn looks at Lyosan as her best chance at happiness. She does not know if she loves him the way he loves her, but she is certain he is perhaps the only youth with a chance to win who values her happiness above the throne. Should he win the tournament and become king, she will certainly have the opportunity to discover her feelings for him. When Shaylynn was alive, she viewed the tournament as a match between Pythyn and Shaylynn. Now that he has passed, she must believe there is another out there capable of defeating Pythyn. Lyosan may very well be the man she seeks, and given their past together, he will always be someone she can trust and tell everything to. He seems to command loyalty from his friends, so he may very well be a good king for the land.

Regardless of the hopes of these two, there are a great many more steps to be taken before the situation reaches any finality. Preparation for these steps cannot be taken lightly, and the time has come to see the duel between Lyosan's two potential combatants. One is a boy the youths know very well – Darrow. Fallon expects him to win the match easily. He faces Jareel who suffered a great injury during the campaign in the south. His recovery has been slow, but he refuses to give up his chance at the throne. Darrow, on the other hand, is in prime condition and has been training as hard as any youth – except maybe Lyosan. This will be rather difficult for Lyosan because he holds Darrow in rather high esteem. Darrow was one of the youths who spoke out against Jorram's offer of peace many months ago, but he was not quick to join the campaign to rescue the princess. It is of course the nature of this business. The tournament is not a friendly competition, and one cannot allow friendship to cloud one's perspective. If the goal is to become king or marry the princess, one must do whatever is required to ensure it happens. If defeating Darrow is one of those requirements, Lyosan must step up to the challenge.

Darrow and Jareel ascend the ladders and take their place on the beams. Fallon pokes Lyosan in the side to focus his attention. Begrudgingly, Lyosan turns away from the princess and follows Fallon to the dueling area. Darrow and Jareel are not in the main stand, but they are close by. Cyrus and Crystalynn can see the duel from where they sit. It is not the most important duel taking place now, but Crystalynn knows what it means for Lyosan.

From the outset of the duel, Fallon realizes Jareel will not win. As he climbed the ladder, Jareel attempted to hide his discomfort. He had done a decent job of doing so, but now that the duel has begun, he can no longer hide his disadvantage. Rather than face Darrow head on, he works to avoid him. As Darrow advances, Jareel retreats. Whatever beam Darrow jumps to, Jareel jumps to the parallel beam to keep the distance between them.

"He cannot win," Fallon comments.

"How do you know?" Faith asks.

"He can barely keep his footing," Fallon replies. Lyosan watches carefully to see the things Fallon sees. "His injury has not fully healed," Fallon continues. "He favors his left too severely. He can continue to dance around and hope Darrow makes a mistake, but he will have to capitalize immediately. After what he suffered, he may not be quick enough or strong enough."

"What happened to him?" Faith asks.

Lyosan answers. "He took an arrow to his side. It went all the way through. He had a terrible time riding back to Langerwitz. I was certain he wouldn't make it, but he did. Darrow was one of the people watching him and tending to him. He has a way with medicine."

"He has a way with a blade too," Fallon adds.

A point which will be proven very soon. As the duel drags on and the crowd begins to boo the duelists, Darrow takes on a more aggressive approach and begins a quicker pursuit of Jareel. Jareel struggles to keep his distance and eventually cannot flee. Once cornered, Jareel steadies himself on a beam and tries to defend himself as best as possible. He puts up a good fight, but the attack from Darrow is clearly too much. When the opportunity arises, Jareel escapes and flees to a different beam, but Darrow quickly catches up to him. All the while, Lyosan, Fallon, and Faith watch the duel with a studious eye.

"See how he advances," Fallon comments, "he uses the best angle while keeping his shield in a prime position. He knows Jareel cannot put up an offensive, so he puts most of his power into his strikes. If he does the same with you, Lyosan, you will have a weakness to exploit."

"Surely, he will not be so foolish," Faith says. "He will know Lyosan is not injured."

"No," Fallon replies, "but he does not see Lyosan as able to put on a strong offensive."

It may seem crass, but the comment is accurate. Darrow has not trained against Lyosan in some time, and he may not have seen Lyosan's first duel. Darrow's opinion of Lyosan's ability may be well out of date. That will present another vulnerability for Lyosan to capitalize on.

As for the duel itself, Darrow keeps it well in hand. With a few more strokes, he manages to displace Jareel from his shield. Without the shield, Jareel cannot protect his weakness anymore. Without meaning to, Darrow strikes Jareel's side with an elbow and sends Jareel crashing down. He stays on the beam, but he clearly cannot continue. Darrow steps away for a moment, perhaps feeling guilt in hitting Jareel where he did. When Jareel says nothing, Darrow steps forward to attack, but before he can get too close, Jareel puts up a hand to stop the assault. Calling for an end to the duel, Jareel yields and moves to the closest beam. Darrow checks on him and even helps him down the ladder – to the approval of the crowd.

Even the king takes note of this chivalry and applauds it. Crystalynn joins him, which only intensifies the noise from the crowd. As the duelists reach the ground, medics attend to Jareel while Darrow acknowledges the praise from the crowd, princess, and king. Humbly, he bows to Cyrus and blows a kiss to the princess. The crowd responds to the kiss with thunderous applause and a loud chorus of approval. Darrow smiles and winks as he steps away. Of all the duelists to fight this day, Darrow has certainly made the best impression.

"Quite a showman," Faith remarks.

Lyosan does not appreciate his showmanship or Faith's impressed response to it. This may have the appearance of a game, but it certainly isn't.

"It takes more than a showman to rule a kingdom," Lyosan says. "This may have won him the approval of the crowd, but I doubt it will do much for him in the tournament."

"Do not doubt the significance of having the people backing you," Fallon says. "They can be a significant ally."

"I do not deny that," Lyosan replies. "I only deny our people can be won over so easily."

Darrow makes his way through the crowd and passes Lyosan, Faith, and Fallon. He smiles at Fallon and Faith and gives a nod of respect to Lyosan. He already knows Lyosan is his next opponent, and just like Lyosan, Darrow holds his opponent in high esteem. Still, he understands the nature of the tournament as well.

"Did you enjoy the match?" Darrow asks.

"I saw what I needed," Lyosan replies.

Darrow smiles. "A good response. I hope your skills are just as good."

He leaves them and goes for home. Many of the duelists have seen what they need for the day and now need to regroup. The next round will be the next day since each participant only fights once a day. So, while many would like to stay and enjoy the festivities, they must also be preparing themselves for the next opponent.

Fallon convinces Lyosan to go home. Lyosan resists at first, especially since his home is so close to the castle. Fallon assumes this resistance has more to do with the princess than simply ignoring Fallon's suggestions. When Fallon finally gets Lyosan to admit as much, it is easier to convince Lyosan to go home. Even Faith agrees it is the appropriate course of action. With both of them against him, Lyosan surrenders and goes home for the day.

Fallon and Faith, on the other hand, stay behind and continue to watch the matches. His dedication to the tournament surprises Faith as he has so little at stake. He will only enter the tournament if all their plans fail. He has made it clear he will marry Faith when the time comes. Unless of course, he has changed his mind. Perhaps after considering the power and wealth which he could attain, he has decided to challenge the winner no matter what. If that is true, Faith will be destroyed. This change in priority would be shocking given all they have been through.

Still, she stays with him for several matches. As the day draws to an end and the sun begins to set, Faith tires of being at the tournament. She hopes she will be able to convince Fallon to come with her, but she worries she will not.

"Walk me home," Faith says.

"In due time," Fallon replies. "The matches will end momentarily."

"It's getting late; I need to be home."

"Well, I need to be here."

"Why?"

The question seems so silly to Fallon. How can she not understand the importance of what he is doing?

"Isn't that obvious?" he asks.

Faith swallows hard. This could turn very quickly. "This goes beyond aiding Lyosan," Faith responds. "It is as though you seek information for yourself."

"What information could I need for myself?"

"I do not know. That is why this scares me."

"Scares you?" Fallon repeats.

Her reaction to this situation makes little sense. Fallon has dedicated himself to this cause for months now. With their only chance to see their plan come to fruition, he must be ever vigilant – especially as he is the only one left to help Lyosan.

"Yes," Faith says. "It scares me. If it was just for Lyosan, I could handle that, but this seems like something else."

"Something else," Fallon says. "I do this only for Lyosan. You must know that. This has always been for him. We planned this for him. We trained him for this. And now that Shaylynn is..."

At the mention of his name, Fallon trembles and stops. Faith too shudders a bit, but it stops Fallon in his tracks. For a long while, he cannot muster the composure to speak. When he finally does, his voice is trembling.

"I should not have mentioned him," he says in broken tones.

"As if he is ever far from my thoughts?" Faith asks. "I think of him every day, I see him every day, and I wish he was still with us every day. We cannot ignore his memory forever."

"I do not wish to ignore him," Fallon replies. "I only wish to finish what he started – what we started. Were he here, I'd not doubt myself, but with him gone, I feel I must do even more than before."

Faith cups Fallon's face in her hand and turns him towards her. "You can do nothing more for Lyosan than you've already done," she tells him.

"You've trained him, guided him, and now scout for him. But do you think you can win this for him? He must do it himself."

Fallon nods in understanding. Faith may have lessened the weight on his shoulders, but quite a burden remains.

"And above all, beloved, allow yourself to grieve for Shaylynn's death. Do not attempt to tiptoe around me because you think his name causes me such hardship. Honor him and remember him as he would want to be remembered. Tell his stories. Speak of him – to me, to anyone."

Tears begin to fall down Fallon's face. "But it hurts," he says.

Tears fall down Faith's face as well. "Yes, it does," she agrees. "For now, but not forever. It will ease, this terrible pain which afflicts us. In time, it will be nothing to us, and all we will have is the happiness he brought us."

Fallon pulls Faith to him, and the two kiss passionately. When they come apart, Fallon agrees to leave for the day. He walks Faith home and returns home himself. Ellisia greets him and asks for everything that transpired at the tournament. She spent the day with Kandessa who, much like Sarin, decided to forgo the tournament for the day. Fallon tells her of Lyosan's match and everything else he saw.

In his own house, Lyosan hears of his own match through the eyes of Steel and Calvin. They stayed out of the way while they were at the tournament, but now that Lyosan is done for the day, they cannot wait to brag about him. They've waited all day because Elle wanted Lyosan to be there when she heard about it. As Lyosan sits at the table and eats his dinner, his brothers go on and on about the sights they witnessed that day. From time to time, he does interject to correct a few of the exaggerations Steel and Calvin put into the telling, but mostly, he sits back and enjoys the attention. Elle smiles at him and enjoys the experience as well. It is not often Steel and Calvin can brag on their brother so much. It is nice to have such happiness in the house again.

After dinner, Lyosan goes straight to bed. He wants to be rested for the next day as he knows Darrow will be a tough task. Perhaps his anticipation of a bigger challenge makes it difficult for him to relax because for several hours, he cannot sleep. Try as he might, he cannot get himself comfortable to the point where he can fall asleep. After a few hours, he hears his door creak open. He sits up in bed to see Calvin standing in the doorway.

"I didn't wake you, did I?" he asks.

"No," Lyosan replies as he goes to light a lamp. Calvin comes in the room and jumps onto Lyosan's bed. "Have you been up this whole time?" Lyosan asks.

Calvin nods in reply.

"Why?" Lyosan asks.

"I don't know," Calvin replies with a shrug of his shoulders. "I guess I'm not tired."

"Well, I am tired," Lyosan says, "and I still can't sleep."

For a few minutes, Calvin sits on the bed and picks at Lyosan's blanket. He has a question he wants to ask, but Steel has told him it would be silly to ask this question. It's far too early in the tournament to be thinking this way. He should wait a few more rounds before he really thinks about asking about this. Still, Calvin is too young to be able to avoid this question.

"Lyosan, can I ask you something?" Calvin finally asks.

"Of course, brother," Lyosan replies. "You know you can ask me anything."

"If you become king, what will happen to us?"

It's not exactly clear what Calvin is asking about here. Lyosan knows it will be a rather big adjustment for Calvin as he and Steel will both technically become princes. At the same time, their lives won't change entirely. They will still have the freedom to make any choice they desire. In fact, a great many more options will open up to them.

"What do you mean?" Lyosan asks.

"Are we gonna have to live in the castle?" Calvin asks.

Lyosan thinks the question over. "You wouldn't want to live in the castle?" Lyosan asks.

"I don't know," Calvin replies. "I always thought this would be our home."

"Well, I kinda did too," Lyosan admits, "but this is something you really can't pass up. If I do become king, I will have to move to the castle. You, Steel, and mom will be invited to come there, but I certainly won't force you. You know, as long as we're together, wherever we are will be home."

Calvin gives his brother a big hug and then leaves his room. Lyosan manages to get to sleep shortly thereafter. When the morning comes, he rises early. Elle has managed to wake before him and already has breakfast on the table for him. He eats heartily as Elle prepares a meal for Calvin and Steel. Lyosan says nothing of the conversation he had with Calvin.

About an hour later, Fallon arrives at his doorstep. Faith and Sarin are with him today. Lyosan is surprised to see Sarin. He certainly understood Sarin might come to the tournament at some point, but he didn't expect it to be this soon.

She looks as she normally does with an expected sorrow still behind her eyes. The looks of it knocks Lyosan out of his comfort zone a bit. He is not sure what to say to her or if he should say anything at all.

Fortunately, she takes the lead. "I hear your duel went well yesterday."

"It did," Lyosan replies.

"I'm glad to hear it," Sarin says. "It will give me something to look forward to."

"I'm glad you're coming."

"Well, I considered staying at home for another day, but I really didn't find it beneficial to sit around and dwell over Shaylynn."

"We do need to busy ourselves," Fallon agrees. "It makes things seem normal when they clearly aren't. So, shall we head to the tournament?"

"I am ready," Lyosan responds.

"Let's go then!" Faith says.

CHAPTER XX

The tournament continues into its second day. The king addresses the youths to begin the day. Firstly, he congratulates them on winning their first respective matches. Secondly, he wishes them luck as the tournament goes on. Lastly, he asks them to continue to fight hard and remember the honor which awaits the winner. When he finishes his speech, Jonas steps forward and announces the matches for the day. Unlike the first round, Lyosan's match will be later in the day. Since there are considerably fewer matches than the first, they will also finish much earlier than yesterday.

The only problem with everyone being there to hear about the order of the matches is it means Pythyn is around. Shortly after Jonas announces the matches, Sarin and Faith catch a glimpse of him. He is in the back, far away from the others. When he arrived, he saw Sarin was with them, and he surely wanted to avoid a confrontation with her. Now, he works to keep his distance from them. Little does he realize, they want to keep their distance from him. As much as they want to see Pythyn get his comeuppance quickly, they want it to come from Lyosan. They would take a shot at him should they get the chance, but they realize it will only help his cause. Right now, the entire city is against Pythyn and wants to see him fail in his quest to become king. Were he to be attacked outside the tournament, even for a justifiable cause, it might garner him some sympathy. Just about everyone accepts the fact Pythyn played some role in Shaylynn's death. Most believe the story Lyosan and Fallon tell. Others think it was merely an accident which should never have happened because the boys shouldn't have been fighting on the wall itself. Only a select few believe him to be totally innocent.

What remains true is the only way they will have justice is by ensuring Pythyn does not achieve his goal. It is the last gift they can give Shaylynn. When the matches begin, they put Pythyn out of their minds and focus on helping Lyosan. Stefen is one of the first duelists to win on the second day. He again wins with ease and seems to be on the best track to getting to the final four.

The match they are waiting for happens shortly before noon. Artimous would most likely be Lyosan's next opponent should he defeat Darrow. Today, he faces Pether. It should be a fairly even match, but Artimous is stronger and in a longer match has the advantage. Pether will have to come out quickly in order to win. If he can get Artimous off balance early in the match, he might be able to steal one.

As they settle in to watch the duel, Faith notices Darrow is sitting across from them to watch the match as well. It is not unexpected to see him there, but it reminds Lyosan of what occurred yesterday. Luckily, Fallon is there to remind Lyosan of the larger picture for the moment. They do not want to overlook Darrow, obviously, but they do want to be prepared once Lyosan wins the match.

Artimous and Pether take their positions on the dueling square. As Fallon thought, Pether attacks early. Artimous fends off the attack with ease, but Pether keeps coming at him. As the duel advances, both combatants lose their shields, and the duel breaks down to a showing of sword play. Artimous advances as Pether begins to wear down. The duel continues for several minutes, but Artimous continues to press his advantage.

"He's big and strong," Fallon notes. "He hopes the duel lasts long. It's almost what cost him in his first duel."

"Pressing him didn't seem to do much," Lyosan adds. "Pether came at him with all he had, and it did nothing."

Fallon shakes his head in disagreement. "It wasn't that Pether came at him; it was the manner in which he attacked. He was trying to end the duel too quickly. Each stroke was meant to be the final blow. Artimous can defend against those too easily. It will take a combination to bring him down."

As Fallon says this, Pether falls from the dueling square and crashes into the hay on the ground. Artimous stands victorious on the square above with his arms raised in victory. His exhibition was truly impressive.

"Any thoughts on what that combination would be?" Lyosan asks.

Fallon only shakes his head.

The crowd acknowledges Artimous's skill by standing as they applaud. Artimous basks in the cheers and shakes a fist. He never fancied himself a king, but with attention such as this, he could certainly warm to the notion. Indeed, he perhaps lingers too long atop the beam as the officials must call him several times before he exits the arena.

With the knowledge of his potential opponent in his mind, Lyosan returns his full attention to the task at hand. Darrow has left the area – no doubt to scout the other potential combatants. There is still a good deal of time before their duel begins, so there is little reason to begin preparing now. When Lyosan first heard his duel would be later in the day, he assumed it would be a good thing. He slept so little the previous night, he felt he needed time to prepare. Now that the time is upon him, he cannot begin to imagine what to do with it. In his mind, he has gone over the duel with Darrow hundreds of times. Fallon has asked him over and over what the likely scenarios are and how Lyosan should react to every attack Darrow might throw. All the possibilities do nothing to ease Lyosan's nerves. In truth, all the preparation could be for nothing. Darrow will know Lyosan and Fallon have studied him closely. He will surely come up with new strategies and methods to throw them off. Perhaps, he has a secret technique he has not shown – knowing full well Lyosan and Fallon have been watching. It is a risky venture, assuming so much about an opponent, but it is all Lyosan can do at the moment.

As the morning hours whittle away, Lyosan and company move throughout the tournament, watching bits and pieces of different duels. They watch many fall who everyone expected to fall. The greatest surprise comes when Kaulow, a youth many were surprised to hear made the field at all, manages to disarm Shawl and force him to yield. Though Shawl was on the other side of the bracket and Lyosan knew he would only face him in the finals, the news remains disheartening. Unless Kaulow can muster the same kind of surprise, he will surely provide an easy passage for Pythyn into the next round. As the crowd cheers for the unlikely winner, Fallon searches the crowd and sees Pythyn with a pleased look on his face. While Fallon would like to remove the happiness Pythyn currently feels, he knows he cannot. Without even taking the stage, Pythyn seems to have earned a small victory.

The tournament pauses around noon for lunch. While the crowds eat, Jonas and his crew work to update the bracket. The first half of the second round is complete. Twenty-four youths remain in the running for the hand of the princess and the rule of Artonia. Pythyn seems to be in a good place, as does Stefen. From the company which went to rescue the princess, only Shawl has been eliminated. Fallon must still wait to see if he will enter the tournament at all.

Lyosan eats quickly, which is no surprise to Fallon. Lyosan's duel is still a ways-off, and the wait is getting to him. It is why Fallon kept the group moving in the morning. The less time Lyosan had to ponder, the better. In keeping with that mindset, Fallon finishes his lunch quickly as well and walks more with Lyosan. Sarin and Faith stay behind as they need more time to finish eating. What's more, they feel it would be better for the two boys to have a few moments alone.

As they walk, Fallon turns them away from the tournament. It will be impossible to ignore it completely, but some distance from the duels might do some good. As they walk, however, they come across a different offshoot of the tournament. Indeed, it has been going on for quite some time, but the youths have always managed to avoid it. Even those participating know the king would not look kindly on their proximity to the tournament. Gamblers have been placing wagers on the duels for months now. As the tournament progresses, small fortunes are being won and lost. With the pause in the action of the tournament, it allows the action of the gamblers to increase.

"Jonas has finished the updates!" one gambler proclaims.

"Give us the latest odds!" another yells.

"Yes! Let's go! Go!" the crowd cries.

At the front of the pack, one man, who seems to oversee the matter, stands and beckons the crowd to quiet themselves. On the one hand, he knows everyone will need to be quiet if he is to be heard. On the other hand, he knows if they draw the attention of the king's soldiers, they will be forced to disband.

"Alright! Alright! Shut it!" the man yells. "Enough of ya! Quiet down or we'll never get business done. We've only a few minutes before the duels commence." The crowd noise dies down as the man looks over a sheet of paper given to him by an associate. "The numbers have been run, and it seems as though Pythyn remains your odds-on favorite to capture the crown!"

A chorus of boos ring out from the crowd. This pleases Fallon and Lyosan, which is nice since the declaration from the man was most displeasing. The man nods knowingly, but he quickly motions for them to quiet themselves.

"I know it's not what you want to hear, but that's the truth of it!" he says. "He's holding down at 5 to 1. Next is Stefen at 8 to 1. After that, you can go with Athen at 14 to 1 or Nycolas at the same…"

The crowd starts to bark out names and numbers, and the man motions for his associates to filter into the crowd and collect bets. Lyosan is not surprised his name was not among the favorites, but it still depresses him.

"I wonder how many would have to go before I was among the top four," Lyosan ponders.

"Do not listen to them as though they have any expertise in the matter," Fallon advises. "If not for the ranking Jonas and the castle put out before the tournament, they would have nothing but conjecture and the whims of desperation."

As they continue through the crowd, the flurry of betting goes on around them. A few times, one of the gamblers recognizes Fallon and asks if he will be entering the tournament. Fallon ignores them all, but they persist. It is only when he and Lyosan begin heading back to the tournament that they desist.

"There is probably not a single bet placed in my name," Lyosan says looking back at the gamblers one more time.

"And the bookies must be relieved," Fallon replies. At first, Lyosan does not understand the remark. If he did not know better, Lyosan would think Fallon is saying no one should bet on him. When it is clear to Fallon Lyosan does not understand, he clasps Lyosan's arm and explains himself further. "Imagine the fortunes they would have to pay out when you are named king."

Lyosan smiles and even lets out a small laugh. He clasps Fallon's arm as well and the two re-enter the dueling area.

The afternoon goes by considerably quicker and the duel with Darrow comes quickly. Nothing unexpected has occurred all afternoon, which means Lyosan must break the trend if he is to win. Since they are one of the last duels in the day, a great crowd has come to watch. Faith and Sarin find a place close to Fallon's spot. Steel and Calvin are near them as well. Some of the members of their troupe are on his side of the square as well, but others are on Darrow's side. It is moot as they are merely seeking a place to watch the duel. Still, it feels as though there is a great division amongst them. Somewhere in the crowd, Pythyn is undoubtedly watching. Despite his hatred for Lyosan, Pythyn has a vested interest in Lyosan going far into the tournament. The further Lyosan progresses in the duel, the less chance Fallon will assert himself. Even if he has to do so as the end, it will no doubt be difficult to suddenly be at the top of his game when Pythyn will have had six duels to ready himself.

Lyosan cannot let outside forces cloud his thoughts now. He must focus on the task at hand. Darrow stands in his way, so Darrow must be dealt with. They ascend the ladders and take their places on the dueling square. Jonas quiets the crowd and announces the two combatants. After a run through of the instructions, Jonas calls for the duel to begin.

Picking up from the day before, when his showmanship garnered him much praise, Darrow begins the duel by playing to the crowd. Rather than attempt to move towards Lyosan, Darrow walks back and forth on his starting beam waving to the crowd and beckoning them to start cheering again. As the row begins to build, Darrow lets a bigger and bigger smile grow on his face. He then begins to dance around on the beam as oh-s and ah-s sound from the crowd. All the while, Lyosan stands in his starting position, unsure how to proceed. For a moment, he looks down to Fallon, who is one of the few people in attendance not impressed by Darrow's showing off. Fallon shakes his head and then turns to Lyosan. Lyosan shrugs to ask how he should proceed. Fallon responds by mouthing the word *attack*. Lyosan nods, readjusts his shield and takes off to the next beam.

Darrow sees Lyosan approach and backs to the corner but does not leave the beam. As Lyosan draws near, Darrow puts his arms behind his back and leaves his front vulnerable. He further entices Lyosan by leaning his chest forward. The crowd quiets as they fear Darrow has lost his mind. What sense could it possibly make to give one's opponent such an easy mark?

Lyosan, however, does not see this as an invitation – at least not an invitation to victory. Darrow has been employing a strategy since the match began; surely, he continues to do so here. But what is his endgame?

Thinking Darrow must be trying to lure him in, Lyosan stays back for a few seconds. When he takes too long, Darrow begins to step forward with his arms still behind his back. Lyosan still does not think he should risk anything, so he remains in his place. Darrow continues slowly moving towards Lyosan, and in a minute, he halves the distance between he and Lyosan. Cries of concern begin to ring out from the crowd, but Darrow maintains his stance. Lyosan keeps his composure and raises his shield in front of him. Whatever Darrow means to accomplish, Lyosan is certain it will come soon.

Finally, when Darrow is only a few feet away, Lyosan lashes out. Brandishing his sword, Lyosan slices with his blade. In a flash, Darrow backs away and retreats to his corner. With a dramatic flourish, he leaps onto the corner post, using one arm to keep himself up on the post and the other to point his blade at Lyosan.

The crowd laughs and cheers at this display. Darrow still means to give them a show. Lyosan means to end it. Having enough, he races down the beam. Darrow drops down to meet him, and the two exchange a few blows. When the chance arises, Darrow leaps to another beam and playfully continues running around the entire square. As the crowd laughs, Darrow feigns fear. It only incites the crowd more. Eventually, Darrow finds himself on the beam which he started. When he comes close to Lyosan, he acts surprised to have come across him again, drops down on the beam, and backs away pleading with Lyosan to give him a moment. At this point, many of the people in the crowd are rolling on the ground, but it still does nothing to further the duel. After a few moments, Darrow rises and nods he is ready to continue. With sword and shield out in front, he comes towards Lyosan. Hoping the games are over, Lyosan steps forward as well.

When they get close enough, Darrow jabs with his sword. Lyosan blocks it easily, but Darrow steps back and raises his hands, as though he's won a battle. The crowd cheers and laughs. The games continue. Again, Darrow steps in. This time, Lyosan swings and Darrow blocks. Again, Darrow steps back and cheers his own success. Rather than play along, Lyosan steps to attack. Darrow must cut his celebration short to block, but he does manage to defend himself. However, in interrupting the show, Lyosan loses a portion of the crowd, and they begin to boo. Darrow shrugs his shoulders as if to suggest he would keep the show going if not for

Lyosan. Lyosan cares not – he has seen enough. Continuing to press, Lyosan moves forward and swings. Darrow continues to block and dodge the attacks, and he keeps his playful attitude throughout.

When he comes to the corner post again, he wraps around so the post is between the two combatants. As Lyosan continues to attack, Darrow swings from side to side on the post to avoid the attacks. While this clever maneuvering keeps the crowd entertained, it also presents on opportunity to Lyosan. Rather than focus his attack on the man, Lyosan swings for Darrow's shield and knocks it cleanly away.

The crowd reacts with a gasp, and Darrow stumbles a bit before he gets back on a beam. The smile lessens on his face as he collects himself. As he does, Lyosan continues to pursue and begins an assault. Darrow manages to block, and the clown gives way to the dueler. He blocks and then presses his own assault. Lyosan uses his shield to his advantage, and after a wild swing from Darrow collides with his shield, Lyosan gives a mighty kick to Darrow's chest and sends him flying back. Darrow lands hard on the beam, but he does not fall. In his hand, he keeps a tight grip on his sword. Not letting Lyosan gain too much of an advantage, Darrow raises his sword to keep Lyosan at bay and quickly gets to his feet. Once upright again, Darrow wipes any trace of a smile from his face. A look of determination and anger comes over him. Lyosan realizes despite all that has happened, this duel has only begun.

Indeed, Darrow comes at Lyosan with a fierceness he did not seem capable of possessing. Despite a shield and sword, Lyosan looks to be at a disadvantage. Darrow's swings come quickly and viciously. As soon as Lyosan blocks with his shield, he needs to be ready to block with his blade. Darrow keeps him pinned in the corner, and Lyosan does not see an opportunity to get himself out of it.

His only hope is Darrow will tire, but it seems unlikely. Lyosan will have to risk his shield if he hopes to regain his advantage. As Darrow swings to Lyosan's sword side, Lyosan brings his shield across him. After blocking with his own blade, Lyosan attempts to disarm Darrow by hitting him with his shield. The blow does knock Darrow back a bit, but he keeps his sword. He also swings around and attacks Lyosan's exposed side. Lyosan counters by wrapping his arm over his head and blocking with his sword. However, it leaves his shield exposed, and Darrow kicks it away. Before the loss can affect him too much, Lyosan lowers a shoulder and bowls into Darrow. Darrow backs away, and Lyosan gets to his feet. The two are at even ground again. Neither can afford a mistake from this point forward.

Though the duel is not over, the crowd begins to cheer. Even without Darrow making a spectacle of himself, the duel has been outstanding. As it continues, they can only hope the end is as dramatic as the beginning.

Darrow begins by flipping his sword in his hand. He comes at Lyosan with an overhead stroke which Lyosan blocks with ease. As Darrow's sword bounces off the block, Lyosan swings for Darrow's stomach, and Darrow ducks away. The two clang swords back and forth for several minutes without either man gaining an advantage. The longer the match progresses, the easier it becomes to see the fatigue in the duelists. They are getting slower, and their swings do not have the same power behind them. Still, a winner must rise.

With a sense of finality, Lyosan comes at Darrow. Darrow blocks and counters, but Lyosan is ready. After blocking, Lyosan grabs Darrow's arm and flings him over his shoulder. Darrow tumbles to the beam and, in trying to keep himself on the beam, loses his grip on his sword, and it falls to the ground below. Lyosan scrambles to his feet and stands above Darrow with his sword at point.

"Who taught you that one?" Darrow asks.

After a moment, Lyosan replies. "Shaylynn."

"You honor him well."

Darrow calls for an end to the match, and Lyosan is named the winner. The crowd cheers again as Lyosan and Darrow come down from the ladders. Steel and Calvin are waiting to congratulate Lyosan when he gets down. Both of his brothers embrace him and almost knock him to the ground. Fallon, Faith, and Sarin congratulate him as well. Rather than wait around for the other duels to end, Fallon convinces Lyosan they should go home for the evening. Perhaps it is because of his talk with Faith the day before or perhaps he realizes Lyosan will need to rest for a match with Artimous, but Fallon does not want to stay.

So, they walk together to Lyosan's house. Steel and Calvin happily recant the story of Lyosan's victory to their mother. Fallon, Faith, and Sarin stay for a bit to revel in the moment, but then they move on. Faith returns home, and in an infrequent occurrence, Fallon and Sarin find themselves together with no one else.

"I've meant to check in on you more often than I have," Fallon says.

"You've been busy," Sarin replies. "I understand."

"It is no excuse. I should have come to you."

"I am not your responsibility."

"You are my friend."

"I am Faith's friend," Sarin corrects. "And you were Shaylynn's friend. That is how it is for us."

Truth, despite its accuracy, and in fact sometimes because of it, is not always welcome. Were Shaylynn still alive, perhaps the comment would not be so hurtful. Indeed, both could attest to its validity and be effected negligibly. How things have changed.

Now, the statement is cutting. It shows the void they should not have allowed to grow between them. It reminds Fallon of the times when Shaylynn would flirt with her, and Fallon would wish so desperately for him to stop. In that way, he garnered a small amount of disdain for Sarin. She would always get in the way and come between the two friends. She would torment him relentlessly, and he would get so angry. What Fallon did not know or understand at the time is how much Shaylynn really loved the attention from her. In fact, the pendulum was swinging to the place where Fallon would be coming between Shaylynn and Sarin. He was becoming the odd-person out at the time of Shaylynn's death. He figured he'd have the time needed to adjust. That his friendship with Sarin could evolve from their connection to Shaylynn. Sadly, time did not give him this chance.

Instead, it gave him this duty. Shaylynn loved Sarin with a fierce passion. He meant to make her his wife and his life. Fallon would always be a part, however small, of Shaylynn's life, so Sarin would in turn be a part of his. However difficult, whatever trials they must overcome, Fallon must keep her a part of his life.

"But that is not how it should be," Fallon replies.

"And how should we be?" Sarin asks.

"You should be as dear as a sister to me," Fallon explains, "and I would be honored should you think of me as a brother."

Sarin considers the idea for a minute. It would be nice. She never had a brother. She does think of Faith as a sister. And yet, there is something which forces her to pause. Something about this arrangement does not feel right to her.

"I do not know if I can accept this," Sarin admits.

It does not hurt Fallon to hear this, but it does confuse him. He is being sincere and genuine in his offer. He understands he has not been a true friend in the past, but he means to atone for that error now.

"Why?" he asks.

Sarin stops for a minute. It will be difficult to explain herself on this issue. "If we do become friends now – in a way we never had been – I will always know it happened because of Shaylynn's death. I do not want anything I am supposed to value to come from his death."

"I understand," Fallon replies. He gives the matter some time to reflect upon it. This concern is more serious than Fallon anticipated. He cannot assume he can solve this puzzle in an instant. "But something good must come of it," he finally says. "Nothing he did in life was without meaning. We must not let his death be meaningless. This city will never forget the name, but they will forget the man. We are the only ones who can keep the smallest pieces of him alive."

"And we are to do this together?"

"I would have no one else with me."

The offer remains sincere, and he is right. Though Shaylynn was taken from them, they can keep him with them if they work together to do so. Death can take so much, but it cannot take everything.

"He would be so proud of Lyosan," Sarin says with a smile and a tear in her eye. "How far he's come. How much of a fighter he is. And you, he'd be proud of you as well. That you have committed yourself to this. That you believe in Lyosan so absolutely."

"He continues to inspire me," Fallon admits. "He gave his life believing in this. I can do no less."

The next day comes quickly. Unlike the night before, Lyosan sleeps easily. He falls so quickly and hard into a dream, he cannot seem to recover from his day. His dream brings back a simpler time. Shaylynn was alive. There was no talk of a tournament or who would be king. School was small and did not seem to have a great impact on their lives. Pythyn was an annoyance in a small measure but nothing to concern themselves with. The three friends ran and played as children do. The princess, Faith, and Sarin came along with them. They were together. They were happy. They were carefree. The day seemed to go on and on with no way for it to end.

And yet, dreams must. As the brief seconds of ignorance drift away, Lyosan recalls all the truths the night hid away. The most important of which is his duel with Artimous lay ahead of him. Since his night does not provide much rest, Lyosan keeps quiet in the morning. He eats quickly and leaves early. Fallon is approaching as Lyosan walks out the door. Either sensing his weariness or sharing in it, Fallon says little to Lyosan as they walk to the castle.

Only sixteen remain to vie for the crown. Most of them are the ones everyone expected to be there. Kaulow is the most unlikely of those who remain. Lyosan would have to be another whom many would be surprised is there, but his showings have been impressive. He defeated a lesser opponent with ease and in a timely fashion. Then, he topped an opponent many thought to be his better. He goes up against another today with Artimous. Artimous is a big body who will not tire easily. After watching one of his matches, Lyosan cannot help but wonder what advantage he will be able to pull against him.

Unfortunately, he will not have much time to figure it out. When Jonas comes forward to announce the duels, Lyosan and Artimous are the first to be named. They are not even given time to hear the other matches. Instead, soldiers come for them and take them to the center dueling arena. As they walk, Fallon stands a step behind barking out instructions and thoughts, but they do not truly sink in. Instead, before he knows it, Lyosan finds himself atop the square, sword and shield in hand with Artimous standing across from him.

And without warning, Artimous suddenly charges around the square and is on Lyosan before Lyosan can prepare himself. Thrusting his shield into Lyosan's, Artimous knocks Lyosan off balance and only continues the assault from there. Back on his heels, Lyosan tries to escape by fleeing to another beam, but Artimous follows. The more Lyosan retreats, the more Artimous advances. For the first few minutes of the duel, it seems inevitable that Artimous will emerge victorious. It is only a matter of how long Lyosan can last.

But with Artimous on the attack so vigorously, his swings are wild and out of control. He keeps his balance because he is a good soldier, but he puts himself in a vulnerable position if something happens he is not anticipating. Such an event happens when Artimous swings and connects with a corner post. Lyosan ducks the swing with ease and hears the loud clang of the shield against the wood. Artimous falls back and almost falls from the beam. If Lyosan had not been so wearied from the onslaught, he might have been able to capitalize. Instead, he takes the moment to recover and try to find his opportunity.

As he does, he looks to the crowd and sees the royal box. Crystalynn sits on the edge of her seat, hands clenching the armrests. A look of concern graces her face. Lyosan has not talked with her since the tournament began. It is odd he should go this long without seeing her – without remembering she is the one he is doing this for. This is no test of his capabilities or his honor. This is a test of his love.

Rising from the beam, Lyosan faces Artimous. Having steadied himself, Artimous nods to resume the duel. Lyosan replies in kind and charges. Artimous takes a few strikes from Lyosan but then quickly gives a few of his own. Unlike the beginning of the match where Lyosan was caught off guard by Artimous's blows, he absorbs them now and continues his own assault. The more they battle, the more Artimous wears Lyosan down. The shield and sword remain, but they become heavy and hindering. In a moment of desperation, Lyosan sheds his shield and elects to continue with only a sword.

The crowd whispers among themselves, and Fallon rises from his seat. This is a concerning move from Lyosan. The shield was the only thing saving him in the early stages of the duel, and he cannot expect Artimous to respond in kind.

Indeed, he does not. After spending a moment puzzling over this move, Artimous shrugs a shoulder and continues his assault. In his mind, Lyosan begins to form a plan. Fallon said it would take a combination to bring Artimous down, and Lyosan begins to see the combination to get him. It will take time, and he will have to weather a storm. Still, it could work.

Artimous swings and attacks. Lyosan manages to block the sword strokes, but he takes a beating from the shield. He cannot get it away from Artimous, but in truth, he does not wish to. Instead, he is getting the timing. Whenever Artimous strikes, Lyosan blocks. And when Lyosan's sword is out, Artimous uses the shield against Lyosan's body. It is effective but will take time to wear Lyosan out. If Lyosan can find his time, he will have just enough strength to make it work.

As Artimous comes to strike, Lyosan beats him to the punch and strikes first. Artimous recovers in time to block, but it gives Lyosan another opportunity to strike. Keeping on his sword side, Lyosan swings wide.

Artimous brings his sword out wide to block and brings the shield to the front of his body. As the swords clang, Lyosan spins away and leaps into the air. Bringing his legs into him, Lyosan strikes out with his feet and catches Artimous squarely in the center of his shield. The blow sends Artimous back, and he falls on the beam. Lyosan cannot watch what happens with Artimous as he must concentrate on staying on the beam himself. Keeping his arms out, he wraps around the beam and hugs it tightly. His legs swing free off the beam, and he must gather himself quickly. The kick may not be enough to win the duel.

As he scrambles to his feet, Lyosan sees Artimous drop his sword to get a grip on the beam. Though he is off-balance, he manages to steady himself and begins to rise. As he does, he finds Lyosan already upon him and making an over-the-top swing. Artimous raises his shield and blocks the first. Lyosan continues to hammer down on Artimous as the roles reverse from when the duel began. In an act of desperation, Artimous gains a small matter of footing and lunges forward. This was the last step in Lyosan's plan. As Artimous comes at him wildly, Lyosan drops down and trips Artimous up. Artimous falls over him, tumbles hard, and loses his place on the beam. Grasping desperately for anything, Artimous drops down to the ground and crashes into the hay.

Still holding fast to the beam, Lyosan looks at his fallen adversary on the ground. As he looks in amazement, the cheers of the crowd begin to find him. Sight and sound tell him his strategy has worked, and he is victorious. In his mind, he still cannot believe it. Slowly, he works himself back to a standing position on the beam. As if called from a great distance, he hears Jonas announce him as the winner. He looks to his side and sees Fallon, Steel, Calvin, and the others on their feet cheering wildly. After a moment, he looks to the princess. She stands and cheers as well. With the moment finally sinking in, Lyosan raises his sword in his hand and acknowledges his own victory.

When he comes down the ladder, Fallon meets him, congratulates him, and praises the strategy. Many come and give Lyosan a pat on the back along with a kind word. Artimous comes forth and shakes his hand. Lyosan will move on.

With his match out of the way, Lyosan can prepare for his next opponent. It will be some time before he learns whom he will face. It will either be Mitan or Athen. In the minds of most, Athen will be one of the final four in the competition, along with Stefen, Pythyn, and Nycolas. Should Lyosan face Athen, he will certainly have to step up his game. He has done so ever since the beginning, but this will be something different entirely. He will truly be at the edge of his limits.

For the moment, he must recover. The duel against Artimous has left him quite drained. After celebrating with friends and family, he takes a quiet moment near a water barrel. Ladling out handfuls of water, he drinks plenty. Fallon takes the others to give Lyosan the quiet he seeks and also to begin scouting the competition. He has seen all the likely candidates multiple times, but he can never have enough information. Whatever the reason, Lyosan is glad to have the silence.

It does not last for long, though the interruption is a welcome one. The princess places a hand on Lyosan's shoulder. He cannot hide the surprise he feels in seeing her. There is a smile on her face he has never seen before. It is quite pleasing.

"I cannot stay long," she says.

"I'm honored you've come at all," Lyosan replies.

Whether the result of the sights she just witnessed or some combination of factors, Crystalynn stands ready to admit a vital truth. She would have never thought she'd be in this position, ready to say such a thing. For the longest time, it seemed Lyosan was meant to be her truest friend but nothing else. Now, fate has shown her how wrong she has been.

"I just missed you," Crystalynn admits. "And since I could steal a few moments, I figured I'd come to tell you something."

"What is it?"

Crystalynn stumbles before she can continue. "Because of my station, I cannot proclaim a favorite in this competition, but it does not change the fact that I have one."

Lyosan could find himself back in a dream should he hear the words he never expected to come. That she may admit now her love for him would be a prize equal to winning this tournament.

Crystalynn takes his hand in hers. "It is you, Lyosan. You are my champion, and I love you."

The moment is too big for him. Lyosan can say nothing in response to this declaration. He sits dumbfounded, questioning whether this is reality or the dream he strayed into last night.

To bring some certainty to his doubt, Crystalynn leans forward and kisses him. After a moment, joy overtakes Lyosan, and he kisses her back. For a few brief moments of passion, they lock lips fiercely. When they come apart, a new life fills Lyosan. His purpose, always singularly driven, now becomes solidified.

As much as he would like to live in this moment, it holds true to all others and is fleeting. To her word, the princess leaves soon after and returns to her box. Lyosan watches her leave and stares after her. Once she is beyond his sight, Lyosan returns to his seat. His thoughts are on nothing but her. Though he stands three duels away from claiming his prize, he feels he has already won a great victory. How can one think of duels and the tournament when he has been given the love of her whom he loves so dearly?

To his benefit, perhaps, Lyosan has others to focus for him. A few minutes after Lyosan's encounter with the princess, Fallon returns with news of the other duels. He also informs him Pythyn will be dueling Kaulow soon.

If anything could snap Lyosan out of his trance, it is news of the one man who means to take his love from him. Pythyn lusts for the crown and victory over those he feels dishonor him. Pythyn knows his life will change should Lyosan become king. After his actions and his part in the demise of Shaylynn, Pythyn can only rely on himself.

Without telling Fallon of Crystalynn's declaration, Lyosan goes with Fallon to the duel between Pythyn and Kaulow. From the outset, it is clear Pythyn does not take his opponent seriously. He does not show off and play for the crowd as Darrow might, but his stance is lazy. He looks at Kaulow as a lesser man. When Kaulow attacks, Pythyn blocks with a sigh and disdain for Kaulow's attempt. He shakes his head, derisively. This is the opponent who comes before him? This is whom they think can defeat him? His arrogance will cost him.

Kaulow did not reach this far on pure luck. He, like all those who taste success, has trained hard and come a long way since talk of the tournament began. Though Pythyn may look to shake him off, Kaulow will not be so easily shook. Whenever Pythyn attacks, Kaulow defends. Although Pythyn may see Kaulow's strokes as simple, Kaulow is ever adapting. Every test into Pythyn's stance shows where a weakness may lie. Eventually, Kaulow finds one.

To the delight of nearly everyone in attendance, Kaulow manages to separate Pythyn from his shield and get him on his heels. As cries for Kaulow come from the crowd, Pythyn scrambles to recover. Eventually, he does, and he also manages to separate Kaulow from his shield. Once even again, Pythyn decides to underestimate Kaulow no longer. Coming at him intensely, Pythyn tries his best moves to finish Kaulow, but Kaulow manages, at times by the narrowest of margins, to keep himself alive on the beam. When his best fails, Pythyn's determination turns to frustration. His attacks lose a bit of their precision. The strokes are a little wilder and harder to control. Every swing takes him a little longer to recover. As those moments grow, Kaulow earns an opportunity to attack. When he does, it leaves Pythyn vulnerable. So vulnerable in fact, he finds himself barely hanging on in the duel.

For after a blow from Kaulow's shoulder, Pythyn falls to his feet and almost to the ground. Only by releasing his sword and grabbing the beam with both hands does Pythyn manage to stay in the match. The crowd cheers loudly as Kaulow stands in disbelief. In his greatest hopes, Lyosan sees the conclusion he dreamt of where Pythyn falls and can no longer haunt his steps towards the crown. For the briefest of moments, he allows himself to believe Pythyn has been defeated and will never again enter his thoughts. Those around him feel justice coming to fruition. The villain who brought their friend to death will be vanquished by the most unlikely of opponents. Pythyn will not even come close to achieving his goal. Shaylynn will be avenged, and even if none of them will be the one who brings him to this justice, seeing it occur will be enough. But they are not so fortunate. In his desire to claim victory, Kaulow makes a critical error. Pythyn will never yield. Everyone knows as much. Kaulow must force him off the beam. When Kaulow moves to attack, he steps too close, and Pythyn manages to force himself up and grab one of Kaulow's legs. With a pull, he rips Kaulow down so Kaulow must hang onto the beam just as Pythyn does.

With the two of them hanging on the beam, it becomes a matter of who can hang on the longest. Of course, Pythyn will not have a competition wherein he does not have an advantage. Once he is steadied, he goes on the attack. Circling his arms around the beam, he turns himself so he faces Kaulow. He begins swinging his feet back and forth, and after a few swings, he kicks out at Kaulow. He catches Kaulow on the hip, and it does rattle his opponent but does not vanquish him. With the stage set,

Kaulow looks to avoid the strikes. Though Pythyn has moved himself into an attacking position, Kaulow does not have the confidence to feel he can do the same. He feels his best chance will come from avoiding the attacks and hoping Pythyn errors again. This hope is misguided. Pythyn is more focused than at any time in the tournament. Though Kaulow manages to avoid the kicks a couple times, he gets hit more than he dodges. With each kick, his will lessens until finally Pythyn connects, and Kaulow falls from the beam.

The victory is not cheered, but many applaud the efforts. Once Kaulow is free of the hay, Pythyn drops harmlessly to the ground. He rests in the hay for a minute, then gets to his feet and leaves the arena. A few shake his hand as he exits, but most look at him with disdain and hate. A much larger contingent goes to Kaulow and congratulates him for his efforts. He is ultimately disheartened by his failure, but the appreciation provides a bit of consolation.

"I thought we had a big coup there," Fallon says to Lyosan.

"He still may fall," Lyosan says. "If we are lucky, Kaulow exposed a weakness someone else may take advantage of fully."

"I hope you are right," Fallon says. After letting the moment pass, Fallon turns to other matters. "I suggest you eat now," he says. "The match between Mitan and Athen will commence in less than an hour."

Taking the advice to heart, Lyosan finds some food and dines with his friends. Their talk is light and deals with matters outside the tournament. Though his heart overflows with love, Lyosan says nothing to them of the princess. It will not help his chances to make her feelings known. He has the feelings in his heart, and the drive remains ever strong.

The hour passes quickly, and the group finds themselves at the match between Athen and Mitan. To everyone's surprise, the match goes quickly. Athen and Mitan waste no time going at each other. Athen gains the upper hand in a few seconds and knocks Mitan off the beam in little less than a minute. The crowd, feeling somewhat cheated, can barely comprehend what they've seen. They cheer, but the cheers are lacking in enthusiasm. Still, Athen comes down proudly. He has accomplished his goal and sent a powerful message to Lyosan.

The rest of the day goes by quickly. At the end of the matches, only eight remain. With the number of duels going down, the king declares a day of rest for the combatants. Furthermore, the matches to determine the last four will all take place in the afternoon and in the main dueling arena.

The news brings a mixed reaction from Lyosan. Rest is always a good thing, but what will he do with his day? How will he be able to think of anything but the tournament?

CHAPTER XXI

In fact, he cannot. Fallon comes over during the day. They train a bit, spar a bit, but mostly, they do odd chores around the house. They talk constantly of Athen's skills and weaknesses. They pour over details Fallon caught in Athen's matches. Granted, there is not much to discuss from the last match, but Fallon speaks of it a great deal.

"You have come a great distance," Fallon remarks, "but there are others who are ahead of you. If you attempt to take them head on, you will lose."

"I know as much," Lyosan concurs.

"You must plan, strategize and take necessary risks," Fallon encourages. "They are your biggest allies here."

Lyosan nods.

"I am certain you will have to face Stefen when you advance," Fallon continues. "This is good. Though Stefen is highly skilled and stands as one of the best available to defeat Pythyn, he is much like Athen. They train together. They spar against one another. Their skills are similar. How you beat Athen may give you the roadmap to defeating Stefen."

As they talk, Faith and Sarin find them.

"Hard at work, boys?" Faith asks.

"Of course not," Fallon replies. "This is his day of rest."

"Day of celebration, I'd say," Sarin adds.

This is an odd comment. Though Lyosan has come far in the tournament, he is certainly not at a place where he can celebrate. He has potentially his toughest two opponents in front of him and his greatest foe waiting at the end. Unless, Sarin knows of the other news Lyosan received.

"Why's that?" Fallon asks.

"Has he not told you?" Sarin asks.

"Clearly, he has not," Fallon replies, looking to Lyosan.

Sarin smiles coyly at Lyosan, but she says nothing. He would have to assume she knows what Crystalynn said to him, but how has she come to know this information? When enough time passes, Sarin addresses Lyosan directly.

"Will you tell him?" she asks.

Fallon interjects. "Someone surely will. I'll not be strung along so."

Lyosan smiles as he has no reason to hide the news. If it were not known, he would still keep it a secret, but he will certainly not deny the truth of it.

"The princess told me she loves me," Lyosan admits.

Faith and Sarin both smile. Fallon's eyes go wide. This is joyous news indeed. Fallon comes over to him and embraces him. Lyosan laughs at Fallon's reaction. The two jump around a bit and revel in the news. When he settles back down, Fallon of course realizes the news has no bearing on the tournament itself. Still, it is a solid motivator.

What's more, it gives them something to use as a distraction from the grind of the tournament. For a few minutes, they can find a reprieve from the thoughts they cannot escape. They can go back to times when love and friends were all their hearts had to deal with. There, they can find true rest.

When the time passes, they still find themselves harkening back to days gone by. Perhaps, each of them have finally come to a place where they are ready to deal with the loss they have suffered.

"I dreamt of him the other night," Sarin admits. Then, she smiles and adds. "Actually, I dream of him every night." Faith smiles as well. "We were younger, all of us. You boys were playing knights with toy swords made from branches off a tree. Faith and I sat in a tree above you. We watched and laughed. Shaylynn became annoyed and demanded to know why we were there…"

"I remember this day," Fallon says. "We should have been doing chores, but Shaylynn said the day was too nice for work."

After a laugh from all, Sarin continues telling her dream. "Faith said we were imprisoned and needed rescuing. Had I said it, I'm certain he would've ignored me and kept playing. But he would not abandon his beloved cousin." The two ladies clasp hands for a moment. "In any event, I offered him a prize should he be able to rescue us. He looked at me quizzically at first, as though I may be trying to deceive him..."

"You were," Faith says.

"I was not!" Sarin replies. "I did have something for him."

Since everyone knows the story already, they chuckle knowing how it will end, but they still want Sarin to finish the telling.

"After I assured him I had a prize for him, he asked how they were supposed to rescue us. I said only one could do it, and it would be the one who managed to beat the other two. With a smile, he turned around and went after the two of you. Lyosan, you threw down your sword and surrendered, but Fallon put up a fight."

"Not much of one," Fallon admits. "He took me down fairly quickly."

"And when he did, he came to the tree to claim his prize. I dropped down in front of him and offered him a kiss. He refused it at first. He started to walk away, but Faith came to my defense."

Faith smiles. "He never could stand it when I cried," she says. "I said I still needed rescued and would not come down until he accepted his prize. He glared at me so."

"But he gave in," Sarin adds. "He came to the tree and stood before me. He said I could kiss his cheek. I agreed. When he came closer, I kissed his lips instead. He turned red in anger, or embarrassment, or something else – I don't know what. The three of you burst into laughter. He looked as if he wanted to run, but he got Faith down instead and turned away. I cannot know for certain, but I like to think he smiled as he had his back to us."

"I am certain he did," Fallon says.

"We will always have those moments, will we not?" Sarin asks. "Since we will have nothing else."

"Yes, I suppose we shall," Lyosan replies. "But no matter what happens to me, I will always feel him with me. He shall stand as the example I wish to be. Whatever trials I face, I will face them wondering what he would do if he were in my place. And I shall attempt to act the same."

"Do not discount your own thoughts so quickly," Faith says. "He would not want that. He wanted you on the throne because of who you are, not because you would try to be him."

"Still, he had a great deal of wisdom and knowledge," Lyosan says.

"So will you, in time," Fallon says.

The day slowly winds away. They continue to tell stories of their younger days. It is ridiculous to think they must consider their younger years as so long ago. They are still young in age, but war, death, love – they add time to the years we live.

The next day, Lyosan and Fallon walk to the tournament after lunch. The other seven competitors – Athen, Stefen, Pythyn, Brynnal, Nycolas, Dragoon, and one Lyosan does not know so well, Hathir – are already at the tournament. Jonas grabs Lyosan and pulls him to the front of the crowd with the other participants. King Cyrus commends them for their efforts and wishes them luck in their next duels. With only four duels in the day, they can afford a little more pomp and circumstance. Rather than rush to get through the events, they let the crowd have a chance to see the duelists up close. They let the duelists have a few more moments in the spotlight since only four will go any further. Then, they announce the matchups. Nycolas will face Dragoon first. Then, Athen and Lyosan will have their battle. Pythyn will go against Brynnal next. Finally, Stefen will battle Hathir.

It is a colder day than most when the duels commence. A biting wind cuts through the air. It nips at the hands of the competitors, and the crowd huddles together to conserve warmth. As Nycolas and Dragoon begin, both look anxious to end the duel quickly. They attack, counter, and stay on the offensive. Neither gains any advantage, and the duel carries on for several minutes without any ground gained or lost.

The more they go at one another, the less anything gets accomplished. Somehow, either by luck or by training, each manages to withstand the attacks of the other without losing sword or shield. When frustration reaches its height, both back away and consider a new course of action. The minutes tick away while the two continue to battle. On and on they go with neither looking like he will be able to earn a victory any time soon. Indeed, an hour passes by with both youths keeping sword and shield. They tire, but they do not give way.

Meanwhile, the other youths become anxious for the duel to end so theirs may begin. The longer the duel progresses, the more they have to wait, and as they started in the afternoon, the sun may come to work against them before the day ends. What's more, the cold of the day already affects them; it will only get colder as the day goes on.

Still, the duel lags on. In the crowd, some wish for one to simply give up, but the prize at the end of the race is far too great. Yes, one of them must win, somehow.

Eventually, Lyosan can watch no more. Sitting for so long has made him stiff, and at any moment, he could be called upon to begin his duel. Though the decree was made for all four duels to happen in the main arena, the king may change his mind if he feels one duel puts the others in jeopardy.

As he walks around, Lyosan carries his sword in hand. He performs several exercises to keep the blood flowing to his hands. In the monotony, they have grown rather numb. He sees many other youths doing the same as him. They keep themselves moving and active. No doubt, each has someone appointed to come alert them when the first duel finally ends. News does not come swiftly. It is nearly twenty minutes later when Fallon and a few others come to find their combatant.

"Is it over?" Lyosan asks.

"Mercifully, yes," Fallon replies. "Nycolas managed to disarm Dragoon and force him to yield. Jonas wants you on the square in a minute's time."

Wasting no time, Lyosan runs to the arena and ascends the ladder. Athen also climbs the ladder, and the two stand across from each other ready to go. Before Jonas calls for the duel to begin, Lyosan looks down to Crystalynn. She smiles at him, and he back. He truly does feel different now – like a new power dwells within him. A power which pushes him forward, knowing nothing will stand in his way. He will gain the victory he so wholeheartedly seeks.

But he does well to not give in to that feeling so completely. If he relents, by even the smallest of margins, he may find himself out of contention. Athen will not cede to Lyosan's desires. Lyosan must fight for them.

Athen comes out on the attack. A flurry of strikes and jabs come at Lyosan, and he manages them fairly well. At times, Athen seems to gain a small advantage, but Lyosan is quick to take it away. As hard as he tries, Lyosan cannot find a place to attack. Athen is as quick as he is careful. He never leaves himself open for long. Whenever he opens up, he seems to be closing off just as quickly.

The duel goes for several minutes with neither gaining ground. Having survived the first wave of attacks, Lyosan looks to go on the offensive, but his attacks are easily blocked by Athen. Not wanting another marathon, Athen turns back to an assault as Lyosan backs away. In this moment, Lyosan surrenders a major point as Athen catches him off guard. Lyosan falls back as Athen comes at him hard. Only by leaping to another beam and putting some distance between them does Lyosan avoid further damage.

On the ground, Fallon does not like what he sees. Lyosan seems passive and only attacking in a safe manner. Athen will not be beaten by care and patience. Lyosan will have to force the issue and soon.

Unfortunately, Lyosan does not seem willing to do so. He stays back on his heels and lets Athen come at him. In his mind, he feels Athen will give him an opening if Lyosan only looks for it, but the longer the match goes, the more Lyosan realizes it isn't so. As Fallon already knows, Lyosan must risk much if he is to defeat Athen.

With hope in his heart, Lyosan prepares for a risky assault. He will leave himself open several times, and if Athen catches him, it could bring an end to the match. With sword at the ready, Lyosan comes in with his shield down. Athen jabs at Lyosan's open side. Side-stepping the blade, Lyosan strikes with his own sword. With his feet at the very edge of the beam, Lyosan cannot put much force behind his blow. Athen blocks with his shield, and Lyosan attempts to knock him back with his own shield. Athen absorbs much of the blow and keeps his balance. To Lyosan's dismay, Athen recovers quickly and launches a counterstrike. While having to regain his footing, Lyosan struggles to defend against Athen's assault. It looks as if the risk may cost him too dearly.

Lyosan manages to withstand the attack with a few well-timed strikes and a lucky guess here and there. Athen comes away shocked he did not even manage to knock Lyosan's shield away, and the two are still evenly matched.

Where his failure might have stifled Lyosan in the past, here it only inspires him to try again. Having risked and not lost, he hopes he can do so again. Leading with his shield this time, Lyosan comes at Athen low. Athen meets him, and the two trade shoves. As they grapple, Lyosan prepares to make his move. After one of his pushes, Lyosan prepares to step back and let Athen fall forward. Then, he should be able to go at Athen from a position of strength. However, as Athen comes forward and stumbles,

Lyosan tries to step on Athen's shield and pin it to the post. He does not get enough of his foot on the shield, so Athen manages to pull it free and go on the attack. When the dust settles, Lyosan loses his shield, and Athen gains a large advantage.

But Lyosan will not accept defeat. Athen presses his advantage, and Lyosan fights him off. Perhaps acting too boldly with his advantage, Athen focuses more on the attack than his own defense. Though he backs Lyosan to a corner post, Athen cannot get Lyosan to yield. As the assault continues, Lyosan begins to see a possible way back into the match. If he can time it just right and survive the blow he might take, Lyosan may turn the tables. As Athen strikes with his sword, Lyosan ducks down rather than block with his own blade. Athen's sword connects with the post and digs into the wood a few inches. It sticks there instead of coming free cleanly. In the meantime, Athen comes in with the shield and gives Lyosan a blow. Knocked off-balance, Lyosan falls against the post. He manages to keep his sword. As Athen strains to free his blade, Lyosan rises and puts a shoulder in Athen's chest. It drives Athen back, and he is forced to let go of his sword. Lyosan does not have an advantage, but he has evened things up again.

Athen's sword remains imbedded in the corner post behind Lyosan. With his shield raised, Athen devises a plan to get his weapon back. He is not beaten with just a shield, but it is difficult to attack with only a shield. He is prepared to do so, but only as a last resort. When it becomes clear Lyosan will not give him a chance to regain his sword, Athen comes with the shield. Trying to jar Lyosan from his sword, Athen jabs with his shield and tries to make hard contact. He must also be ready to deflect any strikes Lyosan makes with his sword. Laying back in defense will have a larger benefit for Lyosan now. The more Athen lashes out with his shield, the more energy he expends. So long as Lyosan can keep Athen from his sword, he should be able to outlast his opponent.

After several minutes, the wear on Athen begins to show. He cannot move his bulky shield with the same precision and force as he did. His sword still remains a world away, and he cannot hope to reclaim it. Lyosan still has a fair amount of energy, but he does not want this to last any longer than it must. Going early and often, he attacks Athen and forces him to expel even more energy in his own defense. Eventually, Athen expends too much. After an attack from Lyosan, Athen mishandles the shield and

Lyosan jumps in. With the tip of his sword at Athen's throat, Lyosan forces a submission, and the match ends. Lyosan jumps with joy at his victory, and Athen raises Lyosan's hand as a sign of respect.

Once down from the square, Pythyn and Brynnal go up to have their duel. After two longer duels, they need to ensure they get the others done in a timely fashion. Lyosan, however, could care less for the duels yet to happen. He merely revels in the victory over Athen. After a quick drink, he returns to the arena to watch the remaining duels. When he comes back, Pythyn has already forced Brynnal to abandon his shield. Brynnal does not appear worried and not at any great disadvantage. Fallon echoes as much.

"Brynnal has to be one of the few participants who prefers to battle without a shield," he says. "When he has a shield, he seems hindered. Now, he seems free, able to move and react better."

Truly, Brynnal does battle with a skip in his step without his shield. He bounces around on the square, which gives added benefit given the cold of the day. He stays loose whereas Pythyn seems to be tightening up. Of course, with Pythyn, tightening up could be a sign he is preparing to attack.

Brynnal is smart enough not to wait to find out. Going on the offensive, he works Pythyn's shield away from him and evens the score. Parted from his shield, Pythyn starts to loosen up a bit as well, and the match becomes an exquisite exhibition of swordplay. They go back and forth with neither giving up an inch. If Lyosan and Fallon were not already so against Pythyn, they might be willing to celebrate the display. Instead, they merely hope Brynnal can keep it up.

Alas, he cannot. After several minutes, Brynnal begins to break down, and Pythyn moves in for the kill. In a few strokes, he disarms Brynnal, and moments later, the duel ends. Brynnal yields, and Pythyn pumps a fist in victory. Again, boos ring out from certain parts of the crowd, but Pythyn ignores them. He has what he wants. He cares nothing for how others feel about it.

Though disappointed, Lyosan and Fallon cannot linger on what might have been. Instead, they need to focus because Lyosan will be facing the winner of the last duel of the day. Stefen and Hathir take their positions, and the duel begins. From the beginning, Hathir looks to be out of his depth. Stefen attacks early and gets Hathir on his heels. Hathir tries to hold his own, but he simply cannot. He loses his shield early and hangs on for a few more minutes. The only interesting part of the match comes when

Hathir tries a desperate attack and his blade catches Stefen in the arm. It seems to be a minor injury as Stefen continues his attack, eventually disarming and defeating Hathir. When he comes down from the platform, medics attend to him, but again, the injury seems minor. It could still be significant considering Stefen will have to duel again tomorrow. Any injury, especially when high on the beam, can be costly.

"He is fortunate it is his shield arm," Fallon comments.

"Won't it make it difficult to wield the shield?" Lyosan asks.

"Perhaps a bit," Fallon replies, "but what is more he will be able to protect it easier. His arm will remain hidden behind the shield. He will only have to worry about it when you take the shield away from him."

Jonas announces the four remaining youths will be needed at the arena in the afternoon again. Pythyn and Nycolas will fight first, and Lyosan and Stefen will be second. Since the action has come to an end for the day, Lyosan and the others go home. A warm meal and fire at home help him recover from the day. He turns in early and sleeps well.

The next day, he goes to the castle with Fallon, his brothers, Faith, and Sarin. Little is said on the walk. They realize how important the day is and how much focus Lyosan must retain. When they arrive, Lyosan goes through the usual festivities. The four stand with the king, but Stefen does not look to be at his best. It is a fortunate turn for Lyosan, but he would rather face his opponents at their best. Something about this circumstance seems to be cheapening his claim.

Fallon, however, refuses to let Lyosan see the down side in this occurrence. Stefen is still a dangerous competitor, and if Lyosan feels the slightest bit sorry for him, Stefen will be able to take advantage.

First, they must watch the duel between Nycolas and Pythyn. Jonas announces the boys and begins the match. Both are aggressive from the outset, and though the duel has a quick pace, it seems the duel will not go quickly. Despite the battles each have gone through in the last four days, they look spry and ready to settle in for a long battle. While they duel, one of the royal guards approaches Fallon and Lyosan.

"The king requests you come to him, Fallon," the guard says.

"I will come," Fallon replies. "May I inquire as to the situation?"

"I cannot help you," the guard replies. "I was only bid to find you."

Fallon nods and leaves his spot. Steel fills Fallon's spot, and the two brothers converse during the duel. The duel does carry on for some time, but the result is exactly what Lyosan did not want to see. Pythyn gets Nycolas off-balance to the point where he cannot stay on the beam, and he falls to the hay. Pythyn lets out a cry in celebration. He will get the opportunity to duel for the crown. It is only a matter of whom he will face.

Once Pythyn leaves the platform, Jonas announces there will be a delay before the next match. He does not give a reason but suggests the crowd take the opportunity to procure a drink and walk around a bit. Lyosan takes his brothers to get a drink, and he also hopes to find out what has happened to Fallon. He has not returned since the guard came, and Lyosan would not like to duel without Fallon in his corner. As they walk about, Lyosan looks for his friend. He turns to the royal box, but the king is not there. Crystalynn is. She looks as beautiful as ever, and she smiles when she sees Lyosan. He smiles back, but he cannot completely hide his concern. Though she might wish to, she cannot console him now.

As he looks in the crowd, Lyosan finds himself face to face with Jonas, who does not look pleased. He rarely does, but here, he seems offended somehow.

"What are you doing?" Jonas asks.

"Looking for Fallon," Lyosan replies.

"You will see him soon enough," Jonas responds. "I suggest you focus on the duel you're about to have."

Jonas rushes Lyosan back to the arena. Apparently, they are ready to begin. Somehow, Lyosan missed the call to return. After one last look for Fallon, Lyosan sighs and ascends the ladder. When he reaches the top, he sees Stefen across from him with his back turned.

At least, he assumes it's Stefen. Something does not entirely feel right about all this. Once more, he looks down to his side. Sarin and Faith have a look of concern on their faces which Lyosan cannot understand. Before he can question it further, he hears Jonas.

"Ladies and gentleman, our princess and king! Our next duel, which will narrow our field to the only other youth to vie for the crown, is between Lyosan Nargin…" Jonas pauses a moment to let the crowd cheer. "…and Fallon Welms!" Again, the crowd cheers, some of them with great vigor. After all he has done for the kingdom, many feel it only right he be given this chance. Those who know him, however, know this is not what he wanted at all. "It is with the greatest regret," continues Jonas when the crowd dies down, "I announce Stefen Greyley will be unable to continue in the field. His wound from his previous match was much greater than realized. However, as decreed by King Cyrus upon Fallon's return from Jorram, he can take the place of a participant who cannot continue. A luxury afforded to him now." Jonas then turns to the duelists. "Let the duel…begin!"

Fallon turns and faces Lyosan. There is a look of disappointment on his face which Lyosan must show as well. Neither wanted Fallon to enter the duel in this fashion. He was only to fight if Pythyn was about to win the crown. He was a safety, a last resort. Every time Lyosan seems to get a break, something else comes to take it away. How are they to proceed? If Fallon does not believe Lyosan can win against Pythyn, he must try to beat Lyosan now. But if he does so, he will end his life with Faith.

"Do not lose your edge," Fallon warns. "You will need it."

Lyosan is not sure how to respond. This is not a sparring match in a training room, nor is it a playful jaunt in the fields of their youth. There are consequences here – dire perhaps.

"I do not expect you to go easy on me," Lyosan replies.

"That is good," Fallon says, "for I will not!"

Moving on to the same beam, the two face each other. Each raises his sword to his face. Once they are ready, they come at one another.

Fallon comes fresh and hard. Lyosan fights him off, but it takes a lot to do so. After his onslaught, Fallon backs away. It is typical of his style. He strikes, retreats, and strikes. It is a style only a few can master. Giving one's opponent a chance to recover can be foolish, but with Fallon, it only incites fear.

Lyosan, after seeing it so many times, will not let the fear take him. He must remain on point and ready for Fallon's next attack. Before it comes, Fallon has more words for him.

"We all agreed Pythyn would not be king," he says.

"I remember," Lyosan says.

"I know you love the princess dearly, but how can I step aside if you cannot beat Pythyn?"

As the question lingers in the air, Fallon steps to attack. Anticipating the move, Lyosan launches forward and attacks first. Fallon is initially surprised, but he recovers easily enough and sends Lyosan reeling after a shot from his shield. As Lyosan falls back, he quickly regains his footing.

"I can beat Pythyn," he proclaims.

"So sure of that, are you?" Fallon asks and then strikes.

Lyosan blocks and defends and gives Fallon a shot of his own. Fallon falls back a bit but regains his footing as well.

"I am!" Lyosan replies.

With a coy smile, Fallon resets himself. "Let's find out."

Coming at him with his absolute best, Fallon does everything he can to rattle his friend. Though the attack is vicious and leaves Lyosan vulnerable for moments, Lyosan never believes himself to be in a position to fail. He counters Fallon at every turn and when Fallon manages to separate Lyosan from his shield, Lyosan does the same only a moment later.

After going at one another for several minutes, Fallon backs away and each combatant takes a moment to recover. In Lyosan's eyes, Fallon sees a fierceness he has never before seen in his friend. There is a determination, a refusal to lose which Lyosan has been lacking all his days. Lyosan has always been a competitor. He has come a long way. Now, he may be at the peak of his abilities. He may be ready to become the king.

With this realization, Fallon remembers the other promise he made to Shaylynn. He would make certain Lyosan was to be named king. Fallon has trained him, pushed him, and now tested him. It is time to let fate take its course. With a smile, Fallon stands and lowers his arms. Lyosan looks at him with confusion. Again, Fallon raises his sword to his chest. Before Lyosan can respond and without another word, Fallon leaps from the beam and down to the hay below.

Lyosan looks to see his friend fall and hears the gasps of shock from the crowd. Regardless of what they think of this unexpected turn of events, Lyosan finds himself in the champion's match. He will vie for the crown against Pythyn.

When Lyosan is announced the winner, a roar rings out from the crowd. Though many would not have expected it, Lyosan has become the people's choice for king. He and his friends are not the only ones who feel disdain for Pythyn. Most in the crowd would see any of the youths in the tournament be named king over Pythyn. If Lyosan is the one to stand against him, he will have all the good will the people can afford. As the crowd calms, Jonas steps forward and announces the final duel of the tournament will take place the next day at three in the afternoon. The king congratulates Lyosan and Pythyn and states his excitement at naming his heir in little more than one day's time.

Though many see Fallon's actions as loyal, not all are willing to concede it was the proper course of action. For some, it is a point of outrage. Where others battled and bled for their chance to compete, Fallon all but ignored his and gave Lyosan his place in the final round. Mitan will not be shy about confronting Fallon for his actions.

"Does the crown mean so little to you?" he asks having grabbed Fallon by the sleeve.

"Watch your tongue, Mitan," Fallon responds. "I do what I do out of love for the crown."

"You have all but given it to Pythyn," Mitan scolds. It matters not to him that Lyosan is nearby. In fact, he probably means for Lyosan to hear him. "How would our captain have felt about that?"

Now Sarin, who also stands nearby, steps forward as she will not have Fallon spoken to this way or Shaylynn's name used in such a way. "If you knew your captain at all," she says, "you would know he intended for Lyosan to be king. He did not seek it for himself."

"But always he would protect it," Mitan replies. "You had the chance to do so, Fallon. You could've protected the crown from Pythyn. Instead, you put our hopes in his hands." Mitan motions to Lyosan as he finishes.

"Careful how you speak of your future king," Fallon warns.

Mitan frowns and shakes his head. "He is not my king," Mitan says as he turns away. "Nor will he be a king."

Mitan storms off, and the group remains silent until he is gone. Once he has left, Fallon turns to Lyosan.

"He is a fool," Fallon says. "Do not listen to him."

"He fears what Pythyn might do," Faith adds. "It is the only reason he says what he does."

"He thinks he could've beaten me," Lyosan says. "That is why he says what he does."

"He underestimates you then," Fallon says, "as so many of them have. As Pythyn still does. Only those few who have stood on that beam against you realize how far you have come. You will show the rest tomorrow when you become king."

While Shaylynn was always willing to talk boldly about his faith in Lyosan, Fallon has never been so forward. Lyosan cannot help but be taken aback by this.

"Have you always believed in me so strongly?" he asks.

"No," Fallon admits. "I have not." He pauses as he fights back his own shame. "That is difficult for me to admit because Shaylynn always told me I should not doubt you. But I did. So, I say this to you, my friend, no more. I will never doubt what you are capable of doing."

CHAPTER XXII

They all part ways for the day. It is difficult for Lyosan to sleep, but he eventually does find peace. When he wakes, he goes to the breakfast table and finds his entire family waiting for him. They set the table and put his meal in front of him. They say little. Every one of them realizes how drastically their lives might change because of this day. They would not dare add any pressure to the load which already weighs on Lyosan's shoulders. As he has been doing lately, Lyosan eats quickly. In his heart, he would wish to ask his mother to attend the tournament, but he knows what she will say. The action, though quite different in nature, would only remind her of Armous. She can have nothing to do with the dealings of knights and soldiers. It is a world which has already taken too much.

A knock at the door comes as Lyosan finishes eating. He goes to the door, expecting Fallon to be there, ready to discuss the upcoming duel. While Fallon is at the door, there is someone else with him – someone Lyosan undoubtedly did not expect to see. With Fallon's hand resting on his shoulder, Daylynn stands with a concerned look on his face. He seems to have grown since Lyosan last saw him. Or it could be a result of the sorrow of Shaylynn's loss no longer plaguing him.

"I am glad to see you," Lyosan says extending a hand.

Daylynn takes it, then draws in to Lyosan to embrace him. Lyosan holds him tightly for a moment, then lets him go.

"Now that you are in the final match, I have a matter I wish to discuss with you," Daylynn explains.

"Certainly," Lyosan replies and bids his guests to enter.

Daylynn enters with Fallon close behind. They enter the kitchen. Elle, Steel, and Calvin welcome Daylynn and Fallon when they enter. Daylynn takes a chair, and Lyosan sits across from him. Elle offers Daylynn some food, but having eaten already, he declines politely. He does ask for a glass of water which Elle is happy to get for him. After taking a drink, he looks at Lyosan and begins his discussion.

"Shay believed you would become king someday," Daylynn begins, "and now, it appears he will be proven right. Since you will take the throne and come into a great deal of power, I would ask some considerations for mother and me."

Before Lyosan can assure Daylynn of anything, Daylynn explains himself further.

"When father and Bey died, there was a great strain put on us," he says, "but I always believed Shay would be enough to make sure we got by. But now that he's died, I fear we will not have enough to make it. I would do all I can to provide, but I am quite sure I cannot fill Shay's shoes."

"A sentiment we all know," Lyosan says, finally cutting Daylynn off. "Daylynn, you are dear to me, like family. Whether I am king or not, I will do what I can for you and your family. We all will."

Daylynn looks around to all the faces present, and they tell the same thing – they will look out for Daylynn and Kandessa. Though they have lost so much in family, there are a great many things they will never be without.

With his fears at ease, Daylynn becomes overcome by his own emotions. Tears begin to form in his eyes, and he is not sure what to do. Just before he loses his composure, he turns to Fallon.

"I miss him so much!" he cries.

Fallon wraps his arms around the boy, and Daylynn digs into Fallon's chest. For a few minutes, he cries hard. Lyosan comes over and places a hand on Daylynn's head. When Daylynn stops crying, he thanks Lyosan and the others. Fallon offers to walk him home, and Daylynn accepts. Lyosan walks them out, and as they leave, Lyosan sees Crystalynn walking towards the house. Seeing her as well, Fallon and Daylynn bow to the princess. She can tell Daylynn has been crying and goes to him immediately. They converse briefly, and Daylynn assures her he is okay. Still, she watches him carefully as he walks away with Fallon next to him.

Long moments of silence ensue after Fallon and Daylynn leave. Though Lyosan is certain the princess has come for other reasons, he will not break the silence and inquire as to why she is here. Instead, he will simply enjoy her company. When they were younger, she would at times come to his house for a moment of silence. The business of the castle was too much for her and she sought quieter places. If that is what she seeks now, it may be the last time his house can offer such accommodations. Once the tournament ends, so much will change. There is no telling how the day may alter their fortunes.

But Crystalynn is not thinking about such matters. Her mind still rests on the boy who left with Fallon. Because the tournament needed to continue and the matter of who would be king must be settled, she could not express her sympathies to Shaylynn's family as she desired. After all he had done for her, Crystalynn wanted to be there for Shaylynn's family as they suffered through another loss. This one in particular. Yes, she did not cause Shaylynn to fall from the castle wall, but he only acted to defend her honor. Had she acted differently that night, his actions may not have been needed.

"I cannot bring myself to go to his house," Crystalynn admits.

"Nor I," Lyosan admits. "Fallon goes. He tells me not to worry, everything is going well with them. I think he tries to stop me from feeling guilty."

"Then I need him to say the same to me," Crystalynn says.

"For the record, it does not work," Lyosan says with a smile.

She appreciates his attempt to pacify her, but she is not ready to feel consoled. For her, there is only one thing which will rectify Shaylynn's death, and Lyosan will give it to her when he wins today.

"You will avenge him," she says, a strong level of certainty in her tone.

"I mean to," Lyosan replies.

She takes her eyes off the road and places them on Lyosan. It is different for Lyosan, to have her look at him knowing she loves him. There is something there which makes his heart leap. To have seen that look one time would be enough to last a lifetime, but he may soon live, getting to see the look in her eyes all his life.

There is something else there as well. Their love, so new and unexplored, is not assured to be able to grow. An obstacle stands in their way, and though each believes Lyosan can overcome Pythyn, his victory, like all matters in the future, is not guaranteed.

"I am afraid," Crystalynn says, as if to answer Lyosan's unasked question.

"What can I do to alleviate it?" Lyosan asks.

"As long as my life hangs in the balance, you can do nothing," she replies. "Until I know whether I will marry you or Pythyn, I will not have peace."

It is terrible to feel helpless to help the one you love. You always hope to defend yourself; you always demand to defend those you care about. Since he can do nothing else, Lyosan takes Crystalynn's hand and holds it in his own. For a long time, they stand in silence, holding hands. When Fallon returns, they have still said nothing more to each other. Crystalynn asks about Daylynn, and Fallon assures her he will be fine. They exchange some pleasantries and laugh a few times. It is nice to be able to have these moments with friends in such tense times.

Eventually, the time comes for the princess to return to the castle. Preparations for the duel will begin soon. Though Lyosan and Fallon do not know it, Cyrus has something special planned. Making it happen will take some doing. Cyrus will want her by his side to ensure the plan comes to fruition. She gives Lyosan a kiss for luck and one for love before she goes. After she leaves, Fallon and Lyosan train with some light exercises. As they spend the morning outside, they see storm clouds come and fill the sky.

When the time for the duel arrives, there has already been a steady rain, and it does not seem to be stopping anytime soon. This changes the strategy of the duel greatly. The beams will be slick and hard to move on. Holding on to sword and shield will also be more difficult. Should the rain pick up, it may affect the eyesight of the duelists. It is a grittier fight in the rain, but the king will not stop it. The man who can master the duel in the rain only strengthens his claim as king.

The rains do not stop the crowds from attending. They fill the main arena and not a seat goes unfilled. On his side, Lyosan finds all his friends and family. To his shock, he discovers his mother has come to the duel. He goes to her and kisses her. Steel and Calvin hug him as they surround their mother. As Lyosan goes to face the king, Mitan steps in his way.

"I was wrong to doubt you," he says.

"You were thinking of the crown," Lyosan says. "I cannot fault you for that."

"I should have been thinking of him whom I thought king," Mitan replies. "If he would have you as king instead of him, then so must I."

"Thank you, my friend."

They embrace, and Lyosan steps forward. Joining Pythyn in front of the king's box, Lyosan readies himself for the match. It has been a number of days since Lyosan has been this close to Pythyn. A part of him would fight Pythyn in this instant, but the rest of him knows he gains nothing by losing his composure. He cannot dishonor the tournament, his family, and the king by giving in to his hatred now. The time will come to unleash his fury. He will wait until that time comes.

Through the raindrops, Lyosan watches as King Cyrus rises from his throne and bids the crowd to quiet. They acquiesce immediately. With a beaming smile, Cyrus looks down at the two remaining combatants and around at the crowd which has gathered.

"My people," he begins, "this is hardly the weather befitting the business we mean to end this day. For, to be named king is a call for celebration and delight. It is an honor to be chosen by a higher power to rule over such well-meaning men and women as it has been my honor to rule over you. Sadly, some day – someday soon – my time as king will end. My sister will become your queen, and one of these fine youths will marry her and become king. It is a calling for only one.

"For that reason, there is some benefit to this rain. It will provide the final test. It will set apart one from all the others who attempted to reach this moment. Verti-dueling is the sport of our people. It is how we define greatness in our knights. Today, it is how we will decide a king."

The crowd lets out a small cheer, but they also realize Cyrus is not done with his speech. After a few seconds, they quiet again and Cyrus continues.

"Now, I am not blind to the sentiment of many who dwell in this city. Indeed, my own heart wonders if we may be witnessing a different match had fate not been so cruel. For there was one who dwelled among us, perhaps the greatest to never be king, whom I gave the opportunity to challenge the winner of this tournament. He was truly a skilled swordsman, a leader among men, and held wisdom beyond his years. He was also quite brash and was not shy in saying he would not vie for the throne.

"It saddens me we will never know if that is true. As a show of my respect and love for this youth, I have asked his mother and brother to sit with me for this final duel..." The crowd begins to stir a bit. This news is surprising. Cyrus holds up his arms to calm them. "…I know I ask a great deal of them, but I also feel it necessary for them to feel the love we feel for them. To remind them, they will never be far from our thoughts, and to let them know we will always be there for them…" Applause comes from the crowd. Cyrus lets them clap as he continues, "…I present to you, Kandessa and Daylynn Storm."

Kandessa and Daylynn come from behind a curtain and step to the front of the box. The crowd stands and applauds them, as does the princess. Kandessa acknowledges their love, but she will not look at the boy who took her son's life. Instead, she smiles and holds her son. Daylynn smiles as well, though his smile looks more forced and insincere. He holds his mother tight and seems to want to be out of the spotlight. After a few minutes, Cyrus offers them a seat, and they step away from the crowd.

"I am also pleased," Cyrus says, "to draw our attention to the dueling square."

As the crowd turns, they see what Cyrus would draw them to. Some additions have been made to the square. At the tops of the corner posts, two beams stretch out over the gap in the square to form an X. In the center of the X, a short rope protrudes from the wood and tied to the rope is a sword.

"In honor of our fallen brother," Cyrus announces, "I have asked for his sword and placed it above the dueling square. May it stand as a reminder to us all of the qualities and characteristics we hope to find in ourselves. May it remind us of Shaylynn Storm!"

A loud cry rings out among the crowd. For several minutes, they stand and cheer. Fallon holds Faith tight, and Faith holds on to Sarin's hand. It is far more than they would have expected a king to do.

Having said his piece, Cyrus steps back and Jonas comes forward. When the crowd finally quiets, Jonas begins.

"Ladies and gentlemen, honored guests, my lady and king! We gather today to honor all those fallen in battle and in this tournament. We honor all those who came before us in this great kingdom and all those who will come after. We prepare to name the next heir to the throne, which will signal a great change in our history. A new bloodline will rise to claim the throne of Artonia.

"Of all who would be deemed worthy, these two stand! In one corner, we have Pythyn Ornol!" Boos ring out among the crowd. Cyrus stands to stop them, but they continue for a short period. When they die down, Jonas continues. "And in the other, Lyosan Nargin!" Now, a chorus of cheers comes from the crowd.

The two bow to the king, then turn and face the crowd. After exchanging a hand, they go to their respective sides and prepare to ascend. Before they go up, Lyosan talks with Fallon.

"Of all the things I might say to you, I choose only one, my friend," Fallon says.

Lyosan waits for his friend to speak again.

"All you have done honors our brother. Now, finish what you have started."

After a nod, Lyosan embraces Fallon, and the two embrace hard. When they separate, Lyosan looks to the princess and smiles. She smiles back, though her nerves still have some power over her. Though he may not like seeing her this scared, it may provide some extra motivation for Lyosan. When he slays this dragon, she will never again need be so afraid.

Slowly, he climbs the ladder with sword and shield. The rain makes the shield heavy, but he will not let it bother him. As he reaches the top, he takes his place on the beam. Looking up, he sees the one man he had always wished he'd never face. Now, he would have it no other way. He will avenge Shaylynn. He will right the wrong Pythyn performed. He will become king over his greatest foe.

"Let the duel begin!" Jonas calls.

Pythyn and Lyosan both take a moment to get a feel for the beams in the rain. Though the rain is steady, it does not impede them as of yet. Once they familiarize themselves with their elements, they begin the duel.

Letting Pythyn close the gap, Lyosan remains on his beam as Pythyn walks around the square. He does not come quickly or rashly. Rather, Pythyn merely brings himself to an attacking position. Shield at the ready, Lyosan puts himself in position and awaits the first attack.

"I will never apologize for what I did to Shaylynn," Pythyn says.

"I would not expect you to," Lyosan responds.

"He stepped in where he did not belong," Pythyn explains. "This fight, for the crown and the princess, is between you and I. Maybe I could not accept that at first, but I do now. It was always you and I, Lyosan. Now, it will be."

"You think you can choose who stands between you and what you want?" Lyosan asks. "You are a fool! You say this now because you are still so certain you can defeat me! You feared him. You still do. But I will show you why you are wrong."

"Then, do so."

Pythyn begins his assault with a series of strikes with his sword. They are fast and powerful and put Lyosan on his heels. Soon, Lyosan finds himself against the corner post, trying to fend off Pythyn's advances. Pythyn is so fast, he leaves only the slightest moments to counter. Lyosan manages to catch one of these moments and catches Pythyn with the brunt of his shield. Pythyn falls back, perhaps more so because of the rain. Either way, it gives Lyosan a chance to recoup and forces Pythyn to yield in his assault. After a quick moment, Pythyn regains his focus and comes in to strike again. This time, Lyosan mounts a stronger defense, but it costs him. Lyosan leaves himself more open to attacks, and Pythyn manages to cut Lyosan on his leg. The sting of the blade weakens Lyosan's stance, and he must retreat for a moment. Only Pythyn does not give him much time to recover. Still working hard to fend Pythyn off, Lyosan favors his injured leg as he goes. In seeing the blood, Pythyn becomes determined to end the duel quickly, but he leaves himself vulnerable in the process.

With as much strength as he can muster, Lyosan raises his shield and launches himself at Pythyn. It is a risky venture, but given Pythyn's aggressiveness, it has a high chance of succeeding. Indeed, as Pythyn raises his sword and begins to bring it down, Lyosan connects with Pythyn's chest and sends him back. The blow rattles Pythyn, and he loses his grip on his sword. He drops the blade, but it does not fall off the square. Unaware of his pending advantage, Lyosan gets up and steps back, assuming Pythyn will be ready to counter. Instead, he sees Pythyn scrambling to the beam to retrieve his sword. Though Lyosan cannot stop Pythyn from picking up the sword, he can take advantage of Pythyn's position. With an overhead slice, Lyosan comes down on Pythyn. Pythyn manages to get his sword and block Lyosan's strike with the blade of his sword. However, he must put both hands on the blade to keep Lyosan from causing severe damage.

Feeling he could end the match, Lyosan grips his sword with both hands and presses down against Pythyn, but he can gain no ground. The more he presses, the more Pythyn finds his place in the duel again. Lyosan is trying too hard to end the duel where the duel cannot be won. After giving Lyosan a false sense of progress by lowering his blade the slightest bit, Pythyn lashes out and pushes Lyosan away. Once he gets a bit of distance, he strikes with his shield and catches Lyosan above the eye. Lyosan falls back and almost loses his shield. As Pythyn gets to his feet, Lyosan scrambles to his. The two trade blows and blocks for several minutes. Each blow brings Pythyn closer to victory as the injury to Lyosan's leg and the blow to his head are taking their toll. And as Lyosan weakens, Pythyn strengthens.

From the ground, everyone sees what is happening. Fallon stands and steps towards the dueling structure. He cannot get too close – he knows – but he cannot merely sit and watch his friend endure this. Sarin and Faith watch with bated breath. Steel and Calvin clutch their mother's hands while Elle prays for her son to be okay. Perhaps worst of all is Crystalynn. She sees her only chance for a happy life disappearing in front of her eyes. As Lyosan falls, her hope fades.

While Pythyn sees victory at hand, Lyosan sees only the end of the first battle of a great war. Pythyn has the early advantage, but Lyosan can take it back in an instant. But when will that instant come?

After waiting for a chance, Lyosan decides to make his own occur. Relying on his sword to defend himself, Lyosan goes back to utilizing his shield. Putting it in front of him, he blocks the blows from Pythyn's sword and starts to recover from the onslaught. Realizing Lyosan is trying to hide behind his shield, Pythyn gives a blast from his shield. Lyosan falls back, but he does not give much ground. Instead, he strikes out with his sword raised over his head. It is a futile attempt as Pythyn catches Lyosan at the peak of his attack and shoves him down. While he's down, Pythyn knocks Lyosan's shield away.

As it clangs to the ground, Lyosan stumbles away and manages to get onto a different beam. Sword raised, he manages to keep Pythyn at bay for a few minutes while he tries to devise a new plan. Without his shield, he will have to rely on his sword to do everything. He has managed to do so before, but against Pythyn, it will be a far different affair.

Eventually, Pythyn works himself over to the same beam as Lyosan. Looking to press his advantage, Pythyn comes at him. Rather than give Pythyn a chance to finish him off, Lyosan comes on the attack. The suddenness and unexpectedness of the attack gives Lyosan a distinct advantage, and as Pythyn reels from the assault, he exposes his shield. Lyosan goes for it immediately and cuts Pythyn's arm. The cut causes

Pythyn to drop his shield, and the two find themselves even again. Now, Pythyn looks for a moment to recover and fends off the attack from Lyosan.

On the ground, hope is restored. Fallon cries out in joy. Everyone who desires to see Lyosan win takes a deep breath and hopes the end will come now. Tears come to Crystalynn's eyes, a mixture of the despair she had felt and the happiness in her hopes restored. But the match is not over.

In fact, it is about to take another turn. Seeing another chance to end the duel, Lyosan comes at Pythyn hard. Though it seems he has Pythyn on the edge, Pythyn is only setting his opponent up. After seemingly knocking Pythyn's hands back, Lyosan winds up for a finishing blow. Lying in wait, Pythyn punches with his weapon and hits Lyosan in the face with the hilt of his sword. Lyosan falls back having taken another blow to the head. Lying on the beam, he finds himself in the same position Pythyn had been in. Pythyn is on top of him, trying to press his blade into Lyosan. Only Lyosan's sword is keeping him from doing so, but Pythyn is stronger and gaining ground.

"Yield!" he demands.

"No," Lyosan responds.

"You cannot win!" Pythyn tells him. "For your desire and love for the princess, you cannot beat someone superior to you."

"You are many things, but my superior is not one of them!"

With a strong head butt, Lyosan gets Pythyn off him, but there is a cost. Another blow to the head, even one of his own doing, rattles Lyosan. He cannot fully recover from the blow. As he rises from the beam, Pythyn lets out a loud cry and swings wildly as he spins around. With all the force in him, he connects with Lyosan's sword and sends it flying away. The hearts of all who watch go dead.

Lyosan backs up against the corner post as Pythyn steps forward. With his blade out, pointed at Lyosan's chest, he breathes heavily. As the distance between the two combatants closes, Lyosan feels failure crush him. He will not be king. He will not marry the woman he loves. He will not avenge his friend. Worst of all, he will fail to keep the crown from his greatest foe. Letting Lyosan truly feel his failure, Pythyn stands before him for a few seconds, then stands tall and proud.

"Yield," he says.

Defeat seems inevitable. Lyosan has no weapon, no protection, and he has no training for this position. Everything logical in him tells him to yield and end the terror. And yet, something else bids him continue. Somehow, someway, there is still a chance he can win this duel. If he can just bide his time, it will present itself. He is certain.

"No," he replies.

Pythyn cannot comprehend this. He has disarmed his opponent. Even now, Lyosan sits in a place of weakness. His leg is cut; his head must be pounding. He cannot expect to claim victory from the jaws of defeat?

"What do you mean no?" Pythyn asks.

Lyosan smiles. "I mean no. I do not yield."

"Would you have me kill you too?" Pythyn asks.

"If you think you can," Lyosan replies.

"Oh, I can!"

Raising his sword high, Pythyn prepares to deliver the killing blow. From below, Lyosan can hear people crying out for him to stop, but he cannot. He will be king, or he will be dead. As Pythyn brings his blade to its highest point, Lyosan's luck begins to win out. A gust of wind blows hard, and rain floods into Pythyn's eyes. He stumbles a bit, and Lyosan charges in. Tackling him to the beam, Lyosan tries to knock Pythyn's sword away, but Pythyn will not be so easily disarmed. Instead, he punches Lyosan in the stomach and flips Lyosan off him. Lying on the beam once again, Lyosan looks up to see Pythyn step above him. Looking away, Lyosan sees Shaylynn's sword hanging above him. If he could only get to it, he could even the score, but how could he get to it?

Even more concerning, Pythyn is preparing for another attack. "You may have drawn this out, Lyosan, but you cannot any longer."

What transpires next will someday be the greatest legend of the land. For, from the jaws of defeat, victory will come. Pythyn raises his blade and prepares for the final blow. Just before he brings his blade down, a bolt of lightning strikes Shaylynn's sword. The flash of light from the blade blinds Pythyn, the clap of thunder stuns his ears, and he stops his attack. Having a small window, Lyosan scrambles to his feet, somehow unaffected by the bolt, and runs down the beam. Somewhere in his mind, he hears a voice telling him he can reach the blade if he jumps. With all his strength, he jumps after the sword. Gasps rings out from below. Though the lightning caused many to look away, the others, including Crystalynn, see Lyosan's desperate leap. With the wind blowing the blade towards him, Lyosan manages to grab the hilt of the sword. Using the rope to swing towards the opposite beam, Lyosan prepares to finish his jump to the other side. By some miracle, the rope breaks just as Lyosan swings forward, and he flies to the opposite beam. After landing, he turns to see Pythyn staring in disbelief. In his own mind, Lyosan cannot believe what he has done. Looking down at the blade, Lyosan sees it still glowing from the strike of the lighting. Throughout his body, Lyosan feels a power flowing through him. His leg no longer hurts – nor does his head. His arms feel fresh, and his legs have new life in them. The rain ends. Light breaks through the clouds. Lyosan will have his day.

Wasting no time, he runs for Pythyn who can only raise his sword out of instinct. With greater speed and precision than he ever had, Lyosan attacks Pythyn with great vigor and purpose. Pythyn cannot defend himself any further, but he will not yield. Knowing this, Lyosan slaps Pythyn's blade away from his body and kicks Pythyn in the chest. The kick knocks Pythyn back to the corner post, and he cannot keep his balance. Crumpling down, he falls from the beam and crashes to the hay below.

The duel is over. Lyosan has won!

The celebration begins as soon as Lyosan reaches the ground. Crystalynn, waiting eagerly for him, leaps into his arms and kisses him. Taken aback a bit, Lyosan quickly recovers as the realization of his greatest dreams comes full circle. Amid the congratulatory slaps on the back, Lyosan basks in the glory of the moment fully believing his life could not get any better. He will ascend to the throne and marry the princess. His family will move from their cottage near the castle into the castle itself. Fallon will become his most trusted advisor and confidant. The sword he holds in his hands, the sword of a fallen friend, will become an heirloom and treasure of the kingdom. Surely, glorious days await him.

But there is one who would not have this day be a celebration. Pythyn, lying on the ground, has failed in his endeavor. What's more, he will never gain favor in the eyes of Lyosan. Lyosan knows Pythyn killed Shaylynn by shoving him off the castle wall. Though he will never condemn Pythyn for this death, Lyosan will ensure Pythyn never outlives the truth of the matter. His life is effectively over.

It cannot end this way for him. Perhaps he has fallen, but he does not have to be the only one who falls.

Reaching for a dagger, Pythyn waits for the moment to come. It would be simple to slip in and kill Lyosan, but Lyosan is not his target. What greater way to ruin Lyosan than by killing the woman he loves?

Darkness fills Pythyn's thoughts as the moment clears in his head. Lyosan may take the throne, but the royal bloodline will be broken. The entirety of the Wuhlfies's heritage will end with the stroke of his blade. If he must, Pythyn will live in infamy as the man who brought the end of a dynasty's reign.

As though it were fate, the crowd begins to open up. Cyrus is making his way to the battlefield. He will shake Lyosan's hand and congratulate him for his accomplishment. Before that can happen, Pythyn will have his opportunity.

Crystalynn is on Lyosan's arm merely a few feet away. The time has come. He can strike and strike now!

With a bloodcurdling howl, Pythyn rises from his spot and charges towards the princess. She does not see him at first though she hears the cry. When she turns to see him, it is far too late. He is a few steps away and none stand in his path. Lyosan cannot react fast enough. Though Fallon has drawn his blade, he will not be able to intervene. As Pythyn raises his arms to bring the blow upon her, there is a flash and all at once, his world goes black.

All who saw the flash shielded their eyes from its striking blindness. Thus, none truly saw what occurred. What many claim, and has thus been named as the truth, is a bolt of lightning cut through the crowd and struck Pythyn before he could attack. Giving credence to this story are the burn marks seen on Pythyn's chest. Whether it truly was lightning or not, the important matter is Pythyn lies dead on the ground immediately after the flash.

For several moments, none react. They can barely process the events which have transpired. Crystalynn and Lyosan hold each other tightly. Cyrus and Fallon gaze at the body of the would-be assassin. Only one looks away from the scene – Sarin. When others notice, they follow her eyes and see a sight none would believe possible if they did not see it with their own eyes – Shaylynn Storm.

But not Shaylynn as he was, Shaylynn as he should be. Healthy, alive, undaunted by the terrors and stresses of this world. More importantly, a Shaylynn bathed in the glory of glimmering light. Glowing, as an angel riding upon a mystical horse which glows the same. Once all are aware of his presence, the horse strides to the middle of the company where Crystalynn and Lyosan stand. Shaylynn, they could now see, clothed in a white robe, dismounts and steps towards his old friends. The light around him lessens, and he seems to be among the living again. Though they are happy to see him, they are not foolish enough to believe him back from the grave.

"How?" Crystalynn can only ask.

"One last glimpse," Shaylynn replies. "One last look at a world I currently hold no place in. A power I gained in Forleen Forest. It can only last for a few minutes, but I am glad I took the time to learn it."

Sarin walks forward and reaches out a hand. Shaylynn slowly reaches out and takes it. She takes his hand and holds it to her chest.

"You always have a place here," she says.

Shaylynn smiles. "And I shall be ever happy to dwell there, my love. And yet, there are journeys that await me which I cannot put off forever."

"You were supposed to share those journeys with me," Sarin says.

"If there were any way I could, I would. I fear I must disappoint you yet again."

"You have never disappointed me – only life has."

Taking him in her arms for what she fears is the last time, Sarin tries to memorize his feel. The strength in his arms. The warmth of his touch. She knows she will never be able to remember everything about him, but she will take as much as she can.

Kandessa and Daylynn charge through the crowd and stop when they see Shaylynn standing in front of them. Daylynn almost drops to the ground in shock, but Kandessa is quick to wrap her arms around him. There is so much they wish to say, but they doubt they have the time to say it all.

"Did they find you?" Kandessa asks holding back her tears.

"Yes," Shaylynn replies, "and they are well."

"Are they coming too?"

Shaylynn sadly shakes his head. "No mother, father and Beylynn are at rest. They wished to see…well, us, before they crossed over, but they were so far from home. We talk of you often. In the only way we can, we watch over you and Daylynn."

"Then, you will give my love to them when you see them next?"

"All except what I keep for myself," Shaylynn says with a smile.

Smiling herself, Kandessa hugs her son again and kisses him on the cheek. When she lets him go, she looks down at Daylynn, who grabs his mother and turns away from his brother.

"I don't want you to go!" Daylynn finally cries out.

Shaylynn drops to a knee and beckons his brother to him. Daylynn will not go at first, but Kandessa pries him away from her. When Daylynn looks at his brother again, the emotion overcomes him, and he charges into Shaylynn's arms. They embrace and hold each other for a long while. Shaylynn whispers things to his brother which bring great comfort to a sad child. Eventually, he makes Daylynn laugh and the two part. Shaylynn then goes to his mother and hugs her one last time.

Finally, he walks back to the new king of Artonia and his soon-to-be bride. Fallon stands with them, and Faith is at his side. Tears have already fallen from their eyes, and more will surely follow.

"My liege," Shaylynn says with a respectful bow.

Lyosan chokes up before he can get a word out. After a second, he manages a few words, "You made me better," he says. "I wish you to know that always."

Shaylynn smiles. "I merely showed you what was always there," he replies. "It was my privilege to do so. May your reign be blessed." Then, Shaylynn turns and addresses the princess. "My lady, I would hope you would consider this atonement for my failure in Jorram."

Crystalynn shakes her head. "Your actions in Jorram could never be considered a failure, my friend. Now, even in death, you hold your place as our kingdom's greatest knight."

Shaylynn bows again, out of respect. Then, he comes to Faith. She cries heavily as he stands in front of her. Shaylynn lifts her chin and tries to make her smile. He cannot. Rather than try to fix a wound which will not heal, he looks to Fallon. "Take care of him," he says to Faith. "I don't know what will become of him without me to guide him."

This does make Faith laugh. "You only led him into peril."

"That will be up to you, now."

As he comes to Fallon, Fallon salutes his fallen captain. The other knights in the courtyard stop and salute as well. Shaylynn scans the crowd for a moment before looking back at Fallon. He is greatly touched to be so highly regarded. He never took the time to as say as much before. Now, this is his last chance.

"I thank you all," he says to his brother knights. "You put your faith in me when I asked you to. You trusted me when you had no reason to."

The other knights thank him and step back. For all his life, Shaylynn was connected to Fallon. They must give them this last moment together.

"You were my brother," Fallon says. "The brother I never had, desperately needed, and always wanted."

Shaylynn clasps Fallon's shoulder. "You were always my brother as well. I'd have no other man protect this kingdom."

There is only Sarin left. Though she has already said goodbye, she will do so again if it is all fate will afford her.

"Do you remember the night you saved me in the river?" she asks.

"It is more dear to me than any other," he replies.

"I believed from that moment you would always be there to save my life and make it worth living," she explains. "I never thought I'd fail to save yours." She cracks at saying this and begins to cry. Shaylynn moves to her and holds her in his arms.

"You could have done nothing for this," Shaylynn assures her. "And you saved me more times than you can imagine. I merely abused the privilege too severely. I was not meant to dwell in this life long, but I am glad I shared as much of it as I could with you. And I will await you in the next life."

Sarin forces a smile as Shaylynn pulls away.

"You better," she says.

They reach for each other and share a passionate kiss. It stands as the kiss for so many things that will never come to be. It is the one moment they still have which will stand as the rest of their lives together. A lifetime to be lived in the warmth and love of a tender kiss.

When they pull away, reality strikes again. The fleeting joy retreats and sorrow fills its place. Shaylynn returns to his horse and mounts him. Before he can take off, Cyrus comes and stands in his path.

"Nothing to say to your king?" he teases.

"I'm afraid my council holds little weight," Shaylynn replies. "After all, I no longer serve the crown."

"And yet you save my sister," Cyrus reminds him. "You cross from death into life to rescue her and our people from darkness. No, Shaylynn, son of Feylynn, leader of the King's Court, your council shall always hold weight here. For you truly are the greatest knight I have ever seen."

Shaylynn nods respectfully as the king steps aside. With nothing more to say or do, Shaylynn rides away and fades to nothing. With him goes the spectacle and dream of so many who saw him. For though he no longer walks on the earth, those who knew him, served under him, and loved him do still keep him in their heart. As such, he will continue to hold sway over the land.

But life cannot be lived in the past. After all they have endured and seen, they must be willing to let go of the past and face the futures which lay in front of them. Their lives will be of great importance. If the kingdom is to thrive, they will all be needed. They must all be ready to make the most of the lives they will get to lead. Lyosan will not become king immediately. So long as Cyrus lives, Lyosan will learn under the current king as a Knight of Langerwitz and prepare for the life ahead of him. When the time comes, he will marry Crystalynn, and they will start a family. Before such time comes, they will be able to explore the love which they have come to find in each other. Fallon will do the same with Faith. In the meantime, Fallon will study to become the captain of the Knights of Langerwitz. Steel and Calvin, as princes of Artonia, will have their choice of how they will serve the crown. Crystalynn will keep Sarin and Faith in her court for all her days. Kandessa and Elle will continue their work but will also find new places in the castle. Lyosan's other friends, Stefen, Athen, and the others, will continue to train until they find their place in the Royal Guard.

Lyosan will see the towns in Artonia affected by the battles with Jorram rebuilt. All that they have knocked down will be restored. The knights will be fortified and made strong again. O'Lyn, Reneel, Delreeve will all come to their former glory. Langerwitz will carry on in glory. Artonia will continue in peace and prosperity. Should the kingdom be threatened and its citizens come under attack, they can always rest assured, the Knights of Langerwitz will come to their aid.

ABOUT THE AUTHOR

Patrick Kennedy lives in Andover, Kansas where he teaches at Andover Central Middle School. Having graduated from Wichita State University with a Bachelor's in Education and a Master's in Literature, he has taught for nine years. A lover of books and movies, he uses inspiration from all around him to create his stories. This is his second book – first in the fantasy genre.

www.ingramcontent.com/pod-product-compliance
Lightning Source LLC
Chambersburg PA
CBHW070751280626
47162CB00016B/156